Palace of the Plague Lord

After the murder of his tribe at the hands of a rival tribe, the fierce Norse warrior, Einarr, finds himself the sole survivor. Seeking revenge for his people and respite from guilt he sets off on a perilous quest deep into the Chaos Wastes, a land of magic and madness that lies far to the north of the world. Hideous monsters, ravenous daemons, even the landscape itself threaten him every step of the journey. What price must a mortal pay to steal the treasure of a god, and will he be able to achieve his ultimate aim, a second chance for his people?

A WARHAMMER NOVEL

PALACE OF THE PLAGUE LORD

C. L. WERNER

To Kenneth and Alfred for their support and assistance.
May the Grandfather's attentions skip you this flu season.

A BLACK LIBRARY PUBLICATION

First published in Great Britain in 2007 by
BL Publishing,
Games Workshop Ltd.,
Willow Road, Nottingham,
NG7 2WS, UK

10 9 8 7 6 5 4 3 2 1

Cover illustration by Les Edwards

Map by Nuala Kennedy and Ian Miller

A CIP record for this book is available from the British Library.

ISBN 13: 978-1-84416-481-3
ISBN 10: 1-84416-481-0

Distributed in the US by Simon & Schuster
1230 Avenue of the Americas, New York, NY 10020, US.

See the Black Library on the Internet at
www.blacklibrary.com

Find out more about Games Workshop
and the world of Warhammer at
www.games-workshop.com

THIS IS A dark age, a bloody age, an age of daemons and of sorcery. It is an age of battle and death, and of the world's ending. Amidst all of the fire, flame and fury it is a time, too, of mighty heroes, of bold deeds and great courage.

AT THE HEART of the Old World sprawls the Empire, the largest and most powerful of the human realms. Known for its engineers, sorcerers, traders and soldiers, it is a land of great mountains, mighty rivers, dark forests and vast cities. And from his throne in Altdorf reigns the Emperor Karl-Franz, sacred descendant of the founder of these lands, Sigmar, and wielder of his magical warhammer.

BUT THESE ARE far from civilised times. Across the length and breadth of the Old World, from the knightly palaces of Bretonnia to ice-bound Kislev in the far north, come rumblings of war. In the towering Worlds Edge Mountains, the orc tribes are gathering for another assault. Bandits and renegades harry the wild southern lands of the Border Princes. There are rumours of rat-things, the skaven, emerging from the sewers and swamps across the land. And from the northern wildernesses there is the ever-present threat of Chaos, of daemons and beastmen corrupted by the foul powers of the Dark Gods. As the time of battle draws ever near, the Empire needs heroes like never before.

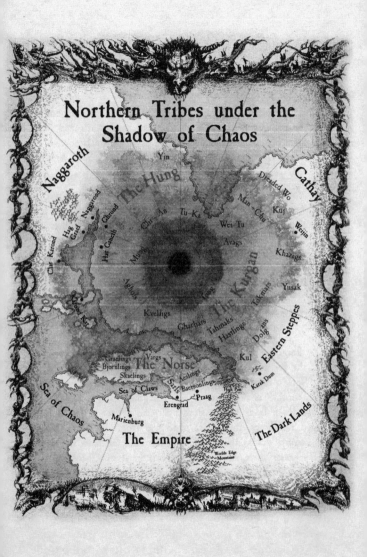

Northern Tribes under the Shadow of Chaos

Naggaroth

Cathay

Yin

The Hung

Dreaded Wo

Man - Chu

Kuj

Chur An

Tu - Ka

Wei-jin

Gad Naggarond

Chrand

Wei Tu

Hag

Hur Gandh

Avags

Khazegs

Char Karond

Ming

Yusak

Aghuls

The Kurgan

Tokmars

Zharr Nag...

Kvellings

Gharbaro

Tahmaks

Hastling

Dolg

Eastern Steppes

Gradlings

Vargs

The Norse

Kul

Bjornlings

Aeslings

Krak Dum

Skaelings

Sarls

Baersonlings

Sea of Claws

Praag

The Dark Lands

Sea of Chaos

Erengrad

Marienburg

The Empire

Worlds Edge
Mountains

CHAPTER ONE

PAIN. IT WAS more than a word, more than a sensation. It was existence itself, the entirety of Einarr's world: day upon day, night upon night of red, searing pain. There were moments of brief respite, when even the Norscan's formidable endurance would break beneath the unremitting torment. At such times, his awareness faded into black, merciful nothingness, fleeing before the kiss of flame and lash. But there was no lasting retreat from his tormentors.

Whether his stupor lasted an hour or a day, Einarr could not tell, but always they were there to drag him back into his agonised flesh, to begin his torture anew. A weaker man might have cried out to the gods, begging them for deliverance or death. Einarr was not such a man. Pain was the price of failure and weakness; the terrible gods of the north had no pity for that which was weak. Better to die with the pride

and honour befitting a warrior of the Baersonlings
and deny his tormentors the victory of seeing him
crawl.

Einarr should have died in the ambush, found a
death worthy of a Norscan on the battlefield, his axe
red and his enemies scattered about his feet, but such
an end had not been the capricious whim of the gods.
Instead he had been rendered insensible by a strike
against his skull and fallen alive into the hands of his
foe. It was as ignoble a doom as any son of Vinnskor
could dread. To fall into the hands of the Aeslings was
more terrible still.

Through the red fog of his misery, memory came
flooding back into the reaver's troubled mind...

THE CHILL HALF-LIGHT of the afternoon cast long shadows across the forest path. The long days of summer
were gone and the icy lands of Norsca were now
falling under the frozen darkness of winter. The sun
was nothing more than a fiery glow smouldering just
beneath the horizon. Even in midday, the stars stood
bright in the darkling sky, lending their distant brilliance to the half-hearted struggle against the
unyielding twilight.

The sighing wind and the drip of melting snow surrounded the winding hunters' trail. Only in the hours
of midday were the sun's rays powerful enough to
warm the land even slightly above freezing. The
morning frost and the evening snow splashed from
the white-shrouded branches of the tall pines while
the trees themselves groaned and cracked as the
frozen sap within them started to thaw.

All but the hardiest, most savage of birds and beasts
abandoned the forests and mountains of Norsca

when winter unsheathed its frozen claws, hiding within their burrows and lairs or retreating into the warmer environs of Kislev and the south. The pine forests were all but stripped of life, only the hungry wolf and the stubborn musk ox still braving the snow-swept terrain.

But it was neither wolf nor ox that prowled along the forest path. Tall, hulking shapes, their powerful frames wrapped in furs and encased in armour of leather and bronze, marched beneath the frozen trees. The flash of steel gleamed from the axes clenched in their brawny fists and upon the weather-beaten face beneath each iron helm was chiselled a scowl of ferocious hate and livid rage. The pale eyes of the Norscans only partially focused upon their snowy surroundings, the minds behind them filled with visions of blood and slaughter and revenge.

Clad in a white wolfskin coat, the foremost of the grizzled reavers was a wiry greybeard, his years written in the scars that pitted his leathery face. The old hunter carried a heavy iron-tipped boar spear in his gloved hands, the weapon following his gaze as he studied the tree line. He paused his cautious steps and held up a fist. Behind him, the Norscan warriors also came to a halt, sullenly staring into the trees, trying to see for themselves whatever sign their guide had discovered.

The old hunter turned slowly and jogged back toward the warriors. One of the hulking reavers strode forward to meet him. He was an immense, bear-like man, a giant, standing a full head above the warriors around him, massive shoulders and deep barrel chest straining against the heavy leather hauberk that covered his torso. Thick ropes of muscle bulged beneath the furs wrapped about his powerful limbs, a broad-bladed sword gripped in one of his paw-like hands. From his massively corded neck rose a head almost lost within the shaggy pale hair that covered it. Bone charms and talismans were braided into the warrior's blond mane, swaying with his every motion. The warrior's face was almost as leathery as that of the hunter, the grey scar of an old wound running across the broad, low brow. Pale eyes shone from the recesses of the reaver's face, colder than the frozen world around them.

'What is it, Svanr? What shadows make you jump this time?' the warrior demanded.

'Shadows indeed!' spat Svanr. 'How many winters have your eyes seen, Einarr son of Sigdan? Can they tell you how long the frost has lain unbroken or when the wolf last walked this path?'

Einarr nodded, understanding the wisdom in the hunter's words. A good war leader was marked not simply by his own strengths but by his ability to recognise the strengths of those he led. If Svanr felt that caution was more important than speed, then Einarr was wise enough to bow to the old hunter's greater experience. It still frustrated him, however, and he could not keep his emotions from his tongue. 'The men are impatient to sink their steel into Aesling flesh,' Einarr said. 'We must make the scum pay a dear price for stealing our cattle and butchering our free-holders and thralls! There will be no rest until we have collected our wergild from the Aeslings – one way or another!'

Svanr shook his head. 'We are in Aesling territory now,' the hunter said. He stabbed a fur-covered finger in a vaguely north-east direction. 'Skraevold lies only a half day from this forest. For all the strength and courage of our warriors, against the entire village it will be the victory of the Aeslings not the Baersonlings that the skalds will sing.'

Einarr nodded, clapping his massive hand against the hunter's shoulder. 'Then we shall need to trust your knowledge of these passes to catch these raiders before they can reach Skraevold. Lead us to them, Svanr. Our steel hungers!'

The war leader's oath had barely been spoken when a sharp cry echoed through the forest. One of Einarr's warriors had dropped to his knees, a heavy spear stuck in his chest. None of the reavers moved to help their stricken comrade, instead turning to face the tree line from which the spear had been thrown. A roaring, howling mob of savage figures erupted from the foliage.

'The Aes!' Einarr hissed as he turned towards the attackers. The vanguard of the marauders had already crashed against the Baersonling warriors, slashing at them with double-headed axes and battering them with massive iron flails. The Aeslings bore the same imposing Norscan physique as their foes, but where the hair and beards of the Baersonlings was pale and gold, that of the Aeslings was dark and crimson. The faces of the snarling attackers were hideously scarred, the runes of the Blood Lord carved into each man's cheek and forehead. The marauders wore heavier armour than the Baersonlings and their arms were covered in bands of steel and bronze. From the belts of many swung the severed heads of those the raiders had slain, offerings they would take back to Skraevold and their gruesome god-beast.

The sight of the heads incensed the Baersonlings, and their momentary surprise was forgotten as a fresh surge of rage energised them. The warriors met the frenzied assault of the raiders with their own brutal fury. War howls echoed across the frozen landscape, punctuated by the shrieks of the maimed and the dying. As Einarr sprinted into the fray, he saw one Aesling pitch into the snow, his neck slashed open by the edge of a warrior's sword. The stricken marauder's blood sprayed across the snow, painting it bright red for a dozen feet and more. Even so, the mortally wounded Aesling tried to regain his feet, tried to return to the battle even as his life jetted from his cleft neck.

One Aesling, his teeth as wicked and sharp as those of any wolf, brought the ball of his flail smashing into the skull of a warrior, striking with such awful violence that his blow cracked the man's skull and his iron helm. Einarr focused on the fanged marauder, sprinting towards him. The marauder turned from his dying victim and locked eyes with the onrushing war leader, swinging his gory weapon in anticipation.

As Einarr approached, the raider swung his flail at the warrior, trying to smash his weapon against the warrior's head. Einarr's sword intercepted the flail, swatting it aside, the heavy chain wrapping around the blade. Before the Aesling could react, Einarr twisted his sword arm, pulling the marauder forward and almost tearing the weapon from his powerful grip. Without breaking his charge, Einarr drove his shoulder full force into the raider, staggering him. The flail was torn free of the marauder's grip as he was driven back and Einarr was swift in pressing his advantage. With the flail's chain still wrapped around it, he brought the edge of his sword smashing into his foe's face, cleaving his nose and severing his jaw.

Bloody froth erupted from the raider's face as he spat broken teeth and torn tissue into the snow. With a second slash of his sword, Einarr tore a jagged line across the Aesling's armour, twisted bronze scales clattering onto the ground. Before Einarr could try again, the raider's massive fist cracked against the side of his head, almost knocking him to his knees. Einarr responded by smashing his forehead into the marauder's already ruined face. He could feel the broken bones cutting into his own skin, but was rewarded by the raider's agonised howl.

Einarr's head was still ringing from the marauder's blow, yet beyond the clamour pounding inside his skull, above even the clamour of the battle raging all around him, he thought he could hear the mournful report of a horn. As the marauder he was fighting wiped blood from his eyes and drew a small hand axe from his belt, Einarr risked a look at the battlefield around him. Of the twenty who had left Vinnskor, only three had fallen to the Aeslings, taking six of the foe with them. Einarr felt his chest swell with triumph, but as he looked beyond the swirling melee, he saw something that put the lie to his hopes for vengeance and victory. One of the marauders had broken away from the combat and was blowing into the long, curved ram's horn he carried. And the note was answered, unless the blow he had taken had left his senses completely shaken. For the first time, cold dread began to tug at the corners of Einarr's mind.

The Aesling charged back towards Einarr and there was no more time to turn his fears into thought. Einarr slashed low as the raider chopped at him with his axe, this time his strike cracking against the armour the man wore over his knee. The reinforced leather prevented the strike from cutting the raider's flesh, but did not completely lessen the force of the blow. The marauder pitched into the earth as his knee popped out of joint and his leg gave way beneath him. Einarr was on the Aesling in an instant, pouncing on him with the ferocity of a sabretusk. The warrior pounded the hilt of his sword into the Aesling's head even as the warrior lifted his axe to defend himself. The marauder slumped beneath the first strike, but struggled to rise once more. Einarr brought the hilt crashing down a second time, then a third. When he struck for the fourth time, there was a sickening crunch and the Aesling became still, the fires of rage fading from his now unfocused eyes.

Einarr rose from the dead Aesling, pausing only to free his sword from the flail still wrapped around it. He looked around him for the next who would fall by his sword, but as he did so, the dread he had felt returned. There were shapes rushing down the path from the direction in which he had imagined the horn had been answered.

The blood-dyed hair and facial scars marked the men as Aeslings from Skraevold. Einarr felt the sickness of shame and fear well up within his stomach. It was not the fear of death that gripped him, for no true Norscan feared escaping the illusion of flesh, but the fear that he had led his men into a trap, the shame that he had failed to exact revenge for his kinfolk. As he watched the Aeslings charge down the path, Einarr realised the mistake they had made. The men of Vinnskor had not been the hunters, but the hunted. The small group of men they had been tracking was nothing more than bait and now twice their number was coming to close the trap. Einarr yelled into the twilight sky, shouting his defiance to the oncoming marauders. If he had made mistakes, he would atone for them now and the Aeslings would pay a dear price for their deceit.

THE HALF-DOZEN Aesling warriors who had survived the battle with the Baersonlings now began to fight defensively, no longer trying to butcher their way through their foes, merely trying to keep them occupied so that the main body of marauders could smash into the undefended enemy flank. Einarr saw the danger, as did his men. Two, young reavers just growing their beards, turned and fled, throwing their axes into the snow in their haste to flee. Einarr watched them run with contempt. If there were not Aeslings to kill, he'd have cut down the two cowards for shaming the honour of Vinnskor. Instead, Einarr tried to gather as many of his men as he could to prepare for the second group of Aeslings. Einarr knew the odds were long; against the weak men of the south, eight Baersonlings might stand against thirty, but, despise them as he did, he knew an Aesling was a worthier foe. The gods were said to look favourably upon those who fought a hopeless fight. Einarr hoped they were paying attention now.

'Look to the man beside you,' Einarr growled. 'Watch his back and guard it well. Don't let yourself become too eager. There are plenty of Aes to go around.' The comment brought a grim chuckle from his men. They knew as well as he that they would all be sitting in the halls of their ancestors before the twilight faded. But they would take many of their foes with them. That much victory they could still hope to wrest from the fists of the gods.

The Aeslings came, roaring like beasts, their scarred faces twisted with bloodlust. Einarr roared back at them and his warriors took up his cry. The marauders smashed into their line and Einarr's sword slashed out, cutting the arm from a bearded Aesling with iron studs through his nose. The raider dropped and the warrior beside Einarr chopped into the man's back with his axe. The mangled Aesling tried to crawl away, but was trampled beneath the iron-shod boots of the raiders rushing to take his place.

Einarr gave the man's death no further thought as his sword batted aside the axes of the man's replacements, snarling brutes with horned helms. One of the marauders recovered from Einarr's parry, turning his axe and chopping at the war leader's shoulder. Einarr sidestepped the blow, slashing his own blade beneath the axeman's guard and slicing into the meat of his leg. The axeman stumbled but did not fall, the bloodlust in his eyes burning still brighter as he brought his weapon up for another strike.

Before Einarr could thrust his blade at the axeman, the other marauder was swinging his own weapon at the reaver. The edge of the axe slammed into Einarr's side, digging into the reinforced leather. Einarr could feel several of the bronze plates woven into the armour pinching against his flesh. Knowing it would expose him to the man's comrade, he twisted around with the marauder as he drew back for another blow, sinking his sword into the Aesling's armpit. Bright blood spurted from the wound and the marauder's arm fell limp as Einarr turned the blade upwards and sliced through muscle and bone. Then he was turning again, ready to face the first axeman, the raider who had amazingly hesitated long enough for Einarr to mutilate his comrade. Einarr found the man already fallen to his knees, his hands clenched around the ragged hole in his throat. Svanr nodded respectfully to Einarr, then thrust his bloodied spear into the mid-section of another charging Aesling. There was no time to be thankful for the hunter's timely assistance, and Einarr turned to finish off the marauder he had wounded.

The roar of battle faded gradually, as the Aeslings overwhelmed the Baersonlings, their greater numbers prevailing. One by one, the men of his village were cut down. Chief among those who had killed his men was an immense raider with a skull-shaped helm, his arms covered in golden bands almost from wrist to shoulder. Touched by the gods this mighty butcher was, stomping across the battlefield on hoofed feet, spitting sizzling death from his fanged mouth to melt the faces of his foes after he had carved them to shreds with his twin swords. Einarr had struggled to face the imposing marauder, to pit his sword against the Aesling champion's blade, but always the press of marauders around him thwarted him.

The murderous attentions of the champion were enough to turn the tide on their own, but there was another fighter among the Aeslings every bit as deadly. Thin and lean, his body cloaked in bearskin, a tall helmet framing his wrinkled face, this was one whom even the Aesling marauders seemed to fear, parting before him as hawks before an eagle. The Baersonling warriors who saw him cringed away in terror, making no move to protect themselves as the scrawny marauder slashed at them with his bladed staff. Every man of the north knew one of the mighty seers when he saw them, the chosen prophet-priests of the Dark

Gods. Every man of the north knew that to raise a hand against a seer was to invite the wrath of the gods. A seer might strike down a warrior, but a warrior did not dare strike down a seer. Not that any mortal could hope to defend against the terrible powers of a seer. The heavy oak staff the shaman carried was tipped with a metal blade, but it was a bright, silvery metal Einarr had seldom seen – the fabulous steel only elves could forge. With his blade, the seer carved through armour as easily as butter, cleaving men from hip to rib when he slashed at them. In his wake, the seer left piles of screaming human debris.

Einarr was thankful for his determination to face the Aesling champion, for the champion and the seer were at opposite ends of the battlefield. The closer he drew to the champion, the further away from the seer he was. Finally, his perseverance told out and Einarr could see the skull-helmed champion looming just beyond the flail-wielding marauder he was currently fighting. Even as he battled the marauder, trying to keep the raider from bashing his brains in, Einarr found his eyes straying again and again to the monstrous champion.

The marauder chief was fighting two Baersonlings; the last of his men Einarr could see anywhere. One was old Svanr, the other a young axeman named Tjorvi. As Einarr swatted back the attack of the marauder fighting him, he saw the champion doing the same with his own enemies. Then, with a speed that belied his armoured bulk, the champion brought his double swords slashing across the body of Tjorvi. The axeman stumbled back, blood streaming down his sides and the champion lunged forward, raking both swords before him in a cross pattern. Tjorvi's head leapt into the air, his face locked in a silent scream as it crashed into the snow.

While Tjorvi was being killed, Svanr charged at the champion's back, his spear aimed at the marauder's spine. Almost as part of the same motion that had decapitated Tjorvi, the champion spun around and brought his blades slashing at Svanr. One sword chopped the hunter's spear in half, the other crunched into the old man's body, nearly severing his leg at the hip.

Einarr shouted in fury, driving his knee into the groin of his own foe. The Aesling crumpled and Einarr did not give him time to recover, bringing the edge of his own weapon cutting across the man's neck. He left the marauder to bleed out and before any of his comrades could close upon him, Einarr was charging towards the champion and the embattled Svanr.

It was too late. Even as Einarr drew near the champion and shouted his challenge to the chieftain, the skull-helmed marauder was dropping Svanr's lifeless body to the ground. The hunter's face was a steaming mess of dripping tissue, burned down almost to the bone by the champion's acidic spittle. Einarr roared again, lunging at the champion. The twin swords were there to block his attack, one swatting aside the warrior's sword, the other slashing toward his neck. Reflexes born from years raiding the northern coasts of the Empire served Einarr well as he recoiled from the champion's deadly blade. It was the first step in a deadly dance as the champion set his impossible speed and strength against Einarr's reflexes and agility. It did not take Einarr long to realise that he was hopelessly on the defensive, pushed back with every attack the champion made. He cringed every time his eyes strayed to the chieftain's skull-helm, wondering when a spray of burning venom would come searing into his own face.

The marauders began to form a wide ring around the combat, watching as their leader dealt with the last of the Aesling warriors. Einarr only dimly heard their jeers and hoots, his every thought fixated upon reacting to the champion's deadly blades. He felt his muscles beginning to burn under the strain of meeting the chieftain's attacks, felt his heart thundering within his chest. It would not be long, he knew, but the gods despised a man who did not fight to his last breath.

The champion drew back as Einarr narrowly avoided a slash that would have cut his arm from its socket. The Aesling laughed deeply, a sound that silenced the marauders watching the combat. 'You fight well, for a Baerson,' the champion laughed, his voice deep and booming. 'What is your name? I shall carve it upon your skull when I offer it to great Kharnath!'

'I am Einarr, son of Sigdan,' this between deep gasps as he tried to recover his breath. 'And it is your skull that shall grace the Skull Throne!'

The champion chuckled again as he heard Einarr's empty bravado.

'It is Kolsveinn, Jarl of Skraevold who sends you to the gods,' he said. 'When you see Kharnath, you will tell him what hand ended your days!'

Einarr braced himself for what he knew would be Kolsveinn's final attack. He could not hope to defend against the jarl much longer and knew he would get no other respite. Yet even as he prepared to meet his ancestors, Einarr felt something crack against the back of his skull. He fell to his knees, then the blow was repeated and he collapsed to the ground. He could hear the voice of Kolsveinn roaring furiously, could almost feel the jarl's armoured feet stomping the ground around him. In answer to the jarl's outrage, a low, wispy voice, like steam rising from a forge, spoke.

'This one has been marked for Kharnath,' the voice said. 'By your own words you have made it so.' Through the swimming stars that sparkled across his vision, Einarr could see the seer standing over him, fresh blood dripping from the blunt butt of his staff.

'He is mine, Alfkaell! Be you bloodfather or no, this one is mine!'

The seer merely smiled at his jarl's fury. 'By your own words, you have offered this one to Kharnath, the great Skull Lord. Would you think it wise to cheat him, especially with your own sword? Enjoy the victory you have won this day, Kolsveinn, for if you cheat the Blood God, it will be your last!'

The champion glared at Alfkaell for a moment, then sheathed his swords and turned away. Even a jarl knew there were powers he did not dare oppose. Alfkaell gestured with his gnarled hands and marauders came forward to lift Einarr from the ground.

'This one comes back with us to Skraevold,' Alfkaell said. 'He will make a fine offering for the god-beast.'

EINARR WAS DRAGGED unceremoniously through the muddy lanes of Skraevold, blood dripping from his wounds. Through his bruised face, Einarr could see the women of the village going about their daily chores, gathering water from the well, and tossing feed to mobs of black-feathered chickens. Children were everywhere, laughing and jeering at the Baersonling, hurling stones at the captive until their aim strayed and the two burly warriors dragging him through the street turned on the whelps and ran them off with threats and curses.

It was a familiar scene for Einarr. Every day he was taken to the squat, cold building that the Aeslings used to butcher meat when they were not using it to torture captives. Long hours under the tender mercies of his tormentors, then his agonised body would be taken back to his cage. Unlike most of the clans of Norsca, the Aeslings of Skraevold did not keep slaves, seeing the practice as a sign of weakness and decadence, taking pride in working their own fields, mining their own stone and felling their own timber. Where another clan might have a stockade to hold its captives, Skraevold had no such structure. Instead, Einarr found himself entombed within the village kennels, a narrow, thick-walled timber building on the outskirts of the settlement. The building was dark and dank, the thick animal smell of the dozens of warhounds and hunting dogs kept by the Aeslings making the air stagnant.

The warriors carrying Einarr forced the Baersonling to his feet as they entered the kennels. Their arrival was greeted by the snarls of the hounds, a din that pounded against Einarr's skull as brutally as the fists and bludgeons of his torturers. The barrel-chested Aesling pushed Einarr forward. After hours of torture, the strength in Einarr's body was all but spent. As he tried to maintain his balance, he stumbled and crashed against the dog cages. Instantly the savage hounds were pressed against the wooden bars, snapping at the prisoner's flesh. Einarr felt sharp teeth dig into his back, felt a fresh stream of blood trickling down his back. Powerful hands closed about Einarr's head, pulling him away from the cage. The treatment was only slightly less brutal than the fangs of the hounds.

'You'll not cheat the gods that way, Baerson!' one of the barrel-chested warriors growled. Behind him, Einarr could see the dogs snapping and snarling; their bloodlust aroused by the scent of his blood. The Aesling warrior turned towards the slavering mongrels, smashing the heft of his flail against the wooden bars, driving the beasts back. 'This one is not for you!' he hissed. The warrior turned back toward Einarr as his comrade pulled the prisoner back to his feet. He leaned into the face of his captive, his ale-ridden breath stinging Einarr's nose.

'Make no mistake, Baerson,' the warrior sneered. 'You will wish we had let the dogs finish you before we are finished.' Einarr smiled at the threat, spitting a bloody froth into the bearded visage of the Aesling. The warrior staggered back, howling as he wiped the filth from his face. His comrade shifted his hold on Einarr, closing his immense arm around the captive's neck. Einarr felt what little energy he still had drain from him beneath the strangler's embrace.

The kennels echoed with the agitated howls of the dogs, excited by the savage emotions of the men outside the cages. The marauder stormed back towards Einarr, glaring murder at the prisoner. The strangler relaxed his hold as his comrade returned, before his grip crushed Einarr's life as well as his defiance. The bearded warrior tightened his grip on his flail as he stared at Einarr, the prisoner's bloody spittle still dripping from his face. For a long moment, the Aesling was silent. Then he smiled and shook his head.

'No, Baerson,' the warrior said, motioning for his comrade to march Einarr to his cage. 'You'll not trick me into cheating Bloodfather Alfkaell from offering you to the god.' Einarr found himself brutally shoved into the timber cage that acted as his cell, the heavy door smashing close behind him as the strangler slammed it shut. The captive struggled to remain standing, but at last gave up the effort, sinking to the icy earthen floor. The bearded warrior grinned at him from beyond the bars. He threw a badly gnawed bone that looked as though it had been stolen from one of the hounds into Einarr's cell.

'Better eat up while you can,' the Aesling laughed. 'The god likes a little meat on its offerings.' The harsh laughter of his captor was all but drowned out by the barking dogs as the warrior withdrew. Einarr waited until the two torturers were gone before reaching for the bone they had thrown him. There was still a faint scrap of meat clinging to the joint and he set about it with ravenous ferocity. He did not trouble himself over what had previously been gnawing at his meal, nor at what kind of meat had once surrounded the bone. All that mattered was the energy and strength his miserable meal could give him, strength that would allow Einarr to live for another day. Strength that might preserve him long enough to make the Aeslings pay for all that they had done.

Einarr gathered the filthy straw littered about his cage in a hopeless attempt to fend off the cold. He felt sharp stabs of pain run up his arms as he reached out to sweep the straw towards him. Einarr pulled back, trying to knead the suffering from his arm with his callused hand. The scabby crust of dried blood cracked beneath his ministrations, a crimson treacle running down his forearms. The renewed scent of blood urged the hounds to renew their excited barking.

'The ymir take your mangy hides!' Einarr cursed, calling on the hoary ice devils of the mountains. He settled back against the cold timber wall of his cage. For all of the injuries he had suffered, he could be thankful for one thing. Despite the agonies they had visited upon him, his torturers were loath to go too far. They intended him as a sacrifice to the gods, and as such he had to be kept relatively intact, for the gods would look poorly upon an offering that was too badly damaged. They had stopped short of breaking bones and tearing muscles.

It was something for which Einarr could be thankful. The backhanded restraint shown by his captors meant that for all his privation and torment, he was still physically intact. If the opportunity presented itself, he might yet wrest from Skraevold a death worthy of a Norscan.

CHAPTER TWO

THE SUDDEN SILENCE that filled the kennels snapped Einarr from the restless sleep that had stolen upon him. The incessant barking and yapping of the dogs had been broken, replaced by an imposing stillness. Einarr rolled onto his back, letting his eyes adjust to the icy gloom that filled the kennels. Two sapphire orbs gleamed at him from the shadows beyond his cage, staring at him with sinister curiosity. Einarr glared back at the shadowy figure, even as his body cringed from the supernatural chill emanating from the apparition. The eyes and the cold were things Einarr knew only too well. The time had come then. Bloodfather Alfkaell had come to offer him up to the gods of Skraevold.

'They tell me it takes much to make you scream, Baerson,' the shaman rasped, his voice like a cold northern wind. 'That is good. Very good. The gods are pleased with those who are strong. It is good to offer them such souls.'

From the darkness, Einarr could see the shaman more distinctly now – the withered, emaciated frame, the heavy bearskin cloak festooned with runestones and bone talismans, the tall elven helm that framed the man's sharp features. The heavy staff Alfkaell carried seemed to glow in the darkness with a strange, smouldering light. Einarr found his eyes straying from the unnatural light to the glistening metal blade that tipped the shaman's staff. He had seen for himself the lethal edge the blade possessed; the impossible keenness only the witch-metal of the elves could keep. With such a blade, the timber poles of his cage would not confine him long.

'That must be why the Aeslings raid and maraud against their neighbours,' Einarr said. 'Because there is none in this maggot nest that the gods would take.'

'Do you know how you will die?' Alfkaell asked, ignoring Einarr's insults. 'Skraevold has been blessed by the gods. In my grandfather's time, the skald was touched by the Skull Lord and changed into a thing of the gods, a living sacrament of their power and might. It is with us still, a temple of flesh to the Skull Lord. We shall offer you to it, that through the beast your soul may be given to mighty Kharnath and feed his mighty hunger. You will scream then, as the great beast strips the flesh from you, as it licks the hot blood from your bones. The beast takes a long time to kill a man – you will think yourself dead a thousand times over before the end finally comes. Suffering pleases great Kharnath, and the beast will see that the Skull Lord is satisfied with our offering.'

Einarr rose to his feet, grinding his teeth against the pulse of agony that throbbed through him as he did so. Bracing himself against the bars of his cage, he forced his way to the front of his cell, glaring into the smirking features of Alfkaell. 'If this beast of yours grew from an Aesling, it is no thing of the gods. I will crush its skull with my hands and spit on its carcass when I am done. You offer it no child this day, crow-caller, but a warrior, a son of Vinnskor!'

The shaman took a step back from the bars of Einarr's cage, but the smile remained on his face. 'It is good that you are defiant, that you shout your idle boasts so proudly. It will make the sacrifice all the more amusing for the Skull Lord. You will shout louder still when the beast's paws flay your flesh, when its jaws chew upon your soul.'

Einarr glared into Alfkaell's luminous eyes. 'When I have strangled the life from your beast, you will be next, carrion-eater. How loudly will you scream when I carve that smirk from your withered face? Tell me what amusement your cries will give the gods as you beg me to let you die.' Einarr could see some of the amusement fall away from Alfkaell's expression, watched as the shaman's features hardened.

'I will take extreme pleasure offering you to the Skull Lord,' Alfkaell hissed.

'Do you not mean offering me up to your beast?' Einarr retorted. 'What is wrong, scavenger-rat, do you need a beast to bring the favour of the gods to Skraevold?' The venomous words were falling from Einarr's tongue faster than his mind could form them, smashing against the shaman's pride. Einarr could see the man's flesh turning crimson, could almost feel Alfkaell's enraged gaze burning into him. A part of him suddenly realised what he was doing, what sort of man he was insulting. This was a shaman, a man touched by the gods, wielder of strange and terrible powers. It was madness to incite such a man, to tempt the awful vengeance a seer could inflict upon a mere mortal. Yet another part of him swelled up within him, filling Einarr with rage. He was already destined to die, what more hurt could befall him by stoking the ire of the shaman. Again, words poured from Einarr's lips, stabbing into Alfkaell's ego. 'Will the gods not listen to the words of the great and terrible Alfkaell? Will even ravenous Kharnath not accept a sacrifice from your own hand?'

'Enough, wretch!' Alfkaell snarled. He gestured with his staff towards the cage, the ithilmar blade fixed to its head gleaming in the meagre light. 'Be silent or I shall cut that wagging tongue from you!'

'How will mighty Kharnath hear my screams then?' Einarr replied, laughing as he saw the shaman become still more incensed. 'The Aeslings are indeed a stupid people not to understand it takes more than a bit of elven steel to make a seer.'

'Fall silent, cur!'

Einarr laughed at the shaman's command. 'Tell me, Alfkaell, what lies did you tell your people about your talismans? Did you tell them stories about some mighty battle in the elf havens, or some great lie about sacking a terrible elven ship?'

'When the god-beast has finished with you, I shall feed your manhood to the crows!' Alfkaell threatened, shaking his staff at Einarr. The shaman's knuckles were white where he held the weapon. Einarr knew he stared at death when he looked into the seer's eyes, but the prospect held no great terror for him and the baiting words continued to roll off his tongue. Nothing Alfkaell could do to him would be any worse than what the shaman already intended.

'Tell me, Alfkaell, did you scavenge your trophies from a wreck or did you earn it as wergild when your woman did not give you a son?' Einarr could see the fury boiling over in the seer's face. Even as far away as Vinnskor the story of Alfkaell's wife had been heard, how she had thrown herself from the cliffs rather than endure the seer's embrace. 'Or was it the woman's fault? Perhaps a thrall such as you is more accustomed to being a consort than taking one!'

Einarr braced himself for the stabbing thrust of Alfkaell's staff. One swift strike and it would all be over, one lethal cut from the ithilmar blade and he would escape the waking dream of the mortal coil and walk among the gods. Yet even as he gritted his teeth against the coming blow, something inside told him to lunge forward, towards the wooden bars of his cage. Einarr stared at Alfkaell, saw the raw hate burning in his eyes. Yet somehow the emotion was muted, indeed there was a sense of dullness about the shaman's cold gaze, a brute quality that reminded Einarr of an ox or goat. Instead of using the great reach of his staff to stab at Einarr from beyond the bars, Alfkaell stepped towards the cage, so close that Einarr could smell the mangy bearskin draped about the seer's shoulders, could smash his fist into the seer's furious face.

The warrior did not hesitate to question the foolishness that had set upon the seer. Instantly, Einarr's massive frame crashed against the bars of his cage, his powerful arm shooting between the timbers to close about Alfkaell's windpipe. The dull quality still filled the shaman's eyes as the captive squeezed and tightened his hold about the man's neck. Alfkaell brought the shaft of his staff smacking against Einarr's arm, but the effort was feeble and painless compared to the days of torture Einarr had endured. His grip tightened and the seer's eyes began to bulge, the dullness beginning to fade as Alfkaell's lungs filled with hot, spoiled breath. The familiar, evil cunning reasserted itself and from the corner of his eye, Einarr could see the shaman adjust his hold on his staff, grabbing it just beneath the bladed tip and pointing it towards the warrior's belly.

With a savage roar, Einarr twisted his arm, snapping the shaman's neck with a grotesque crunch that echoed through the still silent kennels. He heard Alfkaell's staff clatter to the floor, watched as the smouldering life in the seer's eyes began to fade. Einarr let the limp form slip from his hand, watching with apprehension as the shaman's corpse flopped to the floor. It was taboo amongst the tribes of Norsca to strike down one of the god-touched seers, an act certain to bring the vengeance of those same gods upon any who dared such blasphemy. A man might kill a jarl or even a king, but he did not dare raise his hand against one who served the gods.

Einarr shuddered as he considered what he had done. He had thought to goad the seer into attacking him, into giving him a quick and clean death. Instead, it was Alfkaell who had died. The Baersonling stared at the timber roof above him, imagining the angry eyes of the gods glaring down upon him. He held his breath as he waited for their terrible fury to be visited upon him. But long moments passed and slowly his breath grew normal. The fear trickled from his veins, reason subduing the superstition that had paralysed him with terror. Alfkaell was dead, and if the gods had cared so much for the Aesling seer, they had done nothing to stay Einarr's hand. The warrior looked again at the cold, still shape of the seer, crumpled on the filthy floor of the kennel like a pile of discarded rags. Then Einarr's eye was caught by the bright shine of metal. He laughed as he saw it, the sound causing the still cowed hounds in the cages around him to cringe still further into the shadows.

Alfkaell's staff, with its wicked elf-steel blade, had fallen within easy reach of Einarr's cage. The warrior did not even need to stretch to grasp it and pull it through the bars. He lifted the weapon over his head and cracked it against his knee, Einarr's immense musculature allowing him to snap the heavy staff like a twig. He tossed the longer section aside, interested only in the shorter length and the deadly ithilmar edge affixed to its top. Einarr laughed again as he tested the feel of his improvised sword. He had seen for himself the incredible keenness of the elven metal. A weapon that had split iron and cleft steel with such ease would make short work of the timber bars of his cage, and speed was what he needed now. He did not know how long it would be before the Aeslings came for him and discovered what he had done.

The elf steel did its work faster than Einarr could have believed, the wooden bars parting like butter beneath its touch. Soon the only thing that stood between him and his freedom was Alfkaell's crumpled form. Einarr stared down at the seer's corpse and drew a deep breath into his body. Carefully, the reaver stepped from his cage and over the body.

Einarr, son of Sigdan was prisoner of the Aeslings no longer!

THE FUGITIVE MAINTAINED an easy, loping trot as he made his way through the snow swept terrain. Einarr knew there was no sense in tiring himself with a more hurried pace. Though his newly won freedom had done much to strengthen his abused body, he knew he had many leagues to go before he would reach Vinnskor. He also knew that his escape would not go unnoticed for long. The Aeslings would find their seer's body in the kennels or else they would find the body of the warrior Einarr had ambushed and whose clothes he now wore. Once they did, Einarr knew they would come after him, come after him with the very fury of the gods.

Let them come, he thought, throwing his shaggy head back and inhaling the icy night air. They would not find him so easy to capture a second time. Armed with the elf-steel from Alfkaell's staff, even their god-touched jarl might find Einarr a match for him. Einarr's face split in a savage grin as he imagined that contest, as his mind's eye visualised the ithilmar blade slicing through Kolsveinn's swords and ripping through his armour. If he escaped the wilds, if he managed to return to Vinnskor without the Aeslings catching him, Einarr would speak with his own jarl, Tulkir, and encourage him to prepare an all-out attack on Skraevold. The Aeslings would regret taking him captive, carrying him back to their village like some prize beast. For Einarr had seen their village, had seen where it was strong and where it was weak. It would be the women and children of Skraevold who would wail and lament when next their peoples met on the field of battle.

Einarr snapped from his dreams of glory and carnage, freezing as he saw something long and lean slowly steal from the black shadows cast by the trees. Yellow eyes shone from the black shape that began to pace languidly in his direction, gleaming from the darkness like tiny witch-lights. As it paced, the pungent musk of its fur struck Einarr's senses. How long it had been tracking him, the warrior could not say, for it had the sense to stay upwind of him, keeping to the darkness of the trees, far from the light of star and moon. Even now, as he watched it stalking towards him, it made no noise, its paws making no sound as they pressed against the snow. Though its face remained hidden in the shadows, Einarr could see the sharp dagger-like fangs jutting from its lower jaw gleaming in the starlight.

It was an ice-tiger, smallest of the sabretusk breed and the only one of the great cats that did not hibernate during the black Norscan winter. At least Einarr hoped the thing stealing towards him was an ice-tiger. The breath of the gods was strong in the north, its power changing both man and beast. If the predator stalking him had been god-touched, what man could say what strength the Dark Gods might have given it? No, better to think it an ice-tiger, a thing a man could understand, a thing a man could kill.

The creature continued to circle Einarr, and now he could hear its low, threatening hiss. He'd heard the sound before, when hunting as a youth with his father and old Svanr. There had been times when the elk and deer felled by their arrows had been stolen from beneath their very noses by a hungry sabretusk. Some of the hunters told brave stories about savage fights with the massive cats when they took it in mind to hunt the hunter. Even as a child, Einarr had known most of the stories to be nothing but lies, bold tales told to cheer men too old or too infirm to claim real glory by raiding. Yet he'd never been more certain of it than he was the cold winter morning that his father had died, his head crushed between the powerful jaws of a sabretusk. Only a boy of twelve, Einarr had watched the great cat carry off his father, using its claws to scramble up a tall tree where the Baersonling hunters could not follow. Hunting down that cat, by himself and with only a spear and a dagger, had been his rite of manhood.

Einarr brandished the dagger he had fashioned from Alfkaell's staff. He stared into the ice-tiger's hungry eyes. 'Hold, old thief!' the Norscan called. 'I've no spear this day, but you'll find I'm not a stripling anymore. I am Einarr Sigdansson, and you should let me pass.'

The ice-tiger stopped pacing, its body tensing as Einarr's voice split the silence of the night. The great cat scowled at him, baring its fangs. Einarr scowled back at it with an expression equally savage. 'Steal back to your shadows,' he told the beast. 'I've no time for your games.' The ice-tiger almost seemed to understand his words, quickly turning its head in the direction of the trees. But the hunting had been poor and the hunger in its belly great and its head turned back with equal swiftness to snarl at Einarr once more.

'Then one of us meets his ancestors this day, old thief,' Einarr swore. Sabretusk and man lunged at one another in almost the same instant, crashing together beneath the frosty night. The tiger's massive paws scraped against Einarr's body, their sharp claws trying to dig through the heavy furs he wore. The cat's fanged jaws snapped at Einarr's throat, but the warrior's blade was there to meet it. As the keen edge of the dagger slashed against the ice-tiger's muzzle, one of the massive incisors was cut free from its face. The sabretusk yowled in pain, pushing against Einarr's body with all four of its legs. The combined strength of all of the cat's limbs was too great to resist and the cat tore itself free, falling back into the snow.

Before Einarr could react, however, the beast had recovered. Almost as soon as it landed, the ice-tiger was pouncing at him again. Einarr tried to brace himself for the cat's lunge, but its three hundred pound body smashed into him with the might of a thunderbolt. Einarr locked his arms around the sabretusk's body as he felt himself knocked off his feet. He dragged the cat to the ground with him, trying to smash its skull against the frozen ground. The ice-tiger struggled too, scratching at him with its long claws; its frantic efforts to rip itself free shredding the flesh on Einarr's legs. Despite the pain, Einarr held fast to the animal, knowing if he relaxed his grip, it would try for his throat again. He tried to work the edge of the ithilmar blade against the animal's neck, but could only succeed in stabbing the point into its shoulder.

The pain incensed the tiger, causing its efforts to free itself to become even more frantic. Man and beast rolled across the snow, locked in a struggle that could only end in death. Einarr felt small bushes crumple beneath their weight, felt sharp stones and fallen branches dig into his body as they rolled across them. Then, suddenly, the ground gave way and they began to tumble down a sharp incline. The tiger's yowling thundered in Einarr's ears as they rolled down the snowy cliff, the stars and the trees seeming to tumble along with them. Faster and faster they fell, rolling over the frozen hillside. Then came the sudden stop, as the land turned level once more. Dizzy from the fall, Einarr found the tiger springing away from him before he could remember to hold onto it. He could see its lean, pantherine shape staggering in the snow as it too tried to recover its senses.

Einarr tried to clear his head, then realised that both of his hands were empty. The dagger! The seer's blade, he had lost it in the fall! Einarr looked again in the direction of the tiger. The sabretusk was snarling, working its sandpaper tongue against the damaged corner of its jaw. Would it run, retreat to its lair to lick its wounds? No, Einarr could tell there was a malevolence about the beast, a malicious spite that was almost human. As soon as it remembered who had injured it, the cat would be lunging at him again. Without Alfkaell's blade, Einarr did not favour his chances. Sigdan would spit upon him if Einarr allowed a sabretusk to take him. No Norscan could respect a son who did not find a more noble death than his father.

The warrior turned away from the growling beast, keeping one eye on it as he stared desperately at the snow. They had landed in some sort of clearing, almost barren of foliage. Except for where their fall had marred it, the snow stood unbroken all around them. A massive black stone was the only feature of the clearing and as Einarr looked at it he saw its sides were far too smooth to offer him a handhold. He dismissed the idea anyway – anywhere he could climb, the ice-tiger could much better. No, his only hope was to find some sort of weapon.

From the corner of his eye, Einarr saw the sabretusk swing its head back in his direction. It hiss-snarled at him, coiling its body as it gathered its strength. Einarr turned back towards the cat. If he would die, he would die like his father, with his wounds to the fore. At least he could spare that much disgrace from settling upon his ancestors. The ice-tiger growled as it read Einarr's challenge. Something glittering in the snow caught Einarr's eye. Still watching as the sabretusk prepared to charge, Einarr crouched and pulled it from the pristine ground. How it had fallen so far into the clearing, Einarr did not know. All he did know was that with the blade in his hands once more, he again had a chance.

The cat did not wait for Einarr to rise from his crouch. With a teeth-rattling roar, it bounded towards him, its lean muscular frame hurtling through the air. From his crouch, Einarr lashed out at the hurtling cat, the thin edge of his blade raised to ward off the immense mass of the predator. Einarr was knocked onto his back as the ice-tiger crashed against him, every bone in his body quivering from the force of the impact. Yet as he rolled onto his side, Einarr saw that his own strike had been more telling than that of the sabretusk.

The brute shivered in the midst of a patch of scarlet snow, its forepaw severed by Einarr's blade. The warrior stared respectfully at the wounded predator, knowing how near it had come to finishing him. Despite the pain wracking his body, Einarr forced himself to his feet. A lingering death of sickness and injury was no fitting end for such a formidable beast. It was Einarr's obligation to give the ice-tiger a death befitting its ancestor-spirits. The cat scowled at him as he stalked toward it, but when it tried to swipe at him, it merely spilled itself onto the ground. The ice-tiger had lost its balance and with it, its defence. Einarr was careful to strike true as he thrust his weapon into the beast's neck.

Einarr stepped away from the dead sabretusk, slumping into the snow. He was not certain how much time he had lost fighting the cat, but it was time he could ill afford. The Aeslings would be looking for him now, setting their hounds on his trail. He had even less time to indulge in the luxury of rest. He had seen men fall into the snow after a battle and never rise again, their bodies unmarked by any weapon save the icy clutch of the land itself. He would not be one of those men, his spirit condemned to slumber in the ice until the cracking of the world. Against the protests of his battered, bleeding body, Einarr forced himself back up. There was a long way yet to go before he could rest in the warm halls of Vinnskor.

Standing, Einarr found his eyes draw to the massive black stone that rose from the midst of the clearing. He wondered for a moment what it was. It seemed to have letters carved into it, though the wind and ice had all but obliterated them. Was it the marker of some tomb? Had it been placed here to commemorate some long forgotten battle? Einarr considered that it might even be one of the enormous monoliths the Kurgan people raised to honour the gods. Whatever it was, Einarr had no time for its riddles. He turned to leave its enigma behind him, but as he did so he noticed the big black bird perched on its top, its beaked head staring down at the slain sabretusk. Einarr felt a surge of disgust rise within him as he regarded the scavenger.

'Find other bones to pick!' the warrior roared, hurling a snowball at the bird. The missile smacked against the side of the rock just beneath its talons. The bird fluttered its wings in protest, glaring down at him. 'I did not kill that beast just to fill your greedy belly!' Einarr threw another snowball, this time hitting the black bird. It screeched angrily at him. 'Get you gone and earn your own way!' The third snowball exploded against the bird's breast, coating it in white. It was the final straw for the animal and it lifted into the air, screeching its wrath as it flapped slowly into the night.

Einarr scowled at the scavenger bird until it was lost to sight, then made his way toward the trees. He still had a long distance to cover before the feeble light of day again smouldered on the horizon.

THE ORANGE EMBER of the sun again glowed beneath the horizon, starting the day in the Aesling village of Skraevold. The warriors of the tribe had been assembled many hours before, since the discovery of Alfkaell and the escape of the Baersonling captive. Many of the marauders fumed at the inactivity their jarl had forced upon them, eager to begin the hunt and cut down this blasphemer who dared murder their seer. But Kolsveinn would not be swayed. He had risen to be leader of his people not only by his great strength and the favour of the Blood God, but also by knowing his people, by understanding what moved their hearts. Yes, he could have unleashed his tribe, sent the dogs to track down this man, and for a time that would have satisfied them. But soon some minor misfortune would plague the village. A child might get lost in the woods or an ox might be taken by wolves.

When that happened, the people would remember that Kolsveinn had promised the Baerson to Kharnath and that they had killed him before he could be sacrificed, for Kolsveinn knew none of his warriors had the discipline to take the man alive, not after he had slain the seer. Then Kolsveinn would be blamed for bringing the curse of the Blood God upon the village and it would be his blood they would think to give to Kharnath to appease his anger.

No, it was better to do it this way.

Kolsveinn turned his tattooed head towards the hulking Aeslings standing beside the gate that led into the pit. He nodded and the men threw back the iron-banded timbers. A dozen marauders rushed forward, pushing a long log down into the pit, then scrambled away, retreating to where their kinsmen were. Only Kolsveinn stood his ground, holding a long bronze spear, upon the tip of which had been tied the clothing they had stripped from Einarr. The jarl stared into the pit, watching the darkness for any sign of motion. The first he was aware of it was when the sound of claws and fangs splintering the sides of the log reached his ears. Long moments later, a huge shape pulled itself from the pit, bringing with it such a stench of blood and death that even Kolsveinn felt the urge to gag. The hulk heaved itself forward, sliding across the ground on its riot of limbs. Some of the watching Aeslings screamed, wailing like children, forgetting that they were veteran reavers, the victors of countless battles.

Kolsveinn looked into what he thought were the thing's eyes and thrust the spear towards it. A limb slimy with blood coiled itself around the weapon, tearing it free from his grasp. The snake-like member pulled the weapon back towards the heaving bulk. A snuffling sound slobbered its way from the creature's body as it inspected the clothing.

'We would offer that one to Khorne!' Kolsveinn shouted, using the Kurgan name for the Blood God. It was the only name that could control the god-beast of the pit, and as the abomination heard it, a whining chorus howled from its hideous shape. 'He has fled from us, thinking to cheat the Skull Lord! You must find him! You must offer him to Khorne!'

The abomination heaved itself forward, then threw back what Kolsveinn thought might once have been its head. The howl that erupted from it caused blood to trickle from the ears of all who heard it. The echoes of that howl were still rattling the timbers of Skraevold when the oozing horror slobbered across the muddy streets, following the scent of its prey.

Kolsveinn watched it go, almost pitying the foolish Baerson the doom he had brought upon himself. The rest of the village had already hidden themselves, for it took strength to gaze upon the god-beast of Skraevold, a strength that only the mightiest possessed.

The jarl prided himself that he was the only one who watched the god-beast leave. He did not see the large black eagle perched above the kennels, its feathers still stained with snow.

Chapter Three

THE DIM FLICKER of dawn cast its light over the village of Vinnskor. The stone-edged lanes of the village began to fill with people – farmers and herdsmen trudging their way into the fields to tend the tough, shaggy cattle the Aeslings had failed to slaughter or stampede during their brutal raid; women slogging their way through the snow towards the mountain stream that wound its way past the village, heavy hammers to crack the ice held in their arms, ox-hide skins to steal water from the stream slung over their backs; scrawny thralls, their wasted frames barely covered by mangy scraps of cloth and fur, dejectedly marching towards the forest to fell timber for the fires of their masters. Above all the activity prowled the massive warriors of the village, their axes held at the ready, their intense gaze watching the horizon for any warning of the marauders' return. With the destruction of the revenge party that the Baersonlings had sent into the north, the people of Vinnskor knew the Aeslings would be back.

Asta climbed the short earthen steps and emerged from the gloom of her longhouse into the greater gloom of the morning. She sighed as she watched Emla's children racing about the small garth outside her neighbour's home, watching with a tinge of envy as Thorwald, Emla's husband, supervised a pair of thralls as they tended the thatching of their home's roof. She had been so proud to wed a mighty warrior like Einarr, a man who had raided the southlands many times, who had brought the names of many fallen enemies to honour the gods of the Baersonlings. She and Einarr had planned to have children soon, sons who would become even greater than their father.

But Einarr was gone, lost with the others who had gone to avenge the Aesling raids on their pastures and farms. The two who had escaped the Aesling ambush claimed that all the others who had been with them had been slain. Jarl Tulkir had believed the wretches on that matter, but found their stories of their own prowess in the doomed battle insulting and infuriating. He'd ordered the men stripped and when no wounds could be found upon them, not even the faintest scratch to attest to the veracity of their lies, Tulkir had the naked men tied to a gallows and doused with water. Left wet and bare to the elements, by the next day the two were frozen so solid that even the ravens could not make a meal of them. That had been almost two weeks ago and Asta felt the weight of her loss grow with each day. She should have been content with a man like

Thorwald, one who did not seek glory and fortune but was simply satisfied with merely providing for his own.

Asta turned away from her consideration of Emla's home. She smoothed the front of her woollen hanggerrok, and adjusted the balance of the water skins resting over her shoulder. Einarr was gone and she had to accept it. She had to force herself to live on without him, to rebuild the rest of her life. She was still a striking woman, her figure shapely, her long pale hair possessing an exotic quality she knew many of the men in Vinnskor found fascinating. She would need to think about finding a new husband, a new warrior to watch over her and give her strong children. Yes, she would need to think about it, but she would not think about it today.

As the woman passed from the narrow lanes of the village and into the snowy fields beyond, she saw the armoured figure of Rafn standing watch over the women getting water from the stream. He smiled as he saw her, an excited twinkle shining in his eyes. Rafn had always admired her, and now that Einarr was gone the warrior saw an opportunity to expound his unfulfilled affection. The blond-headed sentinel strode towards Asta as she approached, meeting her well before the stream. Asta tried not to meet Rafn's eager gaze and continued to walk towards the stream. She might need to take another husband, but she was in no mind to have the issue pressed upon her so soon after Einarr's death.

Unfortunately, Rafn was no more mind reader than he was mannered. The big warrior kept pace with her, idly swinging his axe as he walked, a juvenile habit that Asta found irritating.

'I asked the gods if they would send you to get water today,' Rafn said, his timid tone at odds with his scarred, bearded face. 'They must be pleased with me, for here you are.'

'You shouldn't bother the gods with such petty things,' Asta warned him, not breaking stride, keeping her eyes fixed on the stream ahead. 'They may become angry.' She shivered as she said the words, for the anger of the gods was not something to be considered lightly. The legends of the Baersonlings were filled with horrible tales of that which befell those who had aroused the ire of the Dark Gods.

Rafn caught her by the arm, turning Asta around and forcing her to look at him. 'I never bother the gods about things that are not important,' he said, tightening his grip on her shoulder. 'But you are right, Asta, a man should not trouble the gods over something he can take for himself.' Rafn's bearded face leaned down towards Asta's. She tried to pull away, but the warrior's grip on her was too strong.

A scream suddenly rose into the dark morning sky from behind them. Soon other women were joining the first voice, shrieking as they fled away from the stream. Rafn pushed Asta behind him, holding his axe at the ready. The other women of Vinnskor were already rushing past them, racing back to the village. Several pointed behind them as they ran. Rafn looked in the direction they pointed. Emerging from the trees he could see a large man, his hulking form covered in furs. He moved with a halting, weary step, shuffling towards the now deserted stream.

'Go back and rouse the bondsmen!' Rafn snarled. 'Tell them the Aeslings are here!' Rafn clenched his fists tight around the heft of his axe and moved to sprint toward the strange figure. Asta grabbed Rafn, restraining him as he started to run off. The warrior pulled away, glaring at her in disbelief.

'Let me be, wench, or that Aesling scum will have both our skulls!' Rafn shouted. Asta didn't even seem to notice his words, watching instead the fur-covered man stagger towards the stream. There was something familiar about him, something that seemed to call out to her. As the man dropped beside the stream a sharp cry rose from Asta's throat and she ran past Rafn towards the fallen man. Rafn cursed and tried to intercept her, but the bulky warrior found himself unable to match her speed.

Asta stopped at the bank of the stream, looking across its icy surface at the stranger. He raised his head weakly and Asta felt her heart tremble with shock as she saw the familiar face. Instantly she was dashing across the frozen stream, ignoring Rafn's desperate shouts. Asta knelt beside the man, turning him onto his back and cradling his shaggy head in her lap.

'Blood of the dragons, woman!' Rafn roared, raising his axe. 'Get out of there and let me finish that Aesling bastard!'

Asta glared defiantly at Rafn. 'Get you gone, Rafn son of Oflati!' she ordered, an imperious tone in her voice. 'Fetch the vitki and tell the people of Vinnskor!' She stared back into the face of the exhausted, scruffy man beside her. Pride filled her voice as she spoke again, the pride born of the devotion and love that bound her to this man.

'Tell them, Rafn! Tell them that Einarr Sigdansson has returned to them!'

* * *

'HE IS TOO stubborn to die,' Spjall, the silver-bearded vitki of Vinnskor pronounced as he rose from administering the pungent poultice to Einarr's wounds. The warrior smiled at the medicine man from the nest of thick furs that covered his bed.

'Too stubborn to die before I see Skraevold burning,' Einarr replied. He looked around the small inner room of his long house, making certain that all within saw he meant what he said.

Spjall chuckled and patted the warrior's shoulder. 'For now think about rest and sleep. You've endured much, it would be a terrible jest to survive what you have and then die in your own bed. Rest, plunder and revenge can wait for another day.'

'Aye,' agreed Einarr, but his words were not intended for Spjall. 'Revenge can wait for another day. So long as it does not wait too long.'

The other men in the room bristled at the obvious challenge in Einarr's words. Bondsmen all, to have a mere warrior and reaver speak to them in such a fashion would have had them reaching for their blades were it not for the presence of their jarl in the room. Even so, Dreng and Oflati, two of the oldest of the bondsmen, looked like they might do so anyway. Only a stern look from Tulkir stayed their hands.

'We have heard your words about the ways of Skraevold,' Tulkir said. 'We have heard you tell us how their village stands…'

'Particularly the kennels,' scoffed Oflati, stroking his be-ringed beard, 'where their people dwell and work.

We have heard you say where the village is strong and where it is weak.' Tulkir nodded his crowned head as he spoke. There was a stern expression on his face as he looked at Einarr. 'What you say makes my sword eager to taste Aesling blood, for it would be an easy thing to strike the dogs down. But what you say also fills me with great fear. I, who have raided the southlands on twenty and ten voyages, who have walked the lands of the Vargs and the Graelings, who have seen the jungles of the dragonfolk, I know fear because of your words.'

Einarr glowered at his jarl, the colour rising in his face. After all he had suffered, after all of the comrades he had seen butchered by the Aeslings, after his miraculous escape from right beneath the noses of his captors, now it would all come to nothing because his jarl was afraid. 'Then let one of your bondsmen lead your people to triumph and glory, Tulkir, or step aside and let a man more worthy of the name bear the title of jarl.'

The insolent words brought snarls of outrage to the faces of the assembled bondsmen and even Asta gave a gasp of horror that her husband had spoken so. Tulkir merely continued to stare at the wounded Einarr.

'It is you who make me afraid, Einarr, son of Sigdan,' the jarl said, stabbing his finger at the man. 'You have dared the wrath of the gods by striking down a seer! No man may defy the gods and live! Ever has it been so. You are cursed, Einarr, by your own hand you are cursed.'

Einarr rose from his bed, ignoring the trembling in his arms as he did so. 'If the gods look so unfavourably upon me, then why am I here? Many times did they have the chance to strike me down when I was captive in Skraevold. Many times I should have died before I ever saw my home again.'

'Only a seer can guess the ways of the gods,' Tulkir said. 'Old-father Ulfarr is casting the runes even now, to find what must be done to appease them. What he says must be done, we shall do. The two curs who returned here with their swords sheathed I had killed for being timid. You, Einarr, I fear I will kill for being too bold.'

The jarl and his bondsmen turned and filed from the longhouse, their visit to Einarr finished. The wounded man watched them leave his home, a great weight pressing upon his chest. He tried to push his doubts aside with visions of hate and revenge, but knew he could not. He knew only too well the unpardonable crime he had committed by killing Alfkaell. A man who killed a seer, even one from an enemy village, rendered his own life forfeit. Tulkir could have had him killed the moment Einarr had admitted his deed. Instead he chose to wait until Vinnskor's own seer had made his divinations. Einarr repented calling Tulkir a coward. It had been wrong to call him such.

'This is a strange thing.' Einarr turned his head to find Spjall looking through the pile of clothing he had taken from the dead Aesling in Skraevold. The vitki held the dagger Einarr had fashioned from Alfkaell's staff, turning the blade in his hand, watching as the light from the hearth danced across the pale elf-steel.

'I took that from the bloodfather,' Einarr said. The words caused Spjall to drop the weapon as though it had suddenly changed into a viper. 'It is an ugly thing,' the warrior admitted. 'I should get rid of it now, but I do not want people saying I did so to try and hide my crime.'

Spjall continued to study the sinister blade. He was an old friend of Sigdan, who had voyaged far with Einarr's father in their younger days. The vitki looked upon the son of his old friend almost as his own kinsman, always trying to help Einarr with whatever wisdom his grey years could remember. The bold warrior was often in need of calmer, more measured advice, but never so much as he did now.

'The people of Vinnskor know you better than that,' Spjall rejoined. He gathered the ox-hide bag that held his herbs and ointments and hobbled towards the exit of the longhouse. 'Einarr Sigdansson would rather die than admit fear, even fear of the gods. It is your strength and your doom.' The old healer paused as he started to leave. He lifted his gnarled hands to his neck, rummaging about in the throat of the heavy fur cloak he wore. When his hands emerged, they lifted a neck ring of silver thread over his head. A motley assortment of bone charms and talismans dangled from the ring, along with stone amulets depicting the sacred runes of the four great gods.

'I will give you this neck ring, in the hopes that it may spare you the ire of the gods,' Spjall said. 'It came from the hoard of a Kurgan prince whose tomb I found in the Troll Lands beyond Kislev when I was still a young warrior.'

'And you think this trinket will make the gods show mercy?' Einarr tried to keep his incredulity from his voice.

'Look well on me, Einarr,' Spjall said. 'I am the oldest man in this village; I have lived beyond the years of my sons and their sons. The gods have looked with favour upon me. The Kurgan prince had many great and wonderful treasures in his tomb, the gods looked favourably on him too.' Einarr and Asta watched as Spjall drew his own dagger and cut the thread. The old vitki began removing the charms and talismans from the thread, stuffing each bit of bone or trinket of metal into his ox-hide bag until at last he was left with only a thread of silver.

'How is this? Not even a wolf-fang to grace my necklace?' Spjall ignored Einarr's humour and twisted the ends of the neck ring together. He stepped towards the warrior's bed.

'It will be up to you to find your own talismans,' the vitki told him, 'just as I had to find my own. You will know them when you find them. The gods will tell you.' Before Spjall placed the neck ring around Einarr's head, he showed the warrior the ends he had twisted together. They were now smooth and unbroken, as perfect as though the vitki had never cut it.

'Why give this to me?' Einarr asked, awed by the magic he had just seen. The gifts of the gods were never less than impressive.

'Because I am old and will walk with my ancestors soon,' Spjall told him, turning back towards the door. 'Because now I feel the same feeling I did when I added my talismans to the ring. It moves me to pass it on to you, Einarr. May its magic see you to glory and doom.'

AMIDST THE HEAVY furs of his bed, Einarr crushed Asta's warm, lithe body against his. His hand caressed the scaly skin that covered the back of her neck and shoulders, the coppery plates feeling smooth beneath his touch. Asta bore the mark of the gods in her flesh, had been marked that way when she had been born. It had been another of the things about her that made her the most pursued woman in Vinnskor. But in the end, it had been Einarr who had caught her.

'You are supposed to be resting,' Asta scolded him, her face turned towards the fire.

'You forget that I have been away for two weeks,' Einarr reminded her, moving his hand to stroke her long pale hair. 'It is a long time to go without a wench.'

Asta tried to stifle the sob of fear that rose within her, but Einarr heard her fright just the same. He turned her towards him, looking into her frightened face. 'Have I learned such harsh manners that you cry so?' he asked, concern in his voice. Asta pressed her cheek against his chest.

'I thought you dead,' she sobbed. 'Slain by the Aeslings, your skull resting on their altar to Kharnath.'

Einarr brushed the tears rolling down his wife's face, trying to soothe her. 'But I'm not dead. I've come back to you. Not even the Aeslings could keep me from coming back. Not even the gods could keep me from coming back.'

Asta recoiled from him, crawling to the other side of the bed, staring at him in horror. 'Don't say such things!' she begged. 'Not now, not when Ulfarr casts the runes and asks the gods what is to be done with you! I can't lose you again, Einarr! I won't lose you again.'

'The runes will show Ulfarr what they will,' Einarr sighed, leaning back amongst the furs. 'Worrying about it will help nothing.' Einarr's calm, resigned words only intensified his wife's terror. She scrambled back across the bed to him, grabbing his hand, pulling at him.

'Then let's be away, Einarr,' she pleaded. 'Take what we can and leave. We can go to the lands of the Sarls or even the southlands. I don't care, so long as we are together.'

Einarr pulled his hand free from her grasp. 'What sort of life would we have among the Sarls? Would you have our children raised among another tribe, or worse reared to be decadent Empire folk? If you fear the gods, do you think you can simply run from their wrath?' He shook his head. 'No, I will not run, Asta. If I am to find my doom here, then here is where I will stand.' He could see the terror in his wife's eyes as he spoke his words. He smiled and tried to calm her. Carefully he removed the silver neck ring Spjall had given him and placed it over Asta's head.

'There, Spjall said this would keep me safe,' Einarr said. 'Now it will keep you safe.' Asta started to protest but Einarr pressed a finger against her lips to silence her words. 'I am the bravest man in Vinnskor,' he said, 'and knowing that you are protected by the gods will make me braver still.'

Einarr started to pull Asta back towards him when both of them suddenly spun around and stared at the door. Outside, in the village, they could hear a great tumult, voices screaming and crying out in alarm. Einarr cursed and pushed himself from the bed, reaching for his wool tunic. He looked around for his axe.

Tulkir had waited too long. The Aeslings were attacking Vinnskor!

SHRIEKS OF AGONY and terror filled the air as Einarr rushed from his long house. The ragged, torn remains of the bondsman Dreng were splashed across the narrow lane. Dismembered limbs and broken skulls were strewn in every direction and the ground itself seemed to have been transformed into a gore-hued slime. The magnitude of the carnage stunned Einarr. How could the Aeslings have visited such violence upon the village in the few short moments it had taken him to fetch his axe?

The answer to his question wallowed amidst the ruin of Emla's home, its shifting bulk caving out the walls as it heaved and oozed its way through the gaping hole it had ripped from the roof. Einarr felt his stomach churn as he looked upon the thing, as its stench of old blood slammed into his senses. Einarr had travelled the mountains and seas of Norsca for many years and seen many strange and terrible monsters, things that had been kissed by the power of the gods. But never had he seen such a thing, a thing that made him want to claw his eyes out so that he might see it no more. A thing that even he, a son of the north, could only call 'abomination'.

The monster was bigger than an ox, bigger than the largest troll or ogre he had ever seen. As it slobbered through the wreckage of the long house, its form seemed to expand outward, pressing against the very walls as though in defiance of the timbers that contrived to contain it. Shape, it seemed to have none, flesh and limbs growing and contracting with the thing's every motion. Tentacles flailed at the air, only to twist into enormous claw-tipped paws and then wilt away into nothing.

Massive legs, thick as a dragonboat's prow and tipped with enormous talons, pushed the monster across the rubble only to collapse into undulating tendrils of formless meat then reform into the scrabbling limbs of a spider. Across its entire body, there was only one constant, the blood-deep hue that saturated its flesh, gore dripping from the multitude of wound-like welts that peppered its hide. As the blood oozed across the abomination's skin, the hide itself seemed to suck it back inside, like a sponge drinking the sea.

The bloodbeast howled as it crushed the building to splinters, the hideous sound shuddering through the village. The sound staggered Einarr, felling him to his knees as blood spilled from his ears.

A great body of warriors had surrounded the monster, threatening it with swords, spears and any other weapon they could find. But even these bold, veterans of numberless battles feared to close upon the thing. The ground was wet with the ruin of those who had tried. A few hardier souls jabbed at it with torches, while a handful of huntsmen tried to pepper it with arrows. The shafts struck the monster's gory hide, shaking as they sank deep into its changeling flesh. Then, to the horror of the bowmen, the monster's flesh seemed to clutch at the arrows imbedded in it and drag them deeper into its body until no sign of them remained.

As Einarr and those warriors who had been closest to the beast's howl recovered from the crippling sound, the monster was in motion once more, pressing its bulk against the front of the house and spilling its twisted mass into the small garth outside. A half-dozen warriors shouted in terror as the thing flopped across the ground towards them, yet for all their fear, they charged it, lashing at it with sword, axe and flail. Einarr could see Oflati and his son among the attackers, their axes biting deep into the monster's shapeless mass. The monster stumbled or reared onto what might have been its haunches and from what should have been its chest, a monstrous face seemed to be pushing its way free. The gory hide burst in a shower of steaming blood as a naked skull, hound-like and a dozen times larger than that of a man, gibbered and shrieked at the stunned warriors. The body of the monster shuddered and collapsed upon itself, reforming behind its new head while the ragged scraps of meat hanging from where the skull had pushed itself free lashed wildly through the air and wrapped themselves around the canine head, swiftly clothing it in blood-hued flesh.

Oflati was on the ground, screaming in agony, half of his own face burned away by the sizzling blood the monster had sprayed across the garth. The thing glared down at him with its eight enormous black eyes, then opened its gigantic jaws and snapped the bondsman in half.

Arrows and torches rained about the beast as Oflati's death cry echoed into the darkness. Einarr ran through the barrage, chopping at the abomination's flank with his axe. The weapon sank deep into its body and Einarr could not shake the impression that the beast's body was built from something more like boiled meat than living flesh. He pulled his axe free, cringing as a spray of steaming blood gushed from the wound. Gallons of the sizzling fluid erupted into the air, yet the beast seemed to take no notice of its hurt, concentrating instead on snapping up the rest of Oflati's men. Einarr chopped again into the beast, howling with frustration as he watched the original wound close upon itself even as his second blow struck home. This time, as blood spurted from the wound, Einarr saw what seemed to be faces shrieking at him from within the gore. He drew back in horror when he saw the face of Thorwald among those trapped inside the crimson sludge.

'The head! Strike at the head!'

Einarr turned to see Tulkir a few feet behind him. The jarl's helmet was dented, one of his arms purple and broken as it dangled useless beside him. Blood was splattered across his armour and his sword, the magnificent blade he had named Fangwyrm and which had seen him through thirty years of battle, had snapped and left him with less than half a foot of weapon.

'Steel and fire don't hurt this thing!' Einarr roared. 'It is touched by the gods. It needs magic to turn it back. Where is Ulfarr?'

'Dead,' wheezed Rafn. The warrior was bleeding in a dozen places where the beast's steaming blood had struck him, one of his legs slashed so deep by the horror's flailing tentacles that Einarr could see the bone. 'The old-father's hut was the first place the thing struck. For all it seems mindless, there is cunning and purpose in the beast.'

Rafn's words struck Einarr like a hammer. It had come here with a purpose, and he was that purpose. Kharnath had sent it to claim him for his blood-drenched realm. All those the beast had killed, all those it would kill, it was because he had thought he could cheat the Blood God.

'It is here for me,' Einarr swore. 'Call off our men! I will lead it from the village!'

Tulkir watched as the monster crushed another Baersonling warrior beneath its talons and licked the man's blood from its paws. While he watched, a screaming youth drove an iron-tipped spear straight into one of the thing's eyes. It did not seem to notice the injury at all and continued to nibble at the man clutched in its paws.

'Get it out of here!' Tulkir snarled. 'And may the gods damn you to the blackest hells for bringing it here!' The jarl looked as though he might take the ruin of Fangwyrm and drive it into Einarr's chest, so great was the wrath in his eyes. Einarr simply nodded and turned to face the beast again. He had brought doom and slaughter to Vinnskor and for that he deserved whatever fate the gods demanded.

Einarr strode towards the beast, then stopped as he became aware he was not alone. Rafn, limping on his mangled leg, was trying to keep pace with him, his axe clenched tight against his chest. Einarr waved him back.

'I must do this on my own!' Einarr growled at him.

'That thing ate my father! The crows take what you must do!' Rafn roared back. The sound of the warrior's rage attracted the attention of the beast. Its long, serpent-like neck arched above its back and its wolfish face drooled hungrily as it glowered down at Rafn. Before Einarr could even move, the beast's jaws shot out from its skull, snapping close in front of Rafn. As the jaws retracted into the beast's head, Rafn toppled forward, the white bone of his skull exposed where the beast's fangs had pulled his face free.

A savage war cry exploded from Einarr as he hurled himself at the beast. His axe chopped into one of the abomination's flailing tentacles, severing it from its body. The mast-like column of flesh crashed to the ground, narrowly missing the enraged axeman. Before his very eyes, it corroded into a stagnant heap of scarlet mush. The beast coughed and croaked with what Einarr hoped was pain and took a swipe at him with one of its enormous paws. Einarr dodged the blow, striking out at the malformed limb as it passed him, the edge of his axe chewing into the back of its foremost talon. The beast coughed again and lashed out once more, this time with a pair of tentacles. Only by

dragging every ounce of speed from his body was the
warrior able to dance between the flailing limbs. The
beast reared back once more, blood dripping from its
fanged muzzle.

'Follow me you blood-worm filth!' Einarr screamed
at the thing. 'I am what you came for!' Einarr jumped
back as the monster struck at him with one of its
panther-like paws. He waited for the thing to surge
towards him. For a moment, the monster's multitude
of eyes stared at him. Then the moment passed. It
swung its trunk-like neck around, closing its jaws
around the shrieking body of a mangled reaver. Einarr
stood in stunned horror as the beast shuddered back
across the garth, towards the warriors assembled on
the other side of the village.

If it had come for him, it certainly didn't seem to
remember. Now its only concern was to feed and to
slaughter, to mutilate and kill. Somehow, that
thought was even more horrible. With a cry of despair,
Einarr raced back across the garth and flung himself at
the beast. He crashed against its slimy back, chopping
frenziedly into its gore-drenched skin. Sizzling gore
splattered across him, but still he hacked and tore into
the thing. The burning blood seared his hands, his
skin coming off in scabby strips as he tried to maintain his hold upon his axe. He saw the screaming,
accusing faces of his kinsmen and his neighbours as
the beast's blood spurted into the black sky. But still
he tore and chopped and ripped and cut.

Only when the blood-slick axe slipped from his
hands did Einarr relent. Gasping, he reached down to
recover his weapon. As he rose once more, he saw the
beast's hound-like head. It was turned back towards
him once more, a hideous suggestion of amusement

about its ghastly features. Einarr looked at the monster's back, watched in despair as the countless wounds he had dealt it oozed shut before his eyes. Then a massive pillar of flesh erupted from the side of the monster, a great tree-like tail tipped with an immense knob of bone. Before Einarr could react, the tail smacked into him, swatting him aside like a bull swatting flies.

The warrior felt himself hurtling through the empty air. Something smashed against his arm, splintering as he struck it, then his head and shoulder were crashing against unforgiving stone.

Then there was only darkness.

Chapter Four

A SHARP, STABBING pain pulled Einarr from the darkness to which his mind had withdrawn. The Norscan likened the sensation to someone jabbing his chest with a dull dagger. He could taste blood in his mouth, feel his bruised ribs and battered shoulder throbbing. His nose was filled with the stink of blood and death, his skin felt oily and unclean. The only sound he could hear was the steady dull thump against his chest and the occasional flutter of feathered wings.

Like a coiled viper, Einarr's hand lunged upwards, closing around the throat of the monstrous black bird he saw perched there through his clouded eyes. It was large enough to be an eagle, though Einarr had never seen one with so thin and crooked a beak. The ugly raptor squawked in alarm as his hand closed around it, beating its massive wings against his face, digging at him with its sharp talons. Einarr was blinded by the flailing wings, crying out as the bird's claws tore into his flesh. But the warrior maintained his grip, closing his hand tighter and tighter, digging his fingers into the eagle's neck. The eagle continued to struggle, and Einarr could feel his blood soaking through his wool tunic. The wings smashed against his head, almost as though trying to smother him with their rancid feathers. Einarr drew his grip still tighter, wincing as he felt the bird's blood dripping down his arm. It was cold, with an almost syrup-like feel to it as it slowly oozed down his hand. Beneath the eagle's blood, his flesh went numb, as though drained of its very life.

Still he maintained his death-grip on the eagle, enduring the agony as its claws dug into his body, as its wings continued to batter his face. He tried to move his other arm, succeeding only in sending a blast of red-hot pain flooding into his brain. It would not move, disjointed in his battle with the god-beast. This realisation forced new strength into his other arm and Einarr willed his fingers still tighter about the eagle's throat. Finally, there came a dull, snap and the bird croaked a final liquid groan. Einarr tossed the filthy scavenger aside, letting its miserable carcass slide onto the floor.

The warrior opened his eyes again, thankful that the eagle had decided to peck at his chest rather than start with his head.

With a grunt that barely voiced the incredible pain that surged through him, Einarr sat up. While his hand felt the tattered mess the eagle's claws had made of his chest, the warrior's eyes scanned his surroundings. He was in a hut of some kind, though it seemed too fine for the thralls and too large for any of the unmarried warriors. The roof had caved in and one of the walls had been collapsed outward in exactly the same way that he had seen Emla's home destroyed. The grisly, half-gnawed skeleton pushed into the remaining timber wall was recognisable as that of Ulfarr only because of the stubby crown of horns that grew from the skull – the same mark of mutation that the seer had borne. The hut then, was the seer's. Somehow, despite the devastation around him and the hideous abomination he had seen tearing apart the village, he felt all his old superstitions about the seer and his home take hold of him. Einarr reached for a half-collapsed timber and used it to pull himself to his feet. He did not know where he would go, he only knew he was not going to linger in the shaman's dwelling.

As Einarr tried to stumble his way free from the wreckage, his eyes fell to the earthen floor of the hut. The seer's runestones were still scattered within a crude circle, lying where Ulfarr had cast them in his divination. Though Einarr could not read the meaning of the runes, there was no mistaking the pattern they had made when they fell. As he stared at the scattered runestones, Einarr saw himself looking at the skull-sign of Khorne, the great Lord of Battles, the ravenous Harvester of Blood.

EINARR LOPED THROUGH the rubble of Vinnskor. Blood was spattered across every stone; the lanes were a sucking morass of crimson sludge. Bodies and bits of bodies were strewn wherever he turned his eyes. Not a man, woman or child, not so much as a dog or a rat, stirred within the silent desolation. Except for himself, there was not even the dimmest flicker of life in the village.

Everywhere the torn remains of once familiar faces, the faces of those he had lived among all his life, stared at him from the muck. Cold dead eyes glared at him with accusation, demanding to know why he had brought such doom upon them. He found Spjall, his body crushed into a little knot of flesh, limbs protruding brokenly in an insane tangle of blood and bone. He found Jarl Tulkir, his skull crushed flat by some enormous weight, the impression of one of the monster's taloned foot-tendrils marring the ground all around his flattened head. Emla, his neighbour for years, whose children his own Asta had helped nurse and raise, was almost unmarred, only the monstrous bite that had pulled her rib cage from her chest spoiling the effect of a weary mother lying at rest.

With every step, Einarr's fear grew. Not terror of where the monster was now, but rather where it had been. He, a crimson-handed reaver who had stormed the walls of Erengrad and ransacked its domed temples and fortified palaces, felt his knees shake as he neared the smoking ruin that had been his home. He did not want to know, above anything, he did not want to know. But he had never given into his fear before, never allowed it to shame him, to give his ancestors cause to curse his name. He could not do so now, not even when every fibre of his soul urged him to flee.

Einarr stepped into the shambles that had been his home, trying not to notice the roof that had been pushed down into the structure, nor the walls that had been collapsed outward. He shambled like a thing without mind or purpose, vanishing into the gloom.

How long he sat there, in the grave of his life, Einarr did not know. When he rose, however, there was no longer room for pain or sorrow or loss in him. In the warrior's eyes there burned a new fire, a flame that only death could quench. He moved towards the splintered timbers that marked where the beast had pushed its way free of his home. He considered the arm lying limp and numb at his side. He positioned it between two jagged logs and pressed his body against the wall. Grinding his teeth together, he pulled his entire body back. With a pop, his arm snapped back into position. Einarr clenched his jaws tight against the shock that stormed through his body as feeling returned to his arm. He would not cry out again. There was no pain greater than what he had already found and it would shame her if he ever gave voice to any lesser hurt.

The warrior scoured the rubble of his home, retrieving what armour he could scavenge. What he could not find in his own home, he took from those of others until he had what he needed. He did not fear the spirits of his kin as he collected the gear. They would understand. He was not looting the dead. He was avenging them.

When Einarr left the sorry, butchered carcass of Vinnskor behind, he embodied the avenging spirit of his people. Tulkir's great breastplate of steel, torn from the corpse of a southland prince, encased Einarr's chest. Over his legs he wore the heavy fur leggings that had been the speciality of Hilga the tanner, a layer of small river stones sewn between the layers of leather beneath the fur to thwart fang and blade. Across his back he wore the monstrous bearskin cloak Raskulf had claimed in a raid against the Vargs, its fur even paler than the snow, the horned skull of the bear covering Einarr's head like a helm. About his hands were the iron gloves of Valbrandr, upon his feet the iron-shod boots of Sorkvir. From his belt hung the axe of Rafn, its haft pitted where the sizzling blood of the beast had struck it. Beside it rested the splintered length of Fangwyrm, the renowned blade of Tulkir. Across his shoulder he carried the ox-hide bag with Spjall's herbs and potions. Around his neck he wore the silver band he had given Asta, the metal stained almost black by her blood, the image of the torn jumble of meat scattered through his home burned forever in Einarr's mind.

One last thing did Einarr take with him as he left Vinnskor, the crude dagger he had fashioned from Alfkaell's staff. There was no reluctance now to touch it; indeed, it seemed almost to slide into his grasp as he reached for it. The warrior tucked the elven blade into his left boot, the metal feeling hot against his skin. He would return it to the people of Skraevold, those who had marked him for the Blood God and who had set Kharnath's vengeance upon his village. He would see if the Aeslings had the strength to take it from him and he would build a mound of skulls from those who failed.

Their bloodbeast had made a mistake, thinking him dead, and Einarr was determined that Skraevold would suffer for that mistake.

BLACKENED TIMBERS REACHED into the dark Norscan sky like jagged teeth in a rotten skull. The wattle walls of garths and pastures were broken and torn, fields trampled into desolation. Even in the murk of the twilight gloom, Einarr could see that there was little of Skraevold still standing. He was under no illusion what had happened here. The tracks of the monster that had destroyed Vinnskor were easy enough to follow, a deep bloodstained furrow that drove straight as an arrow back to the place from which it had come. The bloodbeast had returned to the Aeslings.

Einarr thought of the old admonition his father had always given him about calling upon Kharnath: 'Do not call upon the Blood God, for he cares not from whence the blood flows'. The Aesling had paid the price for not heeding that wisdom. Without their seer, they had no way to control the force they had unleashed.

The warrior continued on into the slaughterhouse that was Skraevold, oblivious to the mangled bodies and splintered bones strewn around him. He prowled among the wreckage like a hungry wolf, eyes watching every shadow for the merest sign of motion. The need to kill was like a fiery fist closed upon his heart, burning inside him every bit as keenly as it had in the monster. The anguish of his frustrated vengeance crashed down upon him the deeper his steps took him into Skraevold. They were dead, all of them. He was too late, too late to claim retribution for his kin, for Asta.

Like a great beast himself, Einarr howled his frustration into the black sky. Long minutes passed while the reaver roared at the stars, the moon and the cruel gods of the north. Vengeance, every drop of blood in him called out for it! Einarr swung Rafn's axe, cleaving the skull of a slaughtered Aesling in half.

'That is my kinsman you butcher.' The cracked, broken voice boomed like thunder in the silent oblivion of the village. Einarr swung around. For the first time he saw movement among the shadows. A hulking shape pulled itself into the light. Kolsveinn, jarl of

Skraevold, was as ruined as his domain. The elaborate armour that girded him was pitted and holed with the caustic burns caused by the beast's blood. His face was a mass of scars; the old ritual signs of Kharnath obliterated beneath the claws marks that now split his visage. One eye was a milky mass, cleft in two down the middle. Half his nose was gone, and a deep gash in his brow gleamed white with the bone beneath. 'You have come too late to find glory here, brigand,' Kolsveinn hissed. 'The Blood God has taken it for himself.'

'I did not come here for glory,' Einarr growled. He pulled back his bear-skull helm, baring his face to the crippled champion. Kolsveinn's remaining eye went wide with shock. Einarr pointed his axe at the mangled jarl. 'I came here for blood and for death.'

'Spoken like a son of Skraevold,' Kolsveinn spat. The jarl staggered forward, his fist closed around one of his deadly swords. But as he moved further from the shadows, Einarr saw the most hideous of the injuries Kolsveinn had suffered. The champion's right arm had been torn from its socket, only a ragged mess of twisted flesh now attached to his shoulder. Einarr did not exult in his enemy's injury; he did not give thought that without his arm and second sword Kolsveinn would be an easier man to defeat. None of that mattered to him. Victory or defeat, survival or death, these were secondary to vengeance.

And now he had something to visit his wrath upon.

There were no more words between them, these last survivors of their people. Einarr rushed at Kolsveinn, slashing at him with his axe. The jarl swatted his blow aside with a parry of his sword, then tried to follow it with a thrust to Einarr's belly. Kolsveinn's attack was slow, awkward; his mind still thinking it should be using the blade held in his missing arm. Einarr grinned savagely at his foe. The fight was already over; the jarl just didn't know it yet.

Kolsveinn slashed his sword at Einarr's face, dropping the sword into a guarding position as Einarr retaliated. But again, the once mighty jarl sank back into habit, expecting a second blade that was not there. Einarr struck at the man's right, just past the guard of his sword. The axe chewed through the rotten, pitted armour, carving a deep gash in Kolsveinn's side.

The champion roared in pain, but even through his pain, he attacked, driving his sword at Einarr's chest. The Baersonling brought his axe up, catching the edge of the sword on its heft. With a grunt, he forced the jarl's weapon aside. He followed up on his block by cracking the end of the axe handle into Kolsveinn's jaw. Teeth flew from the jarl's face and he staggered back beneath the blow.

Einarr firmed his grip upon his weapon and came at the reeling Aesling. Kolsveinn desperately tried to ward off the attack, this time over compensating for his missing arm, leaving his left exposed. Einarr brought his axe chopping down into Kolsveinn's leg. The corroded armour gave way beneath the blow, ripping apart as the axe tore away Kolsveinn's knee. The wounded jarl struck back, slashing at Einarr before the warrior could recover from his strike. The steel scraped along the reinforced fur leggings, a few stones spilling into the mire as the edge tore the leather.

The axe licked out again, barely missing Kolsveinn's head. The red-bearded Aesling dragged his body back, creeping into the shadows, trying to use the gloom to defend him. But there would be no respite, and the Aesling knew it. Einarr slashed at him again, catching the edge of the jarl's sword. Already weakened by the bloodbeast's caustic ichor, notched from its contact with Einarr's axe, the blade broke upon impact, shattering like ice.

Kolsveinn looked in disbelief at his broken sword, then stared into Einarr's face. The Aesling did not ask for quarter for he knew none would be given. Instead, with a howl of rage, he flung himself at the Baersonling, seeking to drive his ruined blade into Einarr's belly. The axe flashed through the twilight one last time, sending the jarl's battered head rolling into the darkness.

AFTER FINISHING THE Aesling champion, Einarr pressed deeper into the wreckage of Skraevold, following the stench of old blood and rotting bones. He had done what he had set out to do; he had visited what vengeance a man might take from his foe. Now he was ready to stand before the grotesque god-beast the Aeslings had called down from Kharnath. He knew it was impossible for one man to prevail where two entire villages had found only death and slaughter. But he was not afraid of death. It was better to die with an axe in his hand and a war cry on his tongue than to wither away, some sulking coward hiding in the wilds. He would make the god-beast understand fear before he would let it take him. He would find a doom that would not bring shame on his ancestors.

It was an easy thing, finding the lair of the god-beast. All he had to do was follow his nose. The stink of rancid blood and the spoil of butchery steadily increased as he neared the great pit that the Aeslings had gouged from the earth. Heaps of offal were splashed across the ground, mounds of glistening skulls grinned at him from every side. The gore-soaked mire he walked upon was so drenched in blood that his boots sank into it with his every step. It was as though the god-beast had tried to recreate a part of the Blood God's realm in the middle of Skraevold.

The walls of the pit were marked with runes and a log palisade, the sharpened ends of the timbers facing inward and pointing down. The one place where the palisade stood open, a massive log had been pushed into the pit, forming a crude bridge into the darkness. Only a small distance from the palisade, the Aeslings had constructed a bier, Alfkaell's robed body lying atop it, the seer's elven helm laid upon his chest.

Einarr strode toward the pit, Rafn's axe at the ready. His eyes tried to pierce the black darkness, but could see nothing. The warrior stopped. The beast already had enough things in its favour; it did not need one more. He drew the broken shard of Fangwyrm, filling his free hand with its comforting weight. Then with a roar he raised his arms above him, smacking axe and sword together. The metal crash thundered through the silence. Einarr thought he could hear something moving in the pit, imagined that the stench of blood grew. He raised his arms again, cracking his weapons together. The third time he did so, he could make no mistake. Something was crawling up from the hole.

Like a gigantic serpent or a vast worm, the blood-beast oozed its way up the log, tendrils coiling around it as the monster pulled itself upward. Its hide was brighter than it had been in Vinnskor, glutted on all the blood it had spilled. It rose, eager for still more, drawn by what its slobbering mind interpreted as the sounds of battle.

This time, the bloodbeast held no horror for Einarr.
He stood his ground as it surged toward him, a gore-
soaked hill of hungry flesh and lashing tentacles. He
watched as the thing's back split open in a burst of
crimson, as a long trunk oozed its way into being, as
the monstrous hound-like head grew from the stump
of the neck. The head swung slowly in his direction,
the riot of black eyes staring down at him. The massive maw with its sword-like fangs dropped open and
from the beast came an ear-splitting howl that shook
Einarr's bones.

The warrior glared at the thing and roared back at it.
The beast surged forward, a great paw growing from
its chest and slashing at him. Einarr dodged the
clumsy swipe, stabbing into the monster's corrupt
flesh with the ragged edge of Fangwyrm. The monster
absorbed the stricken limb back into itself and stumbled forward once more. Einarr backed away as a pair
of crab-like claws shot from the thing on root-like
stalks. The ghastly limbs clacked shut only a hand-
span from Einarr's leg. He spun and chopped down at
the things before the beast could pull them back, the
axe slashing through the meat of the stalks. The dismembered claws writhed in the mire even as they
began to crumble into a blood-black crust.

The beast lurched forward again, growing a gaggle
of mismatched legs to stumble after its prey. A mammoth limb that resembled a flail smashed into the
ground with a sickening squelch, narrowly missing
Einarr. The warrior slashed at the huge knot of bone
and skin, gouging a hole in its side. Even as the monster withdrew it for another strike, Einarr could see the
injury closing upon itself. Even glutted after devouring two villages, the monstrosity had lost none of its

power. Einarr threw himself across the ground as a second giant paw swiped at his head. He rolled across the mire as the paw twisted with a boneless motion and ploughed into the ground.

Einarr glared at the horror as it reared back, clattering in what could have seemed an insane mix of agitation, hunger and amusement. Touched by the gods or no, there had to be a way to hurt it, a way to make it know fear, a way to leave his mark upon it.

A loathsome second head grew from the beast's body, its mouthless lizard-like face spurting a spray of steaming blood from its empty sockets. The filth splashed across Einarr, catching his hand in its lethal wash. Warmth and pain suddenly replaced the numb cold that had claimed his left hand. Fangwyrm fell from his throbbing fingers as he doubled over in agony. The metal glove he had worn was pitted and melted, searing into his flesh. Einarr roared at the god-beast, hurling Rafn's axe at the wretched face. The blade tumbled end over end, then sank into the scaly head. The tiny face tried to shriek without a mouth as its own blood began to consume it. The neck shrivelled and wilted, like a dying flower, leaving a black crust against the beast's breast.

The monster itself seemed oblivious to the fate of the second head it had grown, instead scuttling forward on its mismatched legs. Einarr dashed aside as the thing charged at him, cursing the impulse that had caused him to leap without recovering Fangwyrm from the mire. Now the monster stood between him and the blade. Its body shifted, its neck and head oozing into a new position on its formless mass. Einarr dove behind the only cover he could find, Alfkaell's bier, as the immense bulk hurtled at him.

The bloodbeast crashed into the stack of logs with the force of an avalanche. Einarr was thrown back amidst a cloud of splinters and blood-ridden mud, crashing against the timbers of the palisade. He tried to suck breath into his winded lungs, even as his eyes searched the charnel ruins around him for anything resembling a weapon. Above him, the beast was slithering over the top of the bier, crushing the logs and the body of Alfkaell beneath its enormity.

Suddenly, the god-beast shuddered, retreating from the bier. Its jaws opened in a shriek of agony, smaller mouths rippling across its hide and joining its chorus of pain. Einarr could see a section of its body smoking, the flesh darkening into a black scab-like crust. The outline of the wound at once struck Einarr. It resembled a helm, tall and narrow and straight. He looked away from the monster, spotting the crushed body of Alfkaell and the equally flattened elf helm that had been resting on his breast.

That was the secret, how the seer had maintained control over Skraevold's god. Einarr pulled himself to the top of the smashed bier, dragging the ithilmar dagger from his belt. The bloodbeast gibbered and whined to itself, tongues emerging from its mass to lick its wound. As Einarr stood atop the bier, however, the thing's hound-like face stared up at him. The warrior snarled back at it, shrieking his clan's war cry as he dove down upon it.

Einarr landed atop the hound-skull head, his feet sinking into the quagmire of its substance. He could feel his boots being consumed by the filth of the monster's body, could feel its molten blood dissolving his skin. He put such pains from his mind, driving the ithilmar blade down into one of the black, shimmering eyes of the beast. It shrieked again, the organ exploding beneath his strike. The head reared back, almost throwing Einarr to the ground. He clutched at the side of its face with one hand, then stabbed a second eye, sinking his hand up to the wrist as he drove it deep into the skull.

The beast was screaming from a hundred mouths now. Einarr could see its blood spurting everywhere as he destroyed a third and then a fourth eye. He tried not to look at the screaming faces that shifted and writhed in the thing's blood, concentrating only in working his blade across the monster's obscene bulk. Lashing tentacles whipped around him, flailing idiotically in their desperation to rip him free. As he struck a fifth eye, the head began to ooze back into the body, taking Einarr with it. Einarr braced himself to leap clear, but as he did so, he stared into one of the faces screaming within the beast's blood. A new hate boiled over within him as he saw Asta's tortured features. The warrior held firm, slashing a sixth eye as he disappeared into the oozing hulk.

The bloodbeast quivered and shook, its faceless mass trying to crawl back towards the pit. Legs collapsed into puddles of filth as it moved, organs grew and withered with its every motion. Its immensity began to dwindle as portions of it dropped away and did not reform. The vibrant crimson of its substance darkened, the pulpy structure of its skin hardened and cracked. With a shudder, it slopped down against the ground, the impact causing great chunks of its body to slough away. The thing struggled to rise again, but what strength was in it was no more. It grew a wolf-like paw, raising it imploringly toward the sky. The limb crashed to the earth, crumbling into scabby clay even as the bulk that had spawned it grew still.

The silence and stillness did not linger long. The beast's body shuddered again, great clumps of it falling away, cracking against the earth. From within the gory innards of the horror, Einarr forced his way clear. From head to toe, his battered body was caked in the crusty residue of the bloodbeast, looking himself like some daemonic sending of the Blood God. Einarr lifted his hand into the sky, not in entreaty but in triumph. He shouted his victory to the heavens, to the cold thrones of the gods and the hallowed halls of his ancestors.

EINARR STEPPED AWAY from the quickly crumbling carcass of the god-beast, every muscle in his body feeling on fire. The warrior prowled among the carnage of his battle until he saw the hilt of Fangwyrm shining amid the crimson mire. He bent down to recover it, feeling naked with only the slim length of the ithilmar dagger in his hand. As he recovered the weapon, he saw that he was not alone.

Just beyond the perimeter of the pit and its surroundings, a horseman stood, his shaggy war pony digging restlessly at the crimson earth. The rider atop the animal was clothed in skins and armoured plates of bluish steel. The helm that protected his head was wide and crowned with spikes of bone. Feather talismans dripped from the rider's coal-black hair. The horseman's skin was pale, almost white, his features broad and cruel. He met Einarr's gaze, making no motion to draw the crook-bladed sword at his side.

'For to glory-honour the Tchar-hand!' the horseman called out, his Norse crude and twisted by foreign tones. Einarr made no move to lower his weapon. The accent and hair told him this was no Aesling, nor even a Norscan, but one from the Kurgan tribes. Kurgans in Norsca tended to be raiders and slavers, taking thralls to their own wind swept wastes and steel for their smithies. Keeping one eye on the horseman, Einarr tried to watch the ruined long houses of Skraevold for more Kurgans.

'Make peace with the gods, man of the steppes,' Einarr called back. He had learned the tongue of the Kurgan during the siege of Erengrad. 'I have slain the god-beast of Skraevold. If you think your sword will kill what it could not, the ravens will pick your bones.'

The Kurgan raised his hands, showing that he meant no harm. 'I would not challenge he I have come so far to seek,' the horseman said, returning to his native tongue. 'Many days have I ridden the black wastes and the barren steppes to find you, Hand of Tchar.'

'I am Einarr, of the Baersonlings,' the Norscan told the Kurgan. He continued to watch the buildings for more Kurgans, certain that the horseman's words were a trick.

The Kurgan shook his head. 'You are the Hand of Tchar, the one I have come to seek.' He pointed at Einarr, gesturing to his left hand. Einarr looked down at it, seeing it as though for the first time. The metal glove he had worn was gone, consumed by the searing blood of the beast, but the skin of his hand was largely untouched. Only in places was it marred, coated in molten metal from the ruined gauntlet. There was a pattern to the patches where the metal had adhered, covering only those places where the icy blood of the black eagle had numbed his flesh. Now, as he looked upon the weird metallic skin, Einarr could see the pattern it formed, the rippling moon-shape that was the sign of Tchar, the Lord of Change.

'Who are you?' Einarr demanded. Though his words were directed at the Kurgan, he could not pull his eyes from the change that had seized his hand.

'Vallac, of the Khazags,' the horseman said. 'I heard Tchar whisper your name in the wind, saw your face written in the clouds.' Vallac pulled his helmet from his head. A great patch of his scalp had been shaved and upon it, Einarr could see a tattoo, the tattoo of a rippling moon. As Einarr looked at it, it seemed to him that the tattoo's hue shifted and changed. 'I am a servant of Tchar. I know to read the signs he casts into the wind, and I know to follow the wisdom that is hidden in those signs. That is how I was led here, Einarr Steelfist. How I came to stand here, to witness you smite the mighty beast of Khorne.'

Einarr turned from Vallac, stalking through the crusted remains of the beast, seeing if he could find Rafn's axe. 'The Changer is a trickster, Vallac of the Khazags. He has deceived you. There is no one here called Einarr Steelfist! I am Einarr Sigdansson! I am no champion of Tchar, or any of the gods.' Once the prospect of becoming such would have filled Einarr's mind with wondrous ambitions and mighty visions. Now, with his village gone, his kin slaughtered, the favour of the gods held nothing for him. He had no time for this Kurgan and his delusions.

'But you are marked,' Vallac persisted. 'You are chosen. How else explain your victory over the beast? How else could you emerge unscathed from its fiery belly, your cloak and your armour and your flesh unmarked? Only where the sign of Tchar is written on you did the Changer allow the beast's essence to sear you, so that he might mark you as one of his own.'

The Kurgan's words gave Einarr pause. He looked with new wonder at his unmarked hand, at the leather boots and fur cloak that stood whole on his body. He had seen the monster's blood melt through steel, yet the simple hide of a bear had withstood it. The hairs on the back of Einarr's neck rose. Vallac was right, a great force had guarded him in his fight, preserved him from the bloodbeast. He looked again at his hand, with its metal stigma. He could not doubt what force it was that had watched over him and allowed him to destroy the beast.

Raw, naked hate flared up within Einarr. If such power could protect him against the beast, why had it not done so sooner? Why had it not preserved him in Vinnskor, where such protection might have saved his village? No, there was nothing here worth giving thanks to Tchar.

Einarr found Rafn's axe, stuffing the weapon through a loop on his belt. Without looking back at the Kurgan, he began to stride out of the village, heading north.

'Where do you go?' Vallac asked as Einarr walked away.

'I head north,' Einarr answered without turning. 'There are many Aeslings there, and my axe still hungers.'

Vallac kicked his steed's flank, trotting after Einarr. 'Tchar has guided me here,' he said. 'I do not know why. Until I have solved that riddle, I would follow you.'

'Then follow, Kurgan,' Einarr said. 'There will be enough Aeslings for both our blades.'

CHAPTER FIVE

WITH A GASP, Einarr tore himself from the dreams. Haunting visions of dripping, foul corridors and walls of rotting flesh lingered at the edge of his awareness, refusing to return to the domain of nightmare. A face, at once withered and bloated, glared at him from the edge of sleep before at last slipping back into the shadows. Despite the perpetual chill of the Norscan twilight, a thin sheen of sweat peppered his face. As full awareness returned to him, the bitter wind slammed into his damp features like the frozen breath of a snow giant.

'It is the mark of a mighty warrior that the enemies he has slain stalk him beyond the wall of sleep.'

Einarr took his leathery hand and wiped the frosty residue of sweat from his face, then turned to look at Vallac. The Kurgan sat close to the small fire he had made, roasting a plump rabbit he had killed. The

Kurgan's horse pawed anxiously at the snow behind Vallac, throwing its head from side to side in its agitation. As Vallac cooked his meal his sword stood beside him, thrust point first into the snow.

'I know the face of every man, brute and monster that has bled its last upon my steel,' Einarr replied. The Norscan pushed his way free of the heavy bearskin cloak he'd been using for a blanket. Groaning, Einarr stretched his half-frozen limbs, trying to force feeling back into them. 'The spectres I saw in my sleep resembled none I have sent to see the gods.'

Vallac leaned back from the fire, sucking at his teeth as he considered Einarr's words. His dark features took on a thoughtful cast. 'Perhaps your dreams are not dreams, but the voices of the gods.'

Einarr's harsh laughter greeted Vallac's sagely suggestion. 'The only men the gods speak to are the seers!' he scoffed. 'And they pay a dire price for such a gift. Their minds go strange, the strength passes from their bodies and their seed withers unspent inside them.' The Baersonling shook his shaggy blond mane. 'There are many women in the south who would tell you that Einarr Sigdansson is no seer!'

The Kurgan shrugged his shoulders, reaching to tear some meat from the rabbit over the fire. 'Norsca is a poor land then,' Vallac said, 'that the gods speak to so few. In the lands of the Kurgan, the gods are more free with their power. One has only to open one's eyes to see their might, one only has to listen to hear their words. None among the Kurgan does not feel the will of the gods all around him.'

Einarr crouched down beside the fire, ripping a leg from the rabbit. He tore at the meat with savage hunger, wiping the grease from his beard with the back of his hand. 'Perhaps the gods understand that the Norse are a strong people,' Einarr said between bites. 'They do not need to watch after us like a shepherd watching his herd, for we are mighty enough to survive without them.' Einarr stared into Vallac's dark eyes. 'I pity the Kurgan that the gods must watch them with such vigilance.' He finished stripping meat from the rabbit leg and threw the bone away. 'Perhaps one day your people will be as strong as the Norse.'

Vallac smiled back at the Baersonling. 'Perhaps one day your people will be important enough to interest the gods,' he said. There was no malice in the Kurgan's words. Like Einarr, his belief in the strength of his people was firm enough to endure the other's challenge.

Einarr reached towards the fire again, intending to rip a bit of meat from the rabbit. The symbol branded into his hand reflected the firelight as he did so. Vallac understood it was a deliberate gesture, a reminder to the Kurgan that at least one of the gods was interested in at least one of the Norse. Einarr sank back into a crouch, tearing at the scrap of meat.

'Is it still out there?' he asked, his voice lower with a note of caution in it. Vallac nodded.

'I have heard it prowling among the trees,' the Kurgan said. 'It never comes near enough to the fire to be seen, but sometimes I can catch its eyes shining back at me from the forest.'

Einarr digested his companion's report. Since striking out into the land of the Aeslings three days ago, they had been followed, stalked by something that dogged their every move. Sometimes it would be ahead of them, other times behind them, but always it was there. They could hear it smashing its way through the brush. When the wind changed, its gut-churning stench would smash into them, a rancid combination of rotten meat and a midden heap. Three times Einarr had tired of being hunted, lunging into the forest to confront whatever was stalking them, but always the thing retreated deeper into the forest, trying to draw Einarr into its world. Even with his temper up, the Baersonling knew better than to fight any beast on its own ground. As he returned to the winding trail, he could hear the creature smacking branches against the trunks of trees, almost as if it were daring him to come back.

'You think it to be a troll?' Vallac asked, and there was a note of fear in his question. Einarr did not think any less of the Kurgan's courage, no warrior relished the prospect of fighting a troll. With its immense strength, incredible stupidity and supernatural ability to regenerate, a troll would fight on long after any normal creature would lie down and die. Einarr had seen many men ripped to shreds by a troll with half its head chopped away, its slimy brain dripping onto the ground. No, it did not shame a man to respect the terrible power of a troll.

'No,' Einarr replied. 'I have seen many trolls and none that I have seen have had the discipline for such a hunt. Their minds wander easily, a troll would not stalk prey for days on end.' The Norscan turned and looked into the trees. He thought he could catch the slightest suggestion of movement, but could not be certain.

'The beast-kin might hunt a man,' Vallac said. 'But those of my land lack the patience to stalk what they cannot overwhelm and kill.'

Einarr nodded. 'It is the same here in Norsca. The gors rarely follow prey for any great time. As you say, they either overwhelm their quarry as soon as they are able, or they find easier prey.'

'Whatever it is,' Vallac answered, 'I cannot shake the feeling that it will soon tire of this game. When that happens, our steel had best be sharp.'

THE ATTACK CAME when the dim twilight at last faded into true night. Einarr had broken camp, trudging on into the north, bound for the villages of the Aeslings, to reap such bloody harvest from his ancestral enemies as he might before his spirit went to walk with its ancestors. Vallac followed close beside him, his shaggy Kurgan horse keeping easy pace with Einarr's long strides. The old game trail they travelled followed the contour of the land, rising and falling with each slope and valley, winding around each outcrop of twisted grey rock. It was as the trail circled one of these outcroppings that the nameless thing that had been stalking them for days decided to strike.

There was no warning, just the crash of an enormous boulder as it was flung at the men. The huge stone smashed into the frozen ground, pulverising the ice and earth as it struck. So close had it come, that Einarr's cheek bled from the shreds of pebble and hoarfrost cast up by the stone's impact. The Baersonling was stunned for the moment, awestruck by how near he had escaped being crushed. Had his hand not begun to vex him, had he not paused to soothe it with snow, a far less heroic doom than the one he thought to seize would have been his.

Even Vallac was stunned by the sudden and brutal attack, the Kurgan staring in open fascination at the sheer size of the boulder. It was as big around as a man and the crater it had dug for itself betrayed a weight that was almost inconceivable.

The tremor from the boulder's impact was still resounding in the bones of the warriors when a vile stench overwhelmed them, a reek of dog vomit and festering carrion. There was a great crash among the trees and then a massive shape exploded from the forest. Before Vallac could even draw his sword, before he could register more than an impression of filthy white fur and powerful long arms, the creature was upon him. Towering over the mounted Kurgan, the monster bowled man and steed over with the impact of its charge. Vallac's horse whinnied in fright as it was pushed down on its rump. Vallac found his arm and weapon pinned beneath his animal as the monster turned it onto its side. The horse shrieked in terror, trying to rip free of the creature's powerful grip and regain its feet. The monster growled in annoyance, bringing its fist cracking down on the animal's skull. Vallac's horse wilted under the impact, its head shattered by the beast's blow. As his horse crashed back into the snow, Vallac was pulled down with it, pinned beneath its weight.

Einarr rushed towards his besieged comrade, smacking his axe into the shaggy white back that rose above the Kurgan and his mount. Icy blood streamed down his axe as the monster howled in pain. It spun, glaring at Einarr with ancient, animal hate. It was bigger than a bear, covered not in fur but locks of stringy white hair. The shape was roughly that of a man, twisted by the mass of muscle clinging to its bones. The long arms, longer by far than any man's, ended not in paws but huge hands, each finger tipped with a wicked claw. The face that glowered down at him from behind its fringe of ratty hair was bestial, the nose pushed in against its face, its mouth a great fanged gash. But there was intelligence in the monster's yellow eyes, a cruel cunning and wickedness far greater than any mere beast.

'I've never seen one so big as you, dung-chewer,' Einarr growled at the monster. 'You must be the grandfather of all the ymir.'

The monster threw back its ape-like head. From its mouth there sounded a hideous shriek-scream that made Vallac's blood curdle. Even in the depths of the Wastes, where all was at the whim of the Dark Gods, the Kurgan had seldom heard a sound so terrifying. Einarr seemed unfazed by the high-pitched cry, simply swiping his axe through the empty air, spattering the ymir's mangy hair with its own blood. The brute lowered its head, snapping its jaws at Einarr. The Norscan gestured at it again with his axe, daring it to test his steel. There was more than simple bravado in Einarr's actions. Any man in the north came to know ymir well from the sagas told during the long winter nights. He knew they were cowardly creatures with little taste for battle. If he could intimidate the ymir with a show of force, it might abandon the fight.

The ymir roared, lunging at Einarr, its hands curled into deadly claws. The warrior reacted to its charge, chopping down at it with his axe. The beast turned with the blow, letting the edge of Einarr's blade catch it in the shoulder rather than the skull. The ape-beast's warm blood steamed as it splattered across the snow, but the ymir hurtled onward, its immense weight smashing into Einarr like a living avalanche. The warrior was thrown from his feet, hurtling backward as though kicked by a horse. The ymir loomed above him, snarling. It dabbed fingers into its wound, sniffing the gore that coated its fingers, then shriek-screamed at the man who had injured it.

Einarr heaved himself from the ground with a grunt, hands still clenched tight around the haft of his axe. The Norscan had barely regained his feet when the ymir was lunging at him again. This time he struck low, looking to end the monster's charge rather than its life. The axe chewed into the beast's thigh, scraping against the thick bone of its leg. The ymir collapsed beneath the blow, screaming in pain. Einarr hurried toward the crippled monster while it was still down on its knee, hoping to end the battle with one last strike. But the beast was far from finished. As Einarr closed upon it, the ymir swatted him with its massive arm, tossing him back with such force that the Norscan was certain he'd heard ribs crack beneath the blow.

The Baersonling spat blood from his mouth, pressing one hand against his side where the beast had struck him. He could not tell through the armour just how extensive his injuries were, but the sharp pain that shot through him as he pressed his side told him that they were there. Einarr shifted his grip on the axe, standing his ground as the ymir rose from its own wounds. The beast limped forward, favouring its maimed leg. It snarled at Einarr, baring its enormous fangs. Watching it hobble towards him, Einarr considered that the sagas had seriously overstated the cowardice of these creatures.

Einarr did not wait for the ymir to come at him again, but charged the creature. The ymir slashed at him with its clawed hand, receiving a taste of the axe for its efforts, severed fingers scattering across the snow. The warrior followed upon his attack by chopping the blade into the monster's chest. The ymir howled in pain, rearing back and pulling the axe from Einarr's hand. Instinctively, Einarr lunged forward to recover the weapon stuck fast amid the ymir's ribs. It was a costly mistake. The claws of the ymir's uninjured hand closed around Einarr's arm. The warrior could feel the awesome strength of the ymir as it tossed him through the air like a rag doll, leaving him to crash hard against the icy ground.

Einarr tried to suck air back into his body, even as he reassured himself that he still had an arm. The way the ymir had grabbed him, he had thought the beast had torn his arm from the socket. Certain he was still whole, he drew the jagged length of Fangwyrm from his belt and prepared to face the monster again. He looked aside to see what had become of Vallac. The Kurgan was frantically digging at the frozen ground with his dagger, trying to slide his leg out from beneath his dead horse. There would be no help from that quarter, the earth might as well be solid granite for all the good Vallac's efforts were doing him. No, it would be Baersonling strength and Baersonling steel that would need to deal with the ymir.

Watching the beast hobbling toward him, Einarr began to doubt his faith in either strength or steel. Even with the ghastly wounds it had suffered, with blood fairly exploding from the mangled ruin of its hand, with Rafn's axe still buried in its chest, the ymir still had not lost its murderous hunger.

'I'll split your belly before I fill it,' Einarr cursed as the ymir drew closer. The ape-beast snarled, bloody drool falling from its fangs. If it was intimidated by the battered Norscan with the broken sword, it was certainly not showing any sign.

Suddenly, a grey shape crashed into the monster's side, knocking it flat. Einarr caught an impression of fur and steel as the strange figure straddled the toppled beast, sending its blood flying as his frenzied assault tore into the ymir's body. Again and again, Einarr saw the fur-covered man's axe slash into the ymir, ripping its body into shreds. The beast did little to defend itself – after bowling the crippled giant over, the man's first blow had severed the arteries in its neck.

When the ymir and its slayer grew still, Einarr cautiously approached. The man was shorter than Einarr, but seemed to be even more massively built beneath the patchwork of ragged wolfpelts and animal hides that covered him. Breathing heavily, the man rose from his gory labour, licking the bloody edge of his axe clean. He turned his hairy visage toward Einarr as he approached. Einarr saw that the man's face was thin and sharp, his brow almost as hairy as his chin. Although the man's hair was nearly as grey as the furs he wore, there was nothing about his features that suggested great age; certainly nothing about his sudden and savage attack did.

'You took my kill,' Einarr told the man. The stranger's eyes narrowed at the challenge.

'Five days I tracked it,' the man snarled. 'The kill is mine. Be thankful you're no Aesling, or Orgrim would have let the ymir finish you first.'

'How do you know I am no Aesling?' Einarr asked. If the weird hunter was truly a foe of the Aeslings, he might be useful to Einarr's plans for revenge. He would certainly know better than Einarr where their villages were situated. Besides, there was something compelling about the man, a haunting feeling that Einarr knew him, had seen him before.

The hunter laughed. 'You don't stink like an Aesling,' he said, tapping the side of his nose. The hunter turned back toward the dead ymir. He set his axe down, burying its blade in the snow, and reached towards the weapon still embedded in the beast's chest.

'The kill may be yours, friend, but the axe is mine.' Einarr locked eyes with Orgrim. The hunter had strange pale eyes, like chips of frost. It was not an easy thing to match his gaze, but Einarr forced himself to do so. He had braved the belly of Skraevold's god, he would be damned if he would look away from some scruffy woodsman. Orgrim seemed to appreciate the display of will. The hunter ripped the axe free, offering it to the Baersonling. Einarr reclaimed his weapon, wiping the ymir's gore from the steel. The hunter watched him clean the axe with a suggestion of amusement in his savage face.

'You helped with the kill,' Orgrim said. 'I will share the beast's meat.' For the first time, Einarr noticed the nature of some of the injuries on the ymir's body. The hunter hadn't simply been trying to kill it. After delivering the deathblow to the ymir's neck, he had started butchering it, cutting it into sections even before it was fully dead. The warrior winced at the image of eating any part of the ymir. The hunter shrugged and returned to his labours. 'Suit yourself, more meat for my fire.' Orgrim rose and pointed towards the mountains looming in the east. 'My home is no great distance. If you won't share my food, perhaps you would share my fire?'

'I would be lying if I said a warm fire would be unwelcome,' Einarr smiled and offered the hunter his hand. 'Einarr Sigdansson of the Baersonlings,' the

96   *C. L. Werner*

warrior said. The hunter nodded as he heard the
introduction.

'My nose never lies,' Orgrim said. 'I knew you were
no Aesling. I know their stink too well to be fooled.
The one with you, he is no son of the Aes either.'

Einarr and Orgrim both turned their heads. Vallac
glared back at them, flopped against the side of his
horse, no closer to freeing himself than when he had
started. Horse and Kurgan alike were coated in blood,
having failed to dig into the ground, Vallac had
started to free himself by carving through his horse.

'Show some care, that is our supper you abuse!'
Einarr called back to his companion. They would have
fresh meat, and without accepting the abominable
fodder Orgrim had proposed.

ORGRIM'S HOME TURNED out to be a bleak little cave
pitting the side of a rocky slope. The hunter had made
little effort in the way of comfort, eking out an existence almost as primitive as that of any beast. The
only concession to civilization Einarr could find was a
clay pot filled with salt.

The hunter had made his fire easily enough with
flint and tinder, but Einarr noted that their host barely
let the fat start to sizzle before he withdrew the ymir
meat from the flame and began ripping into it. Vallac
seemed to find the hunter's penchant for raw, salted
meat alternately revolting and amusing. He made a
point of blackening the flesh of his own meal before
starting in on it. The horse had been much too robust
and muscular for its meat to be tender, but Einarr considered that he had eaten far worse and that it was
certainly preferable to the meal Orgrim was wolfing
down. To eat something so similar to a man was one

of the few things that turned even a Norscan's stomach, though Vallac claimed cannibalism was not particularly taboo among his own people.

As they ate, they talked. Orgrim was keenly interested in what had drawn Einarr so far from the lands of the Baersonlings. When he learned of the warrior's mission of vengeance, the hunter laughed with approval. It transpired that Orgrim was an Aesling himself, though an outcast from his tribe who bore his people only the most bitter of hate. He knew quite well the locations of every Aesling village within a hundred leagues and would be more than happy to help turn Einarr loose upon them.

'I knew there was something important about you,' Orgrim said. He tapped the side of his nose. 'I caught your smell on the wind, before even the ymir. There was something special about it, almost as though the wind wanted to lead me to you.'

'The voice of Tchar,' Vallac nodded, touching the mark of his god branded on his flesh. To the Kurgan, it seemed every stray snowflake was the work of Tzeentch. Einarr was beginning to find the man's rampant superstition trying.

'And what does the wind say to do now that you have found me?' Einarr asked. Orgrim shrugged.

'Lead you to kill Aeslings,' he said without conviction. 'Perhaps we can carve our wergild from them together. My own debt with my people has been unsettled for much too…' The hunter froze in mid-thought, his body becoming rigid, his nostrils flaring as he sniffed at the air. In a blur of speed, he drew his axe and leapt toward the mouth of the cave. Einarr and Vallac drew their own weapons and hurriedly followed their host. They found themselves glaring down at a thin, spindly figure bundled in a heavy blue cloak, its collar fringed in bright feathers and glass beads. The figure had been climbing the slope, up towards the cave, but it froze as the men emerged.

Orgrim glared down at the cloaked intruder. The hunter sniffed noisily at the air, his expression growing even more incensed. 'You'll find no shelter from the cold here, Aesling bitch, only pain and a slow death!' As the outcast's anger built, his voice thickened and his features darkened. Einarr found himself backing away from his new ally, an instinctive reaction for anyone who had seen the fury of a berserk. Vallac hesitated, ignorant of the battle-fury that the Norse warriors who walked the path of the berserker could hurl themselves into. Einarr gripped the Kurgan's arm, motioning for him to distance himself from Orgrim. When the hunter slipped into his frenzy, he would be a menace to friend as well as foe.

The traveller pulled back the heavy hood of her cloak, revealing a head of stringy white hair and a face withered by age and the elements. At the centre of the crone's forehead, the skin was puckered and scarred, grey with dead flesh. Into this wound had been placed, or perhaps had grown, a large black stone. Into the rock had been carved an eye-like symbol, one of the signs by which the Windlord Tchar was known. Einarr felt the same haunting feeling that had come upon him when he had faced Orgrim, the eerie sensation that this complete stranger was somehow familiar to him. The crone sensed his scrutiny and he almost felt compelled to look away when he saw the stone shift its position to face towards him, as though it were staring back at him.

The crone tapped the staff she carried against the ground, causing the collection of bone charms and bronze trinkets dangling from it to jangle. Her normal eyes studied Orgrim, watching him with the same caution a man might regard a growling dog. 'When the bloom of youth was mine, you should have eaten out of my hand,' the crone said, her voice thin and scratchy. 'Now I shall be content to have you lie at my feet.'

Orgrim was already in motion, pouncing towards the old woman as though he were a sabretusk. Einarr was struck by the awesome speed and strength in the hunter's lunge and considered that Orgrim's boast about not needing his help to soften the ymir had not been an idle one.

As fast as the hunter was, the crone was faster still. She did not try to flee from Orgrim's attack, did not try to dodge aside from his lunge. Instead, the woman simply struck her staff against the icy ground again. This time the charms did not jangle together, instead the strings of gut and wire seemed to rise as though pulled by the wind, each of the small trinkets reaching out towards Orgrim's hurtling shape. A foot from the woman, Orgrim's body stopped, crashing against some unseen force. The hunter staggered back, his nose bloody from the impact against the invisible barrier. He howled with rage, coiling his body for another charge. There was an expression almost of pity as the crone watched him. She waved her withered hand and Einarr could feel the power erupt as she made the gesture. Orgrim's eyes rolled back in his head and with a whimper, the hunter wilted into the snow.

'I did not come all this way to see my bones gnawed by the wolves,' the crone hissed. She looked up, watching as Vallac and Einarr prepared to face her. The Kurgan too had felt the power that the old woman had used to fell Orgrim, and like Einarr, he did not relish the prospect of fighting a witch.

'Be at peace,' the witch called out to them. 'I mean you no ill. Even that cur lying in the snow is unharmed. He will sleep, for a time, but that is all.'

'He said you were an Aesling,' Einarr replied. He looked aside at Vallac and could see the Kurgan was thinking the same thought as himself. If they both charged the witch at the same moment, perhaps one of them would strike her down before her spells could work their ruin. 'An Aesling is never at peace with a Baersonling!'

The witch pointed at Einarr's hand. 'The mark upon your flesh is more important than the blood in your veins, reaver.' With a flourish, she shrugged back the cuff of her cloak. Upon the thin, wasted arm Einarr could see a patch of skin that had sprouted a growth of brilliant blue and yellow feathers. Somehow, it did not strike the Norscan strange that the growth should be in the same shape as the symbol on his own hand.

Einarr lowered his axe and stepped forward. 'What can you tell me of this mark?' he asked, extending his hand toward the witch. 'I have never given the Wind-lord cause to mark me as his own. Why should he place his sign upon my flesh?'

The witch's laughter wheezed through the few teeth left in her face. 'The gods do not ask, they take!' she sneered. 'Tchar wants you, warrior. Therefore you are his!'

It was Einarr's turn to sneer. 'I have asked nothing of the gods and they have given me nothing. They have little cause to demand my service now.'

The crone shook her head. 'Tchar guided me to you for a purpose. In the entrails of a pig, I saw this place. I saw a man with the mark of Tchar forged into his hand. My divinations told me that the man would not understand what was demanded of him. It would be Urda's task to tell him, and to tell him what Tchar would be willing to give in return for his service.' Urda looked past Einarr, staring at Vallac.

'Let the Kurgan see to the renegade,' she said, turning from the cave. 'There are things I would say that only the ears of Tchar's champion should hear.'

'Am I some cowering thrall to take orders from an Aesling crone?' Einarr growled back. 'Do not think I will balk at cutting the head from a presumptuous old hag who has outlived her days.' He brandished his axe menacingly at Urda. The witch simply smiled at him and turned away. Einarr felt a tremor of rage rush through him at the old woman's haughty airs. Not even the bondsmen of Vinnskor had treated him with such disrespect! Yet even as the urge to strike her down for her arrogance swelled within him, Einarr knew that he would not touch her. He watched the old witch walk back down the slope for a moment, then tucked his axe back in his belt.

'You don't mean to follow that hag,' Vallac said, disbelief in his voice. Einarr nodded his head.

'I have little wit for riddles,' he said. 'If the witch can truly tell me why Tchar has chosen me, then I would hear her words. See to Orgrim, I will not be long.'

CHAPTER SIX

THE OLD WITCH took Einarr a small distance from
Orgrim's cave, into a small stand of gnarled, twisted
trees. Einarr found the writhing, tortured trunks
unsettling, the resemblance of their thin limbs and
scrawny branches far too close to skeletal talons to
escape the Norscan's superstitious attention. His skin
crawled as the unnatural aura reaching out from the
grotesque trees impressed itself upon him. It was the
sensation of cold unearthly expanses, the aroma of
sorcery and magic. Einarr felt foolish, allowing mere
trees to unsettle him so. He tried to tear his gaze from
them, but found them morbidly fascinating. Then, in
his inspection of them, Einarr found a pale blue eye
staring back at him from amid the bark of one trunk.
There was anguished madness in that eye and while
Einarr watched, pallid sap-like tears oozed from its
corners.

'Blood of the old-fathers!' Einarr swore, drawing back from the stand of hideous trees. Beside him, Urda began to cackle.

'Perhaps they were, once,' Urda laughed. Einarr felt sick as he watched the old woman caress one of the branches with her own wasted hand, stroking it as a child might pet a cat. 'Many lifetimes have they stood here, reaver. They came into these lands from the south, to loot and to plunder and to kill. But they offended Tchar the Changer and he brought them low, changing flesh into wood and blood into sap. And here they stand, living testaments to Tchar's wrath.'

'Why have you brought me here?' Einarr demanded. The warrior did not look at the witch as he spoke, his eyes watching the tortured trees, half expecting the abominations to spring into unholy life, to avenge their ancient misery with Baersonling blood.

Urda shook her head, giggling under her breath. 'You don't trust me, Einarr Steelfist?' She laughed louder as Einarr momentarily shifted his suspicious gaze to the witch. 'Good! Good! Trust is the first illusion. None who would navigate the web of Tchar's wisdom should be so easily deceived.' The crone began rummaging through an ox-hide bag, removing small black stones from it. She began pacing through the snow, kneeling and placing the stones upon the ground in a complex pattern.

'Do not fear, reaver,' Urda said. 'I do not think it is Tchar's will to add a new sapling to his grove of the cursed. I brought you here because this is a place strong with the power of Tchar. Places where the gods have left their marks forever draw strength from them. Those who serve can tap into that strength. We are drawn to such places, can feel their call in our bones. It is why that renegade makes his lair in the cave beyond the hill, because the power of this place beckons him.'

Einarr clenched his hand, feeling the metallic flesh groan as he willed it close. 'And what of the men upon whom the gods leave their mark?'

'They beckon too,' Urda said. She set the last stone in place upon the snow and reached into her bag once more. Something sleek and slimy coiled about her forearm as she withdrew it, something that looked to Einarr midway between slug and eel. The witch smiled with her empty mouth as she ripped the thing's throat with her overgrown nails, splashing the snow between the stones with its treacle-like blood. A sharp, bitter smell struck against Einarr's senses as the crone bled the loathsome mollusc dry. Urda tossed the carcass into the woods and turned toward Einarr again.

'You can feel Tchar's strength in you,' she said. 'Others can feel it too and they will be drawn to it, like moths to the flame. Why else do you think the Kurgan and the renegade sought you out? Why else do you think Tchar guided my steps to find you?'

'You promised me answers, witch!' Einarr snarled. 'Not more questions! Tell me why Tchar has done this to me! Tell me what it is the gods expect of me!' Urda stared long into Einarr's furious eyes, then nodded and crouched down, her shrivelled hand reaching into the soiled snow. She approached Einarr, her fist closed around a handful of snow slimy with the life of the mollusc.

Einarr stared at the pungent, soupy mess running between the crone's fingers as the snow melted. It seemed to sizzle as it struck the ground, burning its way into the soil beneath the snow. He shifted his gaze back to Urda's gleaming eyes.

'Eat this, and all your questions will be answered,' the crone said. She opened her fingers, displaying the melting filth that had been crushed into a ball by her grip.

The warrior pulled away, swallowing against his revulsion. 'Was it not you who said that trust is the first deception?'

'So I did,' the witch grinned back, still holding the repugnant mush beneath Einarr's face. 'Perhaps you are not so eager to find wisdom as you profess.' Urda's hollow laughter hissed from her face as she watched Einarr's features twist with disgust as he continued to watch the icy filth melt in the witch's hand. Einarr ignored her gloating, his mind flying as he tried to decide what kind of game Urda was playing with him. Did she mean to poison him, cast some baleful spell upon him? He found his eyes wandering again to the twisted, tortured trees. Perhaps that was what she intended, despite her assurances that such was not the will of Tchar. Sigdan had once told him that the most dangerous lies were those the liar did not bother to hide.

The crone continued to cackle and into her laughter was mixed a menagerie of sounds, human and animal. Einarr felt his head spinning as the noise seeped down his ears. His skull felt on fire, a throbbing agony that echoed Alfkaell's attack upon him. Sweat beaded upon Einarr's brow as he fought to focus his thoughts. The eyes in the trees were wider now, watching him with an air of loathsome expectancy.

Suddenly, amid the babble of the witch's sounds, a set of syllables stabbed into Einarr's mind like a burning blade. The fog of confusion vanished and Einarr lunged forward, his tainted hand closing around Urda's scrawny throat, his other hand holding his axe high.

'What did you say?' Einarr's voice thundered. 'How do you know that name?' Even with Einarr's hand locked about her neck, there was a gloating quality in Urda's toothless smile.

'You know what you must do to find wisdom,' the witch wheezed. Despite the violence of Einarr's fury, her hand still held the ball of filthy snow and she once more extended it toward the warrior's face.

'You said "Asta"!' Einarr growled. 'How do you know that name!' His grip tightened about the witch's throat, her shining eyes bulging in her withered face. Even with death reaching out for her, the smile remained locked on Urda's countenance.

'Daring breeds wisdom,' Urda hissed. 'Death brings only ignorance.'

Einarr roared with frustration, releasing the witch, hurling his axe across the grove. The warrior raised his fists, shaking them at the black sky, hurling curses at the heavens. When he turned, he found Urda standing beside him again, holding the melting filth out to him once more, as though nothing had happened, as though he hadn't come within an inch of snapping her scrawny neck. The rage in Einarr's eyes collapsed into a miasma of defeat. The warrior's shoulders slumped and he nodded his head weakly. Whatever trap the witch had set for him, he did not have the will to escape it.

Urda pressed her hand against Einarr's face. He could feel her paper-thin flesh against his lips as the slimy slush was pushed into his mouth. He could feel the filth burn as it slithered down his throat, could feel its abominable substance racing through his body. Einarr wilted to the ground, hacking as his body tried to vomit the corruption back into the snow. Urda watched his misery for a moment, then slowly made her way back to the ring of stones she had made. She lifted her staff from where she had laid it upon the ground. She stabbed its point into the tainted snow still remaining within the pattern marked out by the stones and began churning the filth like a house-thrall stirring a cauldron.

'Asta...' Einarr gasped as his body continued to heave and convulse.

Urda looked back at the stricken warrior. 'In time, reaver. But there are much greater things we must learn first. You are the chosen, it is upon your flesh that Tchar has forged his mark in steel. It is to you that the will of Tchar has been revealed, even if you are not wise enough to understand. The voice of the gods is spoken in the language of dreams. Tell me what visions have filled your sleep and their shapes will manifest in the blood of the changeling. Tell them to me, that we may both learn how we will serve mighty Tzeentch!'

AN ICY TINGLE worked its way along Einarr's spine as he looked down upon the images that had been captured in the tainted snow. It was not the loathsomeness of the medium, or the fact that Einarr could still taste the filth in his mouth. It was not any level of horrifying detail, for the images were more like the stylistic runes of the seers than pictures torn from life. No, it was the sense of familiarity they evoked as he looked upon them, the certainty that the repugnant ritual had done exactly what Urda claimed it had done. She said the tainted snow had drawn the images straight from Einarr's mind, pulling them from that hidden place where the brain locked away unremembered dreams. Looking upon them, Einarr knew he had seen them before, knew that each figure and each scene had played its part in the long hours of slumber.

Einarr studied each figure, trying to find some meaning, some understanding from them. There was a squat, daemon-like figure, its bearded face split in a wicked grin, its hands extended as though to make an offering of the sword laid between them, heavy chains drooping from its arms. Near the little daemon were two massive figures, their outlines suggesting immense strength, one of them leaning against a gigantic maul. Another figure was that of an armoured warrior, horns curling from his helm, the skull-rune of Khorne emblazoned across his chest.

There were animals too, wild beasts each marked with peculiar signs. There was a griffon, its mighty frame enclosed in armour, great horns framing its visor face. There was a sinister-looking owl, its face sporting three eyes. There was a great falcon with arrows flying from its beak. A loping wolf, an axe clenched tight in its jaws. A shaggy horse, feathers braided into its mane and the mark of Tchar upon its brow. A mighty winged dragon, its wings tattered and torn, its jaws open in a great roar. Above everything, there was a monstrous eagle, its beak crooked, its wings unfurled. Einarr felt his eyes straying again and again to the avian figure, unable to shake the sense of belonging it provoked.

There were scenes as well, places and things that were strange and sinister to Einarr's eyes. He saw a great pillar, its surface covered in writhing figures, a gigantic worm coiled around it. The worm's mouth was open, and strange things danced upon its tongue. He saw an enormous ship, far different from the long-ships of the Norse, listing badly to one side and with great fingers pulling at it from below. There was a tall cliff, its sides jagged and crumbling, seeming to twist and change even as Einarr looked at it.

Einarr stared at the pictures for a long time, trying to make sense of them. But they were too many, too strange in their shape and form. Einarr was a warrior, not a seer or skald. Interpreting the meaning of the signs was beyond him, for all the emotion they evoked in him.

Urda stood beside Einarr. The old crone jabbed at the snow images with her staff, pointing to the three-eyed owl. 'This, I think, must be me.' There was a note of pride in her voice as she made the observation. Einarr considered that for all the witch's gloating, all her talk of conversing with Tchar, there had been doubt in her mind that she had really been guided to him by the gods. Seeing what could be a symbol for herself within the dreamscape of Einarr's nightmares had reaffirmed her convictions.

'If the owl is you, then the stallion is surely Vallac,' Einarr said. He found himself looking once again at the symbol of the eagle. It had been such a creature that had found him in the ruins of Vinnskor that had set him upon this path. He could not deny the sense of kinship it evoked. 'This one,' he said, pointing at the eagle, 'I feel is meant to be me.'

The old crone's face betrayed a moment of shock, her brow lifted in surprise. 'The eagle is the symbol of Tchar,' she pronounced with even more certainty than she had in her own representation among the symbols. As she spoke her words, Einarr felt a twinge of terror as a fragment of his dream seemed to return to him. Running, trying to hide upon a vast, empty plain while above him, its cruel eyes watching his every move, there circled the great black eagle. The horror of the memory caused Einarr's pulse to quicken. Tchar, the Changer of the Ways. Einarr could almost feel the god's eye upon him as he stared down at his symbol. Yet he still could not escape the sense of belonging the symbol made him feel. Somehow he was even more certain than Urda that the witch was wrong, that the eagle was meant to represent himself, not Tchar.

'What of these others, then?' Einarr wondered, trying to change the subject. 'What might they mean?'

'Beware, Steelfist,' Urda cautioned. 'There is both guidance and warning among these signs. Some you are to seek out, others you should avoid.'

'But which are which?'

Urda shook her head. 'The gods are seldom so forthcoming. They leave it for men to find such wisdom for themselves.' Einarr turned away from her and began staring at the symbols again. 'Lock these signs in your mind's eye, Einarr Steelfist. Keep them safe, do not forget them. They are the words of Tchar. When the time is right, you will understand their meaning.'

Einarr digested Urda's speech. Slowly the warrior turned back toward the witch. 'This is how you answer the riddle of my dreams, crone. With more riddles! You promised me answers! You promised me wisdom! Where are my answers, old woman? Why has Tchar cast his mark upon me? What is it he would have me do?' Einarr's voice dropped into a deep snarl.

'And how does the name of my wife come to be on an Aesling's forked tongue?'

The witch gestured at the symbols in the snow again. She indicated a particular cluster on the very edge of the ring marked out by the stones. There was what seemed to Einarr a vast and bleak swamp, from the centre of which rose an immense and crumbling tower. 'Not all of these symbols are unknown to me, reaver. I told you that I understood why Tchar had chosen you and what he wanted from you. I do, but I had to be certain that you were indeed the one Tchar had chosen, that the same visions I had seen in my dreams were also in yours.'

The crone gestured to the figure of a man set beside that of the crumbling tower. The figure was corpulent and bloated, seated upon a lavish throne. 'The Plague Lord Skoroth, favoured apostle of Neiglen the Corrupter, the god of pestilence and decay. This,' she gestured at the tower itself, 'is Skoroth's fortress, the Palace of the Plague Lord. It lies deep within the Wastes, far beyond the lands of the Norse, beyond even the lands of the Kurgan, at the very doorstep of the realm of the gods. Skoroth's palace is a temple to his god, a sacrament to the filth of his master. It is where the great treasures of Neiglen are kept, locked away behind walls of corruption and disease.

'One of those treasures is a sacred relic, an artefact that Neiglen stole long ago from Mighty Tchar. The Windlord has waited many centuries for the time to be right to reclaim what was stolen from him. That time is now. Just as the Corrupter's power waxes, so too does it wane. Neiglen is weaker now than he was when he dared steal from Tchar's holy vaults.'

'Why does Tchar not take his relic back himself?' the blasphemous words were fuelled by Einarr's smouldering anger. The witch was taking the long way around to answering anything.

'Skoroth's palace lies beyond the realm of the gods, existing within the world of mortals. A mortal may enter it and not draw the notice of Neiglen, a god could never do so.' It was the sort of mysterious response Einarr had come to expect from the crone. The witch pointed at the symbols again, this time indicating a large, sickle-shaped claw. 'This is the treasure that was taken from Tchar, the talon of his favoured servant, that which bears the title of "Dark Master". It is a thing sacred to Tchar and filled with his might and power. For it to lie within the fastness of another god is a thing abhorrent and unclean.'

Einarr shook his head. 'Such a small thing for Tchar to ask of me, to storm the stronghold of Neiglen himself and steal one of the plague god's treasures!'

'Not in a thousand years could you gather an army mighty enough to seize the palace of Skoroth,' sneered Urda. 'You must use cunning and deception if you would do this thing. Where an army must fail, a few might succeed.'

'What I must do is cast aside all this talk of gods and relics,' Einarr snarled. 'Let Tchar burn his mark into some other fool! I did not ask for his favour, nor do I want it! All I ask is that I spill the blood of many Aeslings and take vengeance for my slaughtered people.'

Urda's scrawny hand closed around Einarr's arm as he started to leave. 'Wait, Steelfist! I have told you what Tchar asks of you, but you have not heard what he offers in return! Far more than simple vengeance, far more I assure you.'

Einarr glared at the old witch, his temper roused by the desperation in her voice. Was there nothing more behind her talk of gods and palaces than a cheap trick to keep him from cutting his way through the villages of the Aeslings?

'What is there left to me except my vengeance?' he demanded.

'Step within the circle and you shall see for yourself,' Urda replied. The witch motioned for Einarr to cross into the patch of befouled snow. His boots stomped across the images and he waited while Urda pulled a scroll of vellum from beneath her robe. She held the letters close to her face, her eyes squinting as she studied the symbols.

'More sorcery, witch?' Einarr growled. 'I grow weary of your tricks! What would you have me do this time? Milk a maggot, or perhaps drink the piss of a weasel?'

Urda looked up from her scroll. Her eyes glowed with etheric energies. When she spoke, her voice was a subdued whisper. 'The gods do not need such ceremony to impose their will upon the world. The power of a god is but a single word.'

Einarr saw Urda's mouth open again, but such sound as she might have given voice, he did not hear. For when the witch spoke, Einarr's world vanished in a blinding burst of colour and light. Einarr felt every fibre of his being stripped and torn as existence itself collapsed around him.

AMIDST THE HEAVY furs of his bed, Einarr crushed Asta's warm, lithe body against his. His hand caressed the scaly skin that covered the back of her neck and shoulders, the coppery plates feeling smooth beneath his touch. Suddenly his entire body shook, trembling like a sapling beneath the fury of the winter wind. The swordsman sat bolt upright, nearly spilling his wife onto the earthen floor of their home. He stared wide-eyed at the little room, stunned by every unbroken timber. He looked into Asta's pretty face. His massive arms circled her, pulling her against him in a desperate embrace.

'You are supposed to be resting,' Asta scolded him, but her efforts to free herself from his grip were far from genuine.

Einarr tried to stifle the emotion that flooded through his body, but Asta sensed his anxiety just the same. She looked down into his confused eyes. Einarr's breath came in rapid, uneven gulps betraying a fatigue of spirit rather than body. Asta smiled at him, brushing the hair from his brow with her hand.

'I thought you dead,' Einarr finally managed to find his voice. The image of Asta, torn and ruined, her body littered across the shambles of their home... But, no, she was here, in his arms, her breath washing across his face, her scent in his nose. Where had the horrible images, the phantom memories that filled his mind, where had they come from? Visions? Dreams? Nothing more than the ill-sendings of his fever and his wounds?

'It was I who thought you dead,' Asta said, swatting his shoulder with her palm. 'Or have you forgotten your time at Skraevold so soon?'

Einarr felt a cold chill run up his spine. Skraevold at least had been no dream. What of the rest? A warning? A premonition? The chill running up his spine turned to ice as he looked down and saw his hand. He withdrew it quickly, hiding it beneath the blankets before Asta could see.

'Oh! Did I hurt your hand, husband?' Asta reached for Einarr's hand, but the warrior held her back. He didn't want her to see it. If she saw it, then he would know it was real. And if it was real…

'Then let's be away from this place, wife,' Einarr said, forcing his voice to be gruff and steady, to keep the panic that he felt from tainting his words. 'Take what we can and leave. We can go to the lands of the Sarls or even the southlands.'

Asta pulled her hand free from his grasp. 'You are afraid what the runes will tell Ulfarr, aren't you? What Tulkir will decide must be your punishment for killing the seer of Skraevold?'

'No, not Ulfarr, or even Tulkir,' Einarr told her. He pushed her from the bed. 'Don't ask questions. Just move! We have little time! Death is coming to this village!' Einarr surged from the bed and began stuffing supplies into a leather bag. Much to his annoyance, Asta stood beside the bed, staring at him with a perplexed look.

'I don't understand,' she said. 'What do you mean, death is coming to the village?'

Einarr let the length of salted venison he was holding drop to the floor, shuddering as he noted that he had been holding it with his marked hand. His face was a mix of agony and guilt as he looked into his wife's eyes. 'Death is coming to Vinnskor,' he repeated. 'I know because I have brought it here! Now hurry! While there is still time!' The desperation in his voice caused Asta to spring into motion. She raced towards the heavy wooden chests where they kept their furs and clothes, swiftly sorting through them to find the most rugged and durable. Einarr watched her for a moment, then noted the pile on the floor, the cloak and gear he had stolen when making his escape from Skraevold.

The warrior lunged for the pile, startling Asta, causing her to drop the clothes she was stuffing into an old ox-hide sack. Einarr tore through the pile of mangy furs, groping among them for the slender length of silvery metal he now knew could save Asta and his entire village.

Asta watched her husband's strange actions, wondering what sinister spirit had come upon him when both of them suddenly spun around and stared at the door. Outside, in the village, they could hear a great tumult, voices screaming and crying out in alarm.

Einarr bit down on a curse as his fingers closed about the elven dagger, the sharp edge of the metal slicing his hand. Blood spilled down his arm, but he ignored the pain, raising the weapon in triumph above his head. Now he had a chance! Now they all had a chance! He looked into Asta's eyes, feeling his chest swell with hope and determination. The god-beast of Skraevold would not touch her this time!

THE COLD, STINKING snow pressed upon Einarr's face. He recoiled from the muck, straightening himself. He stared all around him, the same shock throbbing through his body. Surrounding him, the ghastly trees seemed to laugh at him, their eyes narrowed as they savoured his despair. A cruel trick! A filthy trap! But the witch had failed in whatever mischief she had thought to work upon him. He knew now what had been illusion and what was reality. Urda would pay for her Aesling treachery with her life!

Einarr could hear the witch croaking with laughter. No, not laughter, she was choking, her breath rattling against her collapsed throat. The Norscan looked in the direction of the noise and found Vallac standing over the witch, his powerful fingers wrapped around her neck.

'Where is he?' the Kurgan was shouting. 'By all the black horrors of Ruin, what have you done with the Hand of Tchar?' Urda beat weakly against Vallac's wrists in a feeble attempt to free herself. Einarr grinned. Good, Vallac was making certain the witch didn't die too quickly. There would be time for Einarr to take his own retribution out of the deceitful bitch's hide. He reached for the shattered length of Fang-wyrm.

The warrior stared in amazement at his hand as he moved it. It was cut, the fresh blood on his fingers and in his palm only now beginning to freeze under the harsh Norscan night. He lifted it toward his face, disbelieving his own eyes. As he did so, a familiar smell filled his nose, a smell he never thought to smell again. Asta's scent still clung to his hand. Then it had been more than a dream!

Horror filled Einarr's mind as he looked back towards Vallac and Urda. The old witch's movements had grown even more feeble, her pale features turning purple as Vallac continued to strangle her. The Norscan shouted, racing toward the combatants. He pushed a startled Vallac away from Urda, almost knocking the Kurgan flat in the snow. Einarr caught Urda in his arms as the witch collapsed. He massaged the crone's neck, trying to will air back into her body.

'Steelfist!' Vallac shouted. 'Where were you? I thought this hag had worked some black sorcery upon you and made you into one of these vile trees!'

'I told you to leave me alone with the witch and see to Orgrim,' Einarr snarled back, desperately trying to minister to Urda. Her breathing continued to be shallow and ragged.

'He is fine,' Vallac said. 'Still sleeping from the hag's spell. It is you I feared for. I should find little glory if you were to find so ignoble an end.'

'A man finds his own glory,' Einarr growled back. 'He does not wait for others to give it to him!' He felt a little easier as Urda suddenly gasped and gulped a great breath into her body.

'Tzeentch guided me here,' Vallac reminded him, a scowl on his tattooed face. 'You play an important part in my own doom, Einarr Steelfist. Until I have seen otherwise, I will go where you go, do what you do.' Vallac's gaze strayed from Einarr as he spoke, looking instead at what remained of the picture-signs Urda had drawn in the snow.

'Then next time you will also do what I say,' Einarr warned him. 'It would sit ill with me if you had travelled so far only to find your doom on the end of my axe.' The Norscan subdued some of the anger he felt. He had no cause to be angry with Vallac, the Kurgan had tried to help, tried to avenge a friend he thought slain by foul treachery. He forced a smile onto his visage. 'If I were forced to kill you, Vallac, who would lead me to all these hot-blooded Kurgan slatterns I've been hearing about ever since we left Skraevold?'

Vallac nodded, accepting the sentiment of both jest and threat. He understood well the strange ways of magic, the many forms and shapes it could take. He also understood that the reason for Einarr's anger was not wholly directed at him, but mainly directed at whatever spell Vallac's attack had broken. The Kurgan turned his head and slowly walked away, his mind wondering what manner of spell Urda had cast over the Norscan and where it had sent him. Einarr seemed unwilling to talk about it, but wherever he had been, it had been no place near the grove and the clearing. Perhaps he would get the truth out of the witch when Einarr wasn't around.

Einarr watched his comrade walk away, heading back towards Orgrim's cave. When he was lost to sight, he looked down into Urda's face. The old woman's eyes were open now, she seemed at least mostly recovered from Vallac's attack. A wry smile puckered the crone's features.

'Now you see,' she said. 'Now you understand. For a moment, Mighty Tzeentch allowed the deceit of time to be cast aside.' Her hissing cackle caused her withered body to shake in Einarr's arms. 'What he has done once, he can do again, any time he wills it. Now you see the reward that Tzeentch offers you, Steelfist!'

CHAPTER SEVEN

THE SNOW DRIFTING down through the Norscan night
shimmered as it fell upon the ground, glowing with
the colours of the rainbow, casting an eerie flickering
light across the pines. The tainted snow felt hot as it
fell against Einarr's skin, causing him to brush it from
his exposed arms in irritation every few yards. For days
they had marched through the hinterlands of Norsca,
their steps slowly but relentlessly drawing them from
the lands known to men.

'The winds blow down from the north,' Urda
observed. The old witch hobbled alongside Einarr,
only too aware that she needed the Norscan's protection. Vallac's distrustful gaze was like a dagger poised
at her back, the Kurgan's eyes always fixed upon her
every time she looked in his direction. Ahead of them,
the renegade Orgrim trudged through the shimmering
snow. When he looked back at Urda, there was no

mistaking the savage, bloody fire that smouldered behind his gaze. Even more than Vallac, Einarr had been hard pressed to keep Orgrim from killing the witch. Several times, he had thought their disagreement would be settled in blood, but Einarr was too cunning to settle for so short-sighted a solution. He needed a guide to pass through the lands of the Aeslings, to reach the Frozen Sea and the Wastes beyond.

'The breath of the gods is in that wind,' Vallac said. 'You can see their fire burning in the snow.' The Kurgan was silent for a moment, as though contemplating his own words. 'It is a good omen', he finally pronounced.

'Not to the herdsmen who tend their cattle, or the shepherds with their flocks,' Einarr said. 'Animals sicken when the power of the gods falls upon them. Many will die when this snow falls into their pastures.' The warrior stopped, lifting his head and staring at the cloudy sky and the shimmering snowfall. 'The herds of the Aeslings will be culled by this snowfall. Perhaps this winter they will starve.' He lowered his head, turning to stare at Vallac. 'It *is* a good omen,' he agreed, a grim smile set on his face.

Urda felt her blood chill as she heard the hate in the Baersonling's voice. She knew that Einarr would have killed her as soon as any other Aesling if he were not terrified that to do so would also kill his only hope of claiming the prize Tchar had promised him. She hoped that the warrior would not take it into his head to force her to try and repeat the ritual. The power had come from Tchar, not her own abilities. It was not something she dare invoke again. When the time was right, the Lord of Change himself would reward Einarr, and when he did, he wouldn't need a tired old Aesling witch to work his magic. She had explained as much to Einarr, but how much he had believed, Urda did not know. The fact that he had forced her to come with him certainly boded poorly for the faith he put in her words.

Ahead of them, the renegade Orgrim suddenly stopped, his head turning from side to side, looking into the trees around them. He dropped to all fours, pressing his face against the snow. Urda could hear him snuffling like a beast as he thrashed upon the ground. Einarr hurried forward to discover what had happened, his axe at the ready. Vallac came up behind the crone, his sword pressing against her side.

'If this is more of your witchery, hag, I'll skewer your heart,' he hissed into her ear, all the menace and malice of his people lurking within the Kurgan's threat.

Einarr stood above Orgrim while he grovelled on the ground. He could hear the man sniffing, his nose pressed into the snow, breathing deeply. The warrior reached down to shake Orgrim from whatever fit had crossed him. The berserker recoiled from his touch like a frightened dog, curling into a knot of tensed muscle and bared teeth. After a moment, reason restored itself to Orgrim's eyes and he relaxed, straightening himself and rising to his feet.

'A woman passed this way,' Orgrim told Einarr. 'Not long ago. Her scent is strange, not the stink of an Aesling.'

Einarr digested the berserker's words. He had already come to trust Orgrim's uncanny sense of smell. But what would a woman, a foreign woman at that, be doing wandering in the wilderness alone and in the middle of black winter? Einarr felt a shudder course through him as he remembered tales of ghosts and spectres that had echoed in his father's longhouse on cold winter nights.

Orgrim pointed his hairy hand to the south. 'She came from there,' he said. His nose twitched as he sniffed at the air. 'But she did not remain alone. They came from the west and took her back with them.'

'Who took her?'

Orgrim's expression was dark as he answered, his face betraying the revulsion he felt as he made his answer. 'The forest folk, the beast-kin.'

'Then your mysterious woman is lost.' Einarr turned to find that Vallac and Urda had joined them. He raised an eyebrow as he saw the Kurgan's sword pressing into Urda's side. Reluctantly, Vallac withdrew his blade and slammed it into its horse-hide sheath.

'Which way did they take her?' Einarr demanded. Orgrim pointed once more towards the west. Einarr nodded his head and began marching toward the trees. Vallac's hand closed around his arm, pulling him back.

'The gors have her, let the matter rest,' Vallac told him. 'While they feast, we may slip through their wood unseen.' Einarr shook his head and pulled away.

'Perhaps a Kurgan might leave his women to warm the bellies of beast-kin, but a Norscan does not,' Einarr said. He could see shame darken Vallac's features as he spoke. 'Even if this slattern were an Aesling slut, I would not leave her to the paws of the beastmen.'

Vallac nodded his head slowly. It was clear that the Kurgan still did not agree with Einarr's decision, but at least now he understood it. Among his own people, there was no dishonour in accepting the harsh whims of the gods, but the Norse were still fool enough to believe they could challenge the strands of fate.

* * *

SHARP AND ACRID, the smell of the cook-fires reached them even before the mangy reek that characterised the beast-kin encampment. Orgrim led the way, gliding noiselessly through the frozen forest, not so much as a branch stirring in his wake. Einarr felt himself as ungainly as a drunken giant trying to match the woodsman's stealth, every twig that snapped beneath his boot seeming to thunder across the silence of the forest, every bush he disturbed seeming to sway with the violence of a war flag on the prow of a longship. Sometimes Orgrim would pause to give him a reproachful glance, but more often the scout ignored his clumsiness, understanding that it could not be helped.

Soon, the sounds of the beastmen broke the silence of the forest, deep-throated roars and high-pitched brays, a mongrel din that grated across Einarr's ears like a knife across bone. The monsters had established their camp in a small clearing nuzzled between two great piles of rock. Einarr could see the filthy bone and gut totems of the gors jutting up from the rocks, boldly proclaiming the presence of the beastmen to anything that had somehow failed to take notice of their stench and sound. One ragged totem, its standard formed by the flayed hide of a man, bore the arrow symbol of the realm of the gods upon it, the scarlet sign still moist with its morbid ink. In the trees above, crows had gathered, draw by the stench of blood and decay, the carrion birds croaking and squawking to one another as they waited for the leavings of the beastmen.

Einarr tested the feel of the axe in his hand, ignoring the flicker of nervousness that raced through his mind. His father had spoken much of the dwellers in

the forest and their savage ways, how it was better for
a man to fall on his own blade than be taken alive by
such monsters. He laughed at his own disquiet. Many
years and much blood separated him from the child
he had been. His eyes had seen much, his body had
suffered much, his spirit had endured much. He
would not let his manhood falter before half-
remembered terrors.

'Ten,' Orgrim growled, the sound low and brutal as
it hissed between his clenched teeth. Einarr nodded as
he heard the woodsman speak. Orgrim continued to
count the monsters prowling the camp, making a
mark in the snow with his finger each time he spied a
new set of horns or his nose caught an unfamiliar
scent. Soon, there were more marks than could be easily counted. They were odds that would set the soft
men of the south quaking in their boots, praying to
their feeble gods for salvation. The Norse were not so
weak. The foe was what it was, the odds already set,
the will of the gods already made. If a man would prevail, then he must prove to the gods that he was
worthy of victory.

'The beast-kin are simple of mind,' Einarr said. 'If
they think we are many, they may lose the stomach for
battle and flee.' He stabbed a finger at Vallac, pointing
to the east. 'Circle among the trees, position yourself
on the right and attack when I attack. Take care to
make no sound, and beware that your scent does not
drift towards their camp.' The Kurgan smiled grimly,
drawing his crooked sword in a slashing motion
through the air. He cast one last suspicious look at
Urda, then crept into the snowy veil of the pines.

'You will take the left,' Einarr continued, pointing at
Orgrim. The Aesling renegade shook his shaggy head.

'The strongest of the beast-kin will be near the fire,' Orgrim protested. 'The fighting will be the hardest at the centre of the camp.'

'That is why I have saved the centre for myself,' Einarr said. Orgrim cocked his head in puzzlement. Einarr turned his hand to display the metal sign forged to his flesh. 'I bear the mark of Tchar. Let us find, here and now, if the god is truly watching over me or if his favour is simply an empty promise.'

'Do not think the beast-kin will show you honour,' the hunter said. 'They will think to draw the god's favour into themselves by devouring your flesh.'

'Then I will teach them fear before I send them to grovel before their ancestors,' Einarr swore.

Orgrim looked anything but convinced by the warrior's words, but still turned and slowly stalked through the trees towards the west of the encampment. Einarr watched him go and breathed deep. It would be a battle worthy of the sagas, if any survived to tell the tale.

'You should not bait the gods.' Einarr turned as he heard Urda's scratchy voice reprimand him. 'It is a terrible vengeance they visit upon those who test their power.' The old witch placed her thin hand on his arm. 'Be careful, Steelfist, lest you tempt the wrath of Tchar.'

Einarr pulled away, turning his head. 'There is nothing worse the gods can do to me that has not already been done.'

Urda's cackling laughter wheezed from her scrawny frame. 'There is always something worse,' she said. 'Even in your misery, respect the might of the gods lest their power bring you so low that even your misery becomes a thing of envy.' Einarr was silent, staring down into the snow as he considered the witch's warning. When he spoke again, his voice was soft.

'You know what has been promised me. If Tchar will not let me save one woman, how can I have faith he will allow me to save my village?' Einarr clenched his hand into a fist, the knuckles cracking under the pressure. He felt the hot rush of anger burn through his body. 'I would have that answer now, not when I stand over Skoroth's broken corpse!'

Rage coursing through him, Einarr launched himself through the trees, his axe at the ready. The corrupt blood of the beastmen would do little to quench his fury, but that would not stop him from trying.

Urda watched the warrior charge through the trees, an enigmatic smile slowly spreading across her features.

WITH A ROAR, Einarr burst through the trees and into the clearing. His eyes swept the squalor of the beast-kin encampment, the piles of excrement festering at the edges of the camp, the bundles of mangy hides and furs scattered about the clearing, the heaps of broken bones, cracked and split where the gors had shattered them to suck out the marrow. At the centre of the clearing, ringed by several large stones, the beasts had piled old branches and bits of dead brush to form their fire. At either end of the fire ring, the monsters had built stands from wood and the antlers of elk, and across the pit a large, blackened pole rested. To this a lithe, pale shape had been tied with tethers of sinew and gut. The captive moaned through the mess of fur scraps that had been shoved down her mouth to gag her and struggled feebly at her bonds. Beneath her, the orange flames of the fire licked up at her flesh.

The beastmen turned away from their cooking meal, staring at the warrior with dull eyes that were cloudy with confusion and surprise. The beast-kin were a mongrel display of animal loathsomeness and human corruption. Their bodies were, for the most part, not unlike that of a man in shape and build, powerful muscles rippling beneath their furred flesh. But these things were no men. Their heads suggested the savage and the inhuman, the faces of many pulled into the long snouts of beasts, their skulls sprouting the horns and antlers of animals. Feet ended in hooves more often than toes and hands might end in claws as easily as fingers. Some of the brutes sported tails and tentacles, others exhibited almost human features made all the more ghastly for their setting amid furred flesh and beneath jagged horns.

The Norscan did not allow the monsters time to gather their wits, but charged straight at the nearest of his foes. The creature, a hulking monster with a goat-like head and elk-like antlers, was cut down almost before it could bleat out a cry of alarm, black blood spraying from the beast-kin's chest as the axe clove it apart. Einarr chopped again into the creature as it crumbled into the snow, breaking its back with the blow.

The death of their pack-mate settled the confusion that had struck the monsters. With brutal roars and high-pitched wails, the grotesque mob lunged into action, some diving for the rusty axes and crude spears scattered about the encampment, others rushing towards Einarr with only their bared fangs and sharp claws. Einarr roared his own defiance at the monsters and charged to meet them.

Before the first of the beastmen could close with Einarr, shouts of alarm and despair sounded from the edges of the encampment. Orgrim and Vallac charged from the trees, their weapons slashing through furred bodies and spraying black blood across the snow. True to the woodsman's statement, the beast-kin on the edges of the camp were small, wiry creatures, their horns mere stubs on their brows. They were a far cry from the massive brutes clustered about the fire. Runts or no, Orgrim tore into them with the same mindless ferocity that had characterised his battle with the ymir, the woodsman's axe crushing bone and cleaving flesh with maniacal abandon. Vallac displayed more restraint, challenging his foes from the edge of the camp, the Kurgan maintaining a position close to the trees and making his enemies come to him. Vallac's curved blade was soon slick with the stinking blood of the beastmen.

While some of the brutes turned to answer the new threats on their flanks, the majority of them still rushed toward Einarr, their bloodlust aroused by the warrior's challenge. A huge beast with the face of an ox and the jaws of a bear closed with Einarr, slashing at him with its long claws. Einarr's axe caught one of the monster's hands, slicing the fingers off. The other claw raked ineffectively across the Norscan's armour, unable to penetrate the tough leather and mail. Einarr answered the creature's attack by chopping into its shoulder, nearly severing its arm. The ruined limb flopped limply at the monster's side as it continued to batter Einarr with the bloody stump of its other hand, an anguished howl that was equal parts pain and hunger bleating from the gor's throat. Einarr silenced the beastman's howls with a slash of his axe, sending its head dancing across the clearing.

Others followed close behind the decapitated brute, their attacks no less feral. One creature with a grinning face and a mass of horns running down the back of its head jabbed at Einarr with a spear of oak and flint while another, bigger beastman snapped at him with its powerful jaws and tried to wrap the slimy rope-like tentacle that served it as an arm around his neck. The warrior found himself pressed to answer the challenge of both creatures when a third howling thing leapt towards him, a crude club of bone clutched in its paws. The howling thing never landed its blow, however. Screaming in agony, the thing dropped into the snow, its body cracking and twisting as its bones and organs shifted and stirred beneath its skin. Before he looked away, Einarr saw the thing's rib cage collapse, then turn in upon itself, pushing one of its lungs through the brute's furry hide.

The tentacled beastman wrapped its noxious limb around Einarr's arm as the warrior turned from eviscerating the spear-wielding bray. Einarr felt the entire arm instantly turn numb as the poisonous member slithered against his flesh. Only by force of will did he maintain his hold upon his axe, refusing to let it slip from his unfeeling fingers. He drew the jagged length of Fangwyrm from his belt. The beastman twisted its body, tightening its hold upon Einarr's arm, almost popping it from his shoulder. Einarr ground his teeth against the pain and surged toward the beastman. The brute tried to protect its tentacle, twisting still further. But Einarr had no intention of cutting the tentacle away, driving Fangwyrm instead deep into the gor's chest, skewering its putrid heart. A great blob of black blood slobbered free of the beast's mouth as it fell to its knees, the tentacle releasing Einarr's arm as the strength left it.

Einarr had no time to watch the beastman spit its life into the snow, already another of the growling monsters was closing on him. Einarr forced his still tingling arm up, catching the rusty weapon of his new foe against the haft of his own axe. The warrior twisted his body around, tearing the rusted flail free from the grip of the goat-faced gor that held it. As he turned, he drove the peen of the axe against the side of the beastman's skull, stunning it and causing it to stagger. Before the brute could recover its wits, Einarr's axe chopped down into its leg, cleaving its knee and spilling the beast into the snow. A kick to its face shattered the beastman's snout, driving bone into its brutish brain.

For the moment, Einarr was not beset by foes. He could see a few beastmen harassing Vallac, but as he watched, the larger of Vallac's foes reeled back as the Kurgan spat into its face. Einarr was struck by the thing's anguished wails and the black smoke running between its paws as it clutched at its features. Yellow grease oozed between the monster's paws as the melted residue of its eyes drooled down its charred face. Vallac did not bother to finish his blinded foe, but focused his attention on his unmarred adversary. Across the clearing, Orgrim continued to slash and rip into the wiry ungors and hulking gors that threatened him, splashing their reeking blood across the snow and howling like a beast himself whenever he sent another foe to find the gods. While Einarr watched, he saw a hornless bray swat at Orgrim with a club only to have the berserker lunge at the creature and tear its throat out with his teeth, seeming to relish the sensation as the filthy blood spilled down his chin.

* * *

WITH THE REMAINING beastmen focused on Orgrim and Vallac, Einarr rushed towards the fire and the captive strung over it. The woman continued to struggle feebly at her bonds, straining to turn her head and observe the battle she could hear unfolding all around her. Her dark eyes went wide with astonishment as Einarr suddenly appeared over her, kicking kindling from the circle and sawing away at the sinew ropes that bound her to the pole. For an instant, Einarr found himself lost in the woman's deep, lustrous eyes, drawn into the enigmatic depths of her gaze. But reason and instinct quickly reasserted themselves, and Einarr attacked the ropes with renewed ferocity. A battlefield was no place to dally over a pair of pretty eyes.

Einarr had barely cut the first hand free when he felt himself struck from behind. The warrior was cast down by the force of the blow, tossed across the snow like a child's toy. He tensed his body and sprang back to his feet, heedless of the pain throbbing from the wound in his back. To let the backstabber slink away without repaying it for its craven assault would hurt him more than torn flesh and bruised bone.

Einarr's attacker had no intention of slinking off, however, but stood boldly beside the fire circle, its gory sword clutched in its massive paw. It stood a head taller than even the largest of the creatures Einarr had killed, its body swollen with its brawn. The monster's head was like that of a goat, a pair of huge fangs not unlike those of a sabretusk jutting from its jaw. Two massive antlers sprouted from the sides of its skull and at the centre of its forehead a great knotted horn curled upwards. The brute already bled from wounds in its arm and belly, but if its injuries pained it, the monster gave no sign. Einarr could tell that the

thing was the leader of this pack, that it was determined to defend the prize morsel Einarr had sought
to free.

The beastlord snarled and shook its head, its massive hooves stomping against the frozen ground.
Einarr cocked his arm back, poising his axe for a
mighty strike and gestured for the monster to charge
him if it dared. The beastlord bellowed its anger
into the darkened sky and ploughed across the
ground towards Einarr, its horns lowered. His body
shuddered as the monster's immense weight
slammed into him and the Norscan was pushed
back across the frozen earth, his boots skidding
through the snow. He heard the brute's right horn
scrape against the side of his helmet, felt the sharp
edge of its sword dig into the meat of his shoulder,
saw the monster's fangs snap close only inches from
his face. But the creature did not assault him with
impunity. Einarr's axe raked down the side of its
head, obliterating its eye and shearing one of its
antlers from its head.

The beastman recoiled from its attack, wailing in
shock as it pawed at the dripping nub of its antler.
Einarr slashed at the reeling creature, but the wound
in his shoulder made the strike sloppy and slow. The
beastman reacted with a quick swipe of its sword and
batted Einarr's blade aside as easily as it might have
swatted a fly. Reminded of his presence, the beastlord
roared its fury and made to lunge at the warrior once
more.

Suddenly, a sharp, trilling sound echoed across
the clearing. Einarr watched in amazement as a
black storm of feathers and talons engulfed the
beastlord's head. The murder of crows gathered in

the trees had descended in a cawing, clawing mob, attacking the monster with an amok ferocity. The beastman staggered back, trying to shield its face from the enraged birds. Einarr forced himself to overcome his wonder. Taking his axe in both hands, a war cry shrieking past his lips, he charged through the swirling swarm of birds to bury his blade in the monster's skull. A look of almost human horror filled the beastlord's face as it suddenly saw Einarr's steel slashing down at it through the blinding veil of black feathers. The edge of the axe bit deep as it crunched through bone, splitting the beastman's face like a wormy log.

Einarr turned away as the crows swarmed over the beastman's twitching carcass. He clutched at the dripping wound in his shoulder, feeling the blood already beginning to crystallise in the frigid Norscan night. He tried to probe the wound with his fingers to see how deep he had been cut, gritting his teeth against the pain. A hissed reprimand pulled him away from his investigation, Urda's scrawny hands pushing his own aside as she examined his hurt.

'Fool of a Baersonling!' she spat. 'I hope this will be a lesson to you that it is madness to test the gods!' The witch fumbled about in her bag, producing an evil-smelling paste, which she pressed into the wound. Einarr looked away as she ministered to him, his gaze canvassing the battlefield. It seemed the beastlord had been the last of its pack, the others of its kind having fled or fallen. He could see Orgrim sitting atop a heap of mangled beast-kin, the berserker's body caked in blood. Vallac was kneeling amid the snow, studiously cleaning his blade with a scrap of fur while elaborate Kurgan prayers dripped from his tongue.

'I should have fared worse had you not worked your sorcery when you did,' Einarr told her between grunts of pain. 'The beast-kin was a worthy foe. If you had not sent the birds when you did...'

Urda paused in her ministrations. 'I did not call the crows,' she said. 'I should not have had the strength to work such a spell after invoking the power of Tzeentch to destroy the one that thought to smack your stubborn brains from your thick skull.'

Einarr felt a thrill of dread race down his spine. If the witch had not summoned the birds...

'Then who did?' The warrior's question lingered in the air for a moment. When it found an answer, it was not in the scratchy tones of the witch.

'I called them.' The words were spoken in a thick, rich voice. Einarr felt his pulse quicken as he set his eyes on the woman who had spoken them. He had found her striking enough even lashed across the cook-fire of the beastmen. Now standing before him, her pale bare body gleaming in the starlight, the wind pulling at her long platinum hair, Einarr found even the dripping wound in his shoulder slipping from his mind. Her lean, feminine shape was the supple, sinuous figure that drove men mad on long sea voyages, filling their minds with vices too long denied. Yet there was strength in her body as well as lure, this was no simple freeholder or farm wench. Even as he admired the curve of her shape, the slope of her thighs and the fullness of her breasts, Einarr noted the grey slashes of old scars and the puckered residue of old wounds. No, this was no meek village wench content to bask in the glory of whatever champion warmed her bed, but a shield maiden of the old sagas, a woman who seized her own glories with her own hand.

Einarr stared into the woman's sharp, comely face, finding himself drawn once more into her dark, alluring gaze. 'You are a witch then?'

The woman laughed and shook her head. 'I am no seer,' she said, and Einarr imagined there was a suggestive note about her tone. 'But I called to them just the same.' She turned her head toward the murder of crows still pecking and scratching at the cooling body of the beastlord. She pursed her lips and again Einarr heard the strange, trilling note echo across the clearing. He could see the woman's tongue as it trembled between her lips. It was long and thin, fluted like that of a bird, as black as the feathers of the crows. When they heard her call to them, the birds rose from their gruesome meal, cawing and croaking as they withdrew back into the trees.

'She is touched by the gods,' Urda whispered, though Einarr could see as much for himself. The woman nodded her head, but when she spoke, her words were again directed to Einarr.

'Since the cradle, I have been able to speak with the creatures of the sky,' she said. 'I can talk with them as easily as I talk to you. They tell me where to hunt and where to shun. There is much wisdom they can give, if only one can listen to them.'

'They did not seem to give you very good advice this day,' Urda observed. 'If Einarr had followed my advice, you'd be warming the bellies of the beast-kin.'

'I was guided by a tale told to me by a falcon,' the woman told Urda. She turned her eyes back on Einarr, stepping toward the warrior. 'He told me that a great jarl with a steel hand had risen in the north, that great glory would fall upon me if I sought him out and pledged my oath to him. I travelled far from the lands of the Sarls to seek this champion, the one with the mark of Tchar written upon his flesh.' The woman reached out, closing her slender hand around Einarr's, her fingers caressing the metal symbol branded into his skin.

'I have spent many weeks trying to find you,' the huntress said. She smiled as she looked away from Einarr's hand and into the warrior's eyes. 'Instead, it is you who have found me.'

CHAPTER EIGHT

FOR LONG WEEKS, the small warband navigated the cold, desolate forests of the north, slowly making their way through the narrow ravines that wound between the craggy slopes of the mountains. Bleak and inhospitable, they saw few traces of either man or beast upon the land. Even in the ever strengthening clutch of winter, it was an unsettling sensation, to be the only things moving beneath the sunless sky.

Only twice, in all those weeks, had they seen any sign of habitation. Once, the berserker Orgrim, ranging far ahead of the group as was his habit, had caught the scent of several men drifting back to him on the wind. With his keen senses, the renegade claimed the smell was that of Aeslings, probably a party of trappers or hunters braving the icy forests in hopes of putting meat on their tribe's tables. Orgrim had described with bloodthirsty enthusiasm the ease with which they could track down the Aeslings and spill their lives onto the snow. Einarr felt the same urge for action, to sink his sword into Aesling flesh and reclaim some of the wergild the northerners owed his vanquished people. He was dissuaded only by the council of Urda. The old witch warned Einarr that, though they saw little trace of them, the settlements of the Aeslings were all around them. If even a single warrior escaped the slaughter that Einarr contemplated, he might bring the entire Aesling nation down upon them. Was Einarr truly willing to risk the reward Tchar had promised him simply to glut his lust for revenge?

The other evidence that they were still very much in the lands of the Aeslings had been discovered by Birna, the pale-haired Sarl huntress they had rescued from the beastmen. Like Orgrim, there was a heavy dose of wanderlust in her heart and she would often range ahead of Einarr and the others, prowling among the trees to find the easiest path. Einarr found himself admiring the skill with which she vanished into the woods, her steps so soft and careful they scarcely marred the snow beneath her feet. After she was freed and had recovered her armour and gear from the paws of her dead captors, Birna had presented a much different figure. Gone was the alabaster-skinned snow goddess that had stood over the dripping corpse of the beastlord calling the crows away from their feast. Instead, Birna's shapely form disappeared into leather tunic and breeches, over which she wore a skirt of chain and a heavy cloak of sabretusk hide. A fat-bladed sword with a whale tooth hilt and an ivory-bound bow completed her lethal appearance, the multitude of feathers she strung through her hair adding a savage, feral quality to the effect. Despite the pain the loss of Asta had caused him, Einarr could not help the quickening of his pulse whenever the striking Birna came near him.

Late one evening, as Einarr and the others prepared to make camp, Birna had stalked back from one of her forays into the forest. Ahead, she reported, was an entire Aesling village. The track they had been following for the past two days would take them right into the settlement. It was a small village, little more than a hamlet and when Vallac pressed her about what she thought their chances might be, Birna had simply shrugged her shoulders, claiming that every victory was at the whim of the gods. Einarr had felt again the drive towards revenge, to stain the earth with Aesling blood and raze the little village the way Vinnskor had been razed. Animal-like growls of agreement came from Orgrim, a bestial light glowing in his eyes as he contemplated the slaughter he would visit upon his hated kinsmen. Even Vallac seemed eager, reverting to the calculating Kurgan raider, having decided that the small village would make easy pickings for the warband. Again, it was the council of the old witch Urda that stayed Einarr's hand. There were many days between them and the Frozen Sea, the borderland of Aesling territory and Norsca itself. Would they throw that away now, simply to indulge in a massacre unworthy of mighty warriors?

'It is the blessing and favour of mighty Tchar that awaits us beyond the Frozen Sea,' Urda said. 'What glory can exceed the praise of a god?'

STILL FARTHER INTO the icy north they travelled, entering lands that were naught but myth in the sagas of the Baersonlings. Einarr could almost feel the breath of the gods washing against his skin with his every step. The trees they journeyed under became increasingly twisted and gnarled, their branches scrabbling at the sky like reedy arms. Einarr saw what looked like a white-furred fox peek at them from behind a clump of snowy rocks, its eyes dangling from thick fleshy stalks, its mane a nest of wiry quills. Even the black veil of night was changing, the eerie light of the aurora shimmering and dancing against the northern horizon.

There was more, something less tangible than foxes and trees, something nebulous and unseen. Einarr could feel it, like cobwebs rubbing against his soul, like a cold flame slithering through his blood. He knew it was the power of the gods, the power that tested everything it touched and destroyed all that was not strong enough to endure it. Even for a mighty Norse warrior, it was an unsettling thing to know that such forces were touching him with invisible fingers, probing his body and testing his worth. He could see that his companions shared his uneasiness, pausing frequently in their steps to scratch at the eerie sensation crawling across their skin, watching the twisted trees and flickering sky with a wide-eyed stare that was more fear than caution. Only the Kurgan, Vallac, seemed unaffected by the strange atmosphere of these hinterlands. If anything, Vallac seemed more casual and steady than Einarr had ever seen him. He was reminded again that the Kurgans came from a land much different than Norsca, but Einarr could not comprehend a people who found basking in the power of the gods a thing of comfort.

At last, the twisted forests gave way to jagged slopes of grey rock where only the hardiest shrubs managed to eke out a miserable existence. The slopes shot rapidly downward until at last they terminated in a sheer drop of several hundred feet, the cliffs so sharp that Einarr could easily credit Urda's muttered words that they had been cut from the mountains by the axe of Kharnath himself. Below the cliffs and stretching out to the northern horizon, its icy expanse shining blue beneath the flickering witch-light of the aurora was a sight that chilled the marrow in Einarr's bones: the Frozen Sea, a dread fable to those reavers and sea dogs that prowled the Sea of Claws and the warmer waters of the south. It was exactly as it had been named, a vast ocean frozen into a world of ice. To a seaman like Einarr, there was something almost unholy about the sight, the rolling waves of the sea turned into a thing as lifeless and still as solid stone. He felt incredibly small and feeble as he looked down at the unmoving waves of ice, appreciating in a way that he never had the awesome power of the gods. They had done this to the mightiest force Einarr had ever known – the sea itself. They had crushed and killed it and left its frozen body for all to see.

What was a man beside such raw, limitless power? How could any man hope to prevail before the omnipotent might of such a force? A man was nothing! A man was less than nothing and all his dreams and thoughts less than the babble of an infant! A man was a fool to think he was anything more, to have the audacity to think his deeds, his hopes, were things of consequence!

Einarr shook his head, trying to clear the sombre thoughts from his mind. He felt Birna's hand fall upon his shoulder and found himself staring into her compelling eyes. Einarr could feel himself being drawn once more into the depths of her eyes, pulled down into whatever secret world existed behind the pretty features of the huntress.

'If that is where you will lead us,' Birna said. 'That is where we shall follow, Einarr Steelfist.' The words were spoken in a voice that seemed wary, almost timid, the tone almost feeling betrayed by what had been said. Einarr drew himself out from Birna's compelling gaze, looking across at his other companions. Urda was staring at the Frozen Sea, her old body shivering beneath its heavy cloak, the talismans fastened to her staff rattling as her arm trembled.

Orgrim was crouched down upon the ground, his head hung low, looking for all the world like a hound chastised by its master. Einarr watched the berserker turning his head from side to side, staring up and down the sides of the jagged slope, staring in any direction except that which would lead his gaze across the Frozen Sea. Even Vallac appeared intimidated, the Kurgan scratching at his chin as he cast a worried look past the side of the cliff. Einarr could appreciate the thoughts he was certain were rolling through the minds of his comrades. It was one thing to consider a place and call it the Frozen Sea, it was another to stand before such an awesome sight and know that it stood in your path.

Somehow seeing the doubt and fear in the faces of his followers strengthened Einarr's own resolve. There would be no turning back. They would find the stronghold of Skoroth and reclaim the treasure that had been stolen from Tchar. Einarr would earn the reward Tchar had promised him. He would save Asta and his people. Not even the Frozen Sea would stop him.

Einarr turned his back to the vast expanse of ice, staring hard at his companions. 'We will need to find a way down the cliffs,' he said, refusing to acknowledge the fear he saw in his comrades. He did not allow the others time to consider or question his decision, instead striding off along the cliffs, following them eastward. He did not look back as he heard first one, then all of his companions following after him. Somehow he knew they would follow. Of all the fears that might be plaguing their minds, he knew none was greater than the shame of being left behind.

'AESLINGS,' ORGRIM'S THROATY growl rumbled in Einarr's ear. The warrior nodded as Orgrim spoke. They had followed the curve of the cliffs for days before at last finding a break in the natural wall, a spot where it would perhaps be possible to climb down to the surface of the ice sea. However, as they grew closer, Orgrim had grown ever more anxious, warning that the smell of men was in the wind. Not long after, Birna had spotted the encampment.

Crouched behind a snow bank, Einarr and the others observed the strange camp. Nuzzled in a deep fissure cut from the side of the slope, it was almost invisible until the observer was almost on top of it. The builders of the camp had clearly appreciated their concealed location, choosing to forego any sort of perimeter wall in the interest of maintaining that concealment. Instead, the builders had situated a pair of watchtowers, ramshackle structures of timber and oxhide, to either side of the fissure's mouth. Beyond these, Einarr could see a pair of long, low buildings, their thatch roofs covered in snow. Beyond these was what appeared to be a smithy, its massive stone forge belching black smoke into the night. Beyond the smithy was the wall of the cliff, pitted and scarred, its face bisected by wooden scaffolds and stone ramp ways. Einarr could see tiny figures pounding away at the cliff, what looked to be chains dangling from their limbs. While he watched, a small cluster of the workers pushed an ox-cart filled to the brim with ore down one of the ramps and toward the smithy. A short, dark figure detached itself from the forge and stomped forward to shout orders and abuse at the men pushing the cart. Einarr could not tell if the sinister apparition were man or daemon, but there was no mistaking the armoured warriors who stood to either side of the imp. Orgrim was right again, the strange quarry was being operated by Aeslings.

'We should go around.' Einarr turned his head as Urda hissed her advice to him. The old witch shook her clawed hand to the west, away from the quarry and the jagged tear in the cliff face that snaked its way to the surface of the Frozen Sea.

'For once I agree with the witch,' Vallac said, though the Kurgan took no pride in his words. 'I have counted at least a dozen warriors in that camp, if they drive their slaves into our swords, then they have four times that number. Too much sword work for the five of us, I fear.'

'They are weaklings!' Orgrim snapped, and it seemed to Einarr that the berserker's teeth were longer and sharper than he remembered them. If the touch of the gods was affecting him, however, the renegade's bloodlust remained. 'Let these cringing vermin hang behind if they will, it will only mean more heads for Einarr and Orgrim to claim!'

Einarr clapped the woodsman on the back. Orgrim was an enigma to him in many ways, but in one aspect he was as firm as though carved from stone. Einarr could always count on Orgrim's eager support if there was killing to be done, no matter the odds. He looked away from the feral eyes of the berserker and turned to face Birna.

'What is your opinion?' Einarr asked. The huntress was quiet a moment, then pulled her bow from the quiver on her back.

'We have marched along these cliffs for three days and seen no other way down to the sea,' she said. 'It would be foolish to think we would find another passage any sooner.' She stared hard at Urda, her stern expression causing the witch to scowl. 'Even if they were my kinfolk, I would say they stand in our way.' She fixed her attention back on Einarr. 'You have asked me, and I say we fight.'

Einarr nodded, drawing his axe from the loop on his belt. 'Then it is decided,' he said. 'If Tchar is truly guiding me, then he has led us here. I cannot believe he did so merely so that we might slink away from it in fear.

'We fight!'

THE GLOW FROM the forge and the flickering torches fastened to the scaffolding made the encampment stand out in vivid contrast to the black night all around it. It gave Einarr an increased sense of security as he crept through the gloom towards the watchtowers. The night vision of anyone within the camp would be compromised by the light from their fires, greatly reducing any chance that the Aeslings would sound an alarm. At least, not before it was already too late.

Einarr kept his body low as he crawled across the snow, his white cloak masking his movements. Only the sentries in the towers presented a real threat of discovery; in their wisdom the Aeslings had ensured no torches burned atop the towers to ruin the night sight of their guards. The sentinels would need to be eliminated before Orgrim and Vallac could work their way to the structure Einarr had decided must be the barracks for the Aesling warriors. Birna would see to the sentries, using her keen sight and skill with the bow to cut down the Aeslings before they even knew they were under attack.

The greatest danger Einarr had taken upon himself. He would work his way to the smithy and confront the dark forgemaster they had seen and those Aeslings he kept near him. While observing the camp and making their plans, they had discovered another obstacle lurking in the smithy. As the slaves unloaded the ore from their cart, an immense shape had risen from behind the forge, gathering the rocks and loading them into a massive wheel-driven grinder. The creature had then used its own mammoth size and strength to pulverise the stone and separate it from the ore. The bulk of the thing had given all of Einarr's companions pause. It was far beyond that of even the largest man Einarr had ever seen. It could only be an ogre, such were its colossal proportions. Although Einarr did not relish the task, he knew defeating such a beast was something he would need to do himself if he were to maintain the respect and obedience of his companions.

Einarr crawled into position and froze, keeping his eyes locked upon the left tower. He could just make out the black silhouette of the sentry, bundled in his heavy furs in a futile attempt to ward off the chill of the winter night. He watched and waited as the

sentinel silently paced the small perimeter of the
elevated platform, his movements regular and precise.
Einarr smiled. It was a common trap for a sentry to
slip into, the drudgery of his duties. The mind and
senses were dulled by the tedium of a long watch,
rendering the guard ever less wary. The Aesling would
enter the halls of his ancestors without ever knowing
what had sent him there.

Einarr did not hear the arrow as it sped through the
night. The first he was aware of it was when the shaft
suddenly sprouted from the sentry's throat. The Aesling gasped a gurgling cry as he choked on his own
blood, trying to shout a cry of warning to the camp.
The effort was beyond his fading strength, and the
Aesling toppled as he stumbled towards the ladder,
which descended from the platform. The dying
marauder hurtled down the steps, crashing to the
ground with a dull thud, his head crooked in an
unnatural pose. Einarr waited a few breaths longer to
assure himself that the guard was well and truly dead.
Even a broken neck was nothing but an inconvenience
to some that had been touched by the gods. The sentry did not rise, however, and Einarr shifted his
attention to the encampment itself. There was no sign
that any of the Aeslings had noticed the demise of
their guard and while he watched, he could see
Orgrim and Vallac creeping their way toward the barracks. For them to be advancing meant Birna had
eliminated the other sentry without incident. The Kurgan and the renegade were to watch for Einarr's signal
once he was near the smithy, but Einarr wondered if
Orgrim would be able to control his feral rage long
enough. He reasoned it was best not to depend on the
berserker's self control. Einarr rose from the ground

and sprinted into the encampment, using the shadows when he could but above all trying to move at speed. If he could catch the Aeslings at the smithy unawares, he might be able to strike down their giant before the beast had a chance to defend itself.

The sound of hammers and picks cracking against the wall of the cliff echoed across the camp as Einarr jogged into the narrow opening of the fissure, the strange acoustics of the defile acting to imprison the noise as securely as the chains imprisoned the thralls. Einarr was pleased by the clamour, it would muffle the sound of his boots crunching across the snow. He swept his gaze across the compound.

He saw no sign of activity around the long structure he had judged to be the Aesling barracks, though a light shone beneath its heavy iron-bound door. A few scrawny slaves clustered around the other building, which Einarr now observed was some manner of kitchen. Under the watchful supervision of a huge pot-bellied Aesling, the slaves were butchering cuts of meat and tossing the flesh into a pair of massive cauldrons. Into one cauldron, Einarr saw the slaves depositing cuts of venison and rabbit, into the other they dropped scraps of pale, pink meat they butchered from the carcasses of thin, wasted things. He could guess that the first cauldron was intended for the supper of the Aeslings themselves, and the second was fodder for their thralls. Einarr felt disgust boil within his gut. To work slaves was no rare thing among the Norse, but to feed thralls flesh from their own dead was something even a Baersonling found abhorrent.

Einarr changed direction, stalking across the camp towards the kitchens. Even if the sight of the kitchens had not evoked his loathing, Einarr knew he would need to kill the Aesling cook. The kitchens afforded a clear view of the quarry and the smithy, and Einarr could not take the chance that the bloated Aesling would see him and sound the alarm. Vallac and Orgrim should have made their way to the barracks by now and were probably waiting for him to reach his own objective before springing into action. He hoped that Orgrim would be able to maintain his calm just a little longer.

The stink of roasting man-flesh overwhelmed the more succulent aroma of the venison. Einarr wrinkled his nose at the smell even as he pressed his body against the supporting wall of the long, lean-to structure that served the camp as its kitchen. The warrior took several deep breaths. Speed would be of the essence, he would need to strike down the Aesling before the scum could even think about reacting. Anything less would bring the entire camp down around their heads.

Craning his head around the corner of the wall, Einarr watched as the Aesling cook swaggered among his slaves, kicking those who were too slow to shuffle out of his way. The obese marauder paused beside the cauldron the slaves were preparing for their masters. He removed a long bronze spoon from where it dangled on his belt and dipped it into the bubbling broth. The cook noisily slurped the efforts of his thralls, greasy brown broth spilling down his face and staining his scarlet beard. The Aesling belched appreciatively, then bent down to fish a cut of venison from the cauldron.

While the marauder was occupied, Einarr lunged into the kitchen, bowling aside those slaves who were not fast enough to leap out of his way. The cook turned as the sound of the commotion reached him. Einarr's axe licked out at the fat Aesling, whistling through the pungent air. The cook's head splashed as it fell into the cauldron, a look of shock frozen on its stiffening features as it sank into the brown soup.

Einarr turned from the cook's mangled body, facing the mob of scrawny thralls. There was no sign of cheer or gratitude among the men, they regarded both Einarr and the bleeding husk of their overlord with the same dull, witless gaze. So long had they been slaves that now, with freedom in their grasp, not one of them recognised it. Whatever they had once been, Norse, Kossar, Kurgan or southlander, now they were all the same – cattle. Einarr spat his contempt onto the floor of the kitchen and pushed his way through the gawking mob. Better to run laughing into the arms of death than to cling to such a sorry excuse for life.

EINARR CONTINUED ACROSS the camp. He could see Aesling warriors prowling along the scaffolding and at the base of the cliff, whipping and haranguing those slaves who tarried in their labours. These were giants of men, their powerful build apparent even from such distance, their bodies covered in bands of blackened iron, heads hidden within horned helms. Their belts were festooned with axes and swords and every man of them had a thick shield strapped across his back. He felt a spark of dread flicker through him. There were more Aeslings abroad than he had hoped for. At least five were moving along the scaffolding, and another four were monitoring the slaves at the base of the cliff. Even if he struck quickly and killed all of the Aeslings at the smithy, the guards at the quarry would soon be after him. Against such numbers the best

Einarr could hope for was a death that would not shame his ancestors. Perhaps the old witch had been right, perhaps they should have searched for another way down.

The moment of doubt passed, burned away by the overwhelming conviction that he was right, that Tchar had indeed guided him here. This was where he needed to be. However mighty the Aeslings were, the might of Tchar was greater. And if the god's power failed him, of what consequence was that to him? Had he not intended to simply slaughter his way through the Aesling nation until one of them at last struck him down? What would it change if he died here or in some forest village, so long as he died with the blood of Aeslings dripping from his axe?

Resolution filled Einarr as he crept closer to the bowl-shaped depression in the ground that contained the Aesling smithy. He would show his strength to Tchar, show the depth of his courage and his conviction. Show to Tchar that nothing would stand between him and what the god had promised.

As Einarr prepared to move around the smithy, to make his way to the forge and the immense shape that slumbered beside it, a sharp, beast-like howl shrieked across the camp. It was soon followed by the clash of steel and the cries of men. Orgrim had grown weary of waiting.

The smithy exploded into life. Two burly Aesling warriors rushed from their burrow-like shelter, wicked axes gripped in their hairy hands. From another hole emerged a squat, broad-shouldered figure, its body encased in blackened steel and scaly strips of leather. A massive double-handed weapon that was at once axe, maul and pick was gripped in the black-garbed imp's hands and as it turned its skull-faced helmet in Einarr's direction, a hateful hiss wheezed from its mouth.

From behind the forge, a great roar sounded and Einarr felt his determination shudder as he saw the immense slumbering shape rise on its trunk-like legs. Easily twice as tall as a man, with arms as thick around as Einarr's entire body, the thing was the largest ogre he had ever seen. The breath of the gods had fallen heavily upon the ogre; upon its shoulders a pair of hideous heads glowered at the world, great tusks twisting their massive jaws. From the centre of the brute's torso, a third arm jutted, its thick fingers clawing at the night as the ogre roared its wrath. Tattered furs and strips of rag clothed the creature's malformed bulk, barely containing the hairy twisted body.

Einarr did not have time to consider the monster further – already the Aesling guards were charging towards him, their mouths open in savage war cries. Behind them marched the sinister forgemaster, its hybrid weapon clutched firmly in its armoured hands. The smith seemed content to allow its guards to close with Einarr first, waiting until they had reached Einarr before putting any great haste in its steps.

The first Aesling swung his axe at Einarr's gut, seeking to disembowel the Baersonling. Einarr blocked the strike with the heft of his own axe, but before he could retaliate, he found himself dodging the sweep of the other guard's weapon as it flashed towards his neck. The Aeslings laughed and came at him again, pressing Einarr back along the perimeter of the bowl, the coordinated attacks of the two marauders keeping him on the defensive, allowing him no respite in which to mount his own attack. Einarr could hear shouts coming from the quarry and knew that the other Aeslings would soon reach the smithy. The guards did not need to press their attack, they had only to keep Einarr busy until their kinsmen arrived.

Sharp, stabbing pain seared its way up Einarr's side. The warrior gasped, flinching away from the attack and almost into the waiting axe of an Aesling. He saw the sinister armoured forgemaster pulling back his strange hybrid weapon, the spike-like point set at the tip of its shaft glistening with blood. The smith laughed behind his mask of steel and Einarr could almost feel the man's sadistic enjoyment of his work. The Aeslings joined the forgemaster in his laughter and came at Einarr again, their axes flashing through the night. Again, Einarr was hard-pressed to match the speed and coordination of his attackers. Once more, as he beat back the weapons of his foes, he felt the forgemaster's spike stabbing into his flesh, digging into his thigh. Einarr forced himself to remain stand- ing even as his leg throbbed with agony and blood began to fill his boot. He knew his foes would finish him in an instant if he showed them any hint of weak- ness.

The Aeslings made ready to come at him again. They were filled with an even greater confidence than before, and the sound of war cries coming from the quarry told Einarr that the other guards must be very near now. He could see the Aeslings smile behind their crimson beards as they prepared to chop him down with their axes. Then an immense shadow fell across the marauders and the smiles withered on their faces. The look of horror that filled the visage of one Aesling vanished as a huge hand closed over his head,

crushing it into a dripping pulp. The ogre reached for
the other Aesling with one of his other arms, causing
the guard to jump back. The manoeuvre brought the
man within easy reach of Einarr's weapon and he
chopped through the marauder's back as though cutting down a sapling. The man screamed and collapsed
into the sooty snow, only to have his screams silenced
when the ogre's enormous foot came crashing down.

In avoiding the attacks of the guards, Einarr had
been slowly circling the bowl of the depression, drawing ever nearer the forge until at last the immense
stone oven smouldered right beside him. The ogre
had waited patiently for the fighting men to draw
near, then when they were within reach, it had acted.
Now the ogre stared intently at Einarr with his four
leprous eyes, an expectant expression spread across
the ogre's hideous faces. Einarr could see now the
chains that dripped from the ogre's limbs, binding
him to the forge. A savage smile spread across Einarr's
features and he nodded to the creature.

The forgemaster read Einarr's intention, rushing at
the warrior with his axe-maul, shouting at the top of
his voice as he did so. Einarr spun as the smith
attacked, his axe glancing off the skull-like helmet.
The smith staggered back, blinking blood from his
eyes, and shouted again. This time his roars were
answered by thick Aesling voices and Einarr could see
red-bearded faces appear at the lip of the depression.
With no more time to lose, Einarr kicked the smith in
his knee, spilling the forgemaster into the snow and
lunged for the massive bronze ring that secured the
ogre's chains to the forge. His arms seemed filled with
an inhuman strength as he drove the edge of Rafn's
axe against the ring. The blade shattered beneath the

impact, shards of steel flying into the night. The sharp, angular runes gouged into the ring flared with unholy fire as he struck it, burning as bright as the heart of a furnace. Then the light died and the bronze ring became a thing of mortal metal once more.

A bellow of monstrous rage sounded in Einarr's ears and he crumpled to the ground as he felt a powerful force crack against his back. He rolled as he struck the snow, sparing himself the savage axe-blade that gouged deep into the ground where he had fallen. The forge-master turned hate-ridden eyes on Einarr as he struggled to free his weapon. Einarr could see tiny skulls woven into the braids of the smith's long black beard, each marked with one of the same dark runes that had briefly flared into life upon the bronze ring. Einarr pulled the shattered length of Fangwyrm from its sheath. He risked a glance away from the forgemaster to see where the Aeslings were. Five guards were rushing down the lip of the depression, axes and swords gleaming in the fitful light of the forge. As Einarr watched, one of the men fell, an arrow sticking from his neck. The others continued to rush towards him.

With an ear-splitting shriek, the bronze ring snapped apart under the renewed efforts of the mutant ogre. Whatever spells had been forged into its substance had been broken by Einarr's axe and the power to restrain the monster had been lost. The charging Aeslings faltered in their steps as they saw the ogre rear upward, his twin heads bellowing with furious jubilation. Then the monster turned his eyes on his former captors and a deep, rumbling hate snarled past his twisted lips. The stunned Aeslings took a nervous step back, none of the marauders eager to confront the vengeful ogre.

The forgemaster, intent upon freeing his axe, did not pay notice to what was unfolding all around him. With a howl of triumph, he succeeded in ripping his weapon free from the icy ground. The sound degenerated into a squeal of shock and horror as the smith found the ogre looming above him. Before the forgemaster could act, the ogre's enormous hand smashed into him, swatting him like an insect and flinging him across the depression to land in a clattering mess of steel and flesh against the far side of the bowl.

Einarr glared at the stunned Aeslings and tightened his hold upon the sword. If they thought the ogre was the only thing that could visit death upon them, then he would show the scum the error of their ways. With a howl, Einarr charged towards the cowed marauders. He heard his cry taken up by the twin voices of the ogre and felt the ground shudder as the huge creature followed after him.

THE PALE, GREASY grey that passed for the arctic dawn stained the eastern sky as Einarr tended his wounds. The blows the forgemaster had visited upon his body were painful, but it seemed the smith had been more interested in agony than injury when he had inflicted them. The villain's overconfidence had cost him dearly. The only enemy it was safe to play games with was a dead one.

The battle against the Aeslings had raged for the better part of an hour, the timely support of the ogre deciding the tide. Even faced with the enraged brute, however, the Aeslings had persisted, fighting to the last against their foes. As much as he despised them, Einarr had to admit they had died deaths worthy of their ancestors.

'You should stay off the leg for a few days,' Urda advised him, her tone petulant. The witch was still sulking from Einarr's decision to have her bound before the attack on the Aesling camp. It had not been an easy decision for Einarr to make, the witch's magic would have been a great boon overcoming the Aeslings. But Einarr had been unable to trust Urda to use her powers against her kinsmen. Every step of the way she had guided them away from confrontation with the Aeslings. In a battle with them, Einarr had simply been unable to trust on which side she would fight.

'You know as well as I that won't be happening,' Einarr grunted as he rose from the ground. 'Now that the way is clear for us to descend to the Frozen Sea, we need to do so before any Aeslings show up to see what has become of their quarry.' They had made camp in the Aesling smithy, a position Einarr trusted more than the confines of the timber structures scattered about the camp.

'At its worst, you could always have your new friend just carry you,' Urda added, a caustic quality still in her voice. Einarr shifted his gaze to the towering ogre. The brute was busy pulling legs from the corpses of the Aeslings and picking them clean of meat. Einarr shook his head at the gruesome sight.

'I think I'll stand on my own feet,' he said. 'I'm not sure how much faith I can put in Thognathog's ability to remember that I'm not for eating.'

'Then why not leave that monstrosity behind?' Urda asked. Einarr admitted that it was a valid question. The ogre was certainly a formidable asset in battle, but he was an equally terrible menace if he were to turn on them. The wisest course was indeed to leave Thognathog to his own devices, but Einarr could not shake the feeling that somehow the ogre was a part of his quest, that he had been meant to free him and thereby earn the monster's service.

'I think the ogre was a part of your vision, that he is the flesh behind the picture of the twin giants you scrawled upon the snow,' Einarr told her. Urda pondered his words, but retained her scowl.

'Remember, Einarr Steelfist,' she cautioned, 'what was shown to you was warning as well as guidance…'

'And wisdom lies in knowing one from the other.' The cryptic games of the gods were a thing Einarr had little patience for. If they would speak to mortals, if they would have them perform services for them, then why could they not speak in ways a simple warrior could understand? 'I confess I do not know. Until I do, the ogre will come with us.'

Einarr looked across the smithy. With its high profile, the smithy had presented the best place to shelter from the chill wind that blew across the cliffs from the Frozen Sea. After the charnel house Orgrim and Vallac had made of the barracks, it was the only shelter that would allow them to keep an eye on the immense Thognathog. Besides, Einarr wanted to have a ready view of the slopes leading down into the fissure. He had no desire to be surprised by more Aeslings. Suddenly he noticed movement near the pile of corpses the ogre had gathered beside him. A black shape gradually wormed its way from beneath the heap of bodies, creeping like a great beetle away from the feasting Thognathog.

Einarr drew Fangwyrm and prowled across the bowl. The abrupt action of their leader drew the attention of Vallac and Birna. They rose from where they had been tending to their armour and weapons and followed Einarr. The forgemaster's attention was fixed on the feeding ogre and the first he was aware of Einarr's approach was when the warrior kicked him in the side, flipping him onto his armoured back. Before the little man could right himself, Einarr planted his boot on his chest and pointed the jagged edge of Fangwyrm at the man's throat.

'Trying to cheat Thognathog of his supper?' Einarr asked. The forgemaster groaned in horror and tried to slither out from beneath Einarr's boot. Einarr pressed his full weight down against the smith's chest, pinning him in place.

'Let me go or you'll suffer for it!' the forgemaster snarled. Einarr smirked at the man's bravado, reaching down and pulling the skull-faced helmet from his head. He immediately wished he hadn't, the smith's face was one of the ugliest he had ever seen. The man's hair was black and greasy, coiled into elaborate rings and festooned with tiny, shrunken skulls, his beard was coarse and wiry, and likewise coiled into rings with little skulls woven into his beard locks. Hoops of gold pierced the thick, hairy brow that shaded the villain's beady orange eyes and gold nails studded his big bulbous nose. Sharp fangs gleamed in the smith's mouth as he spoke, giving his words a hissing, weasel-like tone.

Overall, the man's features were too thick and broad to be human. Einarr was reminded of the dwarfs who sometimes came down from the mountains to trade in the largest Baersonling villages, but the resemblance was as different as that between a falcon and a raven.

'Interesting, little worm,' Einarr laughed. 'Near as I can tell, I am the one holding the sword!' The comment caused Vallac and Birna to join in Einarr's laughter.

'The curse of Hashut will fall on any who dare bring harm to the Dawi Zharr!' the forgemaster snarled, trying to squirm out from beneath Einarr's boot. Einarr's brow wrinkled at the unfamiliar names. He looked aside to Birna, but she was just as ignorant of their import as he.

'He's a follower of the Dark Father,' Vallac explained. 'One of the Fire Dwarfs of the Great Skull Land. My people sometimes trade slaves with his kind for the armour and weapons they make. Strange that one of them should be so far from home.'

Einarr pushed the jagged edge of Fangwyrm against the tip of the dwarf's bulbous nose. 'Well, burrow-rat, what are you doing here? What strange road brings you to the black north and a life among the Aeslings?' The dwarf simply glared at Einarr, his fiery eyes smouldering with hate. Einarr pushed the sword deeper, drawing a bead of blood from the forgemaster's nose.

'The star-metal,' the forgemaster snarled, nodding his head toward the quarry and the pitted cliff. 'But it is useless to you!' he added with venom dripping from his tongue. 'Only the Dawi Zharr have the craft to work it. To barbarian animals like you it is nothing but worthless rock!'

Einarr grinned down at the dwarf, pulling his sword away from the forgemaster's face. 'I have no interest in your black rocks, maggot-breath,' he said. 'And less interest in the curses of your gods.' The warrior turned his head, whistling sharply. The sound caused

Thognathog to raise one of his heads away from his gruesome meal. The ogre's other head soon followed, both faces filling with a wrathful loathing as they saw the figure pinned beneath Einarr's boot. The dwarf's eyes went wide with terror as Thognathog stood and began to stomp toward him.

'No!' the dwarf wailed. 'Keep that thing away from me!' Einarr just smiled down at his captive. After the cowardly way the dwarf had fought him, he was of no mind to be merciful. The forgemaster began to shake with horror as the dark shadow of Thognathog fell across him.

'I'll do anything,' the dwarf hissed. 'I have treasure! Kurgan gold, hidden in the mountains! I can show you where the Aeslings have been sending the weapons I have made for them! I'll teach you the secret of the star-stones!' The dwarf's words trailed into a shriek of absolute fear as the ogre reached down for him with a hand almost as big as the dwarf's entire body. He could see the vengeance burning in Thognathog's eyes and he knew that his death would not be a quick one.

Before the ogre could take hold of the dwarf, Einarr pushed against the monster's hand. Thognathog turned one of his heads to look at Einarr, a questioning look on his monstrous face. 'Just a moment,' Einarr told the ogre. 'Perhaps this scum can be of use to us.' A sudden thought had occurred to him, echoes from the dream-signs Urda had drawn in the snow outside Orgrim's cave.

'You say you make weapons?' Einarr asked the dwarf. He held the broken length of Fangwyrm up for the captive to see more fully. 'Think you could remake this?'

The dwarf nodded his head enthusiastically, his eyes still locked on Thognathog's towering frame. 'Spare Zhardrach's life, and I'll make you whatever you want!' The ogre sneered down at the forgemaster, shaking his enormous heads.

'No!' the brute's voice rumbled. 'Little man makes many screams before he fill Thognathog's belly! Thognathog give little man's liver to Great Maw and let worms eat little man's eyes!' The violence in the ogre's voices made Vallac step back and Birna draw her blade. Einarr smiled indulgently at the immense brute, tapping Fangwyrm against the great steel shackle that still circled the brute's massive wrist. He could see the ogre's leathery flesh was chaffed and scarred by the tight metal band, that the weight of the chains dangling from it caused the ogre no end of discomfort.

'Thognathog,' Einarr said, his tone like that of a parent speaking to a stubborn child. 'If you don't eat the dwarf, he'll take those chains off of you.' Thognathog scowled as his mind slowly turned over Einarr's words. 'Wouldn't that be nice? Make you feel better?' The ogre scratched one of his foreheads, trying to weigh the value of having his chains removed against the pleasure that slowly dismembering Zhardrach would bring him. 'You will remove my friend's chains, won't you?' Einarr added, turning his attention to the dwarf beneath his boot.

'Of course! Of course!' Zhardrach exclaimed. 'It was all the Aeslings' idea anyway! I'd never want to bring any kind of hurt to the big fellow!'

Einarr turned back to face Thognathog again. 'See? He'll take your chains off, make them stop hurting you. Then you can watch him make nice new chains to go around his own wrists.' A sinister look came across Einarr's face. 'Besides, if he decides to try and trick us, you can always eat him later.'

CHAPTER NINE

NIGHT SETTLED OVER the Aesling quarry, darkening the already brooding shadows. Einarr stood upon the cliff overlooking the grey, lifeless world that was the Frozen Sea. Beneath the gibbous light of the swollen moons, it seemed to dance and sway as he gazed upon it, slithering across his vision with sinuous grace. The impression caused his blood to chill. He was reminded of the stories an old reaver had told him while they sailed across the Sea of Claws to sack the city of Erengrad. In his youth, the veteran sea wolf had been part of a voyage to the dark shores of Naggaroth, the land of the elflings. Among the horrors he had related was that which they had encountered as they neared the beaches of Alfland. Great black rocks rose from the sea just beyond the shore, making the approach to the coast perilous. But worse than the rocks themselves had been the things which made their rookeries within the wave-beaten stone. Hideous witch-wraiths with the bodies and faces of nubile young elf wenches, but with the wings of great bats and the clawed talons of enormous vultures. The crew saw the horrible witch-birds as they drew near to the rocks, and the creatures saw them. The reaver had told Einarr how the things had swayed and crooned, how their bodies had gyrated and twisted with lascivious abandon. He related how many of the crew had been powerless to resist the sensuous dance of the fiends, how they had leapt into the sea and swum to the rocks all the while screaming their terror. For even as they surrendered to the call of the sirens, every man of them knew he swam to his death.

The Frozen Sea reminded Einarr of the old reaver's harpies. It beckoned to him, mesmerised him with a serpent's stare and a lover's kiss. Yet even as he felt it working its spell over him, the Frozen Sea could not hide its menace from him. He knew it for what it was – a place of icy oblivion and doom, a place from which no names returned to fill the sagas, where no deeds escaped to grace the songs of the skalds. But even knowing, he could not break free from its call.

They would cross the Frozen Sea.

Einarr turned from his contemplation of the lifeless waste when he heard heavy footfalls crunching through the snow. He smiled as he saw Birna's striking figure stalking up the slope to join him. After contemplating something as forbidding as the Frozen Sea, the sight of the Sarl huntress was a most welcome one indeed. Behind her loomed the immense hulk of Thognathog, his body now freed of its chains, all save the one he now held clenched in one of his mighty fists. The other end of the chain circled the chest of the black-garbed, cursing creature the ogre dragged behind him. Einarr felt a twinge of alarm. If there were any more Aeslings about, they would be able to hear the dwarf's invective from leagues away.

Einarr glared down at Zhardrach as the small procession approached him. If the dwarf noticed the warrior's annoyance, the observation did nothing to stem the tide of abuse and spite spewing from his mouth. Einarr was not the only one who seemed tired of the dwarf's voice. As they came to a halt, Thognathog gave a swift jerk on the chain he held, causing Zhardrach to stumble and crash face first into the slope. The dwarf rose, even more colourful obscenities screeching from his bruised features.

'Still that tongue, burrow-rat!' Einarr snapped. 'Or I'll let Thognathog pull it from that filthy mouth of yours!' The dwarf bit down on the stream of venom he was hurling at the ogre and turned his hate-ridden eyes on the Baersonling.

'We had a deal!' the dwarf spat. He turned his hostile gaze on Birna. The woman shook her head contemptuously at Zhardrach, then stepped towards Einarr, a fur-wrapped bundle clutched in her hands.

'The *slaver*,' she said, the word heavy with spite, 'says that he has finished what you told him to make. He insisted he be freed as soon as it was done, but I reasoned that you had best inspect his work for yourself.'

'Norsling bitch!' Zhardrach snarled, his fangs gleaming in the moonlight. 'You dare insult the craft of the Dawi Zharr!' The fresh stream of threats and abuse was cut short when Thognathog pulled on the dwarf's chain again, spilling him onto his backside.

Einarr paid little notice to Zhardrach's antics, his attention riveted to the bundle Birna held. Gently, almost reverently, he took it from her. Slowly, with the care a mother might show with her newborn child, he unwrapped the furs from that which they covered. The cool, elegant shine of steel winked at him as it caught the moonlight.

After the first teasing glance, Einarr ripped the remaining furs away, exposing the full length of the weapon. The blade of Vinnskor had been reborn, restored from the jagged stump it had been. Einarr held Fangwyrm above his head, as though to show it to the gods themselves. He laughed as he swung it through the empty air, testing its balance, letting his hand become accustomed to the feel of the weapon. It felt purer than any weapon he had ever held, more like a part of his own body than a thing of metal and fire. He knew he was meant to bear this sword, that he had always been meant to carry it into battle. Like the lure of the Frozen Sea, it was a sensation that was beyond the mind, something baser and more primal, something too compelling to doubt.

As Einarr turned the blade through the frosty air, he was impressed by the lightness of the sword, by the ease with which it slashed through the night. He was struck too, by the eerie, silvery sheen that flickered through the metal and was reminded that the sword was Fangwyrm no longer. There had not been enough of the sword left to reforge on its own, Zhardrach had needed something more. Einarr was still uncertain what had moved him to give the dwarf the elf knife he had taken from Alfkaell. It had been a compulsion that had seemed to ignite his brain, almost as though it came from somewhere beyond himself. Once the idea had come upon him, it had been impossible to deny. All of Zhardrach's protestations, his reluctance to have anything to do with the 'devil steel', had fallen on deaf ears. Whatever the difficulties, he knew that joining the elf dagger and Fangwyrm was meant to be. Now he understood. Fangwyrm had been a formidable weapon, but it was like a bread knife beside the sword he now held. He would call it Alfwyrm, he decided, in recognition of the two weapons that had joined to become something still greater.

Zhardrach was silent as he watched Einarr test the blade the dwarf had forged. He scratched at his hairy chin and a sly smile crawled onto his grotesque face. He knew the warrior would be suitably impressed. 'I see my work pleases you,' he said. 'In all the lands of your people, none make finer blades than Zhardrach of the Skull.' The dwarf's face filled with an imperious pride and he held his chains towards Einarr. 'Now, if you are satisfied, as I see you are, I will be on my way.'

Einarr shook his head, sheathing his new sword. 'You do good work, dwarf. So good in fact, I am changing the terms of our agreement.'

Zhardrach lunged for the Baersonling, his fanged face twisted into a savage snarl. 'You back cheating grobi cur!' he roared, hands splayed into claws. Before he could reach Einarr, he was pulled short on his chain by Thognathog, causing the dwarf to nearly strangle himself.

Einarr glared down at the snarling dwarf, staring into the forgemaster's fiery eyes. 'I had intended to make a present of you to Thognathog once you were finished,' he hissed, meaning every word. 'Now, however, I have taken it in mind to keep you around. Whatever gods you honour in the land of the Skull, I suggest you thank them.' Einarr looked away from the cursing dwarf, directing his gaze to Thognathog. 'Tell everyone to make ready, we have tarried here too long already.' The ogre nodded his heads, lumbering back down the slope, dragging the fuming Zhardrach after him. 'And see that his chains are tight,' Einarr called after the hulking brute, knowing that he could trust him to be very attentive about that particular detail.

Birna watched Thognathog go, then stepped closer to Einarr. When she spoke, it was in a tremulous voice. The tone surprised Einarr, until he found that her eyes were not on him, but the vast wastes of the Frozen Sea.

'You still mean to cross it?' she asked.

Einarr was quiet a moment, letting the question dissipate into the frosty air. 'I have seen it in my dreams,' he said. 'This is where they have shown me that I must come if I would do what they would have me do.'

Birna seemed to consider his answer, but the words brought no reassurance to her. 'The Aesling witch says that what the gods show us in our dreams are not only to guide us, but also to warn us. How do you know they did not mean to warn you to stay far from here?'

'How did you know the falcon that spoke to you, that told you to find me, was to be trusted?' Einarr countered. 'We must trust what is inside us, must trust that what our hearts tell us is true, is true. It is all we have, in the end. All the seers and witches in Norsca with all their sorcery and wisdom cannot fathom the riddles of the gods. We must simply accept what we feel to be true or be lost to our own doubts and fears.'

The Sarl huntress nodded. 'I have come this far, I will trust your wisdom, Steelfist,' she said. 'And I will remember what you have said, about placing faith in what our feelings say is true.'

Einarr saw a familiar gleam in Birna's eye as she spoke, an inviting look that had never failed to send a thrill through his blood. But now, somehow, it repulsed him. Perhaps it was the pain of losing Asta, or nothing more than the nearness of something as forbidding as the Frozen Sea. Or perhaps it was the suspicion that it was not he himself that drew Birna's ardour, but what the huntress imagined him to be – the chosen champion of Tchar. Whatever the source, Einarr found himself ignoring the favour of the huntress.

'Check that the provisions are gathered,' he told her. 'I doubt there will be anything to hunt once we walk that wasteland so what we would eat we must carry with us. Be certain there is extra for the ogre to carry. I doubt his appetite is small.'

'What the ogre would eat, none of us would touch in any event,' Birna answered, a ring of petulance in her voice. 'Except perhaps Orgrim.'

'See to it just the same,' Einarr said. Birna nodded again and turned to make her way back down the slope. She had gone only a few steps before she turned back towards him.

'What about the other slaves?' she asked. Einarr barely gave his answer any thought. For days the Aesling slaves had clustered about the quarry and the kitchens, lurking in the shadows like whipped curs, watching Einarr and his companions rummage through the possessions of their former masters with dull, disinterested gazes. Not once had one of them made any move to seize any of the Aesling weapons littered about the snow, nor made any move to approach the forge where Einarr had set his camp.

C. L. Werner

'Leave them,' he declared. 'They did nothing to remove their chains, why should I do it for them? Let them stay here and rot, they are already dead. They have been since the moment they accepted their chains.'

THE CHILL OF the Norscan winter was even more pronounced upon the bleak, undulating expanse of the Frozen Sea. Einarr had never felt such cold before, not in all his years at sea or on land. It was almost as though unseen phantoms were stabbing him with blades of ice every time he took a step, trying to drag him down into their chill world of frozen death with every numbing touch. The blasts of icy wind that smashed into their faces caused their flesh to become as rigid as stone, the spit to freeze inside their mouths and their hair to turn brittle with frost. They found themselves using the rolling landscape to shield them from the northern wind, sheltering within the frozen overhand of the unmoving waves that marked the surface of the plain.

All of them felt the hideous touch of winter slashing through them, but it was Vallac, the Kurgan, who seemed least susceptible to the icy claws raking across his flesh. Indeed, steam seemed to be rising from the man's exposed face whenever Einarr looked at him and Vallac alone did not have clumps of ice clinging to his brow. Einarr was reminded of the burning sludge the Kurgan had spat into the face of the gor and wondered if perhaps this was further evidence of the fires the gods had stoked inside Vallac when they had touched him and transformed his flesh.

At the head of the small procession, his small body dripping with chains, Zhardrach reluctantly tested the ice as they made their passage across the wastes. Close behind the dwarf stalked Thognathog, the end of the dwarf's chain wrapped around the ogre's waist like a belt. Early in their crossing of the Frozen Sea, Zhardrach had tried to eliminate the ogre by finding a soft patch in the ice. Thognathog had broken through the weak surface, nearly drowning and losing much of his supplies before managing to climb out from the frigid waters. Now Zhardrach would need to be more careful – if it happened again he would be dragged down with Thognathog to a watery grave. Einarr noted that the dwarf was much more careful since the new arrangement had been implemented.

The loss of Thognathog's provisions had been a serious setback. A hungry ogre wasn't something even the bravest Norse warrior wanted marching alongside him, ogres had a curious way of placing food before fellowship in even the best of circumstances. Even plundering the provisions of the rest of his warband did little to solve the problem. Einarr was forced to relent and agree to Orgrim's suggestion that the renegade be allowed to break off from the group and hunt whatever game might be found scratching an existence from the ice. The woodsman would stalk off alone, brushing aside Birna's offers to help him. They would watch him vanish into the mists, hunched over and sniffing at the ground as he faded into the icy night. The Aesling would never fail to return the next morning, his beard often matted with blood, his arms filled with the mangled carcass of seals and snow rats. How any man could track game across the windswept ice, Einarr did not know. He might have asked Orgrim, but the renegade was always irritable after his hunts, quick to snap at anyone trying to pry into his habits.

Through it all, the old witch Urda somehow managed to keep pace with the others. Einarr was impressed by the crone's determination and willpower, refusing to allow herself to linger behind, refusing to be far from Einarr's side. He could understand the thinking that gave the old woman such strength. Of all the members of their small warband, only Einarr himself had any reason to keep her around. Orgrim, he knew, would just as soon kill the hag as look at her and Thognathog had little reason to look kindly on any Aesling. Zhardrach blamed the Aeslings as a people for his current predicament, and no dwarf forgave any betrayal easily. Vallac and Birna both distrusted the witch intensely and warned Einarr about the dangers of keeping her around at every opportunity. No, Einarr alone had a vested interest in keeping Urda alive, and the witch knew it well. He only hoped that she did not take it into mind to test just how much control she had over him.

FOUR DAYS AFTER setting out from the Aesling quarry, the undulating, unearthly landscape was broken by the first artificial feature the warband had yet seen upon the Frozen Sea. It was a great smooth furrow, a patch of level ice that cut its way through the unmoving waves. There was no question but that some intelligence had carved the furrow through the ice, it was too regular to be a caprice of either storm or sea. Einarr was at once struck by the immensity of such a feat, of hacking such a road across the Frozen Sea. It wound across the ice as far as the eye could follow in either direction and was wider across than the entire village of Vinnskor. None among them could say who had made such a road, nor why. Einarr did not trouble himself over such questions. It was enough that the path was there.

They made better time, travelling along the path instead of climbing the jagged curves of the frozen waves. The depth of the furrow sheltered them from the worst of the wind, giving them all a much needed respite from the malice of the elements. Yet almost from the first, a nameless dread began to prey upon Einarr's mind as they marched along the ice road, a nebulous terror that set the hairs on his arms shivering yet which refused all effort to quantify and recognise it. Einarr could see that his companions felt it too. Orgrim no longer ranged ahead of the group, the renegade slinking close by his comrades for the first time since they had left his forest cave. Even Zhardrach did not shun them as he had, keeping close to Thognathog despite the rumbling of the ogre's belly. Whatever preyed upon their senses, it was something more than an imagined fear.

On their fifth day travelling along the path, Einarr called Vallac to him. The Kurgan was a seasoned warrior and had seen much in his wanderings. Of all those in his warband, Einarr respected Vallac enough to listen to his council. He needed the advice of another warrior. His question to Vallac was a simple one, one that did not require the cryptic wisdom of witches and seers. Should they abandon the path or should they continue to follow it?

The Kurgan rubbed his fingers against the gold loops piercing his brow as he considered Einarr's question. 'My instincts say to me that we should flee,' Vallac said at last, his voice low, his words for Einarr's ears alone. Even so, he saw Orgrim's head snap around as Vallac whispered, the renegade picking up the hushed conversation even across the dozen yards that separated them. Vallac ignored the berserker's unnatural eavesdropping and continued. 'My mind tells me that we make good time by using the trail. But even I tire of sheltering from the wind beneath the curl of the waves. I weary of huddling together, sucking the warmth from one another's bodies like great leeches. Not a one of us has been spared being cut by the knife-edges of the waves, our blood freezing with every new wound. We have little food and cannot depend upon Orgrim's hunts to get more. There will be game beyond this frozen hell. The sooner we are free of it, the sooner we eat.' The Kurgan shifted his gaze, watching as Thognathog tore a strip of leather from the patch-work jerkin the ogre had stitched for himself and shoved it into one of his mouths. 'I worry that your ogre grows weary of an empty belly.'

Einarr nodded in agreement. 'We might be able to do without for some time yet, but Thognathog is quickly reaching his limit.' The warrior sighed, shaking his head. 'The ogre's strength would be a great boon in overcoming whatever guardians infest the Plague Lord's palace.'

'How many of us will even set eyes upon Skoroth's tower if the ogre decides he wants meat while we are still crawling across this oblivion?' Vallac cautioned. It was a concern that had weighed heavily upon Einarr's mind every time he heard the ogre's belly growl. Even so, he did not want to act until he was certain there was no other way.

'This path leads somewhere,' Einarr said. 'Someone built it. If we follow it, we may find them. If they are people of flesh, then they must eat and if they eat, they will have food.'

The Kurgan nodded in agreement. 'Then we stick to the trail, whatever daemons haunt it.' Vallac smiled, clapping his hand against Einarr's shoulder. 'That is the choice I should have made had Tzeentch's mark been burned into my flesh instead of yours.'

Einarr opened his mouth to reply, but as he did so, he was suddenly struck by an intensification of the crawling dread that had plagued them for so long. It seemed to pass through his body like a tremor, causing his stomach to churn like a storm swept sea. The air around him seemed to take on a malignant, stagnant quality, almost as though all the life had drained out of it. He could see that the others felt it too. Vallac had fallen to his knees, trying to spit his sickness onto the ice. Urda was crumpled into a trembling pile of rags and fur, Birna standing over the witch with her bow drawn and an arrow nocked, her eyes wide and haunted. Thognathog was on his feet again, his heads scanning the trench, trying to find whatever had aroused his fear. Zhardrach cringed in the ogre's shadow, quite willing to put the brute between himself and whatever lurked within the trench.

It was Orgrim's reaction that set Einarr most on edge. The berserker was not scanning the horizon for any sign of a foe, nor crouched against the ground trying to vomit an already empty belly. Instead the renegade stood as still as a statue, his eyes staring intently at the ice some distance from his feet. Every hair on Orgrim's body seemed to be standing erect, from the ratty locks that covered his head to the wiry mass that Einarr observed covering his hands. The woodsman's nostrils were flared wide, like those of some great hound, trying to pick up the scent of what he sensed was near.

While Einarr watched Orgrim, he suddenly noticed something more. The ice was darker where the berserker's eyes were fixed, as though there were some great shadow beneath the ice. As Einarr watched, the shadow grew, blackening the ground as it became larger and more distinct. Something huge was moving beneath the ice, speeding up from the depths towards the surface!

Einarr shouted a warning to his comrades an instant before the ground shook and they were all thrown from their feet. The grinding shriek of splintering ice clawed through the air as great slabs of the trench were tossed into the sky. A putrid stink slammed into Einarr's senses as he recovered from his fall, the stink of rotten fish and the black deeps of the ocean. He wiped at his face as his eyes started to water, concerned that the tears would freeze in the winter wind. Through his frosty gaze, he could see an enormous shape, like a barren tree, lashing against the night sky. It writhed and flailed, crashing against the ice with tremendous fury and nearly knocking Einarr down again. It was grey and scaly, somehow reminding him of a colossal rat's tail. Great green welts marked the back and sides of the thing, but as it rose again into the air, Einarr saw that its underside was puckered with hundreds of plate-sized beaks that snapped and slobbered with an idiot fury.

The ice shuddered again and a second grey tendril exploded from the blackness beneath their feet. It scraped against the wall of the furrow, narrowly missing Birna's head as she crouched low against the ground. The drooling beaks clacked and cracked above her as the hideous limb groped blindly for the prey it could sense was nearby. Einarr did not wait for

it to find its quarry. With a roar, he sprinted across the
trench, Alfwyrm clutched in his fist. Savagely, the warrior hacked into the side of the immense stalk, sinking
the edge of his steel several inches into the blubbery
flesh. Translucent treacle exploded from the wound,
bathing Einarr's body in stinging filth. The tendril
whipped away from Einarr's sword, crashing against
the side of the trench with such violence that part of
the wall crumbled and crashed down into the furrow.
Birna leapt from the frozen debris, narrowly missing
the flailing tentacle as she tried to avoid being
crushed.

Einarr braced himself as the ice groaned and
shrieked once more. A third, then a fourth tentacle
exploded up through the ice, lashing madly against
the sky. Thognathog charged one of the new tentacles,
dragging a protesting Zhardrach after him. The ogre's
huge arms wrapped around the stalk-like limb,
striving to crush it in his powerful grip. The grey
colour of the tentacles darkened into a vivid red as the
ogre attacked. But mighty as the ogre's strength was,
the thing beneath the ice was mightier still. The
tentacle whipped itself ferociously through the air,
pulling Thognathog with it, the violence of its
movements growing more and more frenzied until at
last it shook itself free of the ogre's hold, flinging both
ogre and dwarf across the trench.

The ogre had barely crashed into the wall of the
trench before the ice splintered again and three more
tentacles breached the surface. The floor of the furrow
was now pitted with holes and Einarr could see the
thing's scaly blubber pressing close against the ice it
had not yet destroyed. He could see Vallac and Orgrim
hacking away at the tentacles, splattering the ice with

its greasy ichor. Birna sank arrow after arrow into its blubbery flesh, provoking agitated swipes from the limbs but giving no evidence of any lasting hurt.

'We must flee,' Urda's crackling whisper hissed at Einarr's side. 'You cannot hope to best such a beast with sword and axe.' Einarr shook off the witch's clutching hands, glaring at the flailing pillars of crimson flesh sprouting from the ice. He moved to join Vallac and Orgrim as they chopped and slashed at the noxious things.

'If you would fight the kraken, you will die,' the witch pronounced. 'Your quest will end here and your village will rot in its grave. Tchar will spit your spirit from the halls of your ancestors and you will walk the wastes forever.' The witch's words and the panic with which she said them broke through the battle lust that filled Einarr's mind. He sheathed his sword and shouted to his comrades.

'Warriors of the Steelfist!' he roared. 'We do not fight the beast here! Like sparrows before a hawk, we must flee or die! If we would fight it we must find solid ground to face it on!' His comrades did not think about their leader's words, the wisdom in them was too obvious for thought. Vallac and Birna hurried after him as Einarr led the retreat across the trench. Even Orgrim displayed no great eagerness to linger behind, loping after them as soon as he found himself alone among the forest of flailing tendrils. As they ran, Einarr looked over his shoulder. The tentacles continued to whip across the ice for some time before whatever intelligence guided them decided they had gone. With eerie unison, the hideous limbs shot back beneath the ice, only the great holes they had torn in the surface betraying that they had ever been there.

Einarr should have felt some measure of relief when they withdrew, but instead his impression of dread intensified. He shouted a warning as he saw the immense shadow of the kraken shooting towards them beneath the ice. The warband braced themselves as the trench shook once more and the kraken's hideous limbs erupted through the ice. The monster's blubbery flesh changed from scarlet to purple as its frustrated tendrils clawed at the ice. One of the tentacles whipped across Vallac's back, shearing through his armour and nearly flaying the flesh from his body. The Kurgan roared in pain, trying to avenge his agony by skewering the offending limb with his sword. As he made to strike the tentacle, a second tendril snaked around his waist, lifting him from the ice. Vallac stabbed at the limb that had caught him, trying to force it to release him.

'While it is busy with the Kurgan, we can flee.' The witch's voice had lost some of its panic, a cunning calm entering her tone.

Einarr spun on Urda, repulsed by the hag's cowardice. 'Use your sorcery, crone!' he snarled. 'Or by the Dark Gods, he will not be the only one to feed the kraken.' Urda sneered at Einarr's hostile words.

'You are lost without me,' she said. Einarr grabbed the witch's throat, pulling her close.

'If you would betray him, why shouldn't you betray me?' The question caused fear to return to Urda's eyes. The witch nodded her head in submission, cringing back as Einarr released her.

Birna and Orgrim tried to attack the tentacle that held Vallac, slashing it with their blades. Einarr appreciated the infernal cunning that governed the kraken, as it continued to stretch its captive higher and higher, beyond the reach of his rescuers. At the same time, other tentacles swiped at Birna and Orgrim, trying to catch them within coils of scaly blubber. The kraken was using Vallac as bait to draw more prey within its reach. Einarr glared back at Urda.

The witch had poured her runestones into her hand. While Einarr watched, the stone eye set into her forehead began to glow. He could feel heat drifting from her rune-eye, a sensation so profound that he likened it to Zhardrach's forge. The glow soon transferred from the stone in Urda's forehead to one of those she held in her hand. The witch's face contorted in agony as the blazing stone singed her flesh. Ghastly words slobbered from her withered lips as she clenched her fist. With a final shriek of unholy power, the hag hurled the blazing rock at the kraken.

The stone struck the tentacle holding Vallac, roaring as it exploded into a nimbus of flame. The ice shook as the behemoth beneath it shuddered. The tentacles lashing against the surface recoiled, whipping back down into their holes. The limb that had held Vallac shivered against the ice, its vitality slowly ebbing. Where Urda's runestone had struck it there was now only a twisted mess of charred blubber. Vallac struggled to free himself from the dead weight that was coiled around him, calling out to Birna and Orgrim to help him.

'Collect your Kurgan,' Urda wheezed as she collapsed against the ice, pressing her charred hand against the soothing cold. 'It will not take the kraken long to forget its pain and remember its hunger. If we have not found sanctuary from it by then, its fury will kill us all.'

Chapter Ten

The warband scrambled across the ice, only too aware of the menacing shadow that followed them beneath the surface. For the better part of a day the kraken had pursued them. At first, Einarr had thought they could lose it by abandoning the ice road, emerging from the trench and scrambling across the frozen waves. But they were in the monster's element and it would not be denied. The thicker ice of the Frozen Sea's surface broke before the kraken's tentacles as easily as the floor of the furrow had, the only difference being the inability of its intended prey to see its black bulk haunting them beneath the ice. Not without misgivings, Einarr ordered a return to the trench. He was under no delusion that they could lose the beast, but at least they would have better warning before it attacked. Besides, he was still convinced that the ice road led somewhere, somewhere with solid ground beneath it where they could take sanctuary from the kraken's single-minded pursuit.

They were in sad shape. Vallac, battered and bleeding from his encounter with the kraken, kept an only slightly better pace than the aged and feeble Urda. Thognathog had to carry Zhardrach draped over his massive shoulder, the dwarf still insensible after being flung through the air by the monster's assault. The ogre himself had fallen into a brooding silence, punctuated by the fitful rumbling of his gut. Einarr imagined that the ogre carried the dwarf for no reason beyond a quick snack as soon as the kraken lost interest in them. Orgrim was a jumble of nerves, leaping at shadows, his already feral mind further disordered from being hunted by something he could neither see nor smell. Einarr feared that the time might not be long in coming before the berserker's thin grip on sanity snapped completely and he turned on his comrades. Whenever he locked eyes with Orgrim, they were yellow and bestial with little reason shining behind them. There was no mistaking the unnatural sharpness of his teeth now, nor the lengthening of his fingers into savage claws.

Einarr confided his fears to Birna, the only one of his companions he judged both fit and rational. The huntress accepted his concerns with a grim pragmatism. If either Orgrim or Thognathog snapped, they would most likely fall on Urda or Vallac first. Like any wild beast, they would instinctively strike the weak ones first. That would give herself and Einarr time to slip away. Einarr saw the reason in Birna's words even as they churned his stomach. It would sit ill with him to run from such a battle.

'The path of Kharnath is one that teaches to fight, even when there is no hope of victory,' Birna cautioned. 'But you bear the mark of Tchar and his is the wiser path. Tchar encourages his servants to choose their battles more wisely, to know when to fight and when to hide. It is not sacrifice that pleases Tchar, it is accomplishment.'

THEY TRUDGED ON along the ice road, feeling the numbing north wind howl past them. For hours now, they had eluded the kraken, but none of them doubted that the aquatic horror would find them again. A feeling of despair smashed down upon them as they saw the cliffs of ice looming at the far end of the furrow. There was no bastion at the end of the road, no fortress in which they might take refuge. Indeed, the road, they now saw, was not a road at all.

Its timbers caked in ice, the frozen remnants of its black sails hanging in great tattered sheets from the cracked stumps of its masts, the ship leaned against the wall of the fissure, as dead as the frozen hell all around it. It was huge, a sea-going juggernaut, its hull banded in steel, its sides covered in great scales of bronze. Einarr had never beheld such a vessel, nor dared to imagine that such a brute could ever be put to sea. Its shape struck him as wrong for a ship, wide and bloated compared to the thin sleek longships of the Norse. Yet there was no denying the awesome power the ship's size and majesty, even in death, conveyed. The 'road' they had been following for so many days had been naught more than the trail left behind by this behemoth as it chewed its way through the Frozen Sea.

Vallac stared at the death ship, shaking his head. Like the others, he felt despair that this was the refuge they had thought to find at the end of the furrow. The Kurgan was the first to give voice to his feelings.

'You have led us to our death, Steelfist,' he swore. 'There is nothing here, and nowhere to escape.'

Einarr turned on the Kurgan, glaring down at the smaller warrior from behind his bear-skull mask. 'Has the great Tchar marked your flesh, cur of the Steppes?' He clenched his hand into a fist, the metal fused to his skin shining in the starlight. 'The god has led me here, just as he sent you yapping after my heels!' Vallac scowled at Einarr's words, but he could not hold the Baersonling's menacing gaze. The challenge began to falter in his gaze. Unexpectedly, it was Urda who rose to take up the Kurgan's defiance.

'I warned you, Steelfist!' the witch hissed. 'I warned you that the signs were both guidance and warning, that you must choose wisely which to follow and which to shun!' She spat into the ice at Einarr's feet. 'Baersonling filth! You have chosen wrongly and now we shall be cheated of the glory that should have been ours!'

Einarr stared at the witch, watching as the veil slipped away and the ancient hate between her tribe and his filled her wrinkled features. The rune-eye seemed to glow with a wrathful light of its own, casting her face in an orange light. The urge to run the crone through filled him, to hack her spiteful countenance apart and leave her withered body for the kraken. Just as quickly he fought the urge down. Killing one seer had set him upon the strange path he now travelled, killing another could only make things worse.

'We shall make for the ship,' Einarr declared, stabbing his finger at the distant vessel. The others followed his gesture, but doubt remained on their faces.

'Why should we?' growled Orgrim, the words disfigured by the oversized fangs that now filled his mouth. Einarr turned on the berserker. Without thinking, without willing the motion, his metallic hand smashed into the renegade, knocking him to the ground. The force of the blow caused Orgrim's head to bounce against the ice, almost cracking his skull. The Aesling groaned in pain, clutching at his head.

'Because I say you will!' Einarr roared, the words welling up from within him. Even he was shocked by the force and power within his voice. The others backed away from him, all defiance and doubt gone as their faces filled with something that was more fear than respect. It did not matter to Einarr; all that mattered was that they obeyed.

The spell of authority that seemed to surround Einarr was broken when the ice beneath him suddenly heaved upward, cracking and splintering as an immense shape pressed upon it from below. Almost as colourless as the ice around them, the massive tentacles of the kraken scratched at the sky once more, the beak-like mouths on their undersides snapping and slobbering as they tried to find prey. Einarr was thrown back, crashing against the ice and rolling toward the wall of the fissure. Orgrim leapt back to his feet as another tentacle exploded right beneath him, only the woodsman's inhuman reflexes preventing him from plunging into the hole the creature had made.

Birna drew her sword, watching as a third and still a fourth tentacle burst through the ice. She could see the crusty scars marking where these same limbs had been injured by them during the creature's previous attacks. Whatever pain they inflicted upon the kraken, it simply was not enough to make it give up.

'The witch was right!' Vallac snarled. 'He has led us to our death!' The Kurgan dodged aside as one of the tentacles came crashing down beside him. The kraken had learned a new trick, dragging its flopping arm across the ice, trying to sweep anyone standing upon it into the frigid holes it had made. Vallac winced in pain as he threw himself from the path of the oncoming limb, smashing his already injured body against the unforgiving ice as he landed. The Kurgan did not have time to consider his pain, however, as another tentacle whipped down towards him. Vallac's vision was filled with the tremendous limb's shadow before he rolled aside, so near did it come to crushing him.

'Head for the ship!' Birna shouted as she hacked at a tentacle slithering across the ice trying to find her. The order brought a fresh scowl to Vallac's face. 'Do you see any other cover?' Birna demanded in answer to his unspoken question. Vallac nodded, turning and sprinting across the ice towards the looming bulk of the ship. Birna could see that Urda was already making for the ship with a speed she would have thought beyond the ragged crone.

'Wench-sword listen to what she say,' Thognathog's voices rumbled from beside her. The ogre had a gaping wound in his arm where one of the kraken's tentacles had lashed him but otherwise the ogre looked intact, in better shape at least than the dwarf slung across his shoulder. 'Die stay here!' There was no arguing with the ogre's logic, but Birna found herself hesitating. She looked across the field of flailing tentacles to where Einarr's body lay unmoving against the wall of the fissure. An impulse greater than her urge to reach safety came upon her.

'We need to get Einarr!' she shouted up at the ogre. Thognathog's misshapen faces smiled as he shook his heads.

'Steelfist give Thognathog new life,' the ogre said. 'Thognathog not throw that life away so soon.'

'You have to help me!' Birna roared. 'He might not be dead!' The ogre shrugged and turned away.

'Not dead now, then he dead soon,' Thognathog stated. 'Maybe kraken not hungry after eat Steelfist.' Birna spat in contempt as the ogre began to lumber after the retreating Vallac and Urda. She turned, watching as the kraken's tentacles continued to whip and slash the ice. The bed of the fissure was alive with the kraken's throbbing limbs now, pulsating with its slobbering, unclean life. She gasped as one of the tentacles slithered along the side of the fissure, groping for Einarr's lifeless form.

Every instinct told Birna to leave him, to run and save herself. But what had made her linger, now goaded her on. She had come far to find this man, she would not lose him now.

The kraken's tentacles flailed across the surface of the ice as Birna ran into the midst of the forest of profane flesh. Ice cracked as the tendrils smashed down against the ice. The kraken could sense how near she was and it redoubled its efforts. Birna dove across the ice as one tentacle crashed against the surface where she had been, the violent contact with the ice scraping the flesh from her hands. She did not have time to think about the pain as a second tentacle slithered up from the jagged ice and tried to lash itself around her body. She struck at it with her sword, shattering several of the snapping beaks that puckered its underside. The tendril recoiled in pain, but already a third was whipping across the surface towards her, trying to drive her into the freezing water. Birna waited for the limb to draw close, mustering her strength. Just before it could reach her, she leapt from the ground, clearing the oozing tendril as it swept past her. As she landed, the tentacle shifted, swinging back. Birna noticed its approach and braced herself. Now she was appreciating the madness behind her impulsive decision. Before the kraken had been confused by the variety of potential prey, unable to fix its primitive mind and focus on securing any single victim. Now, there was only Birna and the kraken was without confusion.

Birna jumped again as the tentacle swept towards her. She felt her feet land against something at once scaly and slick with slime. The huntress fought to maintain her balance as the tentacle's momentum caused it to swipe across the ice. The Sarls were great shipbuilders, and few were the villages that did not provide timber for the longships of their tribe. Every able-bodied Sarl in Birna's village had been expected to help herd the timbers down the icy rivers of their land to the shipyards on the coast. Maintaining her footing on the kraken's tentacle was almost child's play in comparison. Birna bided her time, bracing herself to leap off when the tendril changed direction.

A second tentacle whipped toward Birna, seeking to pluck her off the first. The huntress crouched then sprang, feeling a sense of satisfaction as the tentacle smashed against her former position, the sharp beaks snapping into the flesh of the other tentacle. The ice heaved and shuddered as a thrill of pain surged through the kraken. The pale tentacles pulsed livid red, then shot back down into the freezing depths. Birna exhaled her relief. The monster might not be gone long, but any respite was a welcome one.

Einarr stirred weakly as Birna crouched down beside him. She could see that the side of his head was caked in blood, one of the horns snapped off from the mutated bear skull he wore. With one eye on the shattered ice and the frigid pools of water, Birna crooked her arm around the warrior's midsection, trying to lift him from the ice. She stopped as she saw a tattered, bleeding figure staring down at her. Orgrim had survived the kraken's attack, but his chest was a torn mess, the armour stripped away by the snapping beaks of the monster.

Birna shuddered as she saw the feral, bestial state of Orgrim's eyes. The man's entire body seemed twisted, his hands crooked into clawed paws, his face somehow both narrower and broader. The berserker's nostrils flared as he drank in their scent. She could see the jagged scar on Orgrim's brow where Einarr had struck him. Birna looked aside to where her sword lay on the ice, wondering if she could reach it before Orgrim sprang.

'Steelfist is hurt,' Orgrim growled as his nostrils sniffed at the air. The berserker's tongue pushed its way from behind his fangs as he spoke and Birna recoiled as she saw that it was long and sharp, more like that of a dog than a man.

'I won't let you finish him,' she snarled back. Faster than her eyes could follow, Orgrim was in front of her, his clawed hand around her throat. She felt tiny beads of blood trickle down her neck.

'Stupid bitch,' Orgrim's guttural voice rasped. He tightened his grip, almost choking her and threw Birna back. The huntress rolled as she crashed back against the ice, taking most of the impact on her shoulder. She pulled the small dagger from her boot, clenching it in her fist as she lunged back for Orgrim, but came up short when she saw what he was doing. The berserker had picked up Einarr, bracing his body against his shoulders. Orgrim twisted his head around as he smelled Birna approach. 'You're too weak to carry him,' he snapped. 'Follow me and keep a watch for the beast. It is beneath the ice and I cannot follow its scent.'

Birna nodded, retrieving her sword as she wiped the blood from her neck. Orgrim began to lope across the ice. Even laden down with Einarr's bulk, Birna found it difficult to keep up with the woodsman. She wondered at Orgrim's abrupt display of loyalty, unable to trust it, but also unable to question it. There would be time enough for that once they were safely on the ship.

SLOWLY, PAINFULLY, VALLAC pulled himself up the side of the strange dreadnought, the icy bronze plates stinging his flesh as he brushed against them. Closer to the ship, he could see that it had been a vessel dedicated to the gods, bearing their images carved into the wood and branded into the bronze, the runes of the Dark Tongue scratched across the hull. But he could also see that such dedication had not saved it from the ice. The wood was splintered and cracked, great chunks torn away from the sides, exposing the decks within. The massive bolt thrower fastened to the prow of the ship was caked in frost and ice. It was obvious even to a Kurgan from the landlocked steppes that the ship would never sail again, the only thing keeping her afloat was the very ice that had killed her.

Vallac half expected the raised voices he heard coming from the deck of the ship. Both Urda and Thognathog had outdistanced him on the ice, beating him to whatever dubious refuge the ship offered. Perhaps the old hag was trying to talk the ogre out of eating her. But as he came closer and the voices became more distinct, he was surprised to find that the voice arguing with Urda was not the rumbling echo of Thognathog, but the harshly accented spit-growl of Zhardrach. The Kurgan paused as he climbed up the frozen rigging draped across the side of the ship, pulling his knife from his belt and clenching it in his teeth. Whatever devilry the pair was trying to plan, they would not find him an easy victim.

'Help me with these chains, old hag!' Zhardrach was snarling as Vallac pulled himself over the side. 'I'll give you gold! Gems from the Skull Land! Whatever you desire!'

The dwarf was standing near the far side of the deck, Thognathog's body strewn behind him. The ogre's head was bleeding and the stain on the chains in Zhardrach's fists gave mute evidence of what had struck him down. Now he had Urda trapped against the gunwale, unable to get past him. Vallac idly wondered how long the dwarf had been playing dead, letting the ogre lug him across the Frozen Sea, waiting for just such an opportunity.

'Even if I believed your lies, I wouldn't lift a finger for you,' Urda spit at the dwarf. Zhardrach snarled again, jabbing at her with a long boat hook. Vallac could see now that the dwarf couldn't reach Urda, not unless he found some way to drag Thognathog's gigantic body with him. At the same time, the witch couldn't escape her sanctuary without either throwing herself over the side or coming within the dwarf's reach. The red slashes on her arms and face told Vallac that if Zhardrach couldn't reach her, his weapon could. While he watched, Zhardrach ripped a fresh tear in Urda's tattered cloak. 'Perhaps I might lift *one* finger for you,' Urda hissed at him.

'Try any of your witchery and I'll stab you again,' Zhardrach swore. 'Now be sensible and help me get free.'

'So you can kill me?' Urda scoffed. 'You can't bargain with someone when you have nothing to offer them. I have only to lean over the side of this ship and then all your threats are beyond me. It will be a quick death beside what waits you. Tell me, how long do you think you'll be able to live off ogre meat?'

Zhardrach roared, lunging at her with the boathook. As he made to stab at her, Vallac grabbed the boat hook from him, at the same time pressing his knife against the dwarf's hairy throat. The dwarf's rage sputtered into a stream of curses as he froze.

'It took you long enough to get here,' Urda complained. Vallac glared back at her.

'I wanted to hear what kind of offer he was making,' Vallac explained. 'See if it was anything worth listening to.'

'Gold, gems,' Zhardrach wheezed. Vallac pressed the knife more firmly against the dwarf's leathery flesh.

'Yes, I heard all that,' Vallac said. 'If you had anything like that, you certainly wouldn't be working a forge for a bunch of Aeslings.' The pain in his side made him clutch at his ribs. Urda moved towards him.

'I could heal your injuries, Kurgan,' she offered. Vallac smiled at the offer.

'I trust that offer as much as his,' he said. Suddenly another spasm of pain throbbed through his body. Zhardrach acted on the instant, ducking his head and biting Vallac's wrist while grabbing the Kurgan's arm. Vallac tried to pull away while still holding onto the knife, but was unable to do either. The dwarf's strength was easily underestimated and Vallac found himself straining just to tear free from his teeth. Zhardrach let him go, dropping and scrambling for both knife and boat hook at the same time. Vallac kicked at the villain, buckling his leg beneath him and spilling the dwarf against Thognathog's body. The dwarf crashed against the ogre's chest in a tangle of chains and flailing limbs. He lifted his head from the tangle, glaring murder at Vallac. Then the dwarf's eyes went wide with terror and a squeak of fright escaped his lungs.

Thognathog sucked at his jagged teeth as he focused his four eyes on the dwarf spilled across his chest.

'Hashut be praised!' Zhardrach exclaimed. 'You live! I was worried that you had hurt yourself!'

'What happen?' Thognathog growled. The ogre rose to his feet, knocking Zhardrach to the deck. His massive hand reached back to his bloodied head, tenderly testing the knot growing there.

'You slipped,' Zhardrach explained. The ogre favoured the dwarf with an unamused look. Without warning he picked up the dwarf's chains, jerking him into the air and lumbered towards the side of the ship. Soon, Zhardrach found himself dangling over the ice some thirty feet below.

'When see Dark Father, say you slip,' the ogre growled. Zhardrach thrashed about in his chains, eyes

screwed shut as he howled in protest, waiting for the
inevitable plunge down to the ice. When several seconds passed and he was still alive, the dwarf opened
his eyes again. He was surprised to find that Thognathog was not looking at him. The ogre was staring
down into the furrow, as were Vallac and Urda.
Zhardrach followed the direction of their gaze. He
could see Birna and Orgrim running toward the ship
across the ice. The berserker was bent nearly double
carrying Einarr's armoured frame across his shoulders.

'Steelfist live!' Thognathog exclaimed.

'Not for long,' Vallac said as a black shadow
appeared beneath the ice, rushing after the fugitives.
'They'll never reach the ship ahead of that thing.'

Thognathog turned towards the Kurgan, inadver-
tently dragging Zhardrach back on deck. The ogre's
look was pensive, almost as though he were ashamed
of something. 'We help Steelfist,' he said. It was not a
question.

'Of course we will!' Zhardrach was quick to agree. 'I
saw a harpoon thrower in the forecastle of this wreck.
Cut me loose and I can have it working like that.'
Zhardrach snapped his thick fingers. Thognathog
looked over at the frozen wreckage of the bolt
thrower, then back at the dwarf's fanged grin.

'Thognathog has better idea,' the ogre growled.

BIRNA COULD MAKE out Vallac and Thognathog prowling the decks of the ice-bound ship. They were near
enough that she fancied she could even smell the
ogre's rancid stench, but even that was not close
enough. A quick glance over her shoulder showed the
shadow of the kraken speeding after them under the
ice. She shouted to Orgrim to run faster, as though the

berserker hadn't been putting in his full effort already. There was no chance of outdistancing the kraken. She braced herself for the by now familiar sensation of the ice buckling beneath her feet as the kraken forced its tentacles through the ice.

The ice did shudder, but the sensation was less intense than Birna had expected. It also seemed to be some distance away. When the ice shook again, she saw something large crash against the surface a hundred yards away. It looked like a huge spear of all things, as thick around as a man's leg and chased in bronze. The harpoon rolled across the ice where it was soon joined by a second. Birna looked back at the ship. This time she saw Thognathog hurl one of the immense projectiles into the ice.

For an instant, Birna did not understand what the ogre was trying to do. Had the brute's wits deserted him entirely? Then the ice was jolted, not from above but from below. She saw the kraken's crimson arms bursting up through the ice, scratching across the surface. But the kraken had not exploded beneath their feet, it had instead been drawn to the area Thognathog had been hurling his spears. Birna watched for a moment as the kraken's tentacles coiled around a spear and pulled it beneath the ice. She turned and sprinted for the ship. She didn't want to be around when the monster decided it couldn't digest wood.

Orgrim was already at the side of the ship, getting Zhardrach and Vallac's help lifting Einarr over the side. Birna raced to join them, lending her strength to the effort while keeping one eye on the kraken. After what seemed an eternity, Einarr's unconscious body was over the side. Birna lost no time scrambling up after him. The kraken's tentacles had already withdrawn, no longer interested in the junk Thognathog was throwing onto the ice.

The huntress slumped onto the deck, trying to catch her breath after her exertions. She looked across to where Urda was crouched above Einarr's prostrate body. The old witch examined his wounds, shaking her head gravely.

'You might as well have left him on the ice,' she said, turning to face Birna. 'He'll never wake from such a wound. If only he had heeded Tchar's warning, but such is the way the gods rid themselves of those unfit to bear their mark.'

The remark brought a growl of frustration ripping up from Orgrim's jaws, the sound more savage than the howl of a wolf. Birna shook her head in disbelief. After all the signs, all the portents, to have them add up to nothing...

'The beast not like toys now,' Thognathog observed, letting the harpoon he had been preparing to fling overboard crash down onto the deck. 'Maybe it tired.'

Zhardrach spat over the side of the ship, watching his spittle splatter on the ice. 'I can think of a lot of things to call that lurker, but tired isn't one of them!'

'The slaver is right,' Birna sighed. 'It will be back, and probably very soon.'

Vallac nodded his head in agreement. 'We'll just have to make sure Thog has plenty of junk to throw down there for it to play with.'

'I don't think the kraken will be so easily deceived next time,' Urda said. 'Even now, it is down there mulling over how it was tricked. When it resolves its confusion, it will be back.'

'Good thing we aren't on the ice then,' Zhardrach said. 'At least the ship is safe from it.'

'No, it's not.'

All eyes turned to find Einarr standing on the deck, defying the dire pronouncement of the witch. Urda looked at him with a mixture of horror and awe, backing away as though from a raging fire. It was an apt comparison, for the warrior's body seemed to blaze with power, the metal on his hand shining with a molten light. Einarr looked into the face of each of his followers, fixing them with his commanding gaze. Birna wondered if the others felt the same thrill of both hope and dread as Einarr's gaze swept past her.

'The kraken will return, but this ship is no refuge from its hunger,' Einarr said. 'To get us, it will drag this entire vessel down into its black domain. In so doing, it will seal its own doom.' The warrior stabbed his finger at Zhardrach. 'I want you to build a ladder from the prow of this ship to the top of the ice wall, have Thognathog help you. Make it sturdy, dwarf. If the ogre falls, you fall with him.'

Einarr did not wait to hear Zhardrach's protests, but fixed his attention on Urda. 'I need your magic again, crone. A spell to change water to ice. Tell me Tchar has seen fit to teach you such magic.'

Urda nodded her head. 'I know such a ritual, but it is no simple thing to command the powers of the gods! There is much to prepare before such magic can be safely cast.' As proof of her words, she displayed her charred hand to Einarr. The warrior was unimpressed.

'You will climb the ladder first then,' he told her. 'Begin your preparations as soon as you are on the ice. Orgrim will watch over you, to ensure you do not lose your way.' The witch scowled at him, but nodded her head again.

'Birna,' Einarr called to the huntress. She smiled as he said her name, but there was no tenderness in his tone when he spoke, no softness in his eyes as he looked on her. 'Watch for the kraken and sound the alarm as soon as you see it.' Birna's face slipped back into severity and she nodded her understanding of the warrior's orders.

'What of me?' Vallac asked. Einarr's features darkened as he looked at the Kurgan.

'Come with me,' the warrior said, turning and stalking towards the decayed door of the ship's cabin and withdrawing into the gloom within.

THE HOLD OF the ship was a ghastly sight. Bodies were piled together in a great heap at the centre of the hold. Bundled in thick furs, the crew of the ship had at last huddled together, trying to use their combined body heat to stay warm. As they suffered together, so they had died together, frozen into one immense mass of blue flesh and frosty fur. Einarr was surprised to find that many of the men appeared to be Norse, though just as many sported features from lands he could not even begin to name. The only constant were the tattoos and scars, the medallions and talismans that marked these men as worshippers of the Dark Gods in the divine unity of ultimate Chaos.

Even Vallac, an old hand at slaughter and carnage, who had seen his first battlefield while still a babe sucking his mother's teat, even he was struck by the morbid vision. The Kurgan hung back as Einarr circled the heap of frozen men, studying it as a horse trader might study a new foal. Vallac found the sight even more disturbing, recalling the profane bone-callers who sometimes practised their abominable sorcery among the cairns and barrows of his people, instilling unclean life into the husks of fallen warlords.

'You doubt my dreams,' Einarr said as he paced around the pile of bodies. 'You doubt the mark upon my flesh. You doubt the promise that Tchar has made to me.'

'I doubt nothing,' Vallac replied. 'I only questioned if you had interpreted the signs correctly.'

Einarr turned and faced his comrade. 'Do not question me. Do not doubt me. Just follow where I would lead you, Vallac, and you shall have the glory you desire.' He began circling the corpses again, seeming to lose interest in his companion. He touched the wooden support beam that rose amid the bodies, closing his eyes as his fingers traced the runes carved into its surface.

'This ship was mighty once,' Einarr said, his every word booming with force and command. 'The terror of the seas. Many were the nights when the citadels of the elf-lands shivered in fear when the black sails appeared on the horizon. But nothing can resist the Winds of Change. Prey becomes predator and hunter becomes hunted. Chased from the seas, weakened by battle, defeated and wretched, the captain thought he could hide himself in the very lap of the gods. But the gods have no use for the weak. They let him come near enough to think himself safe, then they abandoned him to the ice and snow.'

Einarr stared at the bodies, a strange smile on his face. 'There is a lesson there for mortals, I think. If we are wise enough to heed it.'

Vallac felt the colour rush into his face. 'Einarr, I thought the kraken had killed you, otherwise I should never have left you behind.' The Norscan ignored Vallac's protest, continuing to pace around the bodies. Suddenly he gave a bark of excitement, springing to the pile and attacking it with his sword. Vallac lingered at the edge of the ice-bound hold, wondering what strange mania had seeped into Einarr's skull from his wound.

Einarr struggled at the frozen carcasses, chopping arms and heads free as he ploughed through the pile. At last he forced a huge armoured body free from the corpses clustered around it. He cut away the frozen cape of fur that covered the body's arm. Despite his concerns, Vallac drew close, watching as Einarr dragged the elaborately armoured carcass away from the pile. He could see the intricate runes carved into the blue-black plate that girded the corpse's torso and legs. The powerful arms were bare, however, bound only by thick bands of gold and silver. Einarr had no eyes for these, though, staring intently at the incongruous iron ring that circled the body's wrist.

'Here, as I knew it would be,' Einarr said. He brought his sword cracking down into the corpse's wrist, sending its frozen hand skipping across the hold. Einarr reached down and pried the band from the stump of the arm, holding it reverently in his palm. Vallac could see the eye-like symbols inscribed all along its surface, one of the sacred symbols of Tzeentch.

'What is that, and how did you know it was here?' he asked. Einarr seemed to diminish somehow as Vallac asked the question. When he spoke, the tone was uncertain, almost confused.

'I had a vision of this place, of the frozen captain and the band fastened about his dead arm,' he confessed, staring at the iron band as though seeing it for the first time.

'But what is it?' Vallac repeated.

'Mine,' the Norscan replied, bending the iron band around his own arm. Before Vallac could question him further, both men looked up at the roof of the hold. Birna's voice drifted down to them.

The kraken had returned.

Chapter Eleven

THE ANCIENT SHIP shuddered as it was struck from below, the old timbers cracking and exploding under the strain. Einarr and Vallac fought their way through the rolling passageways as the ship began to disintegrate around them. Fang-like icicles plummeted around them, shaken loose by the ship's violent throes. Slivers of ice slashed at the men as the icicles shattered against the frozen floors, spraying them with debris. Neither man gave thought to the bleeding cuts – far worse waited them if they tarried.

As the timber beneath them began to buckle and crack, the warriors reached the deck. Only a few feet away, the frozen face of the cliff loomed over them, Zhardrach's ramshackle ladder leaning against it, just reaching the top some thirty feet above. The others had already retreated up the ladder, staring down at them from the icy cliff above the furrow. The ship shuddered again, her tortured substance shrieking as the hull began to snap. Almost like a living thing, the deck beneath them heaved and rolled. Einarr pushed Vallac towards the ladder, roaring at him to climb. Nothing more than the toppled mainmast with crude steps pounded into its sides, Vallac struggled to lift himself up the ungainly structure.

'Climb, you damn Kurgan whoreson!' Einarr bellowed, lunging for the ladder himself as the violent convulsions of the ship intensified. He could see the kraken's tentacles, mottled scarlet and black, chewing into the hull of the ship, wrapping about it in a crushing embrace. He turned back towards the faltering Kurgan. 'Climb!' he ordered again.

Vallac continued to struggle to maintain his footing. Einarr snarled, scurrying with a spider-like agility to help his comrade. Long years at sea had left their mark in Einarr, crawling about the rigging of the longships had lent him an unerring sense of agility and balance. The horse-born Kurgan was without such instinct, clinging to the ladder with a desperate grip. Einarr struck Vallac, again extolling him to climb. Beneath them, the ship shuddered again. There was a terrible cracking sound and Einarr looked down to observe the stern crumbling into debris and sinking beneath the freezing water. The ladder trembled and began to slide.

Suddenly, the ladder became stable again, then, impossibly, began to rise. Einarr stared back down at the deck, watching as the destruction that had started with the stern swiftly overcame the rest of the ship. A gaping hole in the ice sucked the wreckage down even as the kraken's vibrant tentacles continued to pull the ship apart. Einarr looked back up at the cliff, smiling as he saw Thognathog's immense hands closed around the top of the ladder, lifting both it and the two men clinging to it to the safety of the ice.

Einarr sprang from the ladder as soon as it cleared the lip of the furrow, turning to stare back at the jagged hole where the ship had been. As he watched, the kraken dragged the prow of the ship down into its watery domain. The tentacles vanished along with its ancient victim, only the jumble of floating debris giving evidence that it had ever been there at all.

'Next time we go around,' Vallac cursed, wilting to the ice as he released his death grip on the ladder. Thognathog stepped away from the recuperating Kurgan. Carrying the ladder with him, the ogre approached the edge of the trench. With a savage grunt, he lifted the massive mast over his head and hurled it like a javelin down into the pool of freezing water that marked the kraken's retreat.

'We should flee before it comes back,' Birna advised, pressing her fur cloak against the worst of Einarr's wounds. Einarr shook his head.

'Crone!' he called. Urda was sitting slouched over her rune stones, a crude circle of symbols and sigils carved into the ice around her. She looked up as the warrior called her, her rune-eye white with frost, her breath a mist of ice. 'Is your spell ready? I want the hole that thing pulled the ship down frozen over again.'

'I waited only for yourself and the Kurgan to get clear,' Urda said.

'Then wait some more,' Einarr told her. 'But be ready. I will tell you when it is time.'

They waited for nearly an hour, feeling the chill Norse wind whip against their bodies, freezing their

noses and eyes. Vallac and Birna urged Einarr to move
on while they could, but the Norscan would not be
moved. The kraken had hunted them for days across
the ice, there was no reason to believe it would relent
now. No, they would settle with it here.

Orgrim was the first to see the beast's return. The
water that had sucked down the doomed ship began
to bubble and froth as an immense body surged
upward from the depths. Einarr called out to the others to be ready in case Urda's magic was less than she
promised.

The water exploded upward in a frigid geyser as the
kraken's tentacles flailed against the ice, scratching
against the sides of the trench. Einarr stared down
into the turbulent pool, watching as the water slowly
filled with the kraken's scaly mass. An eye, hideously
human and the size of an ox, stared back at him. The
kraken rolled its body over, exposing the other eye,
fixing both on Einarr and his comrades. The beast's
drooling, bird-like mouth cleared the water, hissing
and slobbering in its tremendous hunger. For a
moment, Einarr was struck by the enormity of the
kraken, it was larger than the whales of the Sea of
Claws and the hideous prometheans that sometimes
ransacked the fishing villages of the Baersonlings. His
mind rebelled at the thought that such a giant could
live and breathe.

The moment passed and Einarr glared back at the
monster with new eyes. This thing stood between him
and what he had been promised. No matter how
enormous, he would not allow that to be.

'Now, old witch,' Einarr snarled. At his command,
Urda stood, baring arms that were blue from the chill.
The hag circled her hands through the air, as though

weaving the very wind. Sibilant tones wheezed through her shivering lips and she cast a fine white powder of snow into the air. A greater cold clutched at Einarr as the witch worked her magic, a chill of sorcery rather than winter. Einarr pulled his cloak closer and stared back at the kraken.

The monster seemed to sense that something was wrong, stretching its tentacles still higher in an effort to reach the lip of the fissure. The snapping beaks on the undersides of the tendrils dug at the ice, almost as though the beast were trying to pull itself up after them. The kraken's body erupted into a display of livid yellow and black stripes as it angrily tried to pull itself from the water. But if such was its intention, then it was too late.

Ice started to re-form at the very edges of the hole, rapidly expanding to consume all of the water that remained. The liquid froze solid all around the kraken, even as it struggled to free itself. The great beak snapped and slobbered at the ice, trying to crush it within its powerful jaws, but the enchantment would not be so easily overcome. Every sliver of ice the kraken broke free clung to its body, freezing against its scaly flesh. The water that rushed up from the depths to replace the ice froze in turn. Soon the kraken was encased in a solid field far stronger than that which had claimed the ship. The monster's tentacles continued to flail at the ice, but with every passing moment, the beast's exertions became weaker. The vibrant colours on its hide faded into a wretched grey and its eyes clouded over with a film of frost.

A booming war cry bellowed from Thognathog's mighty frame. The huge ogre leaped down from the cliff, his massive hands closed around one of the bronze harpoons from the ship. Like a boulder smashing down the side of a mountain, the immense ogre crashed into the trapped kraken, digging the harpoon deep into its clammy flesh. Thognathog howled again, ripping the spear free and slamming it once more into the imprisoned beast. Purple ichor exploded from the wounds, coating the ogre in greasy ink, but still he stabbed at the beast.

Again and again, Thognathog plunged his weapon into the kraken, rupturing organs with each strike. From the cliff above, his comrades cheered him on, even Zhardrach enjoying the destruction the ogre was visiting upon their terrible foe. Only when there was no life left in the behemoth did Thognathog relent, stabbing the harpoon one last time into the kraken's bulk. He lifted his heads, grinning back at the cheering humans.

'Before you climb back up here,' Einarr called down to him, 'see about cutting some meat off that brute. After trying so hard to make a meal of us, it is only fair we fatten ourselves on it.'

'Are you sure kraken meat is safe?' Vallac asked, a nervous timbre in his voice. Einarr considered the question for a moment.

'Make certain the dwarf gets the first taste,' he answered. 'If he doesn't dry up and die, then we'll know its safe to eat.' Vallac chuckled at the Norscan's response. Einarr shared the Kurgan's humour, fuelling his laughter with the relief that overcoming the kraken had brought. He turned, seeing the others sharing in the joy of simply being alive after such an ordeal. Then his eyes settled on Urda, crouched in the shadow of a frozen wave, her cloak drawn tight around her. As he saw the witch, his own merriment died. Grimly, he marched to where the hag was huddled.

'Well done, hag,' Einarr told Urda. Whatever reply the witch might have made was lost to her chattering teeth. Einarr smiled at the old woman's discomfort. 'Perhaps next time you will have sense enough not to doubt me. Or at least make sure I am dead before you leave me behind.' He did not wait for her to make a response, directing his attention instead to his other companions.

'The beast is dead, but we still have a long way to go before this frozen hell is behind us,' he told them. 'The sooner we start moving, the sooner we shall put solid earth beneath our toes again.'

After their experience with the kraken, the promise of standing on real ground again was all Einarr's warband needed to motivate them.

THE BATTLE WITH the kraken was many days behind them before the craggy cliffs on the eastern boundary of the Frozen Sea loomed upon the horizon. There was little cheer as Einarr's warband laid eyes upon the imposing landscape. It towered hundreds of feet above the surface of the sea, every inch of it looking jagged and lethal. There was no sign of any break in the immense wall of rock and ice, it looked as regular as the wall of a titan's castle, and as imposing. After weeks of hardship and privation on the ice, with nothing but seal meat and ice crabs to sustain them, nothing but snow to drink and little more than good intentions to shelter them from the biting cold, the mere sight of the cliffs was like a physical blow to them.

Einarr paced among them, growling orders, forcing them to move on. It was not that he did not appreciate

their despair, he felt the enormity of what lay before
them as keenly as anyone, but he knew that if they
stopped, if they let the cliffs overcome them, then
they would all die upon the ice.

'Orgrim, you have the sharpest eyes, see if you can't
find the best approach.' Einarr could see that the renegade wasn't particularly hopeful as he loped off across
the frozen waves, but he didn't much care. Lifted by
hope or crushed by despair, they would conquer the
cliffs.

'I'm not climbing that,' Urda stated, slumping down
in the snow. 'And you are mad to even try.'

Einarr stared down at the crone. To be truthful, he
was surprised the hag had lasted this far, he was
amazed she was still breathing, much less able to walk
on her own feet. Whatever force drove her on, it was
powerful.

'Mad or no, we will climb them,' Einarr said, clenching his fist. The witch shook her head.

'Not if the gods gave me back forty of my winters
could I climb that,' she swore. 'Besides, there is my
hand to consider.' Urda held the hand that had been
charred in the fight with the kraken out to Einarr,
reminding him of the change that had come over it.
The breath of the gods had washed over them constantly as they crawled across the Frozen Sea. All of
them sported some degree of change to their bodies,
from tufts of hair where no hair had been to patches
of feathers and fur. Zhardrach had developed a set of
tiny fingers sprouting from his neck while Birna's
nails had lengthened and hardened until they resembled the talons of a bird. In Urda's case, her injured
hand had calcified, changing into something that was
more stone than flesh. The fingers of her hand had

fused into a crab-like claw of stone. Looking at it, he agreed that it was useless for climbing the cliff's craggy face.

'Thognathog will carry you then,' Einarr told her. 'I'll not leave you behind.'

'Your concern touches me,' Urda said. Einarr laughed.

'It is not you that concerns me, it is your magic,' he said. 'A witch will be most useful dealing with the sorcerer Skoroth.'

It was Urda's turn to laugh, her wheezing cackle knifing its way through Einarr's ears. 'Skoroth is the Plague Lord, the scion of Neiglen,' she said. 'One of the mightiest vassals of the Plague God. You vastly overestimate my abilities. Setting me against him would be like setting a rat against a tiger.'

'The tiger may have the power, old woman,' Einarr said, 'but that rat has deceit on her side.'

Urda looked past the warrior, staring at the imposing heights of the cliffs. 'Just now, the rat would be content to have a pair of wings.'

THE CLIMB WAS every bit as difficult as they had expected. Einarr had Thognathog undo Zhardrach's chains, using the dwarf's manacles to tether himself and his companions. If one of them lost their grip, the chain would bind him to the others, arresting his fall. It was an old Norse trick used when climbing their own inhospitable mountains. Einarr had seen the tactic save many an unfortunate climber from plummeting down the side of a mountain. He hoped the trick would serve him well here. Orgrim and Birna were Norse, like himself, and no strangers to climbing up the ragged side of a cliff. He was less certain about

Zhardrach and Vallac, especially since the Kurgan seemed to have taken sick after they left the ship, his body wracked by a cough and his throat swollen to a grotesque degree.

Thognathog carried Urda, lashing the witch's protesting frame to his shoulder. The immense ogre had to climb without the security of the chain – his huge body would pull everyone attached to him into the abyss if he lost his grip. Einarr felt that Tchar had guided his steps so far, but he wasn't about to blindly trust the trickster god.

Long hours they climbed, their hands torn by the icy rocks, their bodies nearly frozen by the wind that howled down upon them from the heights. Twice Zhardrach lost his grip, the dwarf tumbling down the cliff face until the length of the chain arrested his fall. Despite his concerns, Vallac proved an apt, if slow climber. With something more solid than a broken mainmast beneath him, the Kurgan seemed less timid in his movements. With his three arms, Thognathog easily outdistanced even the Norse, crawling up the rocks like some mammoth spider. If the ogre found the passage an easy one, his passenger did not. Urda's thin shrieks of fright drifted down to them every time the wind slackened. The sound would interrupt the string of curses dripping from Zhardrach's mouth as the dwarf chuckled at her discomfort.

Only a few hundred yards from the top, the wind finally died away. Just as they were beginning to appreciated the respite, Thognathog's rumbling voices shouted down to Einarr. He could not make out the ogre's words, but there was no mistaking the alarm in his tone. Einarr craned his head upward, shocked to see Thognathog clinging with one arm to the cliff, his other arms swatting at something with sapphire feathers and scarlet wings. Whatever it was squawked and hissed at the ogre even as it dove at him with splayed talons. While Einarr watched, a second bird crawled free from a little burrow gouged in the face of the cliff. He could see its beaked face stare up at Thognathog, then twist downward and fix its beady eyes on him. The bird dove from its hole, spreading two sets of wings as it plummeted down towards him. Behind it, other birds were emerging from their own holes.

Einarr called out to his comrades and wrapped some of the slack in the chain around a small outcropping, hoping that it would help anchor him a bit more firmly. He could see Birna trying to brace her body against the sides of a small fissure while unslinging her bow. Zhardrach hurled a few particularly colourful oaths into the wind and tried to crush himself behind a jagged fang of rock. Vallac simply pressed himself even closer to the cliff face, trying to tighten his grip on the rock. Above him, Einarr could see Orgrim planting his feet on a small ledge and dragging his axe from his belt.

Then the burrow-hawks were among them, a shrieking mass of sapphire feathers and razor talons. The first closed upon Orgrim, swirling about him in a scratching, clawing riot of lashing wings and snapping beaks. The berserker swung his axe through the swarm, cracking the wing of one hawk and sending it crashing down the side of the cliff. More than this, Einarr did not have time to see, for another pair of hawks dove towards him.

The first of the hawks buried its talons in Einarr's cloak, scrabbling at the heavy bear pelt to gain its footing. The other dove for his face, smacking its sharp beak against his helm. Sparks danced through Einarr's vision as the bird pounded against his head, trying to penetrate it and puncture his skull. The warrior stabbed up at the bird with his sword, sending it squawking back into the air. The second hawk, its talons buried in his cloak, stabbed its beak into his shoulder. Einarr rolled with the blow, twisting his body and crushing the bird against the side of the cliff. The broken, tattered hawk flopped against him, its bleeding wreckage trembling as life oozed from it, its talons locked within the fur of his cloak.

Einarr had no time to free himself of the dying bird's weight. Already the first hawk returned, shrieking its rage as it hurtled down at him. This time it brought three of its fellows to help it overcome the Norscan. Einarr roared up at the hawk, daring it to do its worst.

The air was suddenly filled with a sharp, stringent cry, the shriek of some bird of prey. Yet there was something more about the sound than the cry of a mere beast. Somehow, Einarr thought he could detect Birna's voice within the sound and he thought again of the ravens and the beastman camp.

The burrow-hawks hesitated, beating their blue wings against the air. Einarr could see now that they were hideously twisted in shape and form, beyond their extra sets of wings. None of the birds were alike, each displaying the touch of the gods upon its abhorrent form. One had a grotesque wattle beneath its throat, another had the long, sinuous head of a serpent and a third had sharp thorns growing from its legs. The sight of the severe mutations gave Einarr pause. Against a natural beast, he did not question his courage and his strength, but against things that had been so thoroughly reshaped by the gods he doubted his own abilities.

The hawks did not hesitate long, but gave voice to an ear-shattering clamour of squawking and shrieking. It seemed to Einarr almost as if the things were laughing. The din was silenced when a black-feathered arrow sprouted from the breast of one hawk and the misshapen animal plummeted from the sky. Einarr shifted his gaze, observing Birna nocking another arrow. Then the hawks were on him once more.

Einarr slashed and hacked at the flying predators as they pecked and clawed at him, but was unable to strike the vile birds, successful only in warding off the worst of their attentions. Clinging to the side of the cliff, he was barely able to move while the hawks had complete freedom. It was hardly a fair struggle.

Blood rained down on Einarr's head and he saw another burrow-hawk fall from the sky, this one with Orgrim's axe buried in it. A moment later a savage howl split the air. Einarr saw Orgrim hurtle past him, the berserker's hairy hands locked around the torn mass of a hawk. Einarr braced himself as the chain was pulled tight by Orgrim's weight. With the chain taut, it was all Einarr could do to breathe, much less fend off the hawks. Once again, he felt sharp claws sink into the fur cloak covering his back.

Beneath him, other burrow-hawks dove for Vallac, deciding that the prey higher up was proving deadlier than they liked. One of the birds tore into the Kurgan's back, sending bright rivulets of blood flashing through the air. Vallac howled in pain, tightening his hold on the cliff as he felt the hawk try to pull him away. He twisted his head around, locking eyes with the burrow-hawk's. He opened his mouth and breathed full into the bird's face. His bloated throat collapsed as a fiery cloud engulfed the hawk. The thing shrieked as it pulled away, but already its feathers were alight. Like a firebrand, the burning bird toppled down the side of the cliff.

The attack faltered as the stench of burning hawk drifted upwards. Birna called out again with her bird voice, and this time the hawks found no amusement in her call. Squawking in fright, they shot upwards, scrambling back into their burrows. Einarr wiped the blood from his face as he saw the last of them vanish into their holes. Then he looked down to where Orgrim dangled from his chain. Straining, Einarr began to pull the berserker back up the cliff. From the side of his eye, he could see Vallac climbing up to help him.

'It seems you have learned new tricks,' Einarr called out to him.

'Flesh is but the clay of Tchar,' the Kurgan called back.

'Be thankful Tchar decided to bless you,' Birna shouted from her refuge. Einarr could see that she too had not avoided the attentions of the hawks. Her raiment was tattered from their claws and her frosty hair was dark with blood from a gash in her scalp. 'The filthy things were too wilful to obey me. But like any beast, they fear flame.'

'What did you say to them before they flew off?' Einarr asked.

'I told them we would burn them all, bring fire to their nests and smash their eggs.'

Einarr smiled grimly and shook his head. 'I wish we had time to do that. Remind me on the way back.'

* * *

THE SHORT CLIMB after the attack of the burrow-hawks was harder than the drudgery that had preceded it. Torn and bleeding from the talons of the birds, Einarr could feel his strength draining away every time he stretched his hand and pulled his body upward. But he knew that there would be no rest until he reached the top. If he hesitated now, he would be lost and with him Asta and all of Vinnskor. He would not allow that.

Straining, drawing on reserves of strength he didn't know he had, Einarr finally reached the top. He collapsed on the jagged edge of the cliff, unable even to help his comrades as they finished their own tortuous climbs. Birna crashed down into the snow beside him, too exhausted even to roll onto her back. Einarr mustered the strength to roll her onto her side so that her face wasn't buried in the snow, then collapsed again. He was dimly aware of Orgrim and Vallac slumping against the rocks somewhere to his left. Out of the corner of his eye, he watched as Zhardrach pulled himself over the edge. The dwarf was flushed, his features crimson behind his coiled beard, but Einarr could tell from the way he was breathing that he was in much better shape than the rest of them. He shouldn't have been surprised. The endurance of the dwarfs was renowned, and there was no reason to think the fire dwarfs were any different.

A murderous gleam flickered in Zhardrach's cruel eyes and he began to wrap the chain around his hands and creep towards Einarr. He tried to move but every muscle in his body tensed in protest. Zhardrach smiled as he took note of Einarr's infirmity. Helpless was a condition he preferred his enemies to be in.

The dwarf roared in protest as he was suddenly plucked from the ground. Thognathog's enormous hands crushed the dwarf's arms to his sides. The ogre's hideous faces glared at the squirming captive, ignoring the furious curses streaming from his mouth.

'Thognathog, stop that racket,' Einarr swore. 'Some of us are trying to sleep.' The ogre nodded his left head while grinning maliciously at Zhardrach. With his third hand he smacked the dwarf's head. A fresh stream of obscenities exploded from his mouth as he recoiled from the blow. Thognathog scowled and struck him again. With the third blow, Zhardrach's eyes rolled back in his head and the dwarf slumped unconscious in the ogre's fist.

'Thank you,' Einarr said. 'Make sure he's wearing his bracelets again before he wakes up,' he added. The ogre nodded his understanding and began gathering the chains from the humans sprawled across the snow.

'Wake us up before we freeze to death,' Einarr told Thognathog, every word an effort for his weary mind to conceive, 'and not a moment sooner.'

EINARR AWOKE TO Thognathog's none-too-gentle shoving. His body protested this fresh abuse, but any reprimand he might have made was silenced by the warm glow of the fire the ogre had built. Einarr leaned into the warmth, every cut and bruise in his body forgotten in the simple pleasure of feeling the chill driven from his flesh. As Thognathog stirred the others, they did likewise, Vallac drawing so near to the flames that Einarr thought the Kurgan himself would catch fire.

'The fire was my idea,' Urda said, the witch warming her scrawny frame on the other side of the flames. 'Though I should have just let you freeze. It would be no more than you deserve.'

'Thanks for the kind thought, crone,' Einarr remarked. 'I figured you'd be safe from the hawks. Even a bird knows when something is simply too tough to eat.'

The witch shook her head and tossed another branch into the blaze. Einarr could see that she had quite a collection piled beside her. He wondered how long she had been tending the blaze, how long they had been asleep. Birna's keen eyes found a different question.

'Where did you find this wood?' the huntress asked. She reached forward, taking one of the branches from Urda's collection of kindling. She stared at it in disbelief. Einarr could not understand her anxiety. It was enough to simply be thankful for the fire. Birna made the source of her discomfort clear to him, showing him the tiny green leaf clinging to the side of the branch.

'Noticed that, did you?' the witch cackled. 'I guess there is a brain in that sweet little head of yours after all.' She turned her head and looked across the fire at Einarr. 'It came from down there,' she said, pointing into the distance. Across the flat, featureless expanse of snow-swept plain, Einarr could see a dark, indistinct mass. 'You can't really appreciate it from here,' Urda elaborated. 'But that's a forest... of sorts.'

Einarr stared at the distant mass, trying to pick details from the gloom. 'What is in there?' he wondered aloud.

'That, I decided, was something I would let you find out,' Urda said. 'I have a feeling there is more wrong with the place than green leaves in the dead of winter. Even your ogre felt it, wouldn't go more than a few feet into the trees to collect wood. There is a power there, something older than my magic. Something much more powerful.'

Einarr nodded. 'I'll face your daemons, old hag,' he said. 'But if this is one of your tricks, then pray to the gods I do not return.'

Chapter Twelve

Einarr could feel his skin crawl as he entered the forest, the primordial core of his being sickened with every step he took. Beneath his feet, the soft white snow shimmered with the eerie light of the aurora, yet above him stood mighty oaks, their branches as green and vibrant as the heart of spring. Flowers and wild grass pushed up from beneath the snow, displaying an impossible vitality. Einarr saw tysbast shrubs, luxuriant and ripe, frost dangling from their stems. He saw gigantic marisko orchids, their lush leaves heavy with snow, their roots stabbing deep into the icy ground. So far north of the shores of his own land, even in the depths of summer it should not be warm enough for such flowers to bloom, yet here they thrived with ice dripping from their petals.

A rustling among the shrubs brought Einarr spinning around, Alfwyrm gripped tight in his hand. He had told the others to stay behind at the camp, that he would face whatever secret the forest held alone. It was something he felt he had to do, to show to them that he was without fear. To show them that he was truly the chosen of Tchar. To show them why they should be led by him.

He half expected to see Birna emerge from the undergrowth, defying his command in her eagerness to serve him. He knew the affection she held for him, knew also that much of the emotion stemmed from her own lust for glory and power. By attaching herself to a mighty champion of the gods, she would be able to share in his deeds and his glory. Einarr did not blame her for her ambitions, every relationship grew from the seed of selfish desire. He could not deny that he was tempted by her. She was all a Norscan could want, beautiful and strong, blessed by the kiss of the gods. But she was more, she was strong and fierce, a valiant warrior in her own right. Just being near her, he could almost forget the gruesome memory of Asta's torn remains.

As he thought on Birna's deep, mysterious eyes, Einarr was snapped back to reality when something emerged from the shrubs. It wasn't the lovely huntress he had been half expecting. Instead he found himself looking upon further evidence of the grotesque unnaturalness of his surroundings. The thing crawled along the ground, pushing the snow with its fins, its scaly body caked in tiny crystals of ice. The gills on its neck fluttered rapidly as it sucked air into its abnormal shape. Einarr's mind rebelled at the sight as the beast crawled towards one of the oaks, using its fins to claw its way up the trunk. Only when it had vanished into the verdant branches was Einarr able to tear his eyes away. He had heard tales of the maddening sights the lands of the gods held, now he knew they were more than mere stories. He almost wished he had never left Norsca, where fish understood they were creatures of the water, not of the land.

AFTER HIS ENCOUNTER with the tree-fish, Einarr pressed deeper into the lush forest. The deeper he walked, the stranger and more otherworldly the sights that assailed his eyes became. Stones that scuttled from his path, flowers that devoured the tiny bats that came to drink their nectar, feathered frogs that sang his name as he passed them in their frozen ponds. And always the nameless, crawling evil hovering about the place grew, souring the very air, smothering him with its malignity. Einarr could feel the power of his gods all around him.

He fought down the urge to run, the shrieking fear that slithered through his veins. He was dead and damned already, Einarr reminded himself, nothing in this world held any terror for him now. He bulled his way through the impossibly green shrubs, crushing the lush flowers beneath his boots. Whatever force lurked within this forest, he would not run from it.

The forest finally opened into a clearing and Einarr's breath caught in his chest, his eyes widening with awe. Twice the size of a man, floating a few feet above the ground, was a wondrous prism of crystal. The countless facets of the stone swirled with every colour in creation, bathing the clearing with magnificence. Einarr felt himself overcome, staring with lust and wonder at the incredible manifestation. For a moment he felt the desire to throw himself to the ground, to make obeisance to the apparition. Gods and quests,

women and ancestors, all were forgotten as the
swirling colours washed over him. All that existed was
the prism. All that he wanted to exist was the prism.

Einarr felt his hand growing warm, but he ignored
the sensation, dismissing it beside the mystery of the
prism. The sensation grew, his flesh throbbing with
agony as the heat intensified. He struggled to ignore
the pain even as part of him struggled to embrace it.
His hand felt as though the mark of Tchar were searing its way down to the bone. His nose filled with the
stink of his own burning flesh. With a scream of pain,
Einarr tore his eyes from the prism, plunging his hand
into the soothing cold of the snow. The snow steamed
as the white-hot steel sank into it.

As Einarr tended his hurt, he became aware for the
first time of what lay scattered all around him in the
clearing. Bones and armour littered the ground all
around the prism. He could see the horned helms of
Kurgans and the scale vests of Norsemen. He saw the
rude, savage weapons of orcs and the fanged skulls of
goblins, the twisted remains of beastmen and the carcasses of at least a few Hung. There were dozens,
perhaps hundreds of bodies scattered across the clearing, all curled down against the ground as though in
worship.

Einarr's eyes were drawn away from the corpses,
pulled back to the prism. He felt its power pulling
once again at his mind, but the pain in his hand kept
it from taking hold. He sensed now that it was alive,
alive in some way he could never truly understand.
Perhaps it had been a god once, or something that
had wanted to become a god. The thought gave Einarr
pause. If the thing was a god, even a forgotten one,
then how could any man oppose it?

With his eyes still drawn to the prism, Einarr began to back out from the clearing. As he did so, he suddenly noticed a dark figure watching him from the trees on the other side of the clearing. It was little more than a silhouette, a massive shape of darkness when he first saw it, two fires burning where its eyes should be. Slowly it came forward, emerging from the gloom and into the starlight.

It was a man, or at least something masquerading as a man. Taller than Einarr, encased in a suit of armour so dark that it seemed to devour the light that fell upon it. Einarr could see the intricate runes carved into the pauldrons, the jewelled gauntlets that encased his hands, the skull-shaped poleyns that encased his knees. Upon the cuirass Einarr was surprised to find the eye-rune of Tchar staring back at him, the symbol picked out in bronze and azure. The warrior's head was hidden within the helm he wore, its crown marked with a set of curling horns, its mask forged in the crude image of a bird's beak. From behind the mask, the eyes of the guardian continued to glow red in the darkness. As he stalked into the clearing, the armoured knight threw back the heavy black cloak he wore, exposing the enormous mace swaying at his side. Cruel as death, studded with a riot of spikes and blades, the weapon was as thick around as Einarr's leg, yet the knight hefted it with effortless ease.

Einarr waited for the dark guardian to come to him. There was no thought of flight in the Norscan's mind. He would rather face this foe here than try to elude him in his own forest. A Baersonling died with his wounds to the fore, not in the back.

As the knight advanced, his pace increased, pushing his steel-encased mass forward in a thundering charge.

Einarr braced himself for the attack, rushing in just as the knight swung his gigantic mace at his head. Alfwyrm scraped along the elaborate fauld that covered the knight's waist and hips. The armour screamed as Alfwyrm dug a deep groove through its steel skin, molten blood flying from the edge of the warrior's sword.

If the armour that encased the knight knew pain, the man within did not. The huge mace came crashing down toward Einarr, whistling past his face as it narrowly missed him. In mid strike, the knight corrected, driving the tip of his weapon into Einarr's chest. One of the bladed, claw-like flanges on the mace tore into Einarr's armour, gouging the flesh beneath. Einarr was thrown back by the blow, skidding across the snow and nearly falling over the frozen husk of a Kurgan.

The knight rushed after him, swinging the mace once more for the Norscan's head. Einarr caught the blow with his sword, but strained to hold the force of it. The knight used his greater height and armoured weight to press his advantage, slowly, relentlessly driving the spiked head of the mace downward. Einarr roared his defiance, lashing out with his boot. The kick smacked against the knight's knee, causing him to stagger and nearly toppling him into the snow.

Einarr was quick to capitalise on the knight's momentary weakness, lunging at him with a savage thrust that bore through the join between breastplate and fauld. Again, the sorcerous armour cried out as Alfwyrm chewed through its skin. Blood exploded from the wound as Einarr's sword ploughed through the man inside. He pressed the weight of his entire body behind the thrust, seeking to skewer the guardian's vitals.

Red pain cracked against the side of Einarr's face, knocking him back as the knight's mailed fist cracked against his jaw. The knight swung his mace after the reeling warrior, the weapon smashing against his side and hurling him like a rag doll. Einarr crashed into the snow, feeling skeletons crumble beneath his impact and jagged shards of bone stab at his flesh. His entire side was damp with his own blood where the steel thorns of the mace had stabbed him.

Einarr rolled onto his side, spitting teeth into the snow. He could see the knight stalking towards him once more, the wound in his side steaming as the molten ichor from his armour cauterised his injury. The glowing eyes of the knight regarded Einarr with a cold malevolence as he marched forward. Einarr groped in the snow, his fingers closing around the desiccated skull of a goblin. He twisted his body around, hurling the morbid missile at his foe. The knight didn't pause, merely lifting his left hand. In mid air, the skull exploded into a thousand fragments, a weird blue flame accompanying its destruction.

Grunting with effort, Einarr rose from the ground, hand locked around the hilt of his sword. He quietly prayed to his ancestors, asking them to prepare a place for him in their sacred halls. He spit the blood from his mouth and glared at the approaching knight. 'Mortal, sorcerer or daemon,' Einarr snarled, 'if you want my head, you'll have to earn it!'

The knight rushed forward again, swinging his mace at Einarr's skull. Einarr spun away from the strike, hacking at his enemy's arm as he turned. Alfwyrm slashed deep into the vambrace, chewing into the meat within. Again, the enchanted armour screamed its metallic wail, molten ichor spurting from the torn steel. Einarr followed up his strike by cracking the pommel against the mask of the knight's helm. His foe staggered back before spinning around, a ronard now gripped in his left hand. He punched the round dagger into Einarr's bicep, the searing agony paralyzing his right arm. Alfwyrm tumbled from his now nerveless hand.

Even as he screamed in pain, Einarr drove his helm into the knight's mask, the bear's horns scraping against the steel. The knight recoiled from the headbutt, then locked his hand around Einarr's shoulder, his steel fingers digging into Einarr's flesh. The knight brought the mace smashing into Einarr's back as he held him, the spikes stabbing through the heavy cloak. Einarr felt the electric shock of his agony jolt through him, his vision blurring as black dots circled through his gaze.

Choking back his suffering, Einarr pressed his finger into the wound in the knight's side, sinking it past the knuckle in his enemy's dripping flesh. The knight recoiled, flinging Einarr from him. The Norscan smacked into the frozen ground, the skeletons doing little to lessen the impact. Einarr snarled in rage, forcing his tortured body to obey him. He groped among the bodies, his numb arm twitching with spasms of pain even as he willed his hand to close around the rusty axe of some long-dead Hung.

The knight glared at Einarr as the Norscan struggled to find a weapon. He swung his mace through the air in a gesture of menace, then began to stalk towards his fallen adversary. Einarr felt a slight sense of satisfaction that as he moved, the knight's other hand clutched at the wound in his belly. Perhaps he was mortal after all.

With a howl of pain, Einarr lifted himself to his feet once more and waited for the knight to attack. For his part, the knight seemed to have learned some caution. Instead of bulling his way through, he began to circle Einarr, his glowing eyes giving no hint of the thoughts boiling within his mind. Einarr decided to take the initiative away from him.

Roaring a death cry, Einarr lunged at the knight, chopping at him with the axe. The knight blocked the attack with his mace, the rusted axe head shattering as it smacked against the metal. The force of the impact threw Einarr back and he crashed down into the snow once more. The knight rushed after him, driving his mace down towards the prone man. Einarr's hand slid across the ground, hurling snow into the face of his attacker. The knight flinched, instinctively raising his arms to protect his face. Einarr scrambled back across the snow, kicking old weapons and bones as he went, anything that might impede the knight's advance. The guardian wiped the snow from his steel mask and slowly stalked after his foe.

Dimly, Einarr became aware of something above his head. He reached up with his hand, thinking to use the branches of the tree to pull himself back to his feet. But what loomed above him was no tree, but rather the floating prism. As Einarr's hand connected with it, the mark of Tchar exploded with a pallid light. Einarr screamed as searing suffering shot down his arm, more intense and piercing even than the pain that had broken the prism's spell. He tried to pull his hand back, but it refused to obey, stuck to the scintillating surface of the prism. The colours flooding the clearing strobed with maniacal intensity, ebbing and flowing with every breath. Einarr screwed his eyes shut against the flickering madness, but the insane whirl of colours continued to flash through his mind.

Just when he thought he must go mad, when he thought the colours could not flicker any faster, the world faded into darkness. Einarr felt the prism shatter beneath his hand, soundlessly crumbling away beneath his fingers. He opened his eyes, finding the clearing littered with shimmering fragments of crystal. The fiery glow on his hand began to slowly fade. For the first time since entering the forest, Einarr felt the crawling sense of evil abandon him.

A dark shadow loomed above Einarr and the Norscan sighed. The knight stared down at him with his burning eyes and his steel mask. The spiked mace gleamed wickedly in the starlight and Einarr noted the knight held Alfwyrm in his other hand. He decided he was too exhausted even to rebel against the indignity of being slain with his own sword. He muttered another prayer to his ancestors and waited for the final blow.

Instead, Einarr felt something cold and metal being pushed into his hand. Almost automatically his fingers assumed their familiar grip around the hilt of Alfwyrm. The knight reached down and pulled Einarr from the snow. The Norscan fought to keep standing as he found his feet. The knight watched him, making no move to attack.

'You have my gratitude,' the knight said at length.

'You have a strange way of showing it,' Einarr replied, gritting his teeth as he ripped the knight's dagger from his shoulder. The exertion almost sent him back into the snow.

'I did what the Soul-eater demanded of me,' the knight said. 'Only those strong in the favour of Tzeentch can oppose its will. Only the mightiest of his champions could bring about its ruin.'

'It was luck,' Einarr said, staring at his hand. The glow had faded completely from the metal sigil, taking with it the burning pain it had evoked. Even so, it felt warm to his touch.

'There is no luck,' the knight's steely voice intoned. 'Only fate and the will of the gods. I am Ernst von Kammler, Acolyte of the Purple Talon and Warlord of the Khaigs, if there are any left.' He pointed at Einarr's hand, then slapped the symbol engraved upon his breastplate. 'We are brothers in faith, Norscan, champions of the Change Lord.'

'Einarr of the Baersonlings,' the warrior hissed, taking the knight's hand.

Von Kammler nodded as he heard Einarr's name. 'I warn you, Einarr of the Baersonlings, the tales they tell of the Soul-eater are lies. There is no great reward awaiting the one who would destroy it. Whether you were promised treasure or knowledge, the Soul-eater has none to give. Linger here at your peril.' The knight pointed to the ground. Einarr was shocked to see the shattered pieces of crystal slowly crawling back to the centre of the clearing.

'I lingered too long trying to find its treasure,' von Kammler continued. 'When the Soul-eater was reborn, it bound me to its will. It is a cruel thing, to be commanded to slay the only ones who might set you free.'

Einarr nodded, appreciating the horror of such an existence and wanting no part of it. 'I may have no choice,' he said. 'I doubt I have the strength to crawl,

much less walk, back to my camp and I do not think
any of my comrades would brave the forest to look for
me.'

Von Kammler fastened his mace to his belt once
more, moving towards Einarr and helping to support
the flagging Norscan. 'Your comrades are both wise
and craven,' he said. 'But I will see that you are safely
free from this place. I have not so completely put the
lands of my birth behind me that I would abandon
one who has done me good.'

Too weary to protest even if he wanted to, Einarr let
von Kammler guide him out of the forest, grateful to
be leaving it as the crawling dread of the Soul-eater
began to slowly reconstruct itself within his mind.

Chapter Thirteen

Einarr lay on his belly near the roaring fire that Thognathog had built, his armour strewn around him, his sword close at hand. He grunted sharply as Urda's thin fingers probed his wounds, working a foul-smelling poultice into his injuries. The witch's touch was far from delicate, her finger worming beneath his skin as she clawed damaged tissue and foreign matter free. He endured the torment the witch inflicted on him, he knew Urda was wise in the ways of healing. He smiled as he glanced past Urda, finding the worried gaze of Birna watching him from behind the trickle of falling snow. The huntress stood behind the witch, her scowl darkening every time he winced in pain, her knuckles white where she gripped the hilt of her own sword. If Urda did plan any mischief, at least Einarr could be certain he would not be the only one meeting their ancestors.

The rest of his small warband was also clustered around the fire, gorging themselves on a pair of burrow-hawks Thognathog had plucked from their holes and an oversized rabbit with six legs that Orgrim had discovered on one of his lonesome ramblings. A plate of meat rested beside Einarr's prone frame, slowly freezing in the cold winter night as snow drifted down onto it, but the Norscan had more vital concerns on his mind than the base placation of his animal needs. He turned his eyes away from the fire, staring at von Kammler's immense steel form.

'Now you have heard where it is we go and what it is we face,' Einarr told him. The knight stared into the flames, his glowing eyes seeming to absorb the light. When he spoke, his voice was a deep rumble.

'You have no imagining of where you go or what awaits you there,' von Kammler said, his voice filled with scorn. 'Children and dogs playing at the games of men! Blind, idiot things pretending they can think and see!'

The knight's derision brought a bestial snarl rolling from Orgrim's hairy throat. Birna paced towards him, her hand still gripped on her blade. Vallac stood, glowering at the sinister armoured apparition, his bloated neck pulsing in time with his anger. Thognathog stared at von Kammler, snapping a log in half with his powerful hands. Zhardrach simply chuckled and shovelled another fistful of burrow-hawk into his mouth.

'And you know better?' Einarr asked, his voice low, filled with menace. He would not allow the knight to stop him now, not after they had come so far. Not after he had been promised so much. If that meant finishing their battle, then Einarr would answer that challenge.

Von Kammler nodded his armoured head. 'I do, Norscan,' he said. 'These eyes have seen the place you seek. These feet have stood within its corrupt halls. This mace has tasted the maggot-ridden blood of the tower's master. Yes, I do know better, Einarr Steelfist.'

The statement brought jeering laughter from Vallac. The Kurgan sneered at the knight's words, shaking his head. 'The southlander lies!' he boldly proclaimed. 'I have seen the maps the shamans keep, I have seen the Palace of Plagues marked upon them. It lies thousands of leagues from here, deep in the lands of the Hung! Are we to believe now that a weak southlander could make such a journey, much less return to boast…'

The Kurgan's words died as rings of blazing light suddenly flared into existence around him, swirling and pulsating as they circled him. Vallac fell to his knees, his body throbbing with agony. Einarr could see his flesh peeling away as bony growths erupted from his skin, watched in amazement as his left eye socket began to slide down his face. Across the fire, von Kammler stood with his hand outstretched, his gauntlet pulsing with light. Orgrim pounced at the knight, but a sweep of von Kammler's mace sent the woodsman rolling across the snow. Birna lunged at him before he could recover from the attack. Her blade cracked against the knight's gauntlet, causing the metal to shriek and spraying her with molten ichor. She recoiled from the stinging liquid. The glow faded from von Kammler's gauntlet and the knight turned to face his new antagonist.

'Enough!' Einarr roared, springing to his feet, Alfwyrm in his hand. 'Is this the gratitude you show one who has done you a service? Is this von

Kammler's concept of honour?' The knight glared at Einarr, then at Birna. Slowly, he backed away from the woman, fastening his mace to his belt. Warily, the huntress circled around him, moving to help the still reeling Orgrim.

'Your Kurgan doubted my strength,' the knight said. Einarr looked across the camp to where Vallac writhed on the ground. His arms were a mass of bony knobs, his face distorted by the mutating power of von Kammler's spell. Urda stood some distance from the stricken marauder, watching him intently. Einarr knew what she was watching for, to see if the changes would continue even without the spell, to see if Vallac's entire body would collapse into a mindless, reeking thing of madness and carnage. Beside such a doom, even death was a blessing.

'Vallac knows better now,' Einarr said. 'I do not think any here will challenge you so lightly again.'

'What do you barbarians know of the powers you call gods?' von Kammler growled. 'You understand nothing and imagine much! I sometimes wonder who is more pathetic, the men of the north with their superstitions and legends or the men of the south with their miserable Sigmar!'

'Now you claim to know the gods themselves!' Urda spat, her tone incredulous.

'I know much, wrinkled sister,' von Kammler retorted. He turned towards Einarr again. 'If you would prevail, Norscan, leave behind superstition, it will avail you nothing. Seek wisdom, that alone shall earn you the blessing of Tzeentch. You will need the blessing of the god if you would vanquish Skoroth.' The knight reached to his left hand, pulling away the armoured gauntlet. The hand he exposed was pale and colourless, the veins standing stark beneath the skin. Yet it was the pattern those veins formed that arrested Einarr's attention. There was no denying the shape they formed, the same shape that was seared into his own hand. Von Kammler too bore the mark of Tchar. 'Trust me when I tell you I know of what I speak.'

Emotion swelled within Einarr's bruised frame. Fascination, excitement and something that Einarr almost refused to let himself feel: hope. The Norscan lowered himself back to the ground, eyes fixed to von Kammler's hideous mask and glowing eyes.

'If you have been inside Skoroth's palace,' he asked, 'where is it? How far away? How many days must we travel?'

The knight shook his head. 'Leagues? Days? Such words are without meaning in the lands closest to the gods. Time and distance are deceits the gods place no value upon. If I told you the palace was a thousand, thousand leagues away, it might be a falsehood. If I told you that you should see it before the moons' next rising, it might be truth. There are no "maps" of the Wastes, whatever the Kurgan's shamans might think. Nothing remains where it once was, it finds each traveller in its own measure and its own way.'

Einarr felt the flicker of hope crumbling beneath the knight's words.

'Then how does one find the place?' he demanded, frustrated fury in his voice. 'Can you guide us there?'

'You must guide yourself,' von Kammler replied. 'Distance, direction, navigation, the lands of the gods care nothing for these.' Kammler pointed to his breast, thumping his hand against the gothic platemail. 'It is what is here that the Wastes respect. It is the will and determination that the land measures. If you want something badly enough, if the lust to find it burns brightly enough, *it* will find *you.*'

Einarr listened to the knight's words, not understanding them but believing them. The forest of the Soul-eater and the mythic sagas of the Baersonlings had shown him that in the land of the gods anything was possible. He understood that it was the only answer von Kammler would give him, perhaps the only answer the knight could give him. Yet still he had questions.

'What will we find there, within the palace?' he demanded.

'Death,' the knight's heavy voice intoned. Von Kammler's burning eyes grew dim, as though his very spirit retreated before the memories his mind conjured. 'How is it that Kaanzar the Defiled described it in his tome of abomination? "The lands around the tower are rife with disease and corruption. It is a place where the very ground drips with pestilence and where the rocks spew filth across the earth and the trees weep decay. The very air is abomination, a reeking burning thing that chokes you with its loathsomeness. The plague clans of the Hung make their encampments around the tower and the land is vile with them. They stalk the Wastes like human jackals, eager to infect any clean thing they see with their poxes. The creatures of the Plague God haunt the land in all their bilious shapes, lusting for healthy flesh to rend and defile. About the palace itself festers a great swamp, a place of muck and ruin where the ground is nothing more than oozing corruption that tries to suck you into its embrace. At its centre there lies a great lake of putrescence and rising from the lake, like a sliver of steel in a rotting wound, the Tower of Skoroth stabs up into the leprous sky."'

'Death lurks within that lake,' von Kammler continued, pulling himself from the slithering narrative of the long dead warlock Kaanzar. 'Bubos, the men of the Khaigs called her, a dragon ancient and vile, her body oozing with the power of Skoroth and his god.'

Einarr's companions muttered fearfully among themselves as they heard von Kammler speak of the tower's dread guardian. Einarr refused to let the same fear overcome him.

'What awaits us once we are past the dragon?' he boldly demanded. Von Kammler laughed, the sound like that of scraping steel.

'There is no "after", barbarian,' the knight scoffed. 'Bubos will kill you all. I, with nine thousand Khaig warriors, was unable to prevail against the dragon. We marched on the palace, to cast down Nurgle's loathsome temple, to seize its treasures for mighty Tzeentch. Nine thousand, we marched, neither man nor daemon daring to stand against us. Then we saw that stagnant lake, saw the abomination that dwelt within rise from its putrid depths. I was forced to abandon my army, leave them to the dragon and slink into the fortress like a sneaking thief. Nor did such sacrifice avail me much, for Skoroth was awaiting me. Only a champion of my might could have survived the spells of ruin and corruption the sorcerer cast upon me. Only by the will of Tzeentch did I escape that place at all.'

'We will prevail where you failed, southlander,' Einarr declared. 'We will use cunning and subtlety, the tools of Tchar, not the brute force of an army. We will get past your dragon because she will never know we were there. We will get past the swamp and the Hung and all the other horrors. We will overcome it all. I will not fail as you did, von Kammler.'

'What makes you so certain you will prevail where I was defeated? I, a warlord of the Kurgan, a magister of the Purple Claw! What makes you better than me, barbarian?'

Einarr clenched his fist and as he did so, the mark of Tchar burned with a hellish light. Snow steamed as it struck the blazing fist. 'Because I am the chosen of Tchar!' he roared. 'I will not fail because I will not allow it! What has been promised me will be mine and nothing, not even the Plague God himself, will stand in my way!' Einarr glowered at the knight, staring into the glowing embers beneath his helmet. 'Who broke the spell of the Soul-eater, southlander? Who penetrated the forest only to find the one man who has escaped the place his quest must take him? There is no chance, southlander, only the will of the gods!'

Von Kammler leaned back, seeming to consider Einarr's words. At length, the knight nodded his agreement. 'What you say may indeed be true, Steelfist,' he said. 'You are right to say that nothing is ever merely chance. Perhaps it was the will of Tzeentch that you find me, that I accompany you to the palace. Perhaps in helping your quest, I will reclaim the glory that was stripped from me. Yes, Einarr Steelfist, I will go back there with you.' The knight turned his head, scanning the camp. 'But we are too few,' he lifted his hand to forestall Einarr's objection. 'I do not speak of armies, I speak of numbers. Nine is the sacred number of Tzeentch, the number through which he works his mightiest magic, the number by which his covens and his champions gather. We are seven, eight if your Kurgan lives.'

'Do not worry about numbers, Kammler,' Einarr said. 'If we are too few, then I shall simply have to do twice my share of the work.'

The remark caused von Kammler to shake his head. 'You understand nothing about the ways of the gods. The symbol is the power. It is through symbols that the gods manifest their power, exercise their strength. This prize you seek, why do you think it is of such value to Tzeentch? It is a symbol, a physical incarnation of his power. The Dark Claw, the talon of Be'lakor, the Shadowlord. First among mortals, he was during his life, gathering together all the followers of the true gods to march against the heathen elves and the scaly vermin of the jungles. For his might and valour, the gods raised Be'lakor above all other mortals, sharing some of their own power with him. He became the first mortal to escape the curse of death, became the first man to replace his carcass of flesh for the eternal essence of the daemon. But the gifts the gods bestowed upon him made Be'lakor proud and arrogant in his ways. No longer did he imagine himself as a servant, but as an equal. For his audacity, mighty Tzeentch struck Be'lakor down, stripping him of his power, flaying his mind with such torment that the daemon was driven mad. A shape without form, a wraith without substance, Be'lakor was cast into the winds, to wander the world forever cursed and reviled, an abomination to both man and god.'

Von Kammler turned his head, looking at each of Einarr's followers in turn. 'What you seek is the only remnant of Be'lakor's physical form, the only part of him that Tzeentch allowed to linger in the mortal world. It is the chain that binds Be'lakor's spirit to his curse. Who holds the Dark Claw holds power over the spirit, can use it to command Be'lakor's tortured soul.

'Think of it,' von Kammler hissed. 'The power to command a being even daemons far and dread!'

Einarr's eyes narrowed as he heard the excitement in the knight's metallic voice. 'Is that why you attacked the palace before?'

The knight turned to face Einarr. 'And what noble purpose drives you to seek the Claw?' he sneered. 'What selfless dreams bring Einarr Steelfist and his rabble so far from their homes? I can see your desires written on your faces. The savage woodsman hopes to find a cure for the curse that flows through his veins, to appease the wrath of Tchar. The old witch sees one last chance to prove her worth to Tzeentch, one last chance to earn her god's favour. The Kurgan seeks prestige and glory, to return to his tribe as a mighty champion of the gods in his own right. The huntress looks for something better than her miserable life among the Sarls and marriage to men she thinks unworthy of her. The ogre, he is much simpler in his needs, looking only to repay the man who cast off his chains. The dwarf is simpler still, he'd see every throat in this camp slit.

'But you, Einarr Steelfist, what do you want?' von Kammler asked. 'What purpose drives you into the lands of the gods? I see guilt and loss, desperate hope that you can earn a god's promise...'

'What of you, southlander?' Einarr snapped, colour rushing to his face as he heard the knight mock him.

'I have already said, Norscan,' he replied. 'I seek power.'

IN THE DEAD of night, Einarr awoke with a start. He felt something warm press against his side, rubbing against him beneath the heavy bear cloak he had wrapped himself in. The Norscan scrambled out from beneath his blanket, hand flying to where his sword lay. As the crust of sleep crumbled from his vision, he saw Birna smiling at him. The huntress held the thick fur close to her, wrapped around her lithe frame. Enough of her ivory shoulders and bare arms was left exposed, however, that he found himself wondering how much she was wearing beneath his cloak.

'You'll catch a cold strutting around like that,' Birna chided him. Einarr scowled at her, but relaxed his grip on Alfwyrm.

'I could say the same thing,' he grumbled, stalking back towards the pile of furs he had been sleeping on. He sat down on the hides, looking up at Birna. 'My cloak,' he said, reaching toward her. Birna pouted and snuggled deeper into the folds of fur.

'I don't want to catch cold either,' she said. 'That's why I came over here, to get warm.' Her suggestive smile set Einarr's blood pounding through his veins. The warrior grinned back at her. Eyes still locked to hers, he made a quick lunge, hand closing around a fistful of his cloak. With one swift tug he ripped it away. As he had guessed, the huntress was as bare as a skinned seal beneath his cloak. He chuckled as she gasped in surprise. Einarr let his eyes linger on her a moment, then wrapped the cloak around his body and buried himself in the furs.

Birna stared at him in disbelief for a second, shivering as the night clawed at her skin. Einarr looked up from his feigned sleep and smiled.

'You'd better decide what you're doing before you freeze,' Einarr warned her. 'I'm already one man short according to the southlander.'

Birna seized the invitation, darting under the cloak and squirming close to Einarr's warm bulk. She crooked her head to stare again into his eyes. After a moment, she wrinkled her nose in distaste.

'These furs stink like ogre,' she complained. Einarr pulled her closer his breath hot against her neck.

'Thognathog was the only one I could talk into lugging them across the Frozen Sea,' he said. His calloused hand stroked her smooth shoulder. 'Besides, you have more important things to think about.'

IMPOSSIBLY, A BLOOD red sun glared down at them from the black sky, tingeing the land crimson with its gory rays. Einarr decided that it was the most horrible sight his eyes had seen in the weeks since they had emerged from the Frozen Sea. They had seen rivers of brown soup that slobbered their way across the land only to vanish into nothingness. They had seen trees that crawled across the ground like mighty serpents and which called to one another in the mewing voices of tiny kittens. There had been mountains that seemed to tremble at their approach, slinking fearfully towards the horizon so that every step forward put them two steps further away. They had watched snow lift itself from the ground and fly back into the clouds. There had been colours and sounds and smells without end, coming from nowhere and nothing and vanishing as swiftly as they manifested.

The touch of the gods was on and in everything they saw. The game Orgrim brought back for their fire became stranger every day. Boars without legs, birds with fur instead of feathers, huge mice with fangs the size of daggers and a frill of flesh around their necks.

Once, the woodsman returned with something that might have been a flower save for its size and the scrabbling claws that had replaced its roots.

The change had come upon them as well. Orgrim's ribs had sprouted new extensions, puncturing his sides with spiny fingers of bone. Vallac's misplaced eye had swollen and faded into that of some cave fish. Thognathog's centre arm had withered into a twisted stump while great horns sprouted from his left head. Urda's face had become pinched into something that almost looked like a bird's beak. Zhardrach's skin had darkened into the colour of pitch.

Most unsettling to Einarr had been the changes that had manifested in Birna's body. Every night, the huntress came to him to warm away the chill and worm her way deeper into his affections. At first he did not notice it, trying to dismiss the sensation as some caprice of memory, but after a time there was no denying it. Birna's body was changing, becoming more and more like that of Asta beneath his hands. Even the patch of scaly skin was there, that piece of Asta the gods had touched. Einarr knew it could not be mere chance, that it had to be some mocking gesture of the gods. However much her body changed, Birna would never be Asta.

Did he even want her to be? Birna was a strong, fierce woman, gripped with a determination and force of will that Asta had never possessed. She was a woman that would not be content to linger behind in the safety of some village while her man roamed abroad searching for gold and glory. She was a fighter, a warrior in her own right, one who desired to stand beside him in battle as keenly as lie beside him in the night. Einarr had felt his passion for her overwhelm him, filling his heart almost before he was aware it was even there. The memory of Asta faded from his mind more and more each day, her face only a dim flicker, her voice a distant echo.

Einarr wondered if this too, was naught more than the mockery of the gods. The closer he drew to the Palace of the Plague Lord, the less he cared about the reward he had been promised. He continued because he had sworn an oath and because he knew the others would see the breaking of that oath as a sign of weakness. Birna clung to him because he was strong, because she wanted to share in the glory that could be his. He could not take the risk that she would still care as much for mere Einarr Sigdansson as she did Einarr Steelfist.

THEY CROSSED THE barren tundra of snow and rock, the bloody sun beating down on them fiercely, the snow rejecting its efforts and stubbornly refusing to melt beneath its attentions. Sometimes they saw the bones and weapons of those who had tried to cross these lands before them. Rarely were such remains identifiably human, yet Einarr could not say that perhaps they had not been men before entering the Wastes. Dark shapes sometimes appeared on the horizon, black riders galloping into the distance yet vanishing well before they reached the horizon. Once they saw something that towered above them as it lumbered across the land, its twisted face curled into a feral snarl, its gigantic hands closed around a stone club that looked to have been torn from the side of a mountain. Yet the giant did not see them, walking right through them, its body as insubstantial as mist, its flesh nothing more than thin air. Einarr did not think the thing to be some ghost or spirit, for the vibrancy of life was within it. Von Kammler claimed that it was just as real as any of them, but that it had become out of sequence with the deceit of time and so prowled within its own empty, lonely world.

The incident stayed with Einarr and he considered again the reward he had so proudly demanded from Tchar.

THAT NIGHT, AS they made their camp, Einarr held council with von Kammler. He had done so many times since the knight had joined his warband, but now the Norscan was less willing to accept the cryptic and evasive answers the southlander had given him before. The sight of the ghostly giant had impressed upon Einarr that there were things much worse than death that the gods could visit upon those who displeased them. He was willing to risk much to claim the reward Tchar had promised him, but now he wondered if he had risked more than he had known.

When the fires burned low and even Orgrim settled into a fitful sleep, Einarr joined the knight on the edge of the encampment. Von Kammler stared out at the empty tundra, his fiery eyes scanning the limitless horizon. As they had seen many times since entering the Wastes, the land was never as empty as it appeared.

'What troubles you this night, Steelfist?' the knight asked, not bothering to turn as he heard Einarr approaching. Einarr ignored the challenge in the knight's voice, the tinge of superiority in his words. Such tricks might cow the weak men of the south, but a Norscan respected deeds, not haughty airs and arrogance. He had seen for himself that von Kammler was far from the infallible champion of the gods he thought himself to be. If not for him, von Kammler would still be a slave in the Soul-eater's forest.

Einarr marched up to the knight, seating himself on the frozen ground, following von Kammler's ever-vigilant gaze.

'The Dark Claw,' Einarr said. 'You really think we can steal it from Skoroth?'

Von Kammler chuckled darkly. 'If I did not think so, I would hardly return there with you.' Einarr nodded as he digested the sound reasoning behind the knight's words.

'There is something you are keeping from me,' Einarr said. 'Something that has been bothering me for some time. You spoke of the lake and the dragon. You also spoke of getting past both. I want to know how.' He raised his hand, motioning for the knight to keep silent. 'None of your riddles and half-wisdoms, I want an answer even Thognathog could understand.'

Von Kammler turned his eyes from the horizon, staring down at Einarr. 'You will not like what I tell you. I have seen how you lead this rabble. I do not think you have the stomach for what it will cost you to get into the tower.'

'Tell me anyway,' Einarr growled. Von Kammler turned away, eyes scanning the horizon once more.

'You will need to make sacrifices to get across the lake,' the knight told him. 'There are powers I can call upon that will get us past the lake, but they will demand a price. They will demand blood.'

Einarr digested von Kammler's words, feeling himself grow sick as he considered them. There were few things he would not do to save Asta and his people, but betrayal was one of them. Birna, Orgrim, Vallac and the others, they were trusting him, trusting him to lead them to glory and triumph. Not to feed them to whatever unspeakable power von Kammler decided to invoke. The knight saw the distaste in Einarr's expression.

'It is a talent I have always had,' he said. 'The ability to read a man's soul. The skill to know his limits. It will have to be done.' The knight chuckled again, the sound as malevolent as the growl of a troll. 'If it sits so ill with your conscience, we can always use the dwarf.'

Einarr shook his head. The thought still made him sick. The realisation that using Zhardrach made the prospect almost agreeable made him sicker still. It was not any affection he had for the dwarf, rather the tribal repugnance he felt for anything that smacked of treason.

'There has to be another way,' Einarr said.

'I wish you fortune in finding it,' von Kammler retorted. 'And know this, every moment you tarry beside the lake you risk drawing the notice of the dragon. If that happens, you will have even worse considerations to choke down.'

'What do you mean?' Einarr demanded.

'After my army drew Bubos up from the depths, there was only one way for me to get past her. While she slaughtered my men, I and my closest followers broke away. There was a cave, a tunnel, deep in the swamp. It ran beneath much of Skoroth's domain, eventually opening on the other side of the lake. We dared the dark of the cave, travelling under the swamp to elude the dragon. But the cost was high. A terrible beast, a foul daemon of Nurgle, dwelled within the cave. To get past it cost me many men, their bones stripped clean of meat as the daemon devoured them.'

The knight looked at Einarr again. 'Wake the dragon and we must brave the cave.'

Einarr looked away, staring at the ground. The knight had been right, he didn't like what he had been told. He wondered if he should tell the others, give them the chance to turn back. Then he realised he didn't dare. He needed them, all of them, if he was to stand any chance of stealing the Dark Claw and saving his village.

'We will find another way,' Einarr said. Von Kammler did not reply, simply returning to his scrutiny of the horizon.

EINARR JUDGED THEIR travel across the tundra to be measured in weeks, perhaps as many as three or four, when the Miasma struck. They saw it first as a swirling, pulsating vibrancy against the horizon. Von Kammler shouted a warning to them all, but could offer no advice to defend against what was coming. Like frightened children, they clustered together on the empty plain, clutching to one another as they braced themselves for the terrible power the knight told them was coming.

Einarr watched as the thing skipped across the land. He thought it not unlike a waterspout or cyclone when he first observed it, but no storm he had seen displayed such unnatural character. The thing grew and shrank every instant, sometimes collapsing into almost nothing then swelling so that it stretched across the entire horizon. The light within the storm glowed with putrescence, swirling and dancing in mesmerizing patterns that seemed to decay the soul of those who looked upon it. He could see snow rising from the earth, dancing in the storm's swirling eddies.

As the snow spiralled up into the clouds it began to change, transforming into a dripping slime that infected the very sky with its corruption.

The storm danced across the tundra in a maddening display of directionless uncertainty. Sometimes it would be leagues away, then suddenly skip forward thousands of yards in the blink of an eye. Once, it hopped so far that it was behind them. Before anyone could breathe a sigh of relief, the miasma skipped again, roaring and raging only a few hundred yards from where they cowered before its power. Now Einarr could hear voices in the wind, voices that called and whispered and cursed. If he concentrated, he could hear the words of a particular voice, but every time he did, another voice would shout over the one he attended, trying to drown out the other voices with its own desperate cries.

Then the storm was all around them, its winds tearing and ripping at them, its power pulsating through their bodies. Einarr felt as though his flesh were on fire, as though every scrap of his essence was being stripped away, rotting from his very bones. His mind filled with a hissing cacophony of voices, all clamouring for room within him. He screamed against the maddening din, against the agony pulsing through his body.

All at once, the world was silent again. Einarr's flesh was his own once more, his mind was clear of any voice save his own. For an instant, he had imagined the babble assailing his mind to coalesce into a single shriek, then swiftly explode back into the ether like so many rats smoked from a ship's hold. As he opened his eyes, he saw the fading glow of the symbol branded into his hand, the eye-like rune almost seeming to wink at him as it became dull once more.

He looked around him as his comrades likewise rose from the ground, shaking their heads to try and drive the last echoes of the miasma from their skulls. The snow they brushed from their bodies had turned a stagnant green, dripping from their fingers like oozing scum. Einarr turned his eyes to the landscape around them. It had been transformed from a bleak barren desolation of ice and wind to rolling hills and black canyons. Pools of putrid water steamed up from the ground, spurting their corrupt essence into the air. Even the sky had changed, no longer the black veil of night but a leprous yellow, like a great tapestry of pus and urine. Amid the filth, even the blood-red sun seemed to fade, its rays struggling to pierce the sickness that threatened to consume it.

Flocks of vultures circled in the heavens and Einarr's ears filled with the buzzing of flies. The stench of rot wafted over him. The warrior was overwhelmed by the assault on his senses and he fought to keep his belly from disgorging its contents into the green snow-scum that blanketed the earth. He had just succeeded in his struggle when he felt von Kammler's armoured hand close on his shoulder. He spun on the knight, his hand on his sword, but there was no malice in von Kammler's gesture.

'You must indeed be great in the favour of Tzeentch,' von Kammler told him. 'We have survived the Miasma of Pestilence without our flesh being twisted by the daemons of the withering wind, without our souls being consumed by the poxes of the storm.'

'Where are we?' was all Einarr could find the words to say. Von Kammler laughed, the sound corrupted into a metallic rumble by his helmet.

'Where you wanted to be,' the knight said. 'The Miasma has brought us where you wanted us to be, or perhaps the storm brought it to us.' The knight stretched his arms, gesturing to the filth all around them. 'Behold the domain of Skoroth, the festering realm of Nurgle the Obscene!'

Chapter Fourteen

THE PUTRESCENCE OF the land sucked at their feet as they tried to march across it. For days now they had trudged through a diseased maze of low, mound-like hills. Great fat flies buzzed about their faces, crawling across their lips and scratching at their eyes. The stench intensified, growing from the reek of spoiled fruit to the stink of a sewer. Einarr's eyes teared at the smell, the greedy flies sucking at his suffering as the fluid ran down his face. Orgrim, with his keen senses, was reduced to a whimpering, slinking thing, one hand constantly crushing his nose close.

Disease constantly clawed at their bodies. They could feel it seeping into their flesh. For a time, Urda struggled to combat the plagues, casting her own spells to combat the malevolent power all around them. Her efforts seemed to anger something, rather than keeping the diseases at bay, her magic drew them closer, intensifying their unseen assault. The constant attack wore down the witch's strength, subverting her efforts to keep them healthy.

Urda was the first to develop the cough, the illness settling into her lungs and filling her breath with phlegm and misery. The filth she spat into the snow-scum was green with sickness and red with blood. The corruption spread to Vallac and then Birna and Orgrim before finally claiming Thognathog as its final victim. Strangely, Einarr and von Kammler were almost immune to the pestilence, a fact that did little to comfort their allies. Their march through the mire slowed to a diseased crawl of coughing and spitting as fever ravaged the warband.

Tiny things plopped and slobbered across the ground, cackling and giggling as they savoured the sickness of Einarr's followers. Like living excrement, the grinning daemons slopped along the earth, their bubbling cries tormenting them as much as their fever. Several times, Orgrim broke away to savage the capering daemons with his axe, but for every creature he splashed across the ground a dozen more were drawn by the sound of battle. Eventually even the berserker tired of wasting his energy on the vile things, resigning himself to their ceaseless mockery.

Still they pressed on. Eventually the dung-like hills were behind them, most of the creeping dae-mons reluctant to leave the mounds and enter the stagnant plain that now stretched before Einarr. It was littered with ruined piles of stone and timber, the outlines of walls and roofs nearly obliterated by the mould and slime that clung to them. Great twisted weeds, taller than trees, peppered the land and everywhere Einarr could see tendrils of smoke rising into the mouldering sky and the glow from cook-fires amid the rubble.

'The camps of the plague clans,' von Kammler told him. 'Like lice, they infest these lands. We will need to tread carefully if we would escape their notice.'

'How far is the tower?' Einarr asked. Von Kammler fixed him with his fiery eyes.

'As near as death,' the knight said grimly, 'and as distant as hope.'

CRAWLING THROUGH THE ruins, Einarr was impressed by the scope of the desolation. From the edge of the plain, he had thought it vast enough but he had not appreciated the scale of the architecture buried beneath the moss and mould. No men had reared such structures, men were ants beside whatever had built the primordial ruins. Cyclopean blocks of stone bigger than longships rose from the muck, piled one atop the other in massive walls that sagged sickly from their own ponderous weight. Great pillars wide enough that all of Vinnskor might have fitted comfortably upon their tops stabbed up from the slime, their marble surfaces pitted with decay and corrosion. Ceramic plates, the debris from collapsed roofs of the city were strewn throughout the scum-snow on the ground, every tile larger than a man.

Einarr considered the oldest of the sagas, the tales of the great giants who in the time before man had made war against the gods. Surely this could be nothing if not one of their mighty cities, brought low by the Plague God, its ancient power and glory sucked relentlessly down into the morass of his corruption.

It was this same power that Einarr now dared to oppose. He felt doubt again tug at his mind. Who was he to challenge the Plague God? Von Kammler was a mighty champion of Tchar, a warlord who had led an entire army to this blighted place and seen that same army scattered to the winds. Then he remembered his oath and what he had been promised. His mind turned to Birna and Asta and Vinnskor. A fresh wave of determination coursed through him. The Plague God was mighty, but the Plague Lord Skoroth was only a man.

THEY PRESSED ON through the ruins, vile life slithering through the slime all around them. Flies the size of hawks crawled along the walls, sunning their wings in the crimson sun. Maggots bigger than serpents oozed across their path, blindly crawling across the land in search of carrion. A bloated, slobbering thing the size of an ox but resembling a melted toad regarded them with gem-like eyes from the shadow of a fallen archway but made no move to molest them.

The droning of insects, the scurry of unclean life and the omnipresent cackling of the daemons created such a din that they were unaware of the Hung warriors until they were almost on top of the vermin. It was Orgrim who detected them first, his long-suffering sense of scent picking the smell of men out from the reek that punished him so terribly. The Aesling snarled a warning, lifting his hand and motioning for them all to drop low.

Einarr crawled through the filth to join Orgrim. The woodsman was perched behind a jumble of slime-coated masonry, eyes fixed on what he had discovered. As he drew close to the scout, Einarr could hear the bubbling, slobbering voices of the Hung. Past Orgrim, he could see that a wide expanse of ground had been cleared of rubble and debris, forming an open plaza around the base of an enormous pillar, its sides dripping with yellow treacle. Around the circle was a large group of men and women, their bodies bloated with corruption, their jaundiced flesh split and oozing with pus and disease, their armour rotting on their bodies, their weapons rusting at their sides. They shared a rough semblance in the cast of their features, their faces broad with slender eyes and wiry hair.

'The Hung,' von Kammler said. Even encased within his armour, the massive knight had managed to appear beside Einarr without making a sound. 'They sing their prayers to the Plague God, asking him to perpetuate their suffering, to strengthen the sickness that flows through them so that it might stave off the hand of death.' The knight shook his head in loathing. 'The wretches will grovel and whine for hours. We can go around them and they will never hear our passing.'

Einarr only partially heard von Kammler speak, his attention riveted to the obscene rites of the Hung. He saw a corpulent thing with the head of a slavering insect dressed in tattered green robes moving within the circle, spraying the ground with its filth, making symbols in the slime with the water from its body. Then the vile shaman turned, facing a wooden stake that had been pounded into the earth. Lashed to the stake was a hulking man, his crimson armour standing stark against the pestilential hues of the Hung and the rotting landscape.

'We will go through this rabble,' Einarr decided as he watched the scene unfold.

'Do not be fooled by their rotten bodies,' von Kammler warned. 'They can endure wounds that would kill most men.'

'Nothing should be too easy,' Einarr said. He pointed to the stake and the captive lashed to it. 'He does not look to be any friend of the Hung.'

Von Kammler stared at the prisoner for a moment. 'He's not. A Kurgan, I think. One of Khorne's warriors, whatever his race.'

'We will free him,' Einarr said. Although it was impossible to see emotion in the glowing embers burning behind von Kammler's mask, Einarr felt the bewilderment his words evoked. 'Finding this cannot have been mere chance,' he explained. 'Was it not you who said the sacred number of Tchar is nine? That we are short one sword?' Einarr clapped the knight's shoulder, pushing him back towards where the others were gathered. 'Tell them to ready for battle. We strike…'

His intentions were silenced by the blood-curdling howl from Orgrim. Throughout Einarr's exchange with the knight, Orgrim had remained silent, eyes still trained on the ritual of the Hung. Einarr had put the berserker from his mind, thinking little of his rapt watchfulness. Now he had reason to curse his lack of caution. Orgrim was on his feet, axe raised above his head and roaring his animal hate at the men below. A thick, brute smell seemed to exude from Orgrim's body and before Einarr's stunned eyes, he saw the hair on the man's face and hands begin to thicken and spread. With another howl, Orgrim hurled his axe at the Hung and leapt down into the court, his hands curled into savage claws.

Einarr cursed again, then rushed after the frenzied Aesling. Near the stake, the bug-headed shaman struggled to tear Orgrim's axe free from his breast. He never had the chance. Like a predatory beast, Orgrim pounced on the stricken shaman, ripping and tearing at him with his claws. Ropes of brown entrails and shreds of green flesh littered the air as Orgrim tore the shaman apart. Einarr watched in horrified fascination as Orgrim lowered his head and savaged the shaman's throat. When he lifted his head again, it was no longer that of the Aesling, but the lean, stretched muzzle of a wolf, its fur caked in the unclean filth from the shaman's veins.

'Ulfwerenar,' Einarr gasped, recalling the stories of the were-kin, the men who bore the flesh of the beast within them. The Norscan fought to control his shock; there would be time enough to worry about Orgrim's condition once the Hung were dead.

Fortunately, the Hung were as stunned by the sudden appearance of the werewolf as much as Einarr. The sudden, savage violence that had erupted from nowhere to claim their shaman had frozen them with confusion. But their inaction did not linger long. A huge warrior, his rusty armour struggling to contain the bulk of his bloated body, surged forward from the ranks of the stunned plague worshippers. He turned his pitted helmet in Orgrim's direction, snarling a bubbling cry and pointing his corroded sword at the were-kin. Orgrim reacted to the champion's challenge with a low snarl and launched himself at the armoured warrior.

The plague champion met Orgrim's lunge with a slash of his polluted sword, digging a gory furrow through Orgrim's chest. The werewolf howled in rage at the injury and his claws scrabbled against the champion's armour, tearing into the corrupt metal. The Hung pushed him back with a thrust of his armoured gut, raising his sword for another strike. He froze as the eyes hidden behind his rusting helm watched the wound he had dealt the werewolf closing upon itself. It would take more than diseased steel to overcome the terrible powers that pulsed through the cursed flesh of an ulfwerenar. The champion seemed to realise his mistake, taking a cautious step back.

The other Hung did not seem to notice their champion's distress, however. As the champion had charged, so too had they. Dozens of men and women, their bodies swollen with disease, their flesh leprous and pitted with oozing boils, charged into the plaza and rushed towards Einarr, intent on stopping him before he could reach the stake.

The foremost of the Hung disappeared in a burst of blue flame, their bodies collapsing as the eerie fire consumed them. The head of another burst like an over ripe melon as a shimmering fog appeared around it and then streamed up his nose and ears until the pressure within his skull became too great to contain. By comparison, the few who fell with black-feathered arrows in their diseased bodies were the fortunate ones. Whether they fell from Birna's arrows or the spells of Urda and von Kammler, there were many more to take the place of the fallen.

The survivors kept coming, chanting the obscene name of their god. The sound caused Einarr's stomach to churn, but he kept his grip on Alfwyrm steady. Just as the first of the Hung closed on him, he became aware of Vallac at his side, the Kurgan's mangled face curled into a bloodthirsty snarl. Beside Vallac loomed Thognathog, the ogre's bulk anchoring their flank. Still fastened to the ogre by his chains, Zhardrach cursed and threatened the oncoming Hung with a cruel-looking knife the dwarf had acquired.

Roaring a Baersonling war cry, Einarr met the charge of the Hung, his sword slashing through the belly of the first foolish enough to close with him. The marauder flopped obscenely against the ground, struggling to lift himself on his severed spine. Zhardrach was soon looming over him, plunging his knife again and again into the back of the tribesman's neck.

'Keep putting them down and I'll see they don't get up!' the dwarf croaked, sadistic glee in his deep voice. Einarr and Vallac nodded grimly to the grinning fiend, then put him from their minds as they concentrated on the press of diseased humanity before them.

How long the killing continued, Einarr could not say. His body was caked in blood from his foes. Limbs and heads littered the ground around him, the air was heavy with the stink of death. Flies swarmed all around the carnage, a living curtain of blinding filth.

Somehow, Einarr managed to force his way through the throng, step-by-step cutting his way through the Hung until he had reached the stake. None of the plague worshippers had thought to slaughter their captive, or perhaps like the Aeslings of Skraevold, none of them dared kill one marked for sacrifice. Either way, Einarr found the captive still alive, lashing furiously at his bonds, almost berserk in his impotent rage. The prisoner roared curses on his foes, spitting dark promises of what he would do to them, of the black offerings he would make to the Skull Lord when he was free.

Einarr hesitated for a moment, staring at the raging captive. He was a huge man, bigger even than von Kammler, his armour chased in bronze and stained a bloody red. What looked like bones were somehow

fixed to the heavy metal plates, looking almost as
though they had melted into the steel, giving his mail
an almost skeletal appearance. The face that looked at
Einarr was cruel and savage, hideous runes scarred
into his flesh, his wild hair matted with dried blood.
Through his beard, the warrior smiled at Einarr, his
teeth filed into points and capped with bronze. More
disconcerting were the man's eyes. There was no white
in them, only the blood red of the battlefield and the
shrines of Khorne.

Einarr regarded the bound champion for only a
moment, then his sword was swinging through the
clouds of buzzing flies. Alfwyrm struck the thick cords
of dried entrails that bound the Kurgan, snapping
them beneath its keen edge. The captive pulled his
arms forward, rubbing at his chaffed wrists and then
let loose with a roar of terrible jubilation. He nodded
to Einarr, then flung himself at the press of the Hung.
His hands gouged eyes and tore throats, his armoured
feet smashed knees and shattered legs. Still shrieking
his savage war cry, the Kurgan was soon lost amid the
mob of his foes. Einarr grimly wondered what sort of
madman he had unleashed. Even the bestial fury of
Orgrim had seemed tame beside the wanton blood-
thirst that the unarmed Kurgan displayed.

Then Einarr had no more time for thoughts of
berserkers and beasts. The ground shuddered beneath
him as something monstrous forced its way across the
plaza. Even the clouds of flies seemed to part before it.
It towered above the Hung, even the tallest of the
tribesmen failing to rise to its breast. Its bloated body
was coated in scabs and lesions, its bestial head little
more than a fleshless skull. Mangy patches of fur
dripped off its body and from the sides of its head

great horns, cracked and filthy, jutted menacingly. In its massive paws, the beast carried an enormous hammer, the stone-head caked in slime and sludge. The minotaur fixed Einarr with its beady gaze, the lone eye staring out from its left socket looking like a tiny ball of pus. The plaguebull snorted, smashing its hoof against the ground, and charged.

Einarr leapt aside as the plaguebull brought its mattock hurtling downward, pulverizing the ground and sending shards of earth and stone flying in all directions. The minotaur did not hesitate to even consider its missed strike but with astounding speed swept the hammer up from the crater it had smashed into the ground, trying to catch Einarr with the side of the weapon. The Norscan threw himself flat, ducking under the blow. The hammer crashed against the sacrificial stake, smashing it into splinters. Einarr lashed out at the beast, his sword slashing deep into its side. Putrid water slopped from the wound in the brute's belly, but if the plaguebull felt pain, it gave no sign. Instead it swung around, bringing the hammer about in a deadly arc of ruin. A pair of Hung were crushed as Einarr dove away from the strike, thrown through the air by the impact of the great hammer.

Landing badly, Einarr clutched at his stinging leg. He looked up in time to roll away from the hammer as the minotaur brought it crashing down once more. Splinters of rock tore into his side as the ground shattered beneath the blow. The plaguebull glared down at Einarr, snorting its frustration. A black-fletched arrow suddenly struck the brute's face, quickly followed by a second. The minotaur shook its head, as though trying to shoo an annoying insect, then turned its murderous rage back towards Einarr. The hammer rose again.

Before the plaguebull could bring the hammer down, a hulking shape appeared behind it. Powerful hands closed around the head of the hammer, preventing the mattock from descending. The minotaur spun around, fury in its pustule eye. Thognathog glared back at it and drove his left head into the brute's face. The thick skull of the ogre shattered the minotaur's snout, sending a spray of brown blood and green snot into the air. The beast reeled backward, its hands slipping from the grip of its hammer. Thognathog's faces split into a savage grin as the ogre hefted the stolen weapon and brought it smashing into the minotaur's side.

THOGNATHOG AND THE plaguebull slowly drifted away from Einarr, the battle of the hulks crushing any Hung too slow to give ground before them. The Norscan drove his sword across the neck of a marauder who lunged at him with a morning star then disembowelled a second who came at him with an axe. For the moment, he was free from the press of his foes. He could see his comrades all around him, slashing and smashing their enemies. Orgrim, his shape now almost completely that of a great grey wolf, savaged the Hung with claw and fang, littering the plaza with torn bodies. Vallac plied his curved sword in a murderous arc, hewing limbs from his diseased foes.

Across the plaza, Einarr could see von Kammler. Weary of working his sorcery, the knight now waded through the marauders, crushing bone and rupturing organs with every sweep of his mace. Urda continued to ply her magic, however, sending streams of crackling energy searing into the Hung horde. Beside her, Birna sent black arrows streaking into any of the plague worshippers who took it in their worm-eaten minds to close upon the witch.

Einarr looked away from his comrades, trying to find the Kurgan berserker he had freed. He found the man, his body caked in the blood and filth of his foes, relentlessly slaughtering his way towards the pillar. Einarr could hear the howl of triumph erupt from the warrior's throat as he won his way clear. He pounced towards an altar of green stone that stood beneath the pillar, crushing the skull of one last Hung between his powerful hands. The Kurgan reached the altar, lifting from it a great horned helmet. Even from such a distance, Einarr could see the skull rune of Khorne glowing evilly upon the brow of the skeletal helm. The Kurgan lowered the armour over his head, his scarred visage vanishing behind the beast-skull mask of the helm. With another roar of triumph and fury, he grabbed the enormous axe that also rested upon the altar and turned to face the Hung once more.

The Hung withdrew from the berserker, their ruined faces pale with fear. But it was not the Kurgan that drew their frightened eyes. Einarr could see something descending the column, slowly dripping down the pitted stone pillar. The berserker sensed it too, turning and craning his head upward. Unlike the Hung, the Khorne worshipper seemed to welcome the descent of the abomination.

It was like a worm, Einarr decided as he watched it slither down the pillar, its obscenely fat bulk exuding a purple slime to ease its passage. As thick around as a tree, its head split by a great gash of a mouth, its body pitted with dozens of leprous eyes. The giant worm oozed its way down the column, an aura of pestilence preceding it. The Hung cringed before it and from

their rotting mouths came a wailing chant of suppli-
cation and subservience.

The enormous green maggot slithered its way to the
base of the pillar, its nether regions still coiled about
the structure. The purple sludge drooling from its
belly singed the ground as it reared up and surveyed
the plaza with its slobbering head. None of the Hung
dared meet its gaze, more afraid of setting eyes on
their terrible god than the stabbing blades of their
foes. Zhardrach found easy prey among their prone,
trembling shapes. The worm lurched forward, its
mouth spitting obscenities into the unclean air. The
daemon's voice seemed to defile every ear that heard
it, gnawing at the mind like a jackal's fang or a vul-
ture's beak. Scabrous blood leaked from the ears of
those closest to the worm. The daemon slithered to
the closest of the Hung, licking the crusty gore from
his head with a mottled, whip-like tongue. Like a rotten fruit, the man's head crumbled beneath the
daemon's touch, his flesh corrupting faster than he
could scream. The Hung wailed in horror and devotion as the stench of their decaying tribesman
exploded across the plaza.

The berserker had seen enough. The Kurgan leapt at
the worm, a savage cry booming from his skeletal
helm. The great axe held in his hands seemed to burn
with a crimson light as it swept down towards the
worm's back. The burning edge seared through the
worm's blubbery flesh, spilling stinking brown ichor
across the slimy ground. As the berserker drew back,
the steel on his gauntlets smoked, the filth of the daemon gnawing at the metal. The wound stood raw and
ragged for a moment, then was obliterated by a oozing stream of pus that flooded into the injury. The

berserker roared again and flung himself back at the daemon. Even as his axe bit into it again, the first wound assumed the sickly green of the worm's scabrous hide, showing no sign of the hurt that had been done to it.

Einarr was reminded of the bloodbeast of Skraevold and how it had resisted the violence of sword and axe. Even as the thought came to him, he saw some of his comrades rushing to help the Kurgan oppose the daemon. Vallac appeared at the back of the worm, slashing at it with his curved sword, the edge biting through some of its eyes. For every orb his sword ruptured, three more sprouted across the beast's hide, glaring at him angrily.

Von Kammler approached the thing, the syllables of the Dark Tongue hissing through the mask of his helm. The daemon's flesh quivered and twisted as the sorcery pawed at its substance, but defiantly retained its hideous shape. Thognathog stomped towards the horror, the minotaur's mattock in one hand, the other encased within the plaguebull's horned skull. With a bellow of fury, the ogre punched the skull into the daemon's side, excrement exploding across him as the thing's unclean hide was punctured. Beside the ogre, Zhardrach stabbed at the daemon with a long spear he had stolen from one of the Hung, the dwarf trying to keep Thognathog between himself and the monster.

The daemon barely reacted to the assault of the warriors, its unnatural substance reforming in a burst of pus and filth behind every attack. The drool slobbering from its mouth increased, sending a plume of smoke steaming from the ground. A burst of noxious gas erupted from the skin of the worm, a yellow cloud engulfing its attackers. They staggered back, coughing and retching, their flesh darkening beneath a swiftly spreading rash. Bubbling laughter oozed from the maggot-thing and it swung its head around towards von Kammler.

The worm's body shuddered and convulsed as it spit something from its mouth. Coated in mucous and phlegm, it was only when the thing stood that it resembled a man. A thick, greasy rope of flesh attached the man to the worm, the slimy umbilical vanishing down the maggot's throat. In the thing's hand, the fleshy simulacra of an axe dripped as the plague-zombie lifted its arm and strode towards von Kammler. The knight met the thing's slow, slopping advance, swinging his mace into the thing's head. The weapon struck with a meaty *thunk*, collapsing the man's head. Von Kammler tried to pull his weapon back, but found it embedded in the ruptured ruin of the thing's skull. The zombie withered to the ground, dragging von Kammler's weapon down with it. The worm's body undulated again as it heaved a second zombie from its gullet. The worm's convulsions continued until it had vomited a dozen of the half-digested warriors onto the ground, each still attached to it by a greasy umbilical.

Einarr watched as the plague-zombies marched relentlessly toward von Kammler, then lunged at the abominations, roaring a battle cry. Alfwyrm slashed down at the things, cutting through one of the umbilicals. The zombie attached to the coil of flesh flopped to the ground, quivering as it corroded into a pool of greasy sludge. Einarr shouted to his comrades and darted from the groping claws and flailing meat-bludgeon of a second zombie, slicing through its umbilical as easily as he had the first. His tactic was taken up by his allies, Thognathog wading in and forcibly ripping one of the zombies from its tether, the Kurgan berserker flinging himself at the horrors with his burning axe.

The worm seethed with anger, its rheumy eyes fixing upon Einarr. With a great gulping motion, it retracted the umbilicals and swallowed the remaining zombies. Another burst of corrosive gas sprayed from the daemon's hide as its regurgitated sacrifices slid back into its gullet. Einarr's comrades fled from the pestilential cloud, but the war leader stood his ground. He could feel the band he had taken from the frozen ship throb and pulse as the cloud washed over him. When it had passed, he could see little fingers of rust marring the metal, but on his flesh there was no sign of blemish. He sneered at the perplexed worm.

The daemon hissed again and surged forward, its enormity causing the ground to tremble. Black arrows slammed into its bulk as Birna saw her lover's danger. Thognathog drove his hammer into the thing's side, collapsing its substance like an old bladder. But such wounds were fleeting, the daemon's unholy vitality causing its oozing form to reshape itself around its injuries. Like a relentless juggernaut, the horror drove on towards Einarr.

The Norscan stood his ground, an arrogant contempt filling him. He watched the plague daemon surge towards him, ignoring the frightened shouts of his comrades. He did not even lift Alfwyrm to repel the creature as it reared above him. Instead, almost without any awareness on his part, he opened his mouth and shouted at the daemon, roaring the words that seemed to burn through his brain at the vile abomination. Upon his hand, the steel symbol of Tchar glowed dimly.

'Euooul'th'bueb'ros!' Einarr roared at the worm, the sound of the slobbering name causing the thing to recoil in terror. 'Euooul'th'bueb'ros, be flesh!'

The worm's body shuddered as it heard the command, as its daemonic substance congealed into blood and bone. The purple acid that oozed from its underside sizzled as it burned through the thing's belly. The worm slithered away from Einarr, its body trembling and convulsing as its own excretions consumed it. The Kurgan lunged at it again, this time the huge chunk of flesh that came away with his axe did not knit itself whole behind his blade, but bled freely and darkly. Thognathog followed the warrior's example, smashing the tail of the worm almost flat beneath his hammer.

The daemon's piteous wail shrieked through all who heard it as the retreating horror gained the base of the pillar. Like a mighty serpent, it coiled around the column and began to drag itself upward, struggling on despite the ropes of entrail and organ that dripped from its melting underside. The worm's body shuddered again, becoming almost translucent, wisps of stagnant energies swirling about it as the daemon tried to revert to its etheric substance. Einarr glared up at the fleeing obscenity.

'Euooul'th'bueb'ros, be flesh!' he shouted at it again. The worm wailed piteously as the power of its True Name forced it back into a shape of mortality. The sizzling slime eating away at its body caused the daemon to lose its hold on the pillar. With a last bubbling wail, the worm toppled from the column, smacking into the ground in a great puddle of misery and corruption, its essence splashed across the plaza. For a moment, the wretched sludge tried to cling to life, but the ruin was too great even for the daemon's essence to maintain and it settled into an oozing morass of filth.

Einarr looked down upon what he had done, stunned by the power he had commanded, shocked by his inability to account for it. As quickly as it had taken shape within his mind, the True Name of the daemon had been driven from his brain. He lifted his eyes to find the others staring at him in wonder. Even von Kammler seemed awestruck. The Hung, those that remained, screamed and scattered into the slime-coated ruins.

The Kurgan berserker turned towards Einarr, the dripping axe clenched in his armoured fist. Einarr watched him warily, waiting for the forbidding axe-man to make the first move. Vallac cautiously joined the Norscan, careful to keep his eyes on the berserker.

'You should not have freed him,' Vallac warned. 'He is Veig. My people have fought many wars with the Veigs. They are murderers and cannibals, thinking only of blood and skulls for their gods. The Hung should have killed him. Now we will have to kill him ourselves.'

Einarr shook his head. 'He hasn't tried to kill us yet,' he told Vallac. 'Perhaps he understands that we share a common enemy. He would be of use to us if he joins us against Skoroth.'

The berserker took a step forward, his head rising as he picked the name of the Plague Lord from Einarr's unfamiliar words. He shouted at the Norscan, rage making his Kurgan dialect hard for Einarr to follow.

'Kill worm, much good,' the Kurgan roared. 'Worm no eat Veigs now. Die with fighting, not in worm-gut.'

The berserker lifted his axe, his bloody eyes glaring into Einarr's. 'Kill Skoroth better.'

'The path we walk is the same,' Einarr said. 'We seek the head of Skoroth.'

The bloodthirsty Kurgan lowered his head as he heard Einarr's words, taking some time to consider what he had heard. When he looked at the Norscan again, his eyes shone from behind his skeletal helm with a feral gleam. 'That be fine death, please mighty Khorne! Better than take Norseman skull, take Plague Lord skull!' The Kurgan stared hard at Einarr, then reached forward and took his hand. 'Berus of Veigs.'

'Einarr Steelfist, Chosen of Tchar,' the Norscan said, his tone as imperious as that of any jarl, as firm as stone. He turned towards von Kammler.

'Now we are nine,' he told the knight.

CHAPTER FIFTEEN

IN DEFIANCE OF the sludge of frost that coated the ground, the air became humid and lush as the warband emerged from the cyclopean ruins. Beyond the jumbled heaps of slime-coated stone stretched a vast, seething swamp. The reek of rot grew stifling, every breath scratching the lungs with its taint. Immense weeds rose into the sky on spindly stalks. Vines dripped across the land, choking the ground beneath their decaying foulness. Streams of stagnant water festered and flowed like sewage beneath the scabrous foliage, vermin flitting above its stench. Everywhere, the unclean life of a land remade into the pestilential image of Nurgle flourished. The swamp embodied the diseased whims of the Plague God, his mantra of decay without death, corruption without destruction.

There was no time to pause upon the threshold of the swamp, to allow their abhorrence for the foulness to be subdued by their resolve. The Hung that had scattered after the destruction of the daemon had spread word of Einarr's sacrilege to their kin. It had not taken long for the ruins to resound with the sound of pursuers, to throb to the pulse of Hung war drums. Einarr knew they could not oppose such numbers and live, even Berus understood that if they stayed to face their enemies they would never reach the palace of the Plague Lord alive.

So they had fled, racing through the ruins, trusting more to luck than design to keep ahead of their foes. The slobbering, bubbling voices of the Hung sounded from all around them.

As they scrambled into the stinking morass of the swamp, Einarr looked back to see how near their enemies were. Impossibly, the ruins had vanished behind them, replaced by more swampland, the bog stretching as far as his eyes could follow. Yet he could still hear the sounds of the Hung as they shouted and pounded their drums, ghostly noises that came from nothingness. Einarr did not breathe any easier; whatever force had plucked them from the ruins and into the swamp could just as easily do the same for the Hung. He roared at his retching comrades, extolling them to hasten their pace. There would be time enough to rest when they were dead.

LIKE A LIVING morass, the swamp tried to suck them down into its liquid embrace. The ground gave beneath their feet like porridge, defying their every effort to make speed. Tiny daemons harassed them again, hurling filth at them whenever they stopped, giggling and grinning when the warriors hurled curses back at them. The little nurglings danced across the bog, the ground refusing to drag their filthy forms into its own foulness. The daemons mocked Einarr's suffering comrades, laughing each time a boot became trapped in the mud.

Among the fens and weeds they could hear their pursuers following them, sloshing through the diseased quagmire, eager to avenge their daemon king. Far too soon, filthy spears and arrows began to fall around them as the Hung closed in. Between her hacking coughs, Urda managed to recite words of power as she cast powdered bone across the bog behind them. When the last word hissed through her toothless face, the crone waved the feathered claw that had been one of her hands. The powder burst into flame, licking greedily at the first of the Hung as the plague worshippers charged the warband. The shrieks of the burning warriors echoed across the swamp, silencing for a moment the constant susurrus of insects.

'That will not hold them back long,' Vallac snarled. Even as he spoke the words, two huge marauders forced their way through the flames. Their rusting armour smoking from the fire, the massive warriors stomped towards the warband. Birna sent a black arrow shooting into the visor of one Hung's helmet. The brute fell to his knees as blood exploded from his helm. His comrade did not pause to consider the fate of his kinsman, but rushed at the huntress. Birna tried to dodge back, but not quickly enough to avoid the attack. The Hung's bamboo spear stabbed into the woman's leg, the filthy muck coating it turning her blood black as it bubbled from the wound. Roaring, Birna smashed her bow into the Hung's face, breaking his nose.

Stunned, the marauder staggered back. Before he could recover, Berus swept his axe at the warrior's face, cleaving his skull in half. The berserker roared in triumph as brains and teeth splattered across his armour. Einarr rushed to help the reeling huntress, ripping the bamboo shaft free. He rummaged in Spjall's medicine bag, trying to find a poultice to press against the injury.

Urda turned to von Kammler. 'You have walked this road before,' she said. The knight shook his steel head.

'That is meaningless here,' von Kammler replied. 'Between the pulses of your heart, the entire swamp might change. All is at the whim of the Plague God.'

Einarr cursed the perfidy of the unnatural domain that obeyed no laws and followed no order. Trying to understand it was a thing hopeless and mad, the mere attempt to make sense of the rules that governed this land made his brain burn. This was the essence of the gods, a thing no man could hold within his mind, a thing that was nothing more than madness.

'Sssmelll… ssstrooong,' Orgrim growled. His body was covered in grey fur now, his bestial shape struggling to make words. His axe was gone, lost in the ruins, his armour reduced to a few tatters that stubbornly clung to his lupine form. The werewolf raised something that was more paw than hand and tapped the side of his muzzle, an unsettling reminder of the gesture the Aesling had made so many times before. Watching the grey beast make it caused a sliver of ice to crawl up Einarr's spine. Einarr nodded at Orgrim and the werewolf began to lope into the weeds. Hurriedly, Einarr lifted Birna back to her feet, shouting for the others to follow the ulfwerenar. Vallac laid a restraining hand on his shoulder.

'If eyes and ears fail, why trust a were-kin's nose?'

'Do you have a better plan?' The sounds of the Hung moving through the swamp, circling around the barrier Urda had made punctuated Einarr's words. Vallac shook his head. One by one, the small warband stole through the weeds, following in Orgrim's path.

EINARR STARED IN disbelief at the stagnant swampland that surrounded them. For hours they had followed Orgrim's lead, trusting to the werewolf's keen senses to guide them through the mire. Now, even he seemed confused, pawing at the muddy earth in dismay, turning his head in every direction, trying to pick up some scent that would guide him onward.

'I am really coming to hate this place,' Vallac snarled, kicking at a rotten log. It exploded beneath his boot, hordes of termites scrambling from their broken sanctuary. Zhardrach cursed in shock, straining on the chain that bound him to Thognathog. Einarr could easily see why the dwarf was so agitated. Like everything else, the shattered log was repeated in every direction, right down to the crawling insects. Wherever they turned, it was the same. The same weeds, the same ghastly sky, the same slimy mud, like a mirror reflection of the entire swamp. Even their footprints repeated, giving them the eerie sight of watching marks appear in the mud ahead of them without any visible cause. Only they themselves were not reflected in the etheric mirrors, something that seemed to heighten the horror rather than lessen it.

It was maddening. Einarr could not tell if they were walking in circles, gaining ground or, in a very real sense, moving at all. Even von Kammler seemed agitated, unpleasantly surprised by this new trick the Plague Lord's domain had learned.

Einarr turned to the knight. 'It has to be some kind of illusion. It can't all be the same.'

Von Kammler's steel face scanned the reflected swamp. He reached to the left side of the path, ripping a small bush from the muddy ground. Instantly the same bush was torn from the earth to their right, behind and before them. The knight stormed forward, crushing one of the towering weeds in his mailed fist. Again, the destruction was repeated in the other three directions, an invisible hand snapping the stalk. He roared in frustration, attacking the foliage with his mace. However much he raged, the effects of his violence were dutifully mirrored.

'It seems the great southlander has finally met his match,' Urda hissed, satisfaction in her wrinkled face. 'Good, I hope he rots here.'

'If he rots here, old witch,' Vallac snarled, 'we rot with him.' The hag shook her head.

'Some of us, perhaps, but not all.' She reached into her leather bag, pulling a set of ivory teeth from its depths. The hag closed her eyes, strange words crawling across her lips. The rune eye set in her face began to glow with power. Einarr watched in fascination as the teeth began to slither across her palm, guided by some unnatural life of their own. After a time, they settled and the light faded from Urda's stone eye. The witch opened her mortal eyes and stared at the pattern the teeth had arranged themselves in. She looked up, staring into the swamp.

'It is this way,' she cackled.

'How do you know that, witch?' von Kammler demanded, scorn in his voice. Urda sneered at him.

'Find your own way out, if the swamp lets you,' she chided him.

The knight took a menacing step towards her, the mace still clutched in his hand. Thognathog stepped in front of Urda, placing himself between the knight and the hag.

'Follow witch, leave bad stinky place,' the ogre growled.

Einarr nodded his head in agreement. 'Wandering in this madness will get us nowhere. Following Urda can get us no more lost than we already are.'

The witch scowled at him. 'Your faith in my powers overwhelms me. Perhaps you spend too much time with the southlander.'

'I have not forgotten the hag who abandoned me on the ice,' Einarr retorted. Urda glared at him for a moment.

'We all make mistakes, Steelfist,' she said. 'I can guide you out of the deceit Skoroth has infected this part of the swamp with, but the power to do so is taxing. The ogre will have to carry me.' Einarr gestured at Thognathog and the huge brute reached down, cradling Urda in his enormous arm.

'Walk where I tell you to walk, step where I tell you to step,' the witch cautioned. 'Your eyes will betray you, they will tell you that nothing has changed, that you are still locked within the trap. Do not believe them. Do as I say and you will emerge from this deception.

'Disobey me, and your bones will rot here until the end of eternity.'

THE THICK UNDERGROWTH of the swamp eventually broke, just as the witch had told them it would, the sickly weeds and grasping vines finally yielding before ground too foul even for their fecundity. As Einarr and his followers emerged from the swamp they were struck by the diseased waste that sprawled before them. A great depression in the marshy land, stretching for what looked to Einarr to be a hundred leagues across, filled almost to the brim with filth that could only mockingly be described as water.

A thick green skin of scum floated upon the dead, still lake, like a scab over a festering wound. Rising from the middle of the lake, its foundations lost beneath the stagnant waters, rose a monstrously twisted tower. What stone had been used to build it, Einarr could not say, so thick was the slime that dripped from its walls and battlements. It reared impossibly high from the lake, clutching at the sky like the crooked claw of a corpse, seeming to rise miles into the leprous sky, its topmost summit hidden behind the gibbous moons that hung overhead. As he gazed upon it, Einarr felt his eyes itch and his belly sicken. A tangible aura of despair and decay exuded from the structure, sickening an already sickened land.

Vallac looked out across the vast lake and its rancid water, his face twisted in revulsion. 'Just how in the name of the Changer are we supposed to get across that?' he growled. He looked over at von Kammler, the hate inside him searing into the knight's expressionless steel mask. 'If you say "swim", I'll kill you and I don't care what sorcerer's tricks you have hiding up your sleeve.'

The knight merely nodded his head. 'Swimming is an ill thought,' he growled back. 'Something might notice.'

Einarr set Birna down, taking a moment to check that the old witch was still breathing before turning toward their guide. 'There has to be a way across,' he said, defiance in his voice.

'Yes,' von Kammler agreed, arrogance in his tone. 'There are powers that can be called.'

'Then call on them, southlander!' Vallac snarled back. The knight glowered at the misshapen Kurgan.

'Some things are easier to summon than dismiss,' he said.

'Make boat?' Thognathog suggested. The ogre wore a sheepish look as he voiced the suggestion. Zhardrach spun on his captor, kicking him in the shin.

'From what, you idiot? Mud and weeds?' The ogre stared down at the snarling dwarf, glowering at him. Realising what he had done, Zhardrach backed away as far as his chain would allow. Thognathog lowered Urda to the ground and reached for the dwarf.

'Maybe Thognathog try throw you across?' the ogre said, his immense hand closing around Zhardrach. 'Can you fly, shortling?' Thognathog lifted the squealing dwarf into the air, snapping the thick chain that bound him to the ogre's waist. Zhardrach kicked and struggled to free himself from the ogre's powerful grip.

Von Kammler stepped in front of Thognathog, his spiked mace held at the ready. The knight glared up at the ogre. 'Disturbing the water would be unhealthy,' he warned. Thognathog glared back at him. Einarr hurried to put himself between the two.

'He is right, Thog,' Einarr told the ogre. 'Put Zhardrach down. He might still be useful to us.' The look that Einarr shared with von Kammler did not go unnoticed by the dwarf. Suddenly he wondered if getting thrown into the lake by the ogre was the worst that could happen to him.

Reluctantly, Thognathog lowered the dwarf, a sullen look on his faces.

Berus walked to the edge of the swamp, hacking down one of the immense weeds. He stripped the stalk, flexing and bending the pole-like flesh of the weed. 'Norscan,' he called out. 'This not exactly wood. You think something built of this filth will float?' Einarr stared down von Kammler and Thognathog. Satisfied the two would not come to blows, he stalked over to Berus, taking the stalk from his hand. His brow knitted in thought as he examined the rancid-smelling limb.

'I can't say,' Einarr confessed at last. 'It certainly isn't wood. We put this in water it's likely to lap it up like a thirsty dog.'

Berus took the stalk back. 'One way to find out,' he growled, striding towards the slimy shore of the lake. Von Kammler stepped into the Kurgan's path.

'No one touches the water,' the knight hissed. Berus snorted derisively, moving to step around von Kammler. Before he could go more than a few steps, von Kammler's mace was swinging towards his back. The berserker's incredible reflexes saved him the worst of the blow, the deadly weapon glancing against his armour.

'Swine of Tzeentch, I'll feed your spine to the vultures!' Berus flung the stalk at von Kammler, the crude spear snapping as it struck the knight's breastplate. The force of the blow caused von Kammler to stagger back, long enough for Berus to get a better grip on his axe. With a roar, the berserker threw himself at the knight.

Einarr shouted for Vallac and Thognathog to help him separate the two battlers. This close to the palace, the last thing they needed were their already slim numbers further reduced by infighting. Vallac seemed to take a great deal of delight cracking the flat of his sword against von Kammler's head, though he was less pleased to find the knight not even fazed by the blow. Berus rounded on Thognathog as the ogre reached for him, his axe slashing through the ogre's thigh, causing him to crumple to the ground. Berus lifted his axe again, the fury of animal bloodlust in his eyes. Orgrim sprang to the ogre's defence, leaping onto the berserker's back and smashing him to the ground.

Einarr cursed as the melee quickly slipped past the point of no return.

BIRNA WATCHED IN disgust as her erstwhile comrades fell into conflict. Were they so blind? With glory and the favour of the gods almost within their grasp, they decided to let their own hubris overcome them! It was madness! She drew her sword and tried to help Einarr knock some sense into the fools, but as she did her leg crumpled beneath her. The wound the Hung had dealt her was sticky with blood, the flesh around it putrid with infection. Birna ground her teeth against the pain that threatened to overwhelm her as she looked at the wound. As a huntress, she had learned something of the skill of the vitki. It was a vital skill, alone in the wilds, to heal one's own hurts. She knew a mortal wound when she saw one. The gangrene that had set into the ruptured flesh with impossible speed was even now sending its poison pulsing through her veins. A pleasant little gift from Old Father Nurgle.

The huntress accepted the death coursing through her with the grim pragmatism of the cold northlands. Glory, it seemed, was not to be hers. Yet, as she watched Einarr struggling with von Kammler, she realised that she could still help her man claim the power that was rightfully his. Agony flared through her body as she forced herself from the ground, red misery pounding through her bones. She firmed her grasp on her sword. She would not be weak. She would not shame her ancestors, not now when she could hear them calling her. She would be strong for Einarr, right to the end. Somehow, that was even more important to her now than the lost glory she might have claimed.

Even as Birna gained her feet, the scummy waters of the lake began to boil, the scab of pestilence lying across it rippling and writhing as the water beneath it churned into life. Birna saw Urda standing beside the waters, the old witch backing away from the lake with haste. The crone's eyes met Birna's for a moment and a traitor's grin split the hag's countenance. Then Birna had no more room for the witch in her thoughts. The disturbance in the lake grew, foul-smelling bubbles bursting across the surface. The seething waters slopped upwards in a geyser of filth as an immense form exploded from the putrid depths.

Birna gazed up at the immense shape that reared up from the lake, its decaying hide coated in the clinging scum of the lake. Despite the nearness of her own death, she felt the wormy hand of despair crush her in its terrible might.

A SEETHING HISS, like the snarl of a volcano, boomed across the lake, deafening even the bloodthirsty roars of the men who fought upon the shore. As one, they turned their eyes to the lake, their petty hates forgotten in a moment of awe and horror. They could feel their souls wither as their gaze fell upon the thing, cringing into the black corners of their flesh, desperate to hide from the abhorrence spat up from Nurgle's stagnant hell.

It was like a mountain made flesh, towering above the lake and the swamp, immense despite the great part of it that yet remained beneath the rancid water. Huge legs, immense pillars of bone and scale, rose from the waters, dripping with slime. An armoured body stretched above the megalithic limbs, gradually dwindling into a thick, spiny tail. A massive neck, thicker than a longship, stretched from the front of the monster, terminating in a long, reptilian head.

There was something unspeakable about the neck, as though it was not one but three, all bound together like a pile of logs by the sinews of rotten flesh that coiled around them. The head of the thing was no less repulsive. Withered, almost skeletal, it looked as though the skulls of three monsters had melted and fused into one. Six great horns stabbed from the roof of its skull at irregular and insane angles, and the enormous jaws sported four rows of teeth, as though an extra set had been fused to either side of its proper mouth. Most despicable of all, however, was the thing's eye – a single great, gibbous pool of jaundiced yellow set in the middle of its skull. From behind the milky substance of the orb, six black pupils floated, like beetles floundering in vomit. As the dragon roared, some of her pupils struggled to the fore of her eye, glaring down at Einarr and his comrades.

'I told you not to disturb the lake,' von Kammler growled, shaking free from the suddenly slackened grip of Einarr and Vallac.

CHAPTER SIXTEEN

THE DRAGON'S PUTRESCENT eye scanned the shore, her black pupils rotating madly within the leprous jelly as she focused upon Einarr and his warriors. The reptile took a step towards the shore and the ground trembled beneath her weight. Einarr could see the thing's rotten hide shudder as she moved, the festering flesh alive with crawling maggots and gnawing vermin. The Norscan backed away, his body heaving with revulsion. He was not alone, even von Kammler sickened by the loathsome sight.

'Bubos,' the knight spat, giving a name to the beast.

The dragon seemed to sense their disgust, the pupils swimming within her mammoth eye narrowing with spite. The great sheets of leathery flesh folded against her sides cracked open in a sudden, violent gesture, tattered pinions fanning the stagnant air. The rotten

reek of the dragon smashed into them, the warband's
eyes watering and noses drooling beneath the stench.
Bubos threw her head back, her bubbling roar crawling through the sky. Then she threw herself toward the
shore, her bloated bulk surging forward like some gargantuan seal.

The advance of Bubos broke the paralysing grip of
terror that had set upon them. Einarr roared at his
comrades, thrusting his sword into the air. However
big the beast was, whatever horrors von Kammler
bestowed upon her, she was still a thing of flesh… and
flesh could be slain.

Not surprisingly, it was Berus who took up the call
for battle first, lunging at the dragon as she emerged
from the dripping muck of the lake. The berserker
threw himself at Bubos, his axe smacking into her leg
with a meaty crunch. A spray of stinking brown sludge
erupted from the wound, bathing him in the syrupy
filth that flowed through the dragon's veins. The Kurgan staggered back from the dragon, trying to wipe
the slime from his helm. The reptile's paw rose, swatting him like an insect, hurling the man across the
shore to crash into the mud.

Bubos turned her head towards Berus, jaws dripping
with poisonous slime, but before she could send her
massive neck darting downward to snatch him up in
her monstrous jaws, the dragon snarled in pain. While
distracted by Berus, Orgrim had circled the reptile,
waiting until he saw a weak spot. With the speed of
the beast he had become, the werewolf pounced at the
dragon, leaping onto her left shoulder. Orgrim's claws
tore at the beast, shredding her already rotten hide.
His fangs sank deep into the throbbing vein he found
beneath, the werewolf ripping at it as though

worrying an old bone. Bubos's body shook and writhed, trying to dislodge the painful parasite.

Thognathog limped towards the dragon, his leg still bleeding from the wound Berus had dealt him. The ogre glared up at the dragon and with a savage effort he sent his mattock smashing into her neck. Bones crunched beneath the blow and the leprous hide darkened as blood vessels burst beneath her flesh. Bubos recoiled from the blow, all six of her black pupils focusing on the ogre. The beast roared down at its attacker. Thognathog roared back, smashing his weapon into her jaw, cracking teeth beneath the blow.

With another roar of fury, Bubos lifted her immense paw and drove the clawed foot down into Thognathog, stomping him into the mud. She twisted her head around, trying to catch hold of the werewolf still clinging to her back. Sorcerous lightning crashed against her face, searing the skin and incinerating the legion of maggots crawling across her brow. The dragon paid no notice to von Kammler's attack, fixated on removing Orgrim.

Einarr shared a grim look with Vallac. The Kurgan slowly nodded. They had both seen the terrible way in which Thognathog had been crushed. If the ogre's immense brawn was unable to faze the dragon, there was little chance their own efforts could. Even so, both of them were determined that if they were to die this day, they would die as men, with their wounds to the fore and defiance in their hearts. The gods would expect no less from the worthy.

Einarr struck at the leg Berus had already injured, slashing deep into it with Alfwyrm. Vallac stabbed at the dragon with his own curved sabre, targeting the patch of neck discoloured by Thognathog's assault. More of the dragon's corrupt blood rained down around them as both blows found their mark. Einarr dove aside as Bubos lifted her injured leg and tried to smash him into the ground as she had the ogre. Forgetting Orgrim for the moment, she lowered her head, her jaws snapping at Vallac. The Kurgan leaped back, the immense maw snapping close only a few inches from him. Vallac could feel the dragon's pestilent breath washing over him, so near was her face. The Kurgan glared at the beast and exhaled his own breath, his mutated throat pulsating as he sent a great burst of flame spewing into Bubos's reptilian visage. The pestilent breath of the dragon exploded as the flame contacted it, engulfing her head in fire. Vallac was thrown back a dozen yards, crashing into the mud with a liquid squelch, his armour and hair smoking.

Bubos thrashed across the shore in pain, lashing out madly at everything around her as the flames seared her rotten hide, bursting boils and melting scabs. The dragon's claws ripped apart the muddy shore, her tail thrashing against the lake. In a blind rage, she spun her head around, mouth agape, and sent a blast of her own pestilent fire burning into the swamp. Like mucous, the fire clung to everything it touched, withering and corrupting the already vile landscape. Rocks crumbled into powder, weeds yellowed and wilted, water became naught more than a festering vapour.

Orgrim sprang from the incensed dragon, unable to hold his grip on the furious reptile. The werewolf struck the ground and rolled, narrowly missing the stomping feet of the behemoth. He loped towards Einarr, crouching down beside the Baersonling like an old hunting hound, waiting for the war leader to make the next move.

Einarr glared at the dragon, trying to decide where they could attack that festering bulk where they could have any real chance of bringing her down. There had to be a way past her, and he would find it.

Von Kammler's armoured hand closed on Einarr's shoulder. 'There is no hope here,' the knight warned. 'If you would gain the palace, we must find another way.'

Einarr pulled away from the knight's grip, savage fury filling him. Everything in his culture, everything he'd ever been taught to believe decried fleeing from battle like some whipped cur. His very flesh railed against the idea, but his mind understood the reality within von Kammler's words. This was no different than the kraken, an enemy that could not be fought on its own terms and on its own ground. The only difference was his stubborn perception that there was a difference.

Einarr's choice was made when he looked away from von Kammler and saw the pathetic sight of Birna limping through the mud, desperate to join him, to spend her last moments fighting at his side. The woman's determination and loyalty decided him. He didn't know what had become of Urda and the Kurgans, but he could still try to save the rest of his retinue.

'We'll try and lose her in the swamp,' he told von Kammler. 'If the orm follows us, maybe the bog will suck her down. Even if it doesn't, we'll fare better than we would here.'

'First decent idea you've had since I met you,' Zhardrach griped, the dwarf already sprinting for the swamp. Von Kammler nodded to Einarr and followed after Zhardrach. Einarr watched them go, then looked back at Bubos. The fire licking about the dragon's head had largely burnt itself out, the flesh beneath blackened and cracked. Awareness rather than blind fury seemed to be returning to the beast. It would be a matter of heartbeats before she was after them once more. Einarr shook his head. It was too soon, much too soon. They needed more time to retreat into the swamp, to hide their trail in the tangle of weeds and filth.

Einarr kicked the werewolf crouched beside him. He pointed over to Birna. 'Grab her and follow von Kammler,' he told Orgrim. The werewolf turned and loped over to Birna. The huntress tried to shake him off, but he easily caught her and threw her across his furred shoulder. Birna's accusing stare followed Einarr as Orgrim ran towards the swamp. Einarr felt a weight lift from him. He was under no delusion as to the woman's safety, but at least he would not have to watch her die. Somehow, that had become more important to him than palaces and promises. The realisation made the blood sour in his veins. Why was he here then, if not to save Asta and his village?

Einarr turned to face the dragon. The last flickers of flame dancing across Bubos's festering immensity sputtered and died as they were smothered by oozing pus. She snapped angrily at the empty air, then swung her head downward, glaring at Einarr with reptilian malice. The Norscan fingered his sword, the names of his ancestors a whisper on his tongue. He would see them all soon. The dragon lurched forward, the ground trembling as she moved. Her diseased breath washed across Einarr, causing his eyes to burn and his lungs to crawl. She was near enough that he could see the wiry little worms crawling between her teeth, could smell the reek of charred flesh beneath the dragon's overwhelming stench.

The chill calm of one who knows he is already dead settled over Einarr. The battle was hopeless, but before he died, he would do everything possible to give Birna and the others their chance to escape. Like a watch dog, perhaps the guardian of the lake would not pursue the others if they retreated far enough into the fens.

Bubos almost seemed to laugh at the Norscan's bravery, the air hissing down into her mammoth bulk as she sucked it into her obscene frame. There was no mistaking the malicious intelligence that shimmered in the dragon's pupils. The ground shuddered again as the dragon slithered back across the mud. He had underestimated the dragon's cunning. She wasn't so foolish as to risk Einarr springing an unpleasant surprise on her the way Vallac had.

Einarr's resolve faltered as fragile hope crumbled in his heart. The dragon wouldn't waste more than a heartbeat on him, then she would plunge into the swamps and catch the others. There was no mistaking the satisfaction in Bubos's reptilian smile as Einarr's shoulders sagged and despair flooded through him.

Suddenly, the mud beneath Bubos exploded upward, a bellowing roar booming along the shore. Bloodied, bruised, his armour in tatters, his chest almost crushed flat, Thognathog stubbornly clung to his savage life. The ogre launched himself at the dragon, stabbing the hand still encased in the skull of the minotaur through the reptile's lower jaw, using the plague bull's horned head like some grotesque fist spike. Bubos reared back, bellowing in pain. The ogre roared again, throwing his other arm over the dragon's snout and pulling the monster's jaw closed. Bubos thrashed her head about, struggling to dislodge the ogre clamped around her face. Massive claws flailed feebly as they tried to reach around the bloated, putrid enormity of her flesh, trying to pull the ogre free.

Einarr moved to help Thognathog, but the ogre's heads turned back towards him, fixing him with a sombre stare. 'Thognathog die,' his twin voices rumbled. 'Steelfist live! Find much glory! Remember Thognathog!'

The Norscan hesitated, the idea of abandoning a comrade locked in battle repugnant to everything he believed. As though to decide him, foul green vapour hissed from the dragon's clenched jaws, spilling around Thognathog's powerful frame. As the foul vapours touched him, his skin withered and rotted, the ogre's immense muscles decaying before Einarr's very eyes. Something the size of a man's head dropped away from the shrivelling ogre and it was with disgust that Einarr recognised the blackened husk of the ogre's hand.

Reason demanded that he run, flee while the ogre was still able to distract Bubos. But an overwhelming urge caused Einarr to run towards the hand that had fallen into the mud. He crouched above the desiccated paw, ripping one of the fingers free from the rotting mess. He looked back up at Thognathog, the ogre's left head wasted to little more than a skull by the dragon's fumes. He saluted his friend's sacrifice and reaching to his neck, fixed the ogre's finger to the necklace Spjall the vitki had given him in what now seemed a lifetime ago.

Then he was gone, running into the swamp, the bestial roars of Thognathog and his doom thundering behind him.

URDA PAUSED AGAINST the jagged clump of rock, her body shuddering as wracking coughs again ravaged her withered frame. She spat blood and phlegm into the mire, idly wondering how much she had left to spare. In the distance, she could hear the dragon still bellowing in rage. She nodded her head sagely. Perhaps he really would do it, overcome Bubos. Maybe she had been a bit too hasty in her judgement. The ways of Tchar were many, and even the wisest witch could not hope to see every path that the Changer of Fate laid down before her.

She coughed again, bile spilling down her chin. It had been a bold thing, to carry the carcass of the nurgling hidden beneath her robes, so close to her body. Its diseased essence had oozed into her body, polluting it with a vileness even her magic could not overcome. She knew this, had known it the moment she had killed the thing, but she also knew that the gods did not reward those who wavered in their devotion to them. Flesh was but a prison, it was what reward her devotion would bring to her soul that drove her on.

Urda knew the nurgling's carcass would draw the dragon from the lake. It had been a part of her vision, the same vision that had coloured her dreams since they had emerged from the Frozen Sea and the disgraced champion von Kammler had started to exert his corrosive influence over Einarr. The knight cared nothing for any of them. He cared only about reclaiming the honour and glory that he had failed to claim the last time he had tried to assault Skoroth's lair. He would cheat Einarr of his glory, cheat them all, so that he might reclaim his own lost power. Einarr would never listen to her, he was too deeply under von Kammler's spell, too obsessed with his own promised reward. The others would never listen. There was just enough bitterness in the old witch to rail against the injustice of the deceit Tchar had played on her. To spend her last days travelling across half the world, to bring her chosen champion to the very gates of triumph only to have it all taken from them by a disgraced southlander maggot!

The witch smiled, a raspy cackle wheezing from her body. Well, if her champion could not claim the prize, then no one would. The dragon would make sure of that. There was a grim satisfaction in knowing that if she could not be a part in victory, she could at least be the instrument of defeat.

A sound among the weeds forced Urda to control the spiteful laughter shuddering through her frame. She glanced at the swamp around her, trying to penetrate the veil of diseased filth. Whatever had made the sound, it refused to reveal itself. Even so, the witch decided that she had lingered long enough out in the open. She turned towards a muddy cave just beyond the rocks. It would provide decent enough refuge from whatever was prowling among the weeds and would protect her from the dragon's terrible eye should the great beast take wing in search of stragglers from Einarr's doomed company.

With such speed as she could muster, Urda hobbled towards the cave. The stinking darkness loomed before her and the witch froze, her every sense afire with alarm. She reached into her bag, pulling a pinch of silver dust from a pouch within it. An incantation slithered past her lips as she cast the dust into her eyes. At once they began to glow, piercing the blackness as easily as if she'd called the sun down from the sky to illuminate it for her. A long tunnel stretched through the dripping scum of mud and ooze, human bones beyond number protruding from the slime. The crone shifted her gaze to the slobbering, drooling thing that squatted just inside the cave. Caked in the same muck that made its home, the thing looked like some insane cross between slug and frog. Eyestalks oozed up from the shapeless trunk that formed the thing's head. Flabby webbed paws scrabbling lazily at the mud as the thing shifted its monstrous bulk.

Urda backed away from the plague beast, not eager to join its collection of bones. The daemon seemed to lose interest in her when it became apparent she would not be courteous enough to walk right into its mouth, the eyestalks sinking back into its slimy head.

The Aesling hag turned away from the cave. She would have to find another refuge to hide from the dragon, and quickly if the fading sounds of battle were any judge. The crone had not gone more than a few steps before she found her path blocked by a familiar, if grotesque, face. Covered in his own blood, his scalp torn, his arm slashed, Vallac nevertheless grinned as he stared at the witch.

'You didn't stay to see the dragon, hag,' the Kurgan said. 'One might almost think you saw it coming.' Urda stepped back. The warrior was wounded, that much was obvious. How seriously, that was something it would take her time to decide. There were a fair number of spells she could call upon to rid herself of the Kurgan annoyance, but to cast them she would need to reach into her bag.

'I have the second sight,' Urda reminded him. She lifted a bony finger to indicate her rune eye. Her other hand slowly crawled towards her bag. Vallac took a step towards her and she froze.

'Strange you did not see fit to warn the rest of us,' he observed. 'A suspicious man might even think you planned the whole thing.'

The remark forced Urda into action. She snapped her fingers, the slight residue of silver powder on them igniting into a brilliant flash of powder. Vallac cried out in surprise, throwing his arms to his face as he was momentarily blinded. Urda threw her other hand into the bag, reaching for the powder that would still Vallac's stubborn life. Yet, even as her bony fingers closed around the pouch, her arm was seized from behind. A powerful strength pulled her arm back, snapping it like an old twig. Urda shrieked in pain, but her attacker held fast to her broken limb. Another powerful arm closed around her neck. Urda could feel the clammy touch of muddy steel as the cold armour brushed her papery skin.

Vallac rubbed at his eyes, then stalked towards the witch, a sneer on his twisted face. 'You remember Berus?' he asked. The berserker tightened his hold until Urda yelped once more in pain. 'I found him in the swamp after he crawled out of the hole the dragon put him in. I told him we should find you. If there is one thing Berus despises more than the plague worshippers, it's a traitor!'

Urda spat into Vallac's gloating face. 'This will avail you nothing! The southlander will take all the glory for himself! There will be nothing for Steelfist!'

Vallac's calloused hand closed around the crone's chin, forcing her head upward. He looked over her shoulder at Berus's skeletal visage. When Vallac spoke again, it was not in the tongue of the Kurgans or even the trade patois common between the Norse. It was the brutal, braying notes of the Dark Tongue itself, the language of monsters and sorcerers. 'Your sight does not fail you there, witch!' Berus fixed his eyes on Vallac, trying to discern the meaning of the unfamiliar words by studying the other Kurgan's face. 'There will be nothing for Einarr, but the southlander will not claim the prize either! The glory will be Vallac's and Vallac's alone!' He pushed the hag's chin back still further until her neck snapped with a dull pop. Urda's eyes rolled back in her skull as her head drooped lifelessly against her spine.

'Too bad, hag,' Vallac scoffed at the corpse. 'When you played your games of treachery you didn't realise I was playing too.'

Berus let the broken body fall from his grip.' The witch is dead,' he growled, suspicion in his voice, menace rumbling through the skeletal jaws of his helm. 'Now you will show me the way into the palace, as you promised.'

'In time,' Vallac said. 'We have to wait for von Kammler. He is the one who can get us inside, remember?'

The berserker nodded his horned head. 'You are certain about what you heard the southlander and Steelfist say?'

Vallac nodded his head. The stupid southlander had never imagined that the sorcery he had unleashed upon him had changed more than just his flesh. His hearing had grown to such levels that he heard noises even Orgrim had failed to detect. That had served him well, listening in the dead hours of the night while Einarr and von Kammler made their plans. Now that knowledge would serve them well.

He looked down at Urda's broken body. Had the witch learned something of their plans as well, or was it merely fate that caused her to be here? Either way, her presence was fortuitous and something Vallac was not going to waste.

'Pick up the hag,' he told Berus. 'The crone can keep the thing in the cave occupied while we pass.'

'DOWN!'

For the fifth time, they threw themselves into the muck, sinking into the filthy water as the black shadow crawled across the swamp. Every time, Einarr waited for the earth to shake, for water to explode all around him as the dragon dove down from the sky and descended upon them. Every time, the gods granted them a reprieve, the dragon's hovering bulk sweeping across the pustulent sky to scour some other corner of the desolation for her enemies.

The Norscan rose from the dripping mess as the dragon flew off once more, her tattered wings fanning the noxious air. Convinced that things were as safe as they could be, he lifted Birna from the morass, the huntress leaning on him for support. Growling, Orgrim threw himself to the shore, shaking the filth from his fur.

'One good thing to say for the dragon, she's keeping all the vermin in their burrows,' Zhardrach observed, wringing swamp water from his beard.

Einarr glanced at the dwarf, then at von Kammler. The armoured knight turned his head, scanning the terrain.

'The cave will be near now,' the knight said.

'You are sure it is the best way?' Einarr asked, again looking at the dwarf. Zhardrach smiled back at him.

'Think I'll knife you in the dark?' the dwarf groused. 'Not with that dragon flittering about! Need as much meat to throw between her and me as possible!'

Von Kammler turned back. 'It is the only way.'

Einarr shook his head. 'We can't,' he said. 'We have to think about later.'

'If we don't get past Bubos, there will be no later,' von Kammler reminded him. Grimly, Einarr nodded his head. Von Kammler turned again and forced his way through the rushes.

Zhardrach watched them go, Birna supported by Einarr as he pushed into the weeds. The dwarf sucked at his needle-sharp teeth. There was something he was missing here, something he was certain he didn't like. His hand slipped down to the Hung knife he had hidden within the matted coils of his beard. Maybe the Norscan would be getting that stab in the dark after all.

A low growl snapped Zhardrach from his murderous thoughts. Hackles raised, Orgrim snarled at him, the werewolf's sharp fangs gleaming wetly.

'Allright,' the dwarf sighed. 'I'm moving. See, this is me moving. No need to bite.'

EINARR SET BIRNA down beside a lumpy green stone and joined von Kammler near the opening of the cave. The knight stared grimly into the darkness.

'You are certain this will work?' Einarr asked him in a lowered voice, still uncomfortable with the price they would have to pay to travel this road. Even less comfortable with what it would mean later.

Von Kammler bowed his armoured head. 'There is little mind left in the guardian. Give it prey and it may be too occupied to pay any notice of us.'

Einarr glared at the darkness, his mouth vile with the taste of betrayal. He fingered the edge of Alfwyrm. 'We could fight our way past.' The hollow hiss of von Kammler's laughter echoed from behind his helm.

'Forty of my champions thought the same,' he said. 'A wise man understands when he gains from losing.'

'What about the lake?' Einarr demanded.

'We will burn that village when we come to it,' the knight said. It seemed to Einarr that von Kammler's head turned ever so slightly, as though the knight had started to glance toward Birna before he corrected himself. Disgust pulsed through Einarr's veins, but he bit down on his rage. After they were across the lake would be the time to dissuade the southlander of his unsavoury notions.

Spitting swamp water, his body coated in muck and slime, the curses dripping from Zhardrach's mouth were especially obscene as the dwarf crawled onto the slightly more solid ground around the cave. His eyes narrowed as he spied the dank gloom of the cave, a sinister twinkle in the smile that briefly flashed across his face. To the men, the darkness was forbidding and menacing, but to him it was friendly and inviting. He'd have the advantage now, the humans would be all but blind in that murk while he, with his sharp dwarf eyes, would barely notice the difference. A bit of knife work and it would all be over. The werewolf was the only thing that really bothered him. He wasn't sure how well the beast's other senses would compensate his impaired vision. He'd have to strike the werewolf first then. The southlander next, then the barbarian slut. He'd save Einarr for last. He didn't want to rush when it came to disposing of him. He had many weeks of trial and ordeal to pay the Baersonling back for.

Zhardrach emerged from his dark ruminations, blinking in confusion as he found everyone looking at him. Even von Kammler's steel mask seemed to have an expectant quality about it.

'What? What did I do now?' Zhardrach demanded. Einarr simply gestured towards the cave. Tiny alarms began to clang in the back of the dwarf's mind. He took a step back, nearly sliding back into the mire.

'You expect me to go first?' Zhardrach said, shaking his head.

'You are the dwarf,' Einarr told him. 'Your people riddle the mountains with this kind of burrow. Navigating places like this comes as easily to you as sailing the Sea of Claws comes to me. Lead the way.'

Zhardrach took another step back, this time slipping onto one knee as the muddy bank gave beneath his boot. The unexpected motion drew a deep snarl from Orgrim, but the dwarf kept his eyes focused on Einarr, the alarms banging away as he studied the man's stern visage.

'Not my people,' Zhardrach protested. 'Maybe you are thinking of goblins.' Orgrim's growl deepened and the dwarf could see the werewolf starting to circle him. Einarr took a few steps towards him, one hand closed about the hilt of his sword.

'Do you think me fool enough to have you at my back in the dark?' Einarr said.

Zhardrach clenched one hand into a fist and pressed it against his heart. 'On my father's bones, Steelfist, I wouldn't think of causing you harm.' The dwarf knew

enough about the Norscans to know they found such
oaths impressive. One of his own kind would recognise it for the worthless drivel it was. Unfortunately, it
seemed that Einarr did too. The warrior took another
step towards Zhardrach, a few inches of steel shining
as he started to draw his sword.

Suddenly, the sky darkened and a fell reek came
crushing down upon them. None of them needed to
look skyward to know that their game of cat and
mouse was over. Bubos had found them. The dragon's
seething cry of victory hissed across the swamp.

Zhardrach sprang forward, pushing Einarr aside,
almost spilling himself across the ground in his haste
to scramble into the cave. Orgrim hurriedly loped
after the fleeing dwarf, von Kammler only a few steps
behind him. Einarr turned and hurried to the rock,
helping Birna to her feet. The ground shook as he carried her toward the cave, the impact of the dragon's
descent causing the earth to shudder. He glanced over
his shoulder to find the beast lunging up from the
mire, throwing her bloated bulk towards the cave. The
hot filth of the dragon's breath washed over him as he
gained the foetid gloom of the tunnel. Bubos's jaws
filled the mouth of the cave, snapping in frustration as
she tried to catch her fleeing prey.

Whatever relief Einarr might have felt at escaping
the dragon vanished as he turned his head back
around, the loathsome thing crouched against the
wall of the tunnel turning his stomach. The bloated
slug-toad wallowed in a slop of its own filth, hand-
like tentacles wrapped around greasy bones it slavered
over with a wet, bubbling orifice. As the bubbling
mucus touched the bones, Einarr could see fragments
of sinew and marrow dissolve and be sucked back

into the abomination's ghastly mouth. Putrid eyes on a crown of fleshy stalks spread from the top of the thing's head to watch its mouth feed.

'Tzeentch smiles on us, Steelfist,' von Kammler said. 'The thing has already found prey.'

They began to circle around the feeding daemon, all eyes locked on the loathsome sight, every breath held for fear it might disturb the beast. For some reason, Einarr felt his gaze drawn away from the daemon, drawn to the pile of bones it slobbered over. Shock gripped him as he saw the wet, gleaming skull, the stone rune eye set into its forehead.

'Urda,' he gasped. As he recognised the skull, a mad impulse pounded through his mind, an obsession to take the rune eye from the feeding daemon. Einarr tried to fight the insane urge, but it was all he could do to resist it long enough to hand Birna over to von Kammler.

'Have you gone crazy, barbarian?' the knight hissed.

Einarr shook him off, stalking towards the bloated plague beast. He could see the piled tatters of Urda's clothes and possessions lying beside the bones.

'The witch's bag,' he whispered. 'There may be something in it we can use.' The words sounded hollow even to him. He crept closer to the feeding daemon. Its moist, glistening hide oozed and bubbled only inches from him as he reached for Urda's bag. He held his breath as he lifted it from the pile of bloodied rags. One of the thing's eye stalks twisted slightly at the sound, but it remained content to drool on Urda's femur.

Sweat beaded Einarr's brow as he reached for the skull, unable to deny the urge that had now overwhelmed him. The mark of Tchar glowed faintly as his fingers pressed against the slimy skull, crushing the brittle bone and pulling the rune eye from its socket.

With his prize clenched in his fist, Einarr pulled back, recoiling from the daemon's repugnant presence. But it was already too late. In reaching for the skull, he'd drawn the plague beast's notice, its dozens of eye stalks twisting around to consider him with hungry idiocy. For a moment, man and daemon stared at one another, then a foam of mucus bubbled from the excited beast's gash-like mouth.

Einarr backed away from the daemon, stomach churning as it slithered across the muck of the tunnel towards him. He realised now the terrible position his mad impulse had put him in. At his back was the mouth of the cave and the dragon. Before him, blocking his path, was the gibbering toad-worm. Beyond the daemon he could see von Kammler carrying Birna down the tunnel, herding Zhardrach before him. Orgrim lingered behind, his instinct to flee warring with his loyalty to the warrior.

Einarr slashed Alfwyrm against the plague beast's slimy hide, but the rubbery flesh was thicker than whale blubber, the keen blade unable even to scratch it. For its part, the daemon took no offence at the attack, simply continuing to crawl and drool. Einarr backed away still further, giving ground before the bloated thing.

A whining howl from Orgrim was the only warning Einarr had. How he understood the import of that mournful, bestial cry, he could not say, but the werewolf's howl created an image in his mind as vivid as that of any words. He threw himself to the left as a great scaly claw smashed through the mouth of the cave. Unable to force her head down the tunnel,

Bubos had relented and was now trying to paw her prey back into the open, like a bear picking grubs from a rotten log.

The scaly member smashed into the muddy floor of the tunnel, the talons leaving deep furrows behind as the dragon pulled her leg back. Without Orgrim's warning, more than mud would have been crushed beneath her paw. Einarr did not have time to consider the morbid thought. The daemon continued to ooze towards him, its eyes fixed on the inviting lure of his warm flesh. Between the dragon's claws and the daemon's corrosive maw, there was little to choose.

An idea came to him as he turned to face the dragon. Perhaps this was another unpleasant choice he didn't have to make. Keeping one eye on the daemon's slithering approach, Einarr waved his arms, shouting at the reptilian behemoth crouched beyond the cave. He saw the dragon's eye glare at him from outside. Behind him, the slobbering plague beast drew closer.

Throwing himself violently against the wall of the tunnel, Einarr flattened his body as the dragon's immense claw shot past him into the cave. The gigantic talons smashed down into the daemon's quivering bulk. Bubos hissed with anger as her scales sizzled where the plague beast's corrosive drool touched them. She drew her claw back, dragging the daemon with it, pulling the slobbering idiot thing into the unclean light of the swamp.

Einarr did not linger to listen to the sounds of battle as Bubos discovered just what she had dragged from the cave and it discovered her. Whichever won, dragon or daemon, he did not want to stay around to welcome the victor's attentions. Sprinting down the tunnel, he joined Orgrim and together they hurried after von Kammler and the others.

As he ran, Einarr's hands played with the necklace around his throat, his fingers deftly working a new talisman onto it, Urda's rune eye joining Thognathog's decayed finger.

Chapter Seventeen

Not far from the scum-covered waters of the lake, amid a tangle of reeds and weeds, a small pile of boulders rose up from the muddy earth. Almost completely covered in slime and moss, the stones were all but invisible to an observer until he was nearly standing right on top of them. The gaping hole that wormed its way through the rocks was even more hidden, a black fissure that stabbed down into the dank earth beneath the swamp. Roots and brambles covered the opening, concealing it from even the most careful scrutiny. Yet the path had been found once before, and it had been found again. Hairy grey paws clawed at the curtain of roots, tearing them aside and exposing the mouth of the hole. Wolfish eyes blinked at the harsh light of the sickly sun, trying to adjust after the darkness of the tunnel.

His canine muzzle sniffing at the noxious air, Orgrim crept from the black pit. The werewolf's feral eyes scanned the putrescent sky, watching for any sign of the dragon. After a few tense moments he turned and snarled at the pit. In response, a muck covered hand closed about the lip of the defile. Einarr strained against the slippery sides of the hole as he lifted Birna from the pit. Beside him, von Kammler had a much easier time extracting himself from the hole, despite his armour and the weight of Zhardrach thrown across his shoulder. The knight's display of strength and vitality was not lost on Einarr.

All through the slimy tunnels of the plague beast, Einarr had watched von Kammler with a wary caution. Of them all, it was the southlander who was in the best shape. Einarr knew the knight had his own reasons for coming to this place. If the knight was contemplating treachery, he would do so soon.

The knight dropped Zhardrach into the mud, snapping his fingers and motioning for Orgrim to keep an eye on the dwarf. Then the southlander bent back towards the pit. His steel mask glowered down at Einarr for a moment, then his armoured hands were reaching down and helping him lift Birna from the hole. The huntress groaned as she collapsed into the mud, unable to stand without von Kammler's support. He pulled at her leg, twisting it around to study the ragged wound that ran through it. Black worms squirmed through the meat, pus dripping from the crimson boils that surrounded it. The knight shook his head.

'She belongs to the plague god now,' von Kammler's chilly voice declared. 'It will not be long before he claims her.'

With a surge of strength, Einarr sprang from the pit, fighting his own feelings of fatigue and despair to stay on his own feet as he gained the surface. The Norscan knelt beside the stricken huntress, putting himself between von Kammler and Birna. He reached his hand to brush the damp hair from her forehead. He felt a wave of rage and disgust flood through him. Even now the gods were still changing her, making her into a cruel mockery. Birna's face had become an almost perfect mirror of Asta's, even the expression that suffered beneath her fever was Asta's. Red hate routed the despair that gnawed at his strength. Einarr felt his hand close around the hilt of Alfwyrm. He suddenly realised that his back was to von Kammler. *Let the knight make his move now*, he thought. *I need something to kill.*

'Your woman will die soon, Steelfist,' von Kammler said. 'But she may still be of use to us.'

Einarr looked away from Birna to glare at the southlander. 'There is no need for that,' he growled. Whatever expression the knight wore behind his mask, there was no mistaking the menace and assumed authority when he spoke.

'The dwarf can fight, she cannot,' von Kammler said. 'She is useless to us and will only slow us down. My way, she will still help us.' The expression on Einarr's face darkened. He could feel the grip of Alfwyrm pressing into his palm as his hand tightened around it. Von Kammler's stance remained casual, as though the knight were unaware or unconcerned that the Norscan was a heartbeat from driving his blade into the southlander's chest.

Einarr's hold on Alfwyrm relaxed as he suddenly realised von Kammler was right to be unafraid.

Without the knight, they would never be able to cross the lake and reach the palace. Without the knight, he would never seize the treasure Tchar demanded, never claim the reward he had been promised. He looked down at the sick woman lying beside him, Asta's face looking back up at him. If he failed now, everything would be lost. All their struggles, all their ordeals would mean nothing. He could still prevail, still set everything right. That was the only glory he was interested in – to undo everything he had done.

Von Kammler nodded his armoured head. 'We are agreed then, Norscan?' the knight's grim voice hissed.

Before Einarr could force an answer to his lips, Orgrim spun about, glaring at the wall of dead weeds and twisted trees that rose behind them. The werewolf's hair bristled as an angry growl rumbled from his throat. The weeds parted and two familiar figures strode into the soggy clearing. Vallac made a placating gesture with his hand, trying to appease Orgrim's agitation. Beside him, the hulking Berus glared at von Kammler.

'Lord Tzeentch be praised!' Vallac shouted. 'We are not the only ones to escape the dragon!'

Einarr shifted his gaze from the sinister knight to the pair of Kurgan warriors. He knew he should feel relief to see them, that their strength would be a great asset assaulting the halls of the Plague Lord. Instead, a black dread coursed through his body, a fell premonition of doom. 'We have eluded the dragon, for now,' Einarr told Vallac, every word fighting past the wary caution that filled him. He raised his hand to the band around his neck, his finger brushing against the stone eye fastened there. 'Urda was not so fortunate,' he said. The smile that teased the corners of Vallac's twisted face told Einarr that however the witch had died, it had not been without the Kurgan's help.

'There are others who should not be fortunate,' Berus snarled. The berserker hefted his axe, glaring straight into von Kammler's smouldering eyes. Einarr leapt to his feet, ripping Alfwyrm from its sheath. Orgrim began to prowl around the two Kurgans, his hackles raised. Vallac placed a restraining hand against the berserker's chest. Berus turned his head, glowering at the other Kurgan. For a moment, it seemed he would bury his axe in Vallac before confronting von Kammler.

'The southlander is still important to us,' Vallac reminded Berus. 'After Skoroth has been dealt with, after the prize is ours, then you can take his skull for Khorne.' Berus looked unconvinced, but slowly he lowered his axe.

'After the Plague Lord is dead,' he warned von Kammler. The knight simply nodded.

'I would not stand between a fool and his folly,' he said.

Vallac strode across the clearing, leaving the brooding Berus to his own bloody thoughts. He stepped towards Einarr, hesitating when he saw that the Norscan had not lowered his sword. The Kurgan shifted his attention away from Einarr, looking down at Birna. He shook his head.

'The southlander is right,' Vallac said. 'Your woman is already gone. She will only slow us down.' He tapped the curved sword at his side. 'I can do it, if you like.' There was no malice in Vallac's offer, rather it was spoken in a humble, conciliatory tone. To the practical view of the Kurgan, there was no appreciation of repugnance in a deed that had to be done.

'She will live,' Einarr growled back. He lowered his sword. With his other hand, he pulled the torn remains of Urda's bag from his belt.

'There is no help in there,' Vallac said. 'The witch used it all to keep herself going.'

Einarr crushed the ripped bag in his hands and dropped it into the mud.

'She has to die now, Steelfist,' Vallac persisted. 'Otherwise her spirit will belong to the plague god.'

'No,' Einarr said, the word dripping from his tongue like venom. He reached beneath his bear-skin cloak, removing Spjall's medicine bag. They'd used almost everything to fend off the sickness of the Plague Lord's realm, but there was still something left. Einarr's hand closed around a small bundle of wet, stick-like roots wrapped in sealskin. Vallac's brow knitted as he watched Einarr remove the sticks, grinding them between his hands until they were reduced to a dripping pulp that looked more like blood than anything else.

'An old Norse remedy,' Einarr told Vallac. The Kurgan's expression remained dubious, but he watched with intense interest as Einarr lifted Birna's head and poured the pulp into her mouth. With effort, the huntress swallowed the paste. 'She will not die.'

Einarr heard the words of his lie dance through the swamp, the hollow echoes mocking him as they faded into nothing. He'd done nothing to help Birna, she would thrive or fade at the whim of the plague god. What he had given her was bloodroot, a terrible herb known to the vitkis of the Norse. There was strength in bloodroot, but there was no healing within it. Under its effects, a man would feel strength flood back through his body even as life faded from it.

Einarr had seen warriors fighting with missing arms and collapsed chests under the effect of bloodroot. He'd seen reavers rowing longships back from a raid with their innards spilling from their split bellies. Bloodroot was a thing of death, not of life. It was also the last thing he had to offer Birna.

VON KAMMLER WATCHED Einarr minister to the huntress, then turned and looked up into the sky. The knight raised his arms to the leprous heavens, sibilant notes rasping from behind his mask as he called out to the Realm of Chaos and the forces beyond. The air grew colder, the weeds about the knight's feet shivering as they sprouted new and ghastly growths. A keening wail throbbed above them and even Einarr's eyes were drawn skyward as the leprous tapestry was torn by a pulsating glow of violet and azure. Lightning flashed behind the tear in the sky, lavender clouds spilling through the rupture. The ground shuddered, quivering violently as an undulating earthquake rocked the festering domain. A fierce, silent wind tore through the realm, snapping trees and uprooting weeds as the stagnant air swirled madly across the land. Splotches of pallid putrescence sprouted throughout the leprous sky, like voracious growths of mould.

Einarr held Birna close to him, fighting to rise as the ground quivered beneath them. Orgrim pressed his belly into the mud, howling wildly as his animal instincts were overcome by the awful sorcery pulsing all around them. Berus threw himself from the path of a tree as it crashed into the clearing, its withered bark splitting as organ-like growths of shimmering fungus erupted from it. Vallac abased himself, wailing in his savage language, shrieking the glories of Tzeentch to the heavens.

Then von Kammler lowered his arms and fell silent. As quickly as it had formed, the tear in the sky collapsed upon itself. The silent wind died away, the stagnant air as heavy and humid as ever. The ground, however, continued to tremble, but not with the rolling undulations of an earthquake. The earth pulsed and heaved, bubbling like boiling soup. The ground burst in muddy explosions, showering the warband in filth. Sink-holes opened and closed all around them, sucking trees and rocks down into the blackness beneath the domain. Narrowly, Einarr avoided being sucked down into one of the holes, some sixth sense urging him to leap the instant before the ground beneath him collapsed.

'What have you done, southlander?' Einarr roared as he recovered from his near escape, checking to see that the violent motion had not further harmed the woman he held in his arms.

Von Kammler thrust his steel arm skyward once more. 'I have unlocked the gates of Skoroth's palace!' he bellowed, triumph booming in his voice. 'Behold! They come!'

Descending from the rotting sky were things of nightmare and madness. At first they looked like flickering lights, falling stars that changed colour with each passing breath. As they fell towards the quivering ground, substance could be seen within the shimmering light. What was within the light had mass, but was without shape or form. Einarr could see the rippling substance within the lights twisting and writhing, as though consumed by some inner flame. He had the impression of eyes and fangs, horns and spines, lashing tails and drooling mouths.

Von Kammler strode boldly towards the first of the daemon-lights, stretching his hand towards it. A susurrus of slobbering noises emanated from the thing and it fell still closer to the slimy earth, hovering just above the mud and mire. 'The stallions of Tzeentch!' the knight said, his voice quivering with both excitement and fear. Von Kammler lifted his armoured bulk onto the flattened platform that formed the daemon's back. The thing made wet, hungry noises as it felt the knight's weight pressing down upon it, but made no move to unseat its rider.

'This is how you plan to get into the palace!' The outburst came from Zhardrach, the dwarf perched atop a large stone, unable to decide which he should fear more – the hungry earth or the glowing daemons von Kammler had summoned.

'They will carry us across the lake,' von Kammler said. He looked into Einarr's eyes. 'There is no other way.'

Biting down on his own fear, Einarr carried Birna to another of the slavering, hellish daemons. The feathered skin that covered its shivering form crumbled into ash as he stepped onto its back, a smell of incense rising from the daemon's unclean essence. It gibbered at Einarr. Loathing filled him as he realised that mixed into the thing's lunatic mutterings were mortal words and mortal voices. Thousands of tiny eyes opened up along the daemon's body, each staring up at him with vile hunger.

The earth continued to quiver, the number of sinkholes increasing along with the speed of their onset. Vallac hurriedly mounted another of the floating discs. Snarling his own distaste, Orgrim pounced onto the back of one of the daemons, his claws sinking deep into its flesh in his attempt to secure a firm hold. Berus glared at the things, making no move to mount one of them.

'Stay here and die,' Einarr told him, 'or be a man and conquer your fear.' The Kurgan turned his skeletal helm towards Einarr and the Norscan could feel the Kurgan's hate burning into him. Slowly, heedless of the boiling ground all around him, the berserker strode to one of the daemons.

'You'd better get moving too,' Einarr warned Zhardrach. The dwarf stared at the closest of the daemons and shook his head. Then he felt the rock he was on shudder. With a curse, the dwarf scrambled off his refuge. He had barely cleared the boulder before it was sucked down into the slimy earth. With another curse, Zhardrach flung himself at the daemon, hastily climbing onto its scaly back.

No sooner had Zhardrach mounted his ghastly steed than the entire flock of daemons was in motion, shooting up into the sky like flaming arrows. Before Einarr could even begin to consider their dizzying ascent, the daemons changed direction, speeding out across the swamps. The festering morass passed away beneath them faster than the eye could follow. Then they were flying above the banks of the lake, the scum-covered waters slithering against the shore.

As the daemons flew above those foul waters, however, they began to shudder. Einarr could feel them losing speed, feel the strength draining from them. The foul magics of the Plague Lord were weakening their daemon steeds. He risked a look back, watching as one of the riderless discs lost its glow. The daemon's substance became black with disease and it fell from the sky, sucked down into the noxious embrace of the lake.

The Norscan clutched Birna closer to him, trying not to think what would happen if their own steed were to lose its strength. He turned away from the doom that had claimed the daemon, fixing his eyes on the jagged spire of the palace, watching as it slowly drew nearer. His entire being urged the daemon to fly faster, to close the gap before its own strength failed. Instead, their approach slowed with every heartbeat.

A hideous wail of agony tore Einarr's eyes from the tower. Behind him, another disc plummeted from the sky, diving into the festering sludge of the lake. As it struck the scummy water, a black cloud rose up from the slime. The cloud flew upwards, driving straight towards them. As the speed of the daemons faltered, that of the cloud increased. Soon Einarr's ears were filled with a deafening drone, the buzz of a million flies. The hairy, biting things swirled all around as the swarm-cloud engulfed them. Einarr swatted at the abominable vermin, crushing them beneath his fingers, grinding them into paste. But for every one he killed, a hundred more settled upon him, their jaws chewing at his flesh. His shut his eyes against the biting mass of filthy life, struggling to breathe through the carpet of insect life that crawled into his nose and mouth.

Suddenly, a shrill cry rose above even the buzz of the flies. The sound was repeated from nearby, shrieked into the leprous haze by a hundred voices. A few moments later, the crawling mass that coated Einarr was gone, flying from him as quickly as it had come. He dared to open his eyes. Nearby he could see

a great flock of pallid vultures tearing at the flies with
their beaks and talons even as the gnawing insects
threatened to swarm over them. It was a hopeless
struggle, but at least they would be free of Nurgle's
flies for a time. He looked at Birna. The huntress
smiled weakly back at him, oblivious to the tiny bites
that peppered her entire body.

'I saw the vultures and knew they could help,' she
told him, pointing a shaking finger towards the
palace. The structure had drawn much closer now,
near enough that he could make out its grotesque
details, the polished bone that seemed to form its
walls, the iron spikes that peppered its battlements.
The rotting meat that shuddered on those spikes, even
the most wasted tatters seeming to still cling to some
kind of obscene life.

The daemon steeds descended once more, diving
towards a great balcony that looked out over the diseased lake. The red, glistening mass looked more like
raw muscle than stone or wood. It throbbed with
excitement as the daemons flew across it, for a
moment it seemed that it would sprout arms and rip
them from the sky.

The balcony opened into a great hall, a chamber
more colossal even than the ruins they had seen in the
swamp. Einarr was struck by tales of sky-titans and
their mighty strongholds. Surely no other race could
have built with such enormity. Then he noted the
leathery floor, the walls that wailed and moaned, the
ceiling of dripping foulness, and he knew that no
mortals had built this place. Only daemons used living flesh to construct their castles.

The daemon steeds finally stopped in the middle of
the hall, hovering above the obscene floor. Einarr

forced himself to step down from the daemon's back, he would be the first of them to set foot in Skoroth's palace. His boots scuffed against the leathery floor, drawing blood from the bruised flesh.

Slowly, the others dismounted their own steeds, dropping to the rotting, oozing floor. Zhardrach cursed and kicked at the ground as he stumbled away from his steed, sending what looked like the festering stumps of fingers flying across the hall.

Berus glowered at the vile hall, staring at the moaning walls. Scrawny bodies, fused by some vile magic, struggled to free themselves from the walls, begging the berserker to kill them in a hundred tongues. Even Berus looked disgusted, turning away and staring instead at the hovering discs of Tzeentch. There was a fearsome, expectant quality about the ghastly daemons, their hungry eyes burning even more fiercely than before.

Einarr set Birna against the floor, turning to face the others. He set himself for what was coming, reminding himself that it had to be done. There was no other way.

'They wait for what was promised to them,' von Kammler said. He turned his head towards Zhardrach. Then Einarr saw the knight's gaze shift, his eyes fixed upon Birna.

'Then they will be cheated!' Berus roared. The berserker leapt towards von Kammler, his axe crashing against the knight's arm. The southlander was thrown back, his armour shrieking as its molten blood erupted into the air. Von Kammler drew his mace, moving to block Berus's next attack, but as he turned to attack the berserker, he was struck again from the side. Vallac's face sneered at him from above a dripping sword.

Einarr drew Alfwyrm, but wondered if he should
help the beleaguered knight. The decision was taken
from him as Birna's hand tugged at his leg. 'The
dwarf,' she warned. It was already too late, Zhardrach
crashed into Einarr, spilling him onto the floor. The
dwarf's powerful arms closed around Einarr's own,
pulling them back. The dwarf planted his boot against
Einarr's neck, crushing his face against the rotting
floor, breaking his nose. The floor tore open under the
assault, a lattice of dismembered and decayed arms
pressing against him.

'Feed me to daemons!' the dwarf roared. 'They tried
that in Uzkulak! But Zhardrach is still here!' Einarr
could feel his strength straining against the dwarf's
rage, fighting to keep him from breaking the
Norscan's arms. He felt the dwarf's spittle slap against
his face. The pressure on his neck vanished as
Zhardrach lifted his foot. The dwarf glared down at
him, boot raised above his head. 'Been a long time
since I went grobi-culling,' he laughed. 'Lets see if I
can't cave in that traitorous skull of yours with one
stomp!'

Before the murderous kick could smash down into
his head, a feral growl rumbled across Einarr. The
powerful grip on his arms vanished. Einarr rolled
away from the diseased hole in the floor, spitting his
revulsion from his mouth. He could see Orgrim, a
frenzy of claws and fangs, tearing at Zhardrach, the
dwarf's armour shredding beneath the werewolf's
fury. The jagged knife the dwarf held was wet with
Orgrim's life, but the Aesling renegade did not slacken
his assault.

Einarr recovered Alfwyrm from the floor. He looked
away from Orgrim's frenzied attack on Zhardrach,

wondering if the werewolf would even be able to tell friend from foe in the grip of such fury. Across the hall, he could see von Kammler still struggling against the two Kurgans. The combined attacks of Vallac and Berus had worn the southlander down, it was not his armour alone that now bled onto the rotten floor.

The knight noticed Einarr watching him. The sight infuriated him and he smashed Vallac to the floor with a brutal blow of his mace. He tried to do the same with Berus, but the berserker leapt from the path of his blow. The burning axe Berus wielded flashed through the gloom, cracking down against von Kammler's hand. Steel, flesh, and bone parted beneath the blow and von Kammler's hand fell to the floor, his mace frozen in the now dead hand.

Einarr felt his own hand burn as von Kammler's was cut from his body. The rune seared into his flesh glowed faintly and Einarr recalled the similar sigil that had marked the knight's hand. He was not alone in appreciating what the fallen champion had lost. Berus sprang away from the stricken knight as the hovering daemons converged upon him, enveloping von Kammler. With the mark of Tzeentch cut from him, there was nothing to keep the daemons from attacking the man who had dared call them from the Realm of the Gods.

Von Kammler struggled beneath the biting, ripping mass of the daemons, trying to tear himself free. The air grew chill once more, the entire palace shuddering as once again a hole was cleft between the spheres. The lavender clouds billowed around von Kammler and his destroyers as man and daemon were sucked from the world of mortals. Only the knight's last echoing shriek and his severed hand remained.

Vallac rose from the floor, cradling the wound that dripped from the side of his head. He looked across the hall at Einarr. The two locked eyes for a moment, each man staring into the other's soul, seeing the indomitable force within the other. From the first, Vallac had never intended to share anything with the Norscan, any more than Einarr would allow the Kurgan to stand between him and what he had been promised.

'Berus,' Vallac called to the berserker. 'Now we deal with the other traitor.' Berus nodded, turning his skeletal helm toward Einarr. The berserker gestured at him with his axe.

'Tonight your skull will lie before the Skull Throne,' Berus promised.

Einarr wiped blood from his face, flinging the droplets at Berus. 'For one of Kharnath's butchers, you talk too much.' The Norscan hefted Alfwyrm in his hand and stalked towards the Kurgan. 'Let's make this quick. There are other people I have to kill.'

The berserker roared, hurling himself at Einarr. Before the Kurgan could reach him, however, the entire hall shook, spilling both men to the fleshy floor. For a moment, Einarr thought the hideous daemon steeds had returned, then a sickeningly familiar reek assaulted him.

Turning his head towards the balcony, Einarr saw the opening filled by an enormous shape of festering scales and oozing sores. Bubos's loathsome eye glared down at him and the dragon threw back her head in a hissing roar of satisfaction.

The huntress had found her prey.

CHAPTER EIGHTEEN

THE DRAGON'S BLOATED bulk filled the front of the great hall, her rotting skin peeling where the plague beast's venom had corroded it, her mouth dripping pus where Thognathog's fist had punched through it. Yet for all her wounds, there was no mistaking the awesome power that still pulsed through her enormous frame. As she moved, her claws ripped through the skin of the floor, bones snapping beneath her tremendous weight.

Every eye focused on the monstrosity. Orgrim looked up from the savaged remains of Zhardrach, snarling at the reptilian behemoth. From the floor, Birna weakly raised her head, eyes wide with terror. Vallac stepped back, his misshapen face turning pale as he met the dragon's gaze. In the centre of the hall, even the two combatants were compelled to shift their

attention from their foe to the even deadlier enemy
that now tore her way into the gallery.

Einarr glanced away from the advancing dragon,
locking eyes with Berus. The berserker nodded his
helmed head.

'I will see you in the next world, Norscan,' Berus
growled. Without further pause, he tightened his hold
on his axe and charged the reptile. Einarr watched the
Kurgan for a moment, then turned and rushed at the
dragon from the other side. He hoped the tactic
would divert the monster's attention, force her to
choose between her foes, allow at least one of them to
sink his steel in her diseased bulk. Even as he ran
towards Bubos, he knew how desperate such a hope
was.

The dragon hesitated, her baleful eye fixing on the
blood-mad Kurgan, her lips pulling back from her
fangs. Air sizzled against her teeth as she sucked a
deep breath into her mighty lungs. She drew her head
back, her chest expanding as the malignancy inside
her grew. Einarr could almost see the air turning foul
with corruption. Like a striking serpent, Bubos's head
shot forward, her jaws gaping wide as she sent a cloud
of burning pestilence rushing toward Berus. The
berserker dove through the cloud, sparing himself the
brunt of its terrible power. The floor behind him bubbled as the fume consumed it, skin dripping away as
it was reduced to a greasy slime. The wall behind
Berus shrieked in agony as the dragon's breath struck
it, the wasted bodies that formed it shrivelling before
Bubos's pestilence.

The berserker, his armour steaming as it fell from
him in molten strips, smashed the edge of his axe into
the dragon's snout, crunching through scale and

bone. Bubos's squirming blood vomited from the wound, bathing Berus in her rancid gore. The Kurgan screamed, his cry a hideous mix of agony and exultation. He clung to his axe, his hands locked in a death-grip around the haft of the weapon. Roaring in her own pain, the dragon reared back, shaking her head, trying to rip Berus free.

Einarr seized the dragon's distraction, lunging at the reptile, stabbing Alfwyrm into the wound in her neck. Maggots the size of his fist erupted from the newly opened cut, slithering with loathsome life down his blade. Before the Norscan could recover from his shock and disgust, Bubos's claw slammed into him, hurling him back. The warrior crashed into the wailing wall of flesh, feeling bones crack under the impact. He barely paused to allow the sparks to fade from his vision before lurching back to his feet. The gods continued to smile on him – none of the bones he had heard snap had been his own.

Looking up, he saw the dragon looming above him. Einarr dove toward the beast's belly as she brought her clawed foot smashing down. The lattice of arms snapped beneath her brutal attempt to crush the Norscan and Bubos's enormous body shuddered as she sagged into the hole. Einarr exploited her momentary distress, thrusting upward, exulting as the dragon's putrid ichor slopped from her veins. Bubos reared back from the attack, the palace shuddering as her bloated immensity surged towards the balcony. Something grey and feral sprang over Einarr, pouncing on the recoiling dragon. Orgrim's savage claws tore into the reptile's neck, the spines jutting from his ribs fastening onto her like the spiny legs of a tick.

The dragon's rage built, her tail lashing about, smashing into walls, cleaving them apart like a butcher's blade. Her folded wings slapped against her body, the foreclaws trying to pick Orgrim from her neck, to swipe Berus from her snout. The berserker stubbornly defied her attempts to tear him away, but one of the talons struck Orgrim, ripping into the werewolf and throwing him down onto the floor. Einarr saw the Aesling's leg snap as he struck, bending like a twig beneath the strength of Bubos.

Berus continued to cling to his weapon, striving to rip it free so he could drive it once more into the dragon. The ghastly eye glared at him, the eerie pupils fixed on his defiant frame. The wing talons swiped again and again at him, striving to knock him free, but she could not properly focus her unnatural vision on him, her strikes always aimed too high to connect. The Kurgan snarled at her handicap, spitting at the massive organ even as his armour continued to drip from his limbs. The rage of the Blood God was in him now. If the dragon thought he would simply wilt and die then she knew nothing of Khorne's power. A crimson light of hate and slaughter began to surround his withering body.

With a roar of such fury that even the dragon's eye blinked shut, Berus ripped his axe from the dragon's snout. The blood that steamed against his body, that dissolved his flesh and ate his bones only served to fuel his frenzy. Lifting the axe high over his head, he charged the dragon's eye.

Bubos's head pulled back, instinctively reacting to the madman driving towards her eye. No longer anchored by his axe, Berus lost his footing, tumbling from the dragon's snout. Bubos's head shot forward again, her triple jaws snapping shut on the falling berserker. Legs vanished down the dragon's gullet as Berus was bitten in half. His torso slammed against the pitted floor, guts spilling from the horrendous wound. For a moment, he struggled to lift himself, then even the rage of Khorne deserted him and Berus fell back into the widening pool of his own blood.

Einarr looked away from the berserker's destruction, glaring back at the monster. The dragon continued to paw at her bleeding snout, trying to ease the pain that pulsed through her. For the moment she seemed oblivious to her other foes. Einarr started to approach her again, pausing as his boot struck something lying on the ground. The same unspeakable compulsion he had felt before gripped him, forcing him to lean down and retrieve it, a sliver of metal from von Kammler's gauntlet, the living steel feeling warm against his skin. Einarr hastily stuffed the scrap of armour in his meal bag.

As he rose to face the dragon once more, his world exploded into a sheet of crimson. Sharp, stinging pain flared through the back of his skull. Einarr turned, spinning with the speed a lifetime spent hunting and raiding had given him. He saw the crooked sword slash at him again, twisting so that the blade caught only the edge of his cloak. Vallac's twisted face glared at him, the Kurgan's eyes narrowed with spite and treachery. No, there was something more lurking there, behind Vallac's eyes. Something that had been there from the start, but which Einarr had failed to recognise until now. Envy, jealousy that it had been the Norscan and not himself who had been marked by Tchar, who had been chosen to recover the Dark Claw for the Windlord. Now, with Einarr so near to his goal, Vallac had given in to his wounded pride, striking out at the man who had been given the honours Vallac felt were rightfully his.

The ground trembled as the dragon's foot stamped against the floor. Instinctively, Einarr started to turn back towards the monster. Vallac smiled as he saw the mistake, slashing his sword at the Norscan's belly. Again, the arrogance of the Kurgan caused him to underestimate Einarr's reflexes and agility. From the corner of his eye, he saw Vallac's arm start to move, driving the crooked sword at him once more. He spun with the blow, thrusting Alfwyrm into the arm of his attacker. Vallac backed away, clutching at his injury. Einarr stared at the traitor, death in his gaze. A cruel smile twisted Vallac's mutated features. The swollen sack beneath his chin swelled and Einarr knew the dragon's fire wasn't the only flame he had to fear.

An arrow stabbed into the floor beside Vallac, drawing a wail of pain from the living flesh. The Kurgan spun, scowling as a second arrow narrowly missed him. Einarr lunged at the distracted marauder, driving Alfwyrm towards his enemy's skull. But the Kurgan had not survived so long upon the cold, brutal steppes without his own balance of fortune and fate. Ignoring the archery, Vallac caught Alfwyrm with his crooked blade, blocking the Norscan's blow. A savage kick to Einarr's knee brought the northman low. Vallac started to move in for the kill, but the assassin's face grew pale with horror. Instantly he was on his heels, fleeing down the hall.

Einarr did not have to look to know what had frightened the Kurgan. The warrior dove across the floor, rolling as the dragon's claw came smashing down once more. Like an angry child trying to crush an ant, Bubos's talon pursued him, gouging deep craters in the ground, sending bone and skin spraying through the hall. Some of the gruesome debris struck Einarr, cutting him where cloak and armour failed to protect him.

Bubos's festering eye focused on the Norscan and she lifted her paw once more, determined this time to smash the annoyance into pulp. Einarr heard the reptile's hiss of satisfaction as her claw came hurtling towards him.

Suddenly, the hall shuddered with an ear-splitting cacophony, a keening scream that vibrated through the very bones of everything it struck. Einarr crushed his hands to his head, trying to block out the noise. The dragon reared back, her claw crashing down a few feet from Einarr's body. Bubos raged from side to side, her tail lashing the walls mercilessly, scattering scraps of screaming, festering humanity in every direction. Her talons dug into the floor, digging great pits to swallow her suffering. Her wings snapped open, smashing against the ceiling, causing chunks of flesh and coils of tendon to rain down into the hall. From the dragon's jaws, noxious fumes scorched everything she turned upon.

There was no system or strategy to the dragon's fury, only wretched madness and anguish, the unthinking rage of the maimed and ruined. As her head turned to blast one of the walls, Einarr saw the black arrow sticking from Bubos's eye, the dripping paste that drizzled from the ruptured organ. Blind, the dragon had gone berserk, lashing out at everything around her. Einarr rose to his feet, retreating before she recovered enough of her wits to remember the little man she had been trying to smash.

He found Birna leaning against one of the walls, her bow still in her hands. The huntress smiled weakly as he ran to her. 'I felt I should do my part,' she said. 'I only wish I hadn't missed that Kurgan scum.' She pointed a shaking hand to one of the corridors that opened into the hall. 'He ran into there. I had to choose between stopping him and helping you.'

Einarr pulled her to him, supporting her weakening frame. 'At least you put out the orm's eye.'

'It was too big to miss,' Birna quipped, trying to hide the pain in her voice. Einarr pushed her towards another of the passageways that opened into the hall. He could not say how, but he knew it was the way they needed to take. It was the same impulse that had made him plunge into the forest to find Birna so long ago, that had made him set out across the Frozen Sea. Somehow, he felt he could trust it. Somehow he knew he couldn't disobey the urge even if he tried.

Orgrim's broken body limped over to join them, the werewolf's muzzle singed by the dragon's blood. Einarr looked past Orgrim, into the hall where Bubos still raged. He could see figures running down the far end of the macabre hall, drawn no doubt by the dragon's fury. Let the denizens of the palace try to contain the wyrm's rage, Einarr decided, they had done their best. As he turned to urge his remaining comrades deeper into the passage, his eyes glanced across Zhardrach's torn and mangled form. Another urge swelled up inside him, and like the instinct that drove him on, Einarr knew it was too powerful to resist.

'Stay here,' he growled and before huntress or ulfwerenar could protest, he ran back into the great hall. The dragon's immense claws slashed the floor, digging deep gouges in the lattice, exposing the stagnant depths beneath the hall. Einarr lunged over the crevices, feeling the floor sag beneath him as he crashed against the other side. He pressed himself flat as Bubos's paw swiped the air above him before raking across the shrieking walls, spilling loops of entrail into the air. He was on his feet again in a heartbeat, racing toward the dwarf's carcass. The foremost of the guards rushing into the hall saw him, shouting excitedly in their bubbling voices. Razor-edged javelins slammed into the floor around him as the Hung warriors hurled their weapons at the intruder. The Norscan pressed on through the hail of spears, not slacking his steps even when a bamboo shaft slammed into his arm, shuddering as it glanced from his armour. He kept his eyes fixed on the dwarf, drawn by the urge that burned inside him.

The werewolf had done his gruesome work well, Zhardrach's organs lay strewn around his ripped and mutilated body. Something wet and swollen squelched beneath his boot as Einarr quickly leaned over the dwarf, his hand reaching to Zhardrach's beard. As his fingers closed around one of the coiled beard locks, Zhardrach's eyes snapped open. Einarr hastily drew back as the dwarf's fist came sweeping up, his knife still clutched in his hand. The beard lock tore free as Einarr recoiled from the slaver's last effort, but whatever pain Zhardrach was still able to feel did not diminish the spiteful smile he wore.

An instant later, the dwarf's hate was obliterated as a scaly leg smashed down into the floor. Einarr was thrown back by the impact, watching in awe as the power of the dragon caused Zhardrach's head to pop from his neck and go spinning across the hall like a cork shooting from a bottle. The Norscan froze as the dragon's immense head leaned down, her ruined eye spilling down her snout. The reptile's tongue flickered from her mouth, trying to pick Einarr's scent from the filth of the palace. He held his breath, trying to will the heart hammering away within his chest to grow quiet. For a tense moment, the blind dragon loomed before him, her flickering tongue only inches from his face.

Then the howls of the Hung crashed around them. Bubos reared back, spitting fiery death into the charging warriors. Men shrivelled into ash and cinder beneath the dragon's diseased fire, their bodies immolated by her corruption. Shocked, horrified that the monster had turned on them, most of the survivors fell back, screaming in dismay, or abasing themselves before her in some mad attempt to appease her wrath.

Einarr used the distraction presented by the Hung to make his escape. With the dragon raging above him, he made a reckless charge back across the hall, to the passageway where he had left Birna and Orgrim.

By force of will, Einarr leapt to his feet and ran for the passageway. The Norscan ignored the pain that pulsed through his body, the image of Zhardrach and the Hung warriors giving him more than enough incentive to keep moving. Only the thought of Berus's mutilated torso gave him pause. He turned, looking across the hall to where the berserker's remains lay crumpled against the wall.

He lingered for an instant, watching as the Kurgan's body bled out, waiting for the same mad impulse that had forced him to Zhardrach's side to drive him toward the berserker. When it did not come, he understood why. Von Kammler had made a mistake, they weren't intended to be nine, and that mistake had caused Einarr to make another. Berus had never been intended to be one of them, the proof was in Einarr's own mind, that lack of a fiery urge to rush to the dead berserker and claim from him some manner of talisman, as he had with his other fallen comrades. Einarr cursed his error as he ran back towards the corridor. How very different things might have turned out without the berserker in their midst.

Birna's arms flew around him as he gained the relative safety of the tunnel, her lips crushing against his. Then her fist cracked into the side of his jaw.

'Have the gods made you mad?' she demanded. From where he crouched against the floor, Orgrim gave voice to a low growl, seemingly in agreement with the huntress. 'Why by Tchar's shadow would you go back in there?'

Einarr reached to his neck, fastening the scrap of von Kammler's gauntlet and the beard-lock from Zhardrach to his necklace. 'Collecting keepsakes,' he replied, pushing Birna deeper into the passage. 'But there is nothing more to keep us here. For now what guards this place can muster will be busy with the dragon. It would be unwise to depend on her to keep them so.'

With his grim warning hovering over them, Einarr led his remaining comrades deeper into the palace and whatever nightmares called it home.

BUBOS CONTINUED TO rage through the great hall, her talons and tail ripping into walls and floor, her boiling breath searing the roof and causing it to shred in wet, dripping tatters. The Hung warriors kept their distance, watching the dragon's blind tantrum in silent, mortal terror. There was no thought of trying to contain her fury, they knew only too well what the beast was capable of.

The black terror that filled them was routed by an even greater fear. A crawling, scuttling horror that stole upon them, a foulness that repulsed not merely flesh, but soul as well. The Hung prostrated themselves upon the floor, shivering in dread. The floor shuddered with them and from the wretches entombed in the walls came sobbing wails even more agonised than the ones Bubos had caused.

Into the great hall came a shambling enormity, a stumbling, slithering loathsomeness. Where its shadow fell, blisters sprouted; where its legion of rotting feet stepped, mould sprang into vile life; where its heaving exhalations touched, disease flourished. Those Hung who dared lift their eyes to gaze upon it felt them water, tears of pus running down their faces. Instantly, warriors encased in rusted armour fell upon the heretics, cutting them down where they grovelled upon the floor. The butchered remains they threw before the shuffling feet that marched through the great hall.

It had a body. Thousands of them, naked and writhing, fused into one abhorrent mass by the foulest of sorceries. Every slave's mouth moved in silent agony, displaying the jagged stump where a tongue had been torn from mouth. There was a time to indulge in the sounds of misery, and there was a time to appreciate the silent contemplation of agony. He who was borne into the great hall upon the living palanquin prided himself on understanding that delicate balance.

'Bubos, be still!' the festering voice dripped through the hall from beneath the living canopy of the palanquin. The dragon recoiled at the sound of that voice, even in the grip of her maddened rage, fear had its place. Even in the terror of her blindness, in the madness of her corruption, there were things that still made her know dread. Like a scolded dog, the dragon cringed back, her reptilian head sliding to the floor, seeking refuge behind one of her immense claws.

Skoroth, Plague Lord of Nurgle, Scourge of the Wo and Aghols, emerged from the noxious fume of shadow that filled his palanquin. His bloated body stomped across the backs of the naked carriage, tearing flesh with every step. Atop his obese body, a shrunken, skeletal head surveyed the carnage that had raged through the hall. Cold fury smouldered in the pits of Skoroth's blighted eyes. The rolls of fat engulfing his neck undulated and heaved. From the corners of his mouth, furry black flies crawled free. The insects took flight, swarming about his head. Skoroth stared at them, the rage building inside him.

'The infidels who escaped, the ones who continue to profane this sacred place,' his decayed voice croaked. 'They will be found and made to know despair. Glory to the one who brings me their heads, those who fail will rebuild my great hall.' The Plague Lord surged back into the shadows of his palanquin. The swarming flies sped away, scattering through his fortress, carrying his words in their buzzing drone.

The intruders would be found and when they were, they would curse the mothers who bore them, the fathers who sired them, and the gods who gave them breath.

For a start…

* * *

THE THREE INVADERS plunged into the festering depths of the palace. Rotten arms groped at them from the walls, phlegm-filled voices begging for succour and mercy. Even the hardened Norscans found the wretched pleas infecting them, draining their strength and resolve. Unlike the feeble arms that clutched at them, the voices were not so easily brushed aside.

Einarr found their progress further impeded by the infirmity of his companions. Orgrim dragged his broken leg behind him, his agility and animal speed crushed with the limb. Birna's own pace was little better, only the noxious influence of the bloodroot preventing her from collapsing in a puddle of her own sickness. Einarr knew he should abandon them, press on to the shrine by himself and leave them to their fate. But such a thing smacked too much of treason and cowardice to sit well in his gut. He would leave the running to Kurgan swine like Vallac.

Orgrim suddenly stopped, the werewolf's muzzle curling back in a low snarl. Einarr tightened the grip on his sword and slowly made his way forward. The corridor ahead was filled with a mass of heaving, crawling flesh. With revulsion, Einarr recognised the horror as a gigantic grub, its verminous body coated in glistening slime. Beyond the ox-sized insect he saw two others. One sported gigantic, crab-like claws, which it was using to nip and tear at the living wall. While he watched, the grub cut one of the bodies free from the wall, shuffling aside so that the shrivelled husk could crumple to the floor. Unlike the bodies that still wailed and moaned from their fastenings on the wall, the body on the floor was quite dead.

Morbid fascination gripped Einarr and he watched as the second grub shuffled forward to take the place of its clawed companion. This one was a fat swollen creature. It lifted its massive tail over its slimy back. The tail began to undulate, as though pushing something through its bloated length. From a dripping orifice at the tip of the tail, a scrawny little man appeared, expelled from the grub's body. Before the little wretch could even begin to wipe away the mucous that coated him, the first grub Einarr had seen was scurrying forward. Dozens of arms latched onto the man, pulling him off the second worm's back and pressing him into the hole in the wall. Even as the man screamed, the grub began to cement him into the wall of writhing bodies, coating his arms and legs with a paste-like drool that slobbered from its mouth.

Einarr turned away from the gruesome scene. This, then, was how Skoroth maintained his palace. The hideous grubs were repairing damage in the halls, cutting dead flesh from the walls and replacing it with living bodies. The horror of it made Einarr want to charge the filthy brutes, end their vile existence with clean steel. He also knew that such behemoths would be a long time dying, time he didn't think they had.

But there was another way they might get past the mammoth insects. Einarr looked back the way they had come. There was a side passage connecting into the main corridor. He looked back at the grubs, watching as they continued to attach the screaming man to the wall. His idea was risky, there was a chance he would draw more grubs instead of distracting the three ahead. Einarr pulled Birna from the floor and motioned for Orgrim to follow him. They retreated back down the hall, past the side passage.

'Stay here,' he warned them, then dashed back down the corridor and into the side passage. He looked at the wailing, wretched husks of humanity fused into the walls. Even a Norscan could not help but pity such miserable beings. It was just as well. It made what he had to do easier. It made it mercy instead of murder. Einarr stabbed Alfwyrm into the chest of one man, then plunged the sword into the breast of a woman. Again and again he thrust his steel into the wall, bringing blessed death to the tortured husks. The wailing around him changed into desperate cries, plaintive shrieks for the mercy of the blade. Einarr tried to bring release to as many of them as he could, but he knew he could not linger long. He kept his ears peeled, trying to catch the sound of the grubs shambling towards the passage to repair the carnage he had visited upon the walls. It was difficult to hear with all the moaning voices surrounding him. Instead he felt the insects' advance, their massive bodies causing the floor to shake. Einarr turned away from his grisly work, running down the passageway and back into the corridor.

He froze as he reached the main hallway. One of the mammoth grubs loomed before him, only inches from his face. He could see the thing's beady black eyes, the chitinous parts of its mouth rubbing together. Man and insect stared at one another, neither moving. Finally, Einarr jumped back, bringing his sword up to the ready, prepared to lash out at the grotesque grub. The insect paid him no notice, turning and proceeding into the side passage. Its immense companions followed after it, scuttling away to repair the damage the Norscan had caused.

Einarr breathed a sigh of relief. The grubs didn't have any concern for intruders, only for their own tedious task. He looked down the corridor, smiling when he saw it free of bloated insects. His trick had worked, he had drawn the right grubs. He turned and grabbed Birna's arm.

'We should hurry,' he told her. 'Who can say how many of those things are prowling these halls?'

Birna shuddered at the thought, staring with new horror at the walls around them. 'Promise me a clean death, Einarr,' she said. 'Don't let me wind up like these.'

Einarr looked into her eyes, her words slicing into him like a knife. 'I promise, Birna. If it comes to that…' He didn't need to finish, Birna understood that he would do what had to be done.

SCOUTING AHEAD, EINARR found their advance through the palace was interrupted when the corridor was suddenly split by a great trough that curled between its walls. The channel bisected the passage, sinking a few feet below the level of the floor. He could see the passage continue on the other side some twenty feet beyond, the walls beyond lined with grimy nodules of stone rather than the whimpering bodies of plague-thralls.

It was what filled the trough that caused Einarr to cringe. What filled it was not water or pitch, but a bubbling porridge of what he could only describe as rancid meat. Grey chunks of indescribable filth bobbed about the churning filth, while thick clouds of flies buzzed about it. The warrior muttered an oath to his ancestors as he saw one of the flies touch the surface of the stew and be pulled down into its molten depths. He turned from the trench, to tell his comrades what he had found, and advise that they find some other way around. He was startled to find Birna

already behind him. She looked past Einarr, eyes wide
with loathing as she gazed upon the pestilential soup.

'Orgrim is growing agitated,' she told the warrior,
forcing her eyes away from the pit. 'I think we are
being followed.' As if to emphasise her words, a terrible howl echoed down the corridor. It was not the
wolfish cry of the ulfwerenar, but a lower, cackling
snicker, at once malevolent and wretched.

'We'll have to cross it,' Einarr decided, but there was
no conviction in his voice. He doubted the chances
for healthy men to cross that filth, much less the
injured and the infirm. He reached out across the pit,
feeling the surface of the walls. They were warm,
moist to the touch. The revolting impression came to
him that somehow, against reason and nature, what
was beneath his hand was living meat. Birna removed
a small steel spike from a pouch on her belt, handing
it to the warrior. It was a climbing piton, a tool not
uncommon to the hunters among the Sarls, who
knew how easily the role of hunter and prey could
change and appreciated the value of keeping a safe
distance above snapping fangs and flashing claws.

Einarr nodded and pressed the spike against the
quivering wall. 'This is neither stone nor timber,' he
said. 'I don't know how well it will hold.' The cackling
howl again came to them from up the corridor. This
time it was not one voice, but an entire chorus of bestial whines.

'Either way we die,' Birna told him. Einarr gave her a
grim smile and turned back to the wall. He pressed
the spike once again into the meat, then drove the hilt
of Alfwyrm against it. The walls shuddered with pain,
syrupy blood drooling around the spike. Einarr froze,
almost expecting the entire palace to reach out and

crush him for injuring it. When nothing happened, he grabbed the spike and tested its hold. Despite the ghastly substance that encased it, the piton held firm.

'At least something in this hole favours us,' Einarr said. He took another spike from Birna. One hand clenched around the first spike, he swung himself over the bubbling filth. Refusing to consider the abominable death that lurked just inches beneath his dangling feet, Einarr stretched his other arm out, stabbing a second spike into the wall. He swung back then drove forward once more, pounding the spike in with the palm of his hand. Once again the wall quivered and shuddered, threatening to spill him from his precarious perch. Sap-like gore dribbled from around the piton, sizzling as it flowed down into the trench. Einarr took a deep breath and swung his body out over the pit once more. This time he closed his hand around the second spike. Closing his eyes, he braced himself, half expecting the piton to tear free. Against his fears it held.

'Give me the rest!' he called to Birna, his momentary exhilaration fading as he considered the distance that still separated him from the far edge. He'd need at least five spikes to cover the entire distance, finding the thought of repeating the daring manoeuvre far from appealing. Yet he knew it was the only way.

He had just driven the third spike home when the sound of snarling animals and ripping flesh echoed from up the corridor. Einarr looked back to Birna and hastily swung back across the moat of disease. Their foes had reached Orgrim.

The warrior drew Alfwyrm as soon as his feet touched the floor. Birna already had her blade drawn, bracing herself for the onset of their foes. Einarr shook his head. 'Stay here and guard the way out,' he told her. The huntress started to argue, but her protest was lost in a fit of coughing. Einarr turned away and ran back up the passage to join Orgrim.

The werewolf was at the centre of a snarling maelstrom of violence and savagery. His pelt was torn in a dozen places, bloody strips of fur hanging from his wounds. Around him, a mob of cackling things that looked to be some loathsome mixture of swine and hound snapped at him. Every time the ulfwerenar turned to claw at one of the snivelling mongrels, one from the other side would dart in and sink its fangs into him. Einarr could almost see Orgrim's strength being leeched out of him with each cowardly assault.

'Laugh at this, cur!' Einarr roared, bringing Alfwyrm slashing through the back of one of the carrion-hounds. The crippled beast flopped against the floor, its back smashed by the attack. Einarr did not pause, but swept his sword in a murderous arc that sliced the leg from another hound and opened the muzzle of a third. Plunged into confusion by the Norscan's sudden arrival, the hyenas forgot their old foe. Orgrim lunged at them, sinking his fangs in the throat of the pack leader. The werewolf shook his head from side to side, worrying the wound. The hound struggled in his grip, trying desperately to pull away. Finally, with a wet ripping sound, the hound's throat was torn open, blood cascading from the wound. The maimed beast cringed away, then fell. The remainder of the pack turned, tails between their legs, and galloped back up the passage.

Orgrim shook shreds of meat from his jaws, spitting the taste of polluted blood from his mouth. Something white and sharp clattered across the floor to land beside Einarr's foot. The Norscan was alarmed to find it was a fang, torn from Orgrim's mouth during the battle.

The werewolf sagged against the wall, snapping at the wasted arms as they reached down for him, then started to lick his wounds. Cautiously, Einarr walked toward Orgrim, but the deep growl that rumbled from the werewolf's throat warned him back. He could see the animal fury glowing in the ulfwerenar's eyes, the barely restrained urge to rend and kill. He didn't want to consider what tremendous effort of will allowed Orgrim to restrain himself and keep from attacking the Baersonling.

Orgrim raised his head, sniffing at the air. Far up the corridor, Einarr could hear the cackling howls of the plague-hounds. The craven creatures had recovered from their surprise and were already loping back to glut their bellies and sate their lust for revenge. Einarr started to move down the corridor to meet them. Orgrim pounced ahead of him, snarling at the Norscan.

'Gggooo,' the werewolf rasped through his fangs. Without waiting to see if Einarr would obey, Orgrim turned to meet the charge of the hounds. Einarr hesitated, then stooped and retrieved Orgrim's broken tooth from the floor.

'Die well, Aesling,' Einarr told the werewolf as he turned and ran back to join Birna. He did not know how long Orgrim could hold the plague-dogs back, he could only hope it would be long enough for them to cross the pit.

Einarr rounded the corner and once more found himself gazing upon the putrid quagmire of boiling meat and frothing pestilence. At first he did not see

Birna, then his eyes focused on her, hands clutched
around the last of the pitons. He watched as the
huntress tried to swing herself forward, trying to emu-
late Einarr's feat and drive the fourth spike into the
wall. The warrior cursed aloud. The woman was having trouble standing, the fever must have seeped into
her mind for her to think she could muster the coordination to sink pitons into the wall.

He yelled at Birna, ordering her to stay still. Einarr
slammed his sword into its sheathe and leapt at the
wall, his hands closing around the first two spikes. He
shifted his weight, letting one hand go free and swung
himself around. His hand closed on Birna's, then
slipped around them to fasten onto the spike.

'Grab onto me,' he ordered. Birna nodded weakly.
Einarr did not need to tell her she was too sick to set
the piton, she had discovered that for herself. The warrior grunted as Birna's arms snaked around his neck
and his body felt her weight dragging on it. He
ignored his protesting muscles. Gripping a stake in his
hand, he moved to drive the piton home, to get them
a few feet closer to safety. The sound of battle in the
passage behind them told him there was not much
time.

How little time was borne home when a spindly figure crept from the corridor on the far side of the pit.
Yellow robes that smelled as though they'd been
soaked in urine dripped from the scrawny apparition.
The thing was a man, though the scabs that covered
almost every exposed inch of his frame made it
impossible for Einarr to decide if the man was Hung,
Kurgan or even Norse. Upon the chest of the robe, he
could see the fly-rune of Nurgle drawn in excrement,
upon the man's bald scalp a similar rune had been

branded. The miserable thing turned eyes black with disease in their direction and a sharp-toothed grin split his scabby face. The man lifted his fleshless hand and sickened words slobbered from the sorcerer's mouth as he began his incantation.

Einarr could feel the air around him growing hot and heavy, sticking to him like dampened rags. Birna coughed loudly, her bile dripping down his chest. He could feel her hands growing slick with sweat as the spell strengthened the disease gnawing at her. The wall of meat behind them began to turn green and panic flared through the Norscan as he felt the piton shift slightly. Everything seemed to be withering under the sorcerer's malign magic, everything except Einarr himself. He felt a flash of heat against his arm, watching as the band he had taken from the ship began to grow a bit more corroded with rust and decay. The observation did little to reassure him. The wall would decay and pitch him into the quagmire long before the armband's power was consumed, and long before then, Birna's strength would fail completely.

The sorcerer saw the hopelessness in Einarr's eyes and his grin grew. Filled with unending despair, the last joy for the slaves of the plague god was to see another overcome with the same misery. The warrior felt outrage swell within him, fury that this gloating wretch thought he could overcome the last son of Vinnskor. With one hand, he firmed his hold on the stake, struggling to maintain his grip. The other hand fell to his belt, drawing Alfwyrm in one fluid motion. The plague-wizard's eyes narrowed with dismay and his incantation took on a more rapid, hurried quality.

Einarr glared at the sorcerer, even as he felt the spike shift under his hand. He hefted his sword, tossing it so that he could grip it at the centre of the blade. Then, with a swift pull he crooked his arm forward and hurled Alfwyrm at his foe. Like a spear, the blade plunged through the wizard's chest. A look of disbelief filled the man's features, then with a groan he toppled to the floor, his hand dangling over the edge and into the stinking stew that filled the pit. Smoke rose from the corpse as the volatile filth devoured its flesh.

Birna gave a gasp and Einarr could feel her slipping away. His arm circled her, crushing her against him. Bellowing like a blood-mad troll, Einarr braced his legs against the sickening wall and launched himself across the pit. Huntress and warrior crashed against the floor of the corridor, the diseased bones of the sorcerer cracking beneath their weight. Einarr recovered quickly, glancing down the passage to ensure they were alone. Satisfied, he turned to Birna, doing what he could to comfort her, then stooped above the sorcerer's broken corpse.

'This belongs to me,' he spat, ripping Alfwyrm free and kicking the rest of the sorcerer into the bubbling mire. He looked back across the pit, to the passageway where the sounds of ferocious battle continued to rage. Briefly he considered crossing back and helping Orgrim, but before he could act, the werewolf himself appeared. Not a patch of fur on the Aesling was grey. Every hair on his body was stained with blood. A mob of the plague-dogs continued to vex him, the curs swarming about him like terriers baiting a bear.

The werewolf was pressed to the very edge of the pit. Unable to back away further, he slashed at his adversaries, his claws ripping open the flank of one too slow in making its escape. Orgrim turned, looking over at Einarr, then faced the cackling pack once more. Throwing back his head in one final, defiant howl, Orgrim met their charge, dragging two of them with him as he plunged into the caustic filth. Werewolf and carrion-hounds vanished beneath the boiling soup, steam rising from where they had fallen. The remainder of the pack, torn and mangled by Orgrim's claws and fangs, stared into the pit, even their cackling growls silenced by the spectacle.

Einarr reached into his belt and removed the fang he had lifted from the floor. While he watched the smoke slowly rise, he threaded Orgrim's tooth onto the neckband. Aesling or were-kin, Einarr hoped Orgrim's ancestors received him well when he entered their halls.

EINARR AND BIRNA hurried away from the gruesome moat, the sound of Skoroth's baying carrion-hounds bellowing behind them. The huntress struggled to keep pace with Einarr, the corrupt energies unleashed upon her by the warlock sapping her endurance. As they rounded the corner of the slobbering passageway and the sound of the hyenas faded into the distance, Birna sagged against the wall, coughing blood against the squirming meat. Einarr watched her, the woman's suffering cutting through him as though it were his own. As the wracking attack continued, he looked down at his arm, at the band of pitted steel that had guarded him against the diseased sorcery. He stepped towards Birna, reaching to his arm to remove the band. The huntress laid a restraining hand against his wrist.

'No,' she told him. 'It is too late.'

The Norscan shook his head, struggling to deny the truth in her words. 'It will protect you,' he said. Birna turned her face as another wracking cough seized her. Black fluid dribbled from the corners of her mouth as she looked back at him.

'It is you it must protect,' she said. 'If you fall, then we have all failed.' Her grip grew firm around Einarr's wrist. 'You must win your way through to the shrine, seize the Claw from the Plague Lord! Earn the glory that is your right! Only then can I hold my head high in the halls of my ancestors. I will look in the eyes of my forefathers when they ask me what right I have to sit among the Sarls. I will tell them "I was there when Einarr Steelfist conquered the Palace of the Plague Lord and claimed the favour of Mighty Tchar!"'

Einarr saw the admiration, the fervour in Birna's eyes, undimmed even by the sickness that gnawed at her vitality. He crushed the huntress against him, kissing her fevered face. He held her close, trying to will his own strength into her flagging body, trying to drive the clammy chill from her with his passion. Only when the sound of rushing bodies echoed down the corridor did he allow his hold to weaken. He tightened his grip on Alfwyrm and turned to face whatever new foes Skoroth had sent to die upon his blade.

'Even Einarr Steelfist cannot kill all the plague god's thralls,' Birna warned him. Despite her words, her own sword was in her trembling hand. Einarr looked over at her and nodded.

'We must keep ahead of them,' he told her. He helped her pull away from the wall, then set her running down the corridor. Birna did her best to match the Baersonling's long strides, but Einarr was forced to slow his pace and help her along. Behind them, something howled and the sound of their pursuit grew still louder as whatever beast guided the plague-thralls picked up their scent.

The dripping corridors of meat gave way to halls of bone, diseased-wracked skeletons clinging to one another in a riotous defiance of gravity and architecture. Insects peeked from the pits of skulls, rats chewed splinters of bone within decaying rib cages. The floor was a carpet of loam-like marrow that squelched beneath their feet, bleeding a milky treacle as their boots bruised it. Ahead, two great yawning pits opened in the floor, stagnant vapours rising from their depths.

'Which way?' Birna asked him.

'The left hand path is ours,' Einarr told her without hesitation. The huntress looked at him, her face filled with confusion and doubt. 'Do not ask how I know, woman! Somehow this vile place is more vivid in my mind than the streets of my village! Something guides me, some instinct I can feel in my bones.'

'More of Skoroth's trickery,' Birna spat.

'It does not feel like the Plague Lord's filth,' Einarr said. 'I have felt it for a long time now, since I left the ruin of Skraevold and entered the lands of the Aeslings.'

'Then it has led you far to betray you now,' Birna observed. She limped through the loamy floor, towards the gaping pit. It descended at an angle, a fleshy, tongue-like slope slithering from its lip into the gloom below.

The sound of shouting voices and baying beasts sounded from the passageway, their pursuers rapidly closing the gap. Einarr glanced down the corridor, seeing the shadowy shapes of the plague-thralls rushing toward them. He looked back at Birna.

358 C. L. Werner

'Go,' he said. 'We'll make our stand at the bottom.' Birna nodded and lowered herself into the pit. Einarr turned, watching the passage as the huntress dropped from view. The howling pack increased its speed as they saw the hulking Norscan waiting them. A scrawny jackal-like hound rushed for Einarr's throat, its jaws filled with stinger-like growths. Einarr brought the edge of his sword smashing through its skull, spilling the diseased animal across the floor. Behind it came another, and still another, each more hideous than the last. Einarr broke each in turn, his prodigious strength overwhelming their savage fury. After the first three hounds were littered about his feet, the rest of the pack cringed away in fear, unwilling to confront something that had overcome their leaders. But beyond the cowering curs there were others who did not share such timidity, horned pestigors and sallow-skinned Hung warriors, their mouths shrieking war cries and wrath.

Einarr knew it would be his turn to be overwhelmed if he stayed to wait for the plague worshippers. Numbers alone would drag him down. He might kill a dozen, a score, even a hundred, and his valour would mean nothing. No one would carry his name into the sagas, not even the gods would note his passing. He would simply be another sacrifice before the plague god's festering altar, another speck of sand upon the shores of his corruption.

Tightening his hold on Alfwyrm, Einarr turned his back to the oncoming horde and ran to the pit, diving headlong into its hot, cloying depths. Stagnant air washed over him as the slimy, leathery slope bore him downward. He felt a twinge of panic as he noted the ribbed symmetry of the red, raw walls, unable to rid himself of the image of a gigantic throat sucking him down into its gullet.

The Norscan's slide through the dank blackness ended in a wet, dripping collision with a reeking sheet of velvety flesh. Einarr's body slammed into the loathsome substance, its flexibility cushioning his impact. He scrambled for purchase on the hairy meat, but his fingers slipped from the decaying muck. His flailing hands scraped against the rotting sheet as he hurtled downward. Einarr yelled in protest as he fell to the floor twenty feet below, splashing into a pool of sewage and offal.

Einarr spat filth from his mouth and rose from the obscene water, rancid sludge dripping from his frame. He glared up at the opening through which he had fallen, waiting for any sign of pursuit. For long, tense moments he waited for sallow-faced Hung marauders to drop down after him. It was only when the seconds passed into minutes and still he saw no sign of his foes that Einarr turned away from the opening. Through fortune or fate, it seemed their enemies had lost their trail for the time being.

Einarr stalked off through the slush of scum and detritus that swirled about his feet, eyes struggling to penetrate the gloom. He did not worry that there was no escape from the reeking hole, as he had told Birna, whatever strange instinct had possessed him had led him far only to abandon him in the Plague Lord's oubliette. It was the huntress who was foremost in his thoughts. He worried about her welfare, concerned how well she had weathered the violent descent. He worried too about what else might be sharing the rancid pool with them and despite his concerns for her, he did not call out to his companion lest other ears hear him and be made aware of his presence.

The warrior sloshed through the filth, able to see only a few feet before him in the shadowy stink that dominated the hole. The grainy bed beneath the sludge seemed to crawl under his boots, threatening to spill him face first into the muck with every step. Einarr forced the urgency that filled him to give way to caution and make certain of his footing.

No sooner had he slowed his pace than something black exploded from the waters inches before Einarr's face. Instantly his sword was flashing through the darkness, hacking through the shadowy apparition. Alfwyrm struck the side of the thing with a chopping report, fragments of his adversary spraying across the water. Einarr pulled his sword from the shape, straining to free it from the gash he had drove into the thing's side. No sooner was the sword free than the shape shot back down into the water.

Cautiously, Einarr pressed his foot forward again. Once more, the black shape stabbed up from the water, coils of offal draped down its length. Now Einarr could see what manner of menace he had so narrowly avoided. It was a great black thorn, thicker than a spear and cruelly sharp. Barbs projected from its sides, dripping slime and excrement, and Einarr could see luminous venom dripping from the tip of each spur. He shuddered at how nearly he had given himself to such a hideous and ignoble death.

While he watched, the thorn shot back down beneath the surface, hidden once more beneath the sewage and filth. A gnawing dread quickly grew within Einarr's mind as he watched the water become still once more. No longer concerned with what lurking ears might hear him, he began to call out to Birna. He circled around the sunken thorn, pressing on through the pool, haste once more moving his steps. A second thorn stabbed up, missing him by a hair's breadth. As the slimy spike sank again, Einarr's shouts became a frantic roar, urging Birna to keep still, warning her of the gruesome menace that lurked in the water.

He strained his ears for the faintest hint of a whisper, but only the dripping slime answered him. Einarr pressed on, turning back towards the opening through which he had dropped. Again, a ghastly spike burst from the water, diseased sludge crusted about its deadly frame. Einarr chopped at it with his sword and the thorn retreated once more. Panic churned in his stomach and the Norscan roared Birna's name, until his throat was raw. The warrior slogged through the filth, hacking at the thorns as they erupted around him.

A black spine shot up beside him as he raged through the mire. Einarr swung Alfwyrm at the lethal spike, but his arm froze in mid stroke. Strength drained from Einarr's body and he slumped down before the thorn, scarcely able to retain his grip on his sword. The world faded into a bleary smudge as tears spilled from the Norscan's eyes.

The outline of the thorn was all but lost, only the gory spike at its tip visible. The rest of it was embedded in a lean, lithe body, driven through thigh and belly and breast before ending its murderous passage by punching through the side of the neck. The ruin of the woman's head sagged against the edge of the thorn, eyes frozen in a moment of shock and agony. There was an abominable irony in that face as Einarr gazed into it. The last vestiges of Birna had been driven from it. Looking upon her he saw again the maimed debris of Asta lying strewn about their home. The loss of one lover was magnified with the loss of the other. Einarr felt himself being crushed beneath the pitiless sorrow that ground him beneath its heel.

How long he sat beside the lethal trap, Einarr did not know. What words dropped from his tongue, he could not say. Whether he mourned Birna or Asta, even this refused to burn through the icy numbness that closed around him. He was aware, dimly, of regaining his feet, of trying to pull Birna from the thorn. Every effort only succeeded in maiming her further as the spurs tore deeper. At length, he relented, drawing back, resigned that he would have to leave his companion behind amid the squalor and filth of the pit.

There was a cold distance between mind and action as Einarr reached to Birna's mangled head. He cupped her face in one hand and raised the edge of Alfwyrm toward her mouth. For an instant, he tried to resist the impulse, but he could no more fight against it than he could when he had taken talismans from the other comrades he had lost. Instead, his mind retreated into some black corner of his being, watching with cold detachment as his fingers pried the woman's mouth open and the sharp edge of Alfwyrm did its gruesome work.

He felt his hand fumbling at his neck, opening Spjall's band and added the new charm to the others. He could feel Birna's sharp, bird-like tongue dripping against his neck, but refused to admit the horror the sensation evoked. He crushed his revulsion into a knot of hate, husbanding the emotion with all the care of a wet nurse. He would use it, use it against Sko-roth, against the fell Plague Lord. The sorcerer would feel that hate, when Einarr clove open his skull and ground his brains beneath his boot.

The Norscan turned away, vengeance glowing in his eyes as, alone, he stalked off into the shadows. Behind him, the impaled remains of his last comrade faded back into the stagnant pool as the thorn withdrew once more.

Chapter Nineteen

EINARR STALKED THROUGH the festering halls of the palace, a thing of pain and regret. Birna's death pulsed through his mind, a crimson phantom of anguish, her lifeless eyes staring at him, her dead lips set in silent accusation. She had trusted him to lead her to glory, had followed him here from Norsca only to find death, to have her soul devoured by the gluttonous plague god. He felt guilt rip through him like the edge of a sword, bile churning in his belly. Within his mind, other faces appeared, glowering at him with accusing stares. Thognathog, his double heads rotted to the bone by Bubos's pestilence. Orgrim, his flesh melted and torn. Even old Urda, her skull crushed and broken. All glared at him, demanding recompense for their deaths. Black despair flooded through Einarr and he crumpled to his knees, the fleshy floor quivering as he sank against it.

What was the purpose? What was the use? He had dared everything in this mad adventure, this vain attempt to seize an impossible promise. Those who had followed him were dead now, those who had trusted him to lead them to glory and triumph. Asta, Spjall, his entire people would remain as they were – butchered offerings to ravenous Kharnath. There would be no redeeming them from the Skull Lord's realm, no righting the terrible doom Einarr himself had brought down upon his village. All was carrion and the laughter of the cruel gods.

In his hand, Einarr could feel the cold grip of Alfwyrm pressing against his flesh. It would be so easy to end this hopeless farce, to cheat the gods of their sadistic entertainment. What was death, after all, but an escape from suffering, release from the horrors of a wicked world?

Einarr turned the sword he held, pointing its blade at his own belly. One quick thrust, and his misery could be over. He closed his eyes, seeing the approval in the mangled visages that filled his mind. This was what Birna and the others wanted. This was what would satisfy them.

The mark of Tchar forged into his flesh blazed with fiery brilliance and Einarr's hand felt as though he had thrust it into the mouth of a furnace. Alfwyrm dropped from his smouldering grip, flopping against the floor. The faces swirling within his mind shrieked as a blinding light exploded through his consciousness, the visages collapsing into one another until only a single face remained – the rotting skull of the Plague Lord. It scowled at him in cold hate as the light burned even his true face from Einarr's brain.

The Norscan doubled over in sickness, spitting his stomach against the throbbing wall. As the Plague Lord's fell influence was purged from his mind, Einarr's flesh crawled with revulsion at the sorcerer's obscene violation of his soul. The black despair that Skoroth had evoked within him withered, overwhelmed by his rage at the sorcerer's deception.

Strangely, the Plague Lord's mental attack emboldened Einarr, firming his resolve to bring about Skoroth's ruin. If the sorcerer was trying to use such tricks, trying to force him to kill himself, then Skoroth did so because he was afraid. He did not trust the palace's gruesome defences to stop Einarr. The Norscan smiled at the thought. Nothing would stop him now. He would carve his wergild from Skoroth's withered carcass and hear him wail for mercy before he allowed the sorcerer to die.

The glistening, meat-like wall shuddered and Einarr watched with disgust as a drooling mouth formed within it. It slopped open and, from its putrid depths, shambling, wailing things that could only mockingly be called human emerged. They turned desiccated, disease ravaged faces towards him, their corroded axes and swords as pitted with decay as the skeletal hands that clutched them. The moaning, wretched horde advanced on him, the slime of their own excretions dripping from their feet.

Einarr glared back at the zombie-like horrors. He stooped and retrieved Alfwyrm from the quivering floor. His other hand closed about the necklace he wore, feeling the talismans against his skin. One man against such a horde, even a horde of such miserable things, could never hope to prevail. But Einarr was more than one man. He could feel the strength of his

dead comrades filling him, surging through his body.
They were with him still, they could still share his triumph and his glory. That was how he would satisfy
their spirits, by giving to them their victory.

With a roar of feral savagery that might have torn
itself from the canine jaws of Orgrim, Einarr charged
the plague-thralls. The first he decapitated, the second
he disembowelled. The third he cut in half with
Alfwyrm's shining blade and crushed its mangled
bones beneath his boots as he began the slaughter in
earnest.

FROM THE SLAUGHTER of the plague-thralls, Einarr
pressed onward. The rotting halls of the palace oozed
and throbbed all around him. Walls of raw meat alive
with maggots, floors of oozing mucous that clung to
his body and tried to suck him down into their filth.
He saw pillars of fused bone, alive with gnawing vermin. He heard the shrieks and howls of the damned
as he passed. His nose was assailed at every turn by
the mephitic vapours he could feel blackening his
lungs as he drew them in. Through his very bones he
could feel the throbbing vibrations that pulsed
through the palace, the abominable life that infested
every corner of the hideous structure.

Einarr endured it all, the thirst for revenge, the lust
for triumph, steeling him against the worst the palace
could inflict upon him. He could feel Skoroth's pestilential sorcery trying again to thrust diseased fingers
into his mind. But he was aware of the Plague Lord's
trickery, steeling himself against his magics. He
mocked Skoroth's efforts, daring the decayed sorcerer
to face him with steel instead of tricks. The fury of the
Plague Lord thundered across Einarr, boils and oozing

sores erupting from his flesh when the sorcerer found he could no longer infect his mind. The armband Einarr had taken from the Frozen Sea grew still more decayed as it drew the worst of the pestilential sorcery into it.

As Einarr jeered at Skoroth's efforts to bewitch him, the ceiling overhead began to pulse and throb. The glistening meat that formed the roof peeled back with a wet, sucking sound, exposing thick ropes of coiled intestine so large Einarr doubted if even a mammoth's gut could contain such enormity. The leprous organs quivered and swelled, expanding until they flopped from the ceiling, dangling disgustingly into the corridor. Einarr felt dread gnaw at his mind as the organs continued to swell. He looked back the way he had travelled but found that it too had been overtaken by the bloated loops of intestine.

'Is this all you have?' Einarr growled to the unseen sorcerer. At that instant, the nearest of the organs reached the point at which it could expand no more, its swollen skin splitting as the intestine burst. Green, stinking juice sprayed across the hall, steaming as it struck the fleshy walls and the shivering floor. Einarr howled in pain as the acid sizzled against his skin, his cloak and armour smoking where the intestinal filth struck them.

Einarr bit down on the pain and set his eyes on the corridor ahead. Already more of the intestines were reaching the bursting point, the acid from the first seeming to speed the process. He started to turn his head around, then stopped himself. Whatever happened, he would not take one step back. The heart of the palace lay ahead of him, the prize Tchar demanded from him would be there, triumph would be there. Behind him was nothing but shame and death. Before him was vindication.

Howling like a thing spit from the blackest hells, Einarr lunged down the corridor, charging past the drooping sacks of acid. Some burst before he reached them, showering him with a burning spray, others exploded behind him, singing his cloak and gnawing into his armour. His body railed against the pain, against the abuse, but Einarr would not heed it.

Blood seeped from his ravaged flesh, his armour hung in tatters, his bearskin cloak was reduced to smoking rags, and still the Norscan refused to falter in his purpose. For what seemed an eternity he rushed down the corridor, roaring as the acid rained down upon him. He felt his strength ebb, his limbs grow cold and heavy, yet still he forced his body onward. When endurance failed him, Einarr's indomitable will sustained him. When even this reached its limit, spite alone kept him moving.

At last, Einarr won his way clear of the deadly hall, crashing to his knees as he emerged into a chamber of fused bone and reeking moss. The warrior sucked deep breaths into his starved lungs, even the stinging stench of the palace a welcome respite after the burning mist that had assailed him. The Norscan reached his hands to his head, removing the bear skull helm. It was pitted from the acid, even its unnatural strength overcome by the burning filth. Einarr hurled it from him, then began peeling away the shreds of cloak plastered to his back by his own blood. The tattered ruin of his armour was next, dregs of acid still eating through the toughened leather and steel.

Fatigue tugged at Einarr's body, trying to crush him to the floor. He raged against it, lurching to his feet.

With the weight of his ruined armour gone, he felt light, almost wisp-like. He shrugged aside the sensation of vulnerability that came with it. After the punishment dealt it by the acid, his armour would not have protected him from the claws of a weasel, much less anything that lurked within these diseased halls. It would only have slowed him down, taxed his already waning strength with its bulk. Einarr cast aside the rest of his gear, the meagre remains of his rations, the last dregs of his waterskin, the empty hollow of Spjall's medicine bag. Only the necklace of talismans, the corroded armband and the deadly edge of Alfwyrm did he retain.

Einarr turned away from his cast-offs, studying the chamber in which he found himself. Grotesque mouth-like doorways littered the room, rotten teeth forming the frame of each opening. The Norscan studied them for a moment, then shook his head. Some unnatural instinct had guided him this far, leading him by the nose when reason should have left him hopelessly lost. He would continue to let it guide him.

Without further pause, Einarr sprinted towards one of the openings, darting past the jagged teeth, half expecting the immense jaws to snap close as he passed beneath them. Beyond the doorway he found a hall of rippling muscle, red and raw in the stagnant light that filled the palace. As he approached, the muscles heaved and pulsed, the walls smashing together with wet, meaty slaps, the ceiling and floor rushing together in a crushing embrace. After a moment, the muscle-walls withdrew, quivering with anticipation. Another step, and they crashed together once more, the force of their impact shaking the entire corridor. Einarr had no illusions as to the fate of anything trapped by such an impact. He also knew it was beyond the strength of a mere mortal to summon the speed and agility to surge past the walls before they reacted and smacked together.

The mark of Tchar smouldered against his hand, its glow barely seen by Einarr's eyes. Thoughts rushed through his mind and he felt the impulse to close his hand around Orgrim's fang. Einarr seized the talisman and with a fluid motion, he tore it from the neckband. The warrior stared at the sharp, savage tooth, imagining again the feral shape of the were-wolf. He saw the ferocious spirit that had lurked within Orgrim's flesh, the terrible power that had coiled within his body. Throwing his head back, Einarr shouted the werewolf's name and plunged the fang into his arm.

The sharp tooth bit through his flesh, ripping deep into his body. Einarr collapsed as he felt a force pulse through him, racing through his veins like wyvern venom. He howled in anguish as his bones ground against one another, twisting and stretching beneath his flesh. His skin darkened, throbbing in pain as hair erupted all across his body. His screams thickened into a bestial growl as his face was pulled into a muzzle, as his teeth lengthened into knife-like fangs. His entire being was stripped away, twisting into the feral form of the ulfwerenar, only the hand bearing the mark of Tchar stubbornly resisting the change that thundered through him.

Einarr slowly rose from the floor, feeling the savage power of his new form pulsing through him. Fatigue was forgotten, injury was forgotten. All that he felt was a terrible strength, a strength that made his old body feel like a weak, simpering thing. It was a wolf's howl that rumbled through Einarr as he revelled in his power. The lust for blood, the urge to feel flesh tearing beneath his fangs burned in his veins. Einarr turned his head, sniffing at the stagnant air, overwhelmed by the riot of sensation that flooded his nose. He could smell them, the festering slaves of Nurgle, crawling through the halls of the palace like so many maggots. With his new strength, he could kill them all, leave the corridors littered with their chewed bones and make the halls echo with their screams.

Before the beast could overwhelm his mind, Einarr recovered himself. He fought back the bloodlust that pounded through him, clinging to his retreating intellect as the wolf threatened to consume him. He stretched his still human hand, closing his fist around Alfwyrm's cold steel. The touch of the sword seemed to lessen the grip of the beast, its savagery slinking into the black shadows of his mind.

Einarr turned back towards the quivering corridor, at the moving walls of muscle and slime. He had seen Orgrim, he knew what one of the ulfwerenar could do. But would it be enough, would even the were- wolf's animal strength and speed be enough?

The Norscan choked back his doubts and flung him- self down the hall. The walls crashed together behind him, clapping together in a crushing embrace. Einarr did not pause, continuing to lope down the hallway as ceiling smacked into floor, wall drove against wall. He could feel the air being sucked back around him, so near did the writhing structure come to crushing him. It was as if the palace itself were trying to destroy him, possessed of a hideous, malevolent intelligence all its own. Einarr growled, sensing the sorcerous hand of Skoroth. But if the villain thought he would grind him into paste, he had not reckoned upon the Norscan's determination.

THE QUIVERING MAZE of moving walls at last emptied into a gargantuan hall, a jagged fissure that cut its way through the palace. As Einarr gained the canyon of rotting flesh and dripping ooze, he could see the leprous sky festering overhead. The mangled, pathetic bodies that formed the walls of the canyon groped blindly for him, moaning in despair as they sensed his approach. The faces that gibbered from the walls were little more than shrivelled skulls, great wounds marking where eyes had been ripped from their sockets. Yet there was life, foul and vile, within each of them, the misery of men who discover too late the true nature of the god they served.

The stink of carrion wafted down from the heights of the canyon, and Einarr's ears rang with the croaking of crows. His sharp eyes could see them, bloated and black, swirling about the upper reaches of the fissure, a great murder of carrion-eaters prowling the sky in search of more eyes to ease their abominable hunger. Warily, Einarr watched the crows circle as he stalked into the canyon, his every sense tuned to the rapacious birds and their croaking cries.

But the danger that set Einarr's nerves on edge, the threat that tugged at his animal senses, did not lie with the greedy crows. Distracted by the murder swirling above him, the first Einarr became aware of his true foe was when a musky, rotten reek filled his nose. Einarr spun around as the familiar stench threatened to overcome him with terror. He felt the palace shake as something tremendous surged toward the canyon. The wall of fused, moaning bodies to his

left exploded outward in a shower of ruptured meat
and rancid blood as the reptilian behemoth ripped
her way through the wall. Einarr cringed away from
her, his hubris withering, his pride in his new strength
crumbling as he again saw the awful shape of Bubos.

The dragon's body surged through the rupture in the
wall, heedless of the stinking blood that washed
across her, oblivious to the broken, shrieking things
she pulverised beneath her mass. The dragon swung
her head about, her rotten tongue flicking from her
jaws as she tasted the air. Einarr drew back as she lowered that frightful visage. He could see the dripping
ruin of her eye, but seated within the filth was a
ghastly figure. Robes of leprous flesh clothed his obese
bulk, his withered, almost skeletal face looking
impossibly small atop the bloated mass. Pockmark
scars littered the man's flesh, forming hundreds of fly-
runes, the sign of Nurgle. Worms sprouted from the
man's arms, like a growth of squirming hair, while fat
ticks clung to his chest. From the sides of the man's
head, ropy tentacles dripped, stabbing down into the
jelly of the dragon's broken eye.

Here, Einarr sensed, was the master of this obscene
place, the Plague Lord himself, the loathsome horror
that hid behind the name Skoroth.

The sorcerer turned his gaze to Einarr, and as he did
so, Bubos's head turned with him. His cracked, pallid
lips pulled back from a mouth black with disease and
decay. His rotten smile spread as other, smaller
mouths opened along his cheeks and neck.

'The stink of your hope offends my master,' Skoroth
told him. 'There is no place for it here. Despair is the
only salvation, to embrace misery and corruption, to
praise the defiled and the decayed. From the moment

you profaned my lord's domain, your every breath was but futile pride. Bow to the inevitable, barbarian, for it has come to claim your soul.'

The dragon took a thundering step towards him, her claws shredding the carpet of bone that formed the floor of the canyon. A scathing hiss seeped past Bubos's fangs, staining the air with her putrid hate. Einarr glared back at the dragon, at the sorcerer nested within her broken eye. The sneering, condescending smiles that pitted Skoroth's face cut into him, fanning the embers of despair that still festered inside him.

Einarr railed against the sorcerer's malignant spell. Tightening his grip on Alfwyrm he charged toward the dragon. Bubos pulled back in surprise, her immense bulk grinding against the screaming walls. Einarr struck at her, slashing her foreclaw with his sword's keen edge. The dragon's sludge-like blood bubbled from the wound as her rotting scales split beneath the blow.

The Norscan darted back as Bubos's jaws snapped at him. The air grew cold and vile around him, taking on a green luminance. Beneath the fur of the wolf, he could feel his skin crawling. Atop the dragon, Skoroth's hand was stretched towards him, blazing with a sorcerous light. Einarr ground his teeth as the malevolent magic washed over him, the armband growing a bit more blackened with each passing breath. Skoroth's face twisted with frustration as he saw Einarr withstanding his sorcery. Scowling, he snarled at the dragon. Bubos surged forward, swiping at Einarr with her claw. The attack slammed into the wall of the canyon, ploughing through the moaning bodies like blood-filled twigs.

Bubos roared, sharing Skoroth's frustration as Einarr slashed her leg again. With a mighty heave, the dragon launched herself at him, her entire ponderous bulk undulating forward in a great mass of scales and teeth. Einarr sprang at the wall, his bestial paws sinking into the tortured flesh that shrieked beneath him. He dug his claws into the rotting flesh and propelled himself upward, scrambling over the wailing bodies nimbly and rapidly. The dragon smashed into the floor below him, her enormity tearing through the layers of bones and flesh. The ground collapsed beneath her, sucking her down into a shallow pit of her own creation. The jagged bones that lined the crater stabbed into the dragon's sides, digging deeper as she struggled to free herself.

Skoroth glared at Einarr as he scrambled up the wall of the canyon. He roared again at Bubos and the dragon lifted her head. Her jaws parted and she sent a sheet of cloying, sizzling pestilence shooting upward. The dragon's aim was off, her deadly breath consuming the wall a dozen feet to Einarr's right. Skoroth fixed Einarr with his gaze, concentrating even more fully than before, willing the blind dragon to see through his own eyes. Again Bubos spat death at Einarr, the fused bodies only a few feet below him withering into smoking husks that crumbled into decayed ash. Einarr dug his claws deeper into the canyon wall as the entire structure shuddered. The dragon opened her jaws a third time, horrible fires of disease and ruin gathering in her throat.

Einarr reached his hand to his necklace and tore the blackened stump of Thognathog's finger free. Howling the ogre's name, he flung the desiccated thing down at the dragon. Skoroth covered his head as the withered finger bounced off Bubos's snout, rolling across the splintered floor. The sorcerer sneered and pointed a fat finger at Einarr, urging Bubos to finish him.

Neither dragon nor sorcerer noticed Thognathog's finger smouldering on the floor. They did not see the glowing liquid that spread from the blackened stump, the viscous oil that shimmered with fell energies. The bones that littered the floor began to pulse with their own eerie glow, matching the rhythm of the luminous oil. Shards of bone tore from the ground, scuttling across the floor to sink into the shining muck. Soon entire skeletons were sucked into the pool, the glowing liquid darkening as more and more bone sank into it. As it darkened, the pool grew in size. Then, when it had lost almost all of its brilliance, the black pool began to bubble and foam. Einarr watched in amazement and disbelief as from the froth a huge skeletal hand emerged. A second soon followed, grabbing at the bony floor as it strained to pull free from the sludge.

It was then that Skoroth noted the taint of sorcery exuding from the pool. With alarm in his rheumy eyes, the plague worshipper bellowed commands to Bubos. The dragon gave one last blast of diseased fire, annihilating the wall beside Einarr, and swung her head towards the pool. From the blackened sludge, an enormous figure was rising, its skeletal limbs dripping shimmering slime, the sockets of its massive skull staring emptily at the reptile. Bubos roared at the undead thing, her hissing shriek echoing through the canyon. The immense skeleton simply stared back, taking a lumbering step towards her. Skoroth gestured at the abomination, a swirling stream of burning vomit exploding from his dozens of mouths, crashing against the skeleton in a wave of searing corruption. The dripping slime that coated the skeleton evaporated into smoke under the sorcerer's attack, but still the horror lumbered onward. A second skull slowly pushed its way up from the undead thing's collarbone, joining the first in its pitiless consideration of the dragon and her lord.

Einarr had no time to spare for dragons and undead ogres. As the skeletal monster closed upon Bubos, the Norscan struggled to keep his hold on the swaying, ruptured walls. The bodies beneath his hands crumbled and rotted, dripping down in liquid foulness to splash the floor below. The dragon's pestilential flame continued to eat away at the living walls of the canyon, devouring them with insatiable hunger. The crows, agitated by their quaking rookeries descended in a black cloud of mangy feathers and rusted beaks to peck and claw at him. Einarr felt their talons ripping into his flesh, felt their stabbing beaks pounding against his bones. He howled and raged, striving to both maintain his grip and fight off the furious flock. Then his hand closed around his necklace once more and he knew that he was not alone. He knew what he had to do.

There was no time to consider the horror as he ripped Birna's tongue from the necklace. He screamed the huntress's name, tearing the sound from the depths of his heart. His canine jaws snapped closed around it, devouring it with the raging hunger of a true wolf. Einarr sucked the abominable meat down, struggling against the revulsion that shuddered through him. When the taste of flesh was gone from his mouth, he opened his jaws once more. It was not the howl of a wolf that thundered from his muzzle,

but the sharp, keening cry of a bird. The frenzied murder that swarmed around him flew away, obeying
without question the shrill cry he had uttered.

Einarr turned his head, glaring downward at Bubos
and Skoroth. The skeletal ogre was straining against
the dragon, its thin arms wrapped about the reptile's
snout, its bony fingers tearing into her flesh. From her
head, Skoroth continued to send bursts of fell magic
slamming into the monster, but spells alone did not
seem enough to stop it.

The Norscan watched the struggle for a moment, then
glanced back at the enraged crows still filling the sky
above the canyon. He threw back his head once more
and an avian shriek wailed through the fissure. A storm
of black feathers shot downward, descending upon the
dragon in a tempest of animal fury and rage. The dragon
vanished beneath the croaking, cawing mass. Einarr
could hear her painful cries as she writhed beneath the
assault. Her noxious flame flicked through the swarm,
hundreds of crows burned from the sky. Skoroth's diseased sorcery flashed from the thick of the flock,
splattering feathers and bones across the canyon. Yet for
every hundred that fell, a thousand more dove down
upon them, squawking and slashing.

The wall shuddered beneath Einarr once more. He
looked upward, feeling his hope wilt as he saw the
great distance that yet lay between himself and the
top. He looked back down at the floor of the canyon.
The mark of Tchar glistened on his hand and Einarr
reached to the band around his neck once more. His
fingers closed around Urda's rune eye. Again, some
instinct beyond himself told him what to do. Howling like a beast, Einarr leapt down from the wall,
plummeting toward the dragon fifty feet below.

Einarr crashed through the swarming cloud of crows, slamming into the top of the dragon's head. He drove Alfwyrm into Bubos's skull before his impact caused him to roll away. The reptile shrieked in agony as his sword punctured her festering brain. Einarr saw Skoroth turn away from his assault on the crows, watched as he struggled to control the dragon's agony. The tentacles dripping from the sides of his head throbbed as he tried to force his will into her mind.

With a roar of rage, Einarr lunged at the sorcerer, smashing into his bloated bulk. Still trying to control the dragon, Skoroth feebly raised his hands to ward off the Norscan. Einarr drove his claw into Skoroth's belly, ripping strings of rotting organs from his gut. Skoroth shrieked in agony, green energy spilling from his ghastly wound. His eyes snapped open as he abandoned his efforts to control Bubos, fixing his hideous gaze fully on Einarr. For an instant, the warrior felt again the noxious touch of Skoroth's sorcery against his skin. The arm band crumbled beneath his power, fading into a crust of decay as it drew the awful power into it. Einarr snarled in pain as the magic ward snapped and he was left exposed to the sorcerer's power. He grabbed Skoroth's arms, feeling the putrid skin slough away beneath his touch. Another roar of fury exploded from his jaws as, with inhuman strength, Einarr ripped the sorcerer from the cloying goo of Bubos's eye socket. Skoroth flailed madly in his grip as Einarr lifted him overhead and hurled him to the shattered floor below.

Purple sludge gushed from the torn tentacles and the dragon thrashed wildly as she was plunged fully into a world of blindness. She lashed her head from side to side, striving to dislodge the warrior clinging to the edge of her eye socket. Einarr felt his arm almost pulled from his shoulder, such was the dragon's desperate panic. He felt the rune eye burning against his palm. Shouting Urda's name, he pushed the stone into the rotting jelly of the dragon's eye. Then his hold on the dragon's skull failed him and he was sent flying through the air. He slammed into the moaning, shuddering wall of flesh and withered to the floor.

Bubos lashed furiously against everything around her as molten agony coursed through her body. Her claw smashed down into the skeletal ogre, pulverizing the undead thing. Her fiery breath sprayed through the air, incinerating thousands of crows. Her powerful limbs ripped and tore at the ground, pulling her free from her pit, ignoring the stabbing fingers of bone that gouged her sides. Her forked tongue flickered from between her jaws, struggling to taste Einarr's scent on the air. The dragon heaved upward, grinding the last remains of the ogre beneath her armoured belly. Einarr spat the blood from his mouth and watched the gigantic reptile begin crawling towards him.

Then light began to shine from the dragon's ruined eye, a searing, blinding light that was at once all colours and no colour. The brilliance exploded from the dragon's skull, her veins glowing within her body, shining through her scaly flesh as burning agony coursed through her entire bulk. The dragon flailed against the pain, her claws ripping into the walls, her immense tail crashing against the floor, smashing bones into powder. Smoke began rising from Bubos as she burned from the inside out. Steaming blood erupted from her maw, dissolving her fangs as her jaws decayed into brown slush.

Einarr saw Skoroth lifting himself from the splintered floor. The sorcerer looked up at the dying dragon, then glared at the Norscan. In the same instant, the behemoth reared back, crashing onto her side and rolling miserably across the canyon as pain assaulted every shred of her being. The sorcerer's body exploded into a mist of flies and maggots as the dragon's enormity crushed him. Einarr grinned at the justice of it, the mighty plague master slain by his own creature.

Bubos slammed back into the pit she had gouged, more broken bones stabbing into her ravaged frame. The dragon tried to rise once more, but greasy froth spilled down her crumbling face and the last of her lower jaw pulled free of her wasted skull. For a time, the dragon's body continued to shudder and writhe, but whether there was still intelligence behind such agonies, or merely the last suffering of tortured muscles and nerves, Einarr could not say. Even so, he watched until the frightful force ravaging the dragon had consumed her utterly, leaving behind only a puddle of reeking filth.

Despite the pain that filled his own battered body, Einarr forced himself to rise and stride to the site of the dragon's dissolution.

'This time I think you don't come back,' he growled, spitting into the brown slush.

CHAPTER TWENTY

EINARR STALKED ONWARD through the reeking gloom of the palace, through the diseased corridors and chambers. There was a terrible quiet about the infernal structure now, as though the entire palace was holding its breath, shuddering in fear. Accustomed to the rustle of vermin, the gibbering cackle of nurglings and the squealing of rats, Einarr found the silence somehow even more horrible. Even the wailing things that had been fused into the walls were still, their decaying faces set into moribund masks. The Norscan could feel their eyes staring at him, could feel the ruin of their minds scrutinizing his every move. For good or ill, he could not say. Perhaps the poor mad things weren't even capable of such a distinction after squandering their miserable lives for the plague god's diseased whims.

He had not travelled far from the canyon where he had wrought the destruction of Skoroth and Bubos when the strength Orgrim's fang had endowed him with began to fade. Einarr screamed in pain as his bones shrivelled back into their proper shape, as the fur that covered his limbs shrank back into his skin. He fell to his knees, writhing in pain as his face collapsed back into a human visage. He felt diminished as the power of the wolf left him, a great emptiness inside him. The dulling of his senses made him feel almost blind and deaf, such had been the keenness of the wolf's awareness. He understood now the terrible lure the bestial spirit had, the grim power that had made Orgrim embrace the feral life of the ulfwerenar and shun that of his kin.

Eventually the warrior rose once more, prowling through the silent, brooding corridors, guided by the uncanny instinct that had led him so far for so long. When the corridor branched, there was no delay, he knew which path to take. When the halls degenerated into a labyrinth of narrow passages and shivering walkways, he unerringly sensed which steps to take. Einarr wondered if even Urda, with her witch-sight, could have guided him as well as the urges that tugged at his mind.

At length, he sensed he was drawing close to the very heart of the palace, the place where the Claw had been locked away by Nurgle's thralls. It was so close now, he could almost taste it, almost feel its black power vibrating through the passages. A dull throb pulsed through the meat-like walls, almost like the pounding of a drum. The sound boomed through Einarr's ears, thunderous after the silence of the halls. His pace quickened and he rushed onward, desperate now to seize the Claw in his hands, to secure the prize Tchar had demanded from him. To claim that which the Lord of Change had promised him.

It was an old story, among the Baersonlings, the struggle between Tchar the Eagle and the Worm Nurgle. The cunning schemes of Tchar constantly threatened by the rapacious appetite and mindless hunger of Nurgle. Sometimes the Worm would be too powerful, too swollen with plague-infested meat, for the Eagle's talons to carry off. At such times, terrible diseases ravaged the land, felling mighty and meek with the indifference of a blind axeman. The careful plans of Tchar would be upset by Nurgle's gluttonous feast, his mortal servants struck down along with the rest, his unwitting puppets cut from their strings. Of all the gods, it was Nurgle that Tchar reviled, for the Plague God was too unpredictable even for the Great Manipulator to coerce.

The Norscan's hurried pace faltered as he neared the end of the corridor. The passage was blocked by a gate. Not a thing of bone and flesh, not a portcullis of quivering daemonic pestilence. After all the horrors he had endured, all the terrors he had overcome, a simple fence of steel bars separated him from that which he had struggled so long to win. Einarr shook his head in disbelief, unable to accept that this was the last obstacle that stood in his way.

Einarr strode towards the gate, seizing its bars in his hands. Instantly pain flooded through him, blazing agony that coursed up his arms in red misery. Beneath his touch, the steel bars were white-hot. Flesh melted from his fingers, fusing to the gate. But he refused to release his hold, the promise of what lay beyond greater than all the agony his body could endure.

Black specks flared through his vision, the stink of his own cooking flesh filled his nose, and still he kept hold of the bars, straining to force the gate open. His teeth ground together, his muscles burned in protest as he strained them beyond their limits.

Finally even Einarr's tremendous endurance crumbled beneath the strain. Screaming he pulled away from the gate. The warrior clenched his bloody fists, raging against the cruel caprices of the gods. He would not be denied, not now. Not when he had come so close.

The symbol of Tchar on his hand began to glow once more. He raised his gory fist to his neck, pulling free the scrap of armour he had taken from von Kammler's gauntlet. He glared at the defiant gate. Bellowing the knight's name, he flung the metal shard at the barrier. The missile blazed with chromatic energy as it struck the steel bars. The blinding light spread through the steel, rushing all across the portal. Before Einarr's eyes, the bars began to twist and change, their skins of steel warping into scaly flesh, their pointed tips changing into serpentine heads. The hissing of vipers wheezed across the corridor as the snakes dripped away from the portal, slithering across the floor in a squirming carpet.

Carefully Einarr made his way past the hissing snakes, the reptiles still glistening with the energy that had transformed them. Gingerly he picked a path between the serpents, his bare toes curling as cold reptilian flesh brushed against them. By degrees, he won his way clear of the vipers' nest, the pulsating hall beyond the gate standing unguarded and unbarred before him.

* * *

THE THROBBING RHYTHM that pounded through the walls and floor grew still more distinct as Einarr approached the shrine. Unerringly, his instincts had led him here, but now the unnatural guidance had nothing more to offer him. They had failed him because there was nowhere left to lead him.

He had arrived.

The meat-like walls vibrated with the pulse that ran through them, quivering and shaking as Einarr strode past them. A framework of rotting bodies rose before him, decayed hands clutching at him weakly, faint moans sighing from the wasted corpses. Einarr brushed the feeble grip of the wretches from him, sparing no thought for the damned slaves of Nurgle. There were others he would save, others who were worthy of life.

Past the archway of festering corpses, Einarr found himself standing within the shrine, the very heart of the palace. The room was lit by a golden light, a diseased magnificence that made his eyes water. Here the walls were a lattice of veins and arteries, the fleshy tubes quaking as black filth shot through them in chaotic spurts. The floor was an expanse of stretched sinew, a quilt of flayed human flesh. Faces stared up at Einarr from the floor, watching him with insane, maddened eyes. Upon the ceiling, glowing with its malevolent power, was the fly-rune of the plague god, branded into the quivering flesh of the palace, dripping with luminous pus, alive with squirming maggots.

By force of will alone did Einarr tear his eyes away from the sign of Nurgle, retching as the after-image of the diseased rune continued to infect his vision. When he recovered, he tightened his hold on Alfwyrm, the sword's grip chewing into his mangled hands. He glanced about the noxious shrine, looking for the prize he had been told would be here.

Against the far wall, he could see a curtain of slimy gossamer, looking for all the world like a great sheet of mucous. Around the alcove were littered the bodies of dozens of Hung and pestigors, their corrupt bodies cut and burned. Blood still seeped from their grievous wounds, pooling in a stagnant mess upon the blinking floor.

Einarr strode towards the butchered guards, watching the black shadows that crawled at the corners of the shrine for any trace of what had killed them. Every nerve in his body on edge, Einarr stalked towards the alcove and the prize he had come so far to claim.

A dark, twisted shape emerged from the side of the alcove, its torn arm dripping against the curtain. A misshapen face grinned wickedly at Einarr as mismatched eyes struggled to focus upon him.

'So, Steelfist continues to enjoy the favour of Lord Tzeentch,' Vallac spat as he strode into the light. 'By steel and strength and the lives of those foolish enough to follow him, he at last reaches out to claim his destiny!'

Whatever shock Einarr felt when he saw Vallac standing in the shrine was quickly smothered by the hate that swelled up inside him. He could well guess how the Kurgan had been able to reach this, the inner sanctum of the palace. Skoroth had been frightened of Einarr, obsessed with destroying the one who bore the mark of Tchar upon his flesh. He'd been so driven to destroy Einarr that the Plague Lord had ignored the other rat scurrying through the walls. Every ordeal he had endured, every foe he had slain had made Vallac's passage through the palace that much easier, drawn that much more attention away from the Kurgan and focused it upon Einarr.

Einarr glared at the Kurgan, studying the wounds that marked Vallac's body, trying to determine how much strength was left in the man, how much fight he could still muster. 'And the brave Vallac, like a thief in the shadows, comes to steal what is not his to take!'

The Norscan's words were intended to provoke Vallac, but the Kurgan's reaction was not what Einarr expected. Instead of some reckless fury, bitter laughter took hold of him, wracking his mangled body like an ague. He raised his hand, closing his bloodied fingers around the rotten curtain. With a savage pull, he tore the gauze-like decay from its fixture, letting it wilt against the floor.

'What is there to steal, Norscan! Where is the great treasure Lord Tzeentch told you to reclaim!'

Einarr stared in horrified fascination as Vallac exposed the depths of the alcove. Instead of chests of treasure, instead of altars of gold and silver, instead of piled gems and hoarded wealth, there was only a mass of greasy, dripping muscle. For one final time, disbelief seized Einarr's heart, crushing it in an icy fist. The warrior became oblivious to everything, the pestilential light, the crying floor, the glowing fly-rune, even the Kurgan who glared at him and fingered his bloodied sword. All that existed for him in that black moment was the alcove, what it contained, and what it did not.

The Norscan stepped towards the mass of quivering muscle. He could see the slime dripping from it, the black sludge that flowed through it. Bones poked from its surface, decayed limbs and splintered ribs, the ruin

of a skull locked in one final scream. At the very centre of the mass, a brown, putrid thing pulsed and
throbbed, its rhythm racing away into the walls. But
of the Claw, the treasure he had come so far to find,
there was no trace.

Pain flared through Einarr's body as he felt steel
slash against his back. Only the weakness of the strike
prevented the attack from severing his spine, even so
there was enough strength behind it to make Einarr
reel from the blow. He staggered back, lifting Alfwyrm
in time to swat aside the crooked blade clenched in
Vallac's grimy fist.

'You have cheated me!' the Kurgan roared. 'Cheated
me of everything!' He brought his blade crashing
down, the edge biting into the floor as Einarr parried
his strike. Before Einarr could press his own assault,
the Kurgan's sword was flashing towards his belly
once more. Strength might have withered within Vallac's arms, but the marauder had lost none of his
speed.

'The favour of Tzeentch is lost to me!' Vallac raged,
bringing his sword slashing down into Einarr's leg,
tearing deep into the calf. 'Glory is lost to me!' he
screamed, and Einarr felt the edge of Vallac's sword
cut into his arm. 'Life is lost to me!' he howled and his
sword swept towards Einarr's head. The Norscan
ducked beneath the furious attack, bringing Alfwyrm
slashing through Vallac's forearm. The Kurgan's arm
flopped to the floor, the sword still clutched in its
dead fingers.

'At last, something we agree on,' Einarr snarled,
plunging his sword into Vallac's chest. He felt ribs crack
beneath his strike, organs rupture beneath his steel. The
Kurgan's hot blood drenched his hand and Einarr

sneered into Vallac's stunned countenance. The marauder scowled back at him, his face splitting in a spiteful smile. Einarr flung himself to the floor as Vallac spat fire from his mouth an instant too late to consume the Norscan. Einarr scrambled across the ground, rolling away from the fiery exhalations that Vallac sent shooting after him. The skin coating the floor shrivelled and blackened beneath the Kurgan's fire, but his opponent remained stubbornly just beyond his reach. Finally, even Vallac's hate could not keep him standing. The fires sputtered and died, the Kurgan's knees folded and he fell, the blade still thrust through his chest driving even deeper as it struck the floor.

Einarr stared at the Kurgan's twitching body, watching his life drain from his ruined carcass. He felt a sense of triumph swell within him. After all he had endured, he could still find some satisfaction in life's smaller pleasures.

THE SOUND OF buzzing flies tore Einarr's attention from the dying Kurgan. From the tiny spaces between the pulsing veins that formed the walls, great blue flies crawled into the light, hairy legs rubbing together in an almost human expression of glee. The insects took to the air, gathering in a cloud of flittering vermin. Einarr watched in horror as the tiny bodies slowly melted together, coalescing into a terrible new form. Skoroth's skull-like face grinned at him as the melting flies gave him shape once more.

'Thank you for removing the Kurgan,' the sorcerer said, the tones still tainted by the hum of insects. 'I did not care for his fire. It was most troublesome.'

'You'll find me more troublesome,' Einarr growled. He stooped to the floor and lifted a rusty axe from a dead Hung. 'I do not know how you cheated death before, maggot-kin, I only know this time I will do better!' Snarling, Einarr charged towards the bloated plague master.

Skoroth lifted his pudgy hand, filthy sounds belching from his throat. Einarr felt himself hurled back, as though some slimy fist had smashed into him, throwing him to the floor. The sorcerer stared down at him, eyes smouldering with a fanatic's intensity.

'Somehow, I fail to be impressed,' he hissed. He stretched his hand again and the axe in Einarr's fist began to rot, metal and wood dissolving into a paste that oozed through his fingers. Einarr's flesh smouldered beneath the sludge. The sorcerer strode towards him, the floor wailing in revulsion beneath his loathsome tread. From the tips of Skoroth's fingers, whip-like tentacles shot across the room, lashing Einarr's body, tearing into his skin. Gangrenous sores spread from the welts as diseased venom pumped through Einarr's body. Screaming, the warrior struggled to control the spasms that wracked him, striving against his rebelling body to lift himself from the floor.

'Yes, Norscan. Scream. Shriek. Feel the suffering and sorrow flow through you!' Skoroth's skeletal grin spread to the dozens of tiny mouths that drooled open across his withered head. 'Know despair, know agony, know desolation! Beg, grovel, bow your head as it rots from your body! Quail before the power of Nurgle!'

A scum of blood trickled from Einarr's eyes, his lungs filling with stinging filth. His flesh crawled with pestilence, maggots sprouting from his wounds, burrowing still deeper into his flesh. By inches and degrees, he could feel himself dying, feel his life being drained away by the sorcerer's fell magic. A wheezing cough wracked his body and torn scraps of lung erupted from his mouth.

Through the agony, through the slow death, Einarr forced his arm upward, his hand to close around the last charm dangling from his neckband. Blood and tissue dripped from his mouth as he forced his head off the floor and glared into Skoroth's smirking visage.

'Zhardrach,' the warrior growled, hurling the dwarf's beard-lock at Skoroth. The sorcerer lifted his arms instinctively to ward off the missile. The hairy coil bounced harmlessly from Skoroth's hands, but as it struck the floor, it exploded in a burst of scintillating colour. From the beard-lock, great chains of iron shot upward, swirling around the sorcerer's body, engulfing him in a cocoon of crushing, clinging metal. Soon, where the sorcerer had stood, there was only a pillar of twisted links that swayed and shuddered as the thing trapped within struggled against its prison.

Given a respite from the sorcerer's stinging tendrils, Einarr plumbed the depths of his being to summon whatever vitality remained within him. He felt the now empty neckband, the last charm now used. All of his comrades had left him now. Now there was only Einarr of the Baersonlings, and somehow he doubted that would be enough. He turned his head to where Vallac's body lay upon the floor, the cold blade of Alfwyrm still buried in the Kurgan's chest. Painfully, Einarr dragged himself toward Vallac. The Norscan's ravaged body screamed in protest, urging him to lie still and accept death. He fought back the weakness of his flesh. A Norscan fought until his last breath, and beyond if need be. He did not sit back and quietly let death claim him like some miserable southlander. To do so was insult both to the gods and his ancestors. Now, so close to the grim halls of the afterworld, now was the time when it was most important to be strong.

Like a worm, Einarr slithered across the staring floor, fingers gouging eyes as he gripped their sockets to pull his body forward. Vallac's body slowly came nearer, inch by agonising inch the carcass of his treacherous comrade came closer. Einarr risked a look back at the pillar of chains that had encased Skoroth. The sorcerer's struggles no longer caused the pillar to sway. Instead, Einarr could see a green mist rising from the column, the links rusting and corroding within the cloud. Desperation swelled the flagging strength in the Norscan's body. If he did not reach Vallac's body before the chains encasing Skoroth rotted away, he knew that he never would.

Einarr refused to look back at Skoroth, forcing himself to keep his eyes on his goal. Slowly, ever so slowly, the body of the Kurgan drew nearer. Vallac's caustic blood stung Einarr's maimed body as he crawled through the pool of gore trickling from the carcass. The burned floor crumbled beneath his fingers as he dragged himself onward. Finally, his hand closed around the Kurgan's leg. His muscles aflame with pain, Einarr pulled himself up Vallac's body.

For a moment he stared down into the mutated face of the traitor. Einarr lurched back in alarm as Vallac's eyes flashed open. The Kurgan croaked and gagged, trying to summon a gout of fire to incinerate his killer. All that came was a dry, hacking gargle. Acidic phlegm slobbered over the Kurgan's lips, searing his skin.

'Come… to… take back… your… sword,' Vallac hissed. His eyes closed on the neckband around Einarr's throat. His broken face contorted into a sneer. 'What… what trophy… do… you steal… from Vallac…?'

Einarr glared down at the Kurgan. He heard the first rusty links of chain clatter to the floor as Skoroth's prison began to collapse. The Norscan's features darkened into a mask of stone. The symbol of Tchar on his hand glowed with power. 'From you, Vallac of the Khazags…' Einarr slammed his glowing fist into the Kurgan's chest, feeling ribs crack beneath his hand, flesh split before his fingers. 'From you, I take everything!'

The Kurgan's shriek echoed through the chamber as Einarr ripped his fiery soul from Vallac's body. The marauder's eyes collapsed into cinders, his flesh blackened and crumbled into ash. Einarr tore his hand from the smoking corpse, his fist wrapped in Vallac's inner fire. He watched the ghostly flames swirling about his hand for a moment, then spun about, staring at the corroded pillar of chains.

With a final, mournful crack, the chains shattered, spraying across the room in an explosion of rusted iron and putrid mist. Skoroth's bloated body emerged from the shambles of his prison, his skeletal face hideous in his rage. Then his eyes fastened onto Einarr. The rheumy orbs grew wide with fear as Skoroth saw the wraith-fire pulsing around the Norscan's fist.

'Burn, sorcerer!' Einarr spat. 'Burn with all your filth and horror!' He threw his hand forward, the ghastly fire leaping from him to streak across the room. The flames slammed into Skoroth's obese bulk, engulfing him in a spectral inferno. The sorcerer's shrieks thundered through the shrine, causing veins to burst and rotten slabs of flesh to fall from the ceiling. Einarr glared at Skoroth's blazing figure as he writhed in torment. He stooped once more to Vallac's mangled body and pulled Alfwyrm free from the ashes. In his mind's eye, he saw Thognathog, consumed by the pestilential fumes of Skoroth's dragon. He saw Orgrim, dissolving in the bowels of Skoroth's palace. He saw Birna's bloodied face, her body pierced by Skoroth's trap. He saw Asta and Spjall and Sigdan, all awaiting him in the halls of their ancestors.

Even with his body enveloped in flame, Skoroth tried to summon his magic to protect him as the Norscan stalked grimly back across the shrine, murder in his eyes. The fleshy floor snapped and snarled beneath Einarr, struggling to bite his feet as he strode across the faces. Maggots rained from the ceiling, burrowing into his flesh as he passed beneath the oozing fly-rune of Nurgle. Tiny daemons, like a stream of living excrement, slithered from the walls and wrapped slimy arms about the Norscan's legs. From Skoroth's fingers, black tentacles lashed at him, searing his flesh where they struck, sending disease sizzling through his body.

Like a juggernaut, Einarr strode through everything the sorcerer cast upon him. Pain was banished from his mind, fatigue and injury vanquished by the adamantine will that thundered within his soul. Hope and despair, fear and courage, these were things that had lost all meaning for him. The only thing left in him was the determination that he would see his quest through to the bitter end. If he could not offer the Claw to Tchar, then he would offer the skull of Skoroth to his ancestors.

Skoroth watched Einarr advance upon him, disbelief in the sorcerer's eyes. He opened his mouths, spewing a stream of worm-infested bile from his bloated innards. The corruption sizzled against Einarr's skin, gnawing through flesh and muscle. The gleam of bone shone from the festering wounds, yet still the Norscan came. No scream sounded from him; no cries of agony and pain. Only a quiet, whispered litany as the names of his forefathers found purchase one last time upon his lips. Soon, the name of Einarr Sigdansson would be among them.

Panic seized the sorcerer as Einarr forced his tortured body towards him. The warrior pulled his arm back, Alfwyrm's blade reflecting the dancing flames that swirled about Skoroth. With his concentration fully broken, the magics that kept the worst of the fire's fury at bay vanished and the greedy flames began to consume his obscene bulk. Einarr sent his sword driving down into Skoroth's withered head.

The sorcerer exploded beneath the blow, his body disintegrating into thousands of flies. The fire continued to engulf the noxious insects as they flew through the air, darting back into the nest of veins that formed the wall of the shrine. Einarr roared in fury, slashing his sword through the retreating flies, refusing to let the stricken sorcerer escape.

As the flies burrowed back into the gaps between the pulsing veins, the rune upon Einarr's hand glowed once more. Something beyond his own will compelled him to stagger to the wall, to stretch his hand and seize the last of the flies before it could vanish.

Words formed on his tongue, but the voice was not his. Sounds rumbled from his throat, but they were not those of a man. The syllables that left his mouth scorched the air, blazing with power as they transformed from idea into purpose. Somehow, without understanding the ghastly sounds, Einarr knew their meaning. *Be flesh*, the shrieking notes said. *Be flesh*.

Beyond all the other horrors he had experienced, the wailing scream that sounded from within the nest of veins stabbed into Einarr's mind, offending his very soul with its unearthly depths of agony. A gory paste of meat and bone oozed from the gaps in the wall, dripping down the lattice of veins in a runny slime. Putrid blood fell from his hand and opening it he found that where once had been a fly, now he held a decayed human finger. Disgusted, he let the digit drop to the floor. Even for one of the plague god's slaves, Einarr could not help but be sickened by the horror of such a death.

THE NORSCAN TURNED from the loathsome ruin that had claimed Skoroth and sagged to the floor. His last foe vanquished, now he felt the weight of his wounds, the enormity of his suffering. He let Alfwyrm fall from nerveless fingers. His vision became a fog of weariness, the shrine and everything within it fading into grey shadows. Only the sound of the throbbing heart and the diseased sludge pulsing through the vein-walls remained clear and distinct to him.

His hand burned with energy once more, and Einarr forced his tired eyes to focus on the now numbed member. The metallic symbol that had been seared into his flesh was moving, slithering across his skin with a life of its own. He watched it drip from his arm, pool on the floor and continue to crawl away. Gradually he became aware that it was growing larger, the metal sheen darkening to the black of pitch. He blinked away the shadows as feathers sprouted from the sludge, as the oily tendrils formed into wings. Rising from the slime, he saw a great black eagle, its beak crooked like a sickle. He had seen such a bird before, the carrion eater that had perched upon his chest after the destruction of his village, the scavenger who sat atop the boulder and thought to feast upon the sabre-tusk he had slain .

Even as the memory came to him, the black bird was changing again. Its beak opened in a savage cry, its shape swelling like a gathering storm. The eagle's scaly legs grew, rippling with energy as they expanded. Tiny gemstones twinkled from the pillar-like limbs, a scintillating skin of sapphire and diamond. The eagle's body stretched and twisted, the feathers folding in upon themselves until they vanished back into the creature's leathery skin. Hundreds of eyes blinked from the mottled chest, no two sharing a kindred colour. Flames of white fire flashed through the raptor's wings and its thin bones thickened into the clawed arms of a giant. New wings, translucent, almost glass-like, spread from the eagle's back, tinkling like tiny bells as they snapped open. Einarr could almost see landscapes and creatures moving within the smoky depths of the wings, and turned his eyes away, lest he discover his impression to be true.

Only the eagle's head resisted the change that consumed the rest of it. Throughout the metamorphosis, it retained its cruel avian shape. Though he could not say he had seen it grow, somehow the bird's head remained in proportion to its body. Its eyes, changing size and shape with each passing breath, stared down at Einarr, an air of amusement in the daemon's pitiless gaze.

Einarr looked again at his hand, the hand that no longer bore the curled sign of Tchar upon it. Now he understood, now he knew why he had been chosen. This was why he had not claimed a talisman from Berus's torn body. The berserker was not a part of them, they had already been nine when Einarr had freed Berus from the Hung. The ninth warrior, the one who completed the sacred number of Tzeentch, that one he had carried within himself. From the moment the foul thing's blood had seeped into his skin, it had been there inside him. Guiding him. Manipulating him. Protecting him. All the foes he had faced, the trials he had overcome, he had conquered only with the daemon's unseen help. The comrades he had gathered, the enchanted talismans he had claimed from their mangled bodies, these had been nothing but tools in the daemon's game, puppets dancing upon its strings.

Einarr felt his soul crack as the enormity of the deceit crashed around him. Everything had been a lie, everything he had been told had been a trick. The rune he had seen in the snow, the image plucked from his own dreams – the black eagle had not represented the man, but the thing the man carried inside him. The quest had never been about recovering the Claw, it had been about bringing the daemon into the shrine. He was not the champion, not the hero who would claim glory from the gods themselves! He was nothing more than a horse to carry his master whither he willed.

Did you really think you could come so far alone, little mouse? The daemon's words scraped against Einarr's consciousness like a knife across bone. *Did you think flesh and steel were enough to challenge the gods themselves?*

Einarr's head swam as the daemon's voice crawled through his skull. The abomination seemed to still be growing, its impossible enormity filling the entire shrine. Or perhaps it was the room itself that was expanding, growing to accommodate the daemon's power. His senses rebelled against the violation of perception that the daemon embodied and he ground his hands against his eyes, trying to block out the awful sight.

One more thing you will do for me, little mouse. The thing I brought you so very far to do. Einarr's body trembled in revulsion as the daemon's gigantic claw closed around him and he was lifted from the floor. He could feel his flesh running between the daemon's talons, his blood curdling as its ghastly essence seeped down into his veins. *You refused to leave an offering before my monolith. Now you shall make amends.*

'But the Claw is not here!' Einarr protested through trembling lips. The daemon laughed.

Of course not, little mouse! It is safe with my master as it has been for thousands of your years. It is a different prize that brings me here, little mouse, one I did not see fit to trust to the weak mind of a mortal, lest some other daemon tease the knowledge from your fragile flesh.

The daemon set him down in the little alcove. Einarr fell to his knees, his body twisted and mangled by exposure to the daemon's aura. His arms were curled like the horns of a ram, his legs buckled and bent, the bones melted beneath his dripping skin. Einarr struggled to move, but his muscles refused to work in the ways he knew.

The heart, little mouse. Give it to me and then I will let you die.

Einarr felt the daemon's malice lash through him, a sensation a thousand times more terrible than even the sorcery of Skoroth. He tried to force his body to move, sliding across the alcove like some dripping snail. Tears wept from his eyes as he willed his crippled arms to lift, only succeeding in making the hands flop uselessly against his chest. He screamed as he felt the daemon's talon stab into his back, as he felt flesh and bone erupt from his wound, flowing together in some new and abominable growth.

Reach with your paws, little mouse. Do not make me ask again.

The Norscan wailed with impotent fury, crying in agony as he tried to force his maimed body to obey him. Despair flooded through him, the despair of the damned. Before him, the knot of muscle quivered, pulsating in tune with the tiny heart that pounded within it. Einarr stumbled forward on his useless limbs, flopping against the side of the alcove. He watched as the heart faltered, skipping a beat before resuming its pulsations. Even in the pits of desolation that filled him, Einarr noted the change in the rhythm, a change that vibrated throughout the shrine and the palace beyond. The disembodied heart now beat in time with his own!

Now, little mouse, take it now.

Einarr's crooked arm slapped uselessly against the knot of flesh. Straining, he lurched closer to the heart, craning his head against the quivering, throbbing obscenity. Its oozing skin slapped against his face, its dull pounding throbbing in his ears. Weeping from the effort, Einarr brought his mangled arm up, pinning the heart between it and his head.

Good little mouse. A mortal placed it there, it needs a mortal to take it away. Take it now, little mouse, and your suffering will be at an end.

Einarr screamed as he pulled his twisted body away from the greasy mass of muscle. For an instant, the heart held fast, clinging stubbornly to its fastenings of sinew and artery. Then, with a wet tearing sound, it ripped free. Einarr crumbled upon the floor of the alcove, the still beating organ gripped in his teeth. Black filth cascaded from the ruptured veins, showering the Norscan in diseased sewage. All around the shrine, the throbbing, quivering life faded, the walls grew still as the sludge no longer shot through the vein-like coils.

You have done well, little mouse. Now bring it to me.

Einarr lifted his head, forcing his eyes to fasten onto the daemon's grotesque presence. His disfigured face curled into a snarl of defiance.

'No,' he spat through clenched teeth.

The daemon's wings opened wide, the images struggling for substance within their smoky depths turning into tongues of flame. The eyes that glared at Einarr from its mottled chest turned red with inhuman fury. The floor beneath the daemon's clawed feet screamed in horror as its unholy rage thundered across the shrine.

The little mouse dares to defy me, Yth'nitzzilik the Maleficent! Yth'nitzzilik the Enduring! Yth'nitzzilik the Great Abomination!

'You made a promise to me, daemon,' Einarr snarled, teeth falling from his mangled jaw. 'Black claw or festering heart, you will keep your oath to me.'

The daemon's eyes glowered down at the tiny, broken mortal.

You cannot begin to imagine the paths that have led to this moment, little mouse. The many centuries that have faded away waiting to bring me here. From the instant when the plague god crowned the first Plague Lord and built from his mortal shell this palace, the strands of fate have conspired to give shape to this moment. My master waits to feel the Festerheart in his hand. The gods plan their great war, little mouse. They need only the Festerheart to bind the plague god to their cause. All existence waits upon this moment, and one heartsick mortal thinks to stand in the way?

'You promised to turn back the hours, to open the gate between days! You swore to send me back, back to Vinnskor, back to the time when the bloodbeast attacked my village! I can save my people this time! I can save Asta and Spjall and all the others! I can save my people! I can stop Birna and the others from ever coming to this pit of death and horror! I can change it all!'

Yth'nitzzilik stepped closer to Einarr, its enormous shadow falling over him, making his skin crawl with unclean changes. Despite the burning torment in his eyes, Einarr continued to glare at the daemon. The crooked beak twisted, impossibly forming itself into a smile.

So like a mortal, obsessed with such petty dreams. There is a jest here even the eternal can appreciate. The daemon's mocking laughter shuddered all around Einarr's broken body. *Very well, Einarr Sigdansson, I shall keep my promise.*

The daemon's clawed hand stretched down towards Einarr, shimmering light growing from the centre of its palm...

EPILOGUE

A SAVAGE WAR cry exploded from Einarr as he hurled himself at the beast. His axe chopped into one of the abomination's flailing tentacles, severing it from its body. The mast-like column of flesh crashed to the ground, narrowly missing the enraged axeman. Before his very eyes, it corroded into a stagnant heap of scarlet mush. The beast coughed and croaked with what Einarr hoped was pain and took a swipe at him with one of its enormous paws. Einarr dodged the blow, striking out at the malformed limb as it passed him, the edge of his axe chewing into the back of its foremost talon. The beast coughed again and lashed out once more, this time with a pair of tentacles. Only by dragging every ounce of speed from his body was the warrior able to dance between the flailing limbs. The beast reared back once more, blood dripping from its fanged muzzle.

'Follow me, you blood-worm filth!' Einarr screamed at the thing. 'I am what you came for!' Einarr jumped back as the monster struck at him with one of its panther-like paws. He waited for the thing to surge towards him. For a moment, the monster's multitude of eyes stared at him. Then the moment passed. It swung its trunk-like neck around, closing its jaws around the shrieking body of a mangled reaver. Einarr stood in stunned horror as the beast shuddered back across the garth, towards the warriors assembled on the other side of the village.

With a cry of despair, Einarr raced back across the garth and flung himself at the beast. He crashed against its slimy back, chopping frenziedly into its gore-drenched skin. Sizzling gore splattered across him, but still he hacked and tore into the thing. The burning blood seared his hands, his skin coming off in scabby strips as he tried to maintain his hold upon his axe. He saw the screaming, accusing faces of his kinsmen and his neighbours locked within the beast's blood.

THROUGH EYES CLOUDED with blood, through a haze of madness and fury, Einarr watched his past self chop and slash at the bloodbeast. He tried to hold the monster back, tried to stay its murderous claws, but his efforts were as futile as his attempts to turn the beast back as it slithered toward the village. His was but one soul among many trapped within the blood-beast's body, one voice among the screaming throng that tried to command the brute's formless mass. The spite and hate and psychopathic rage of the others was too much for him to overcome, the legion arrayed against him too vast to conquer. He could only watch as events unfolded, following the pattern he had struggled so vainly to break. He pressed against the flesh of the bloodbeast, struggling to warn his past self, to warn the man that had been Einarr about the treachery of hope and the lying tongues of daemons.

Einarr felt the flesh of the bloodbeast bubble and change as he strove against it, the gory hide transforming into the rude semblance of his own features. Tears of blood bubbled from his eyes, his mouth moving in silent cries of warning to his past self, desperately striving to make the man he was turn back before it was too late.

THE AXEMAN SLASHED the blade of his weapon deep into the bloodbeast's blubbery hide. Steaming blood cascaded from the wound, showering Einarr in scalding liquid. The warrior ground his teeth against the pain and raised his axe for another blow.

For an instant he froze, mesmerised by the image of one of the shrieking faces that bubbled up from the monster's wounds. The face seemed almost to be his own, locked in some nameless, unspeakable torment, screaming in limitless agony.

Einarr tore his eyes from the shrieking soul, forcing himself to plunge his axe once again into the bloodbeast's vile flesh. He did not see the crimson tears spilling from the eyes of the tiny face as damnation consumed its last, fragile hope.

IN THE SKY above, a gaunt black eagle circled and croaked with amusement as it watched slaughter consume Vinnskor. The eagle's talons were wet with blood and clutched in its claws was a throbbing, pulsing heart. Its laughter drifted down to the carnage, its mocking notes dripping from the sky like burning rain. The bloodbeast raised its misshapen trunk, trying to find the source of such caustic notes. The eagle laughed again and gradually flew away into the darkening gloom, abandoning the village and its would-be saviour to their fate. Slowly the daemon faded from the star-swept sky, vanishing back into its own terrible realm to bear its prize to its master.

ABOUT THE AUTHOR

C. L. Werner has written a number of
Lovecraftian pastiches and pulp-style horror
stories for assorted small press publications
and *Inferno!* magazine. Currently living in
the American south-west, he continues to
write stories of mayhem and madness set in
the Warhammer world.

THE BLACK LIBRARY

BRINGING THE WORLDS OF WARHAMMER AND WARHAMMER 40,000 TO LIFE

Check out all the action happening on the Black Library website!
All the latest news, downloads, special offers, articles, chat forums, online shopping and much more.
Miss it and miss out!

WEB STORE

Pre-order new releases, buy available products and Collector's Editions.

NEWSLETTER

Sign up and receive latest news and special offers!

DOWNLOADS

Free wallpapers, first chapters of all our novels and loads more.

FORUM

Chat with fellow Black Library fans and post fan fiction.

Visit: www.blacklibrary.com